The GIRL WHO NEVER GAVE UP

BOOKS BY KATE HEWITT

Far Horizons Trilogy
The Heart Goes On
Her Rebel Heart
This Fragile Heart

Amherst Island Series
The Orphan's Island
Dreams of the Island
Return to the Island
The Island We Left Behind
An Island Far from Home
The Last Orphan

The Goswell Quartet
The Wife's Promise
The Daughter's Garden
The Bride's Sister
The Widow's Secret

The Inn on Bluebell Lane Series
The Inn on Bluebell Lane
Christmas at the Inn on Bluebell Lane

The Emerald Sisters Series
The Girl on the Boat

The Girl with a Secret
The Girl Who Risked It All

STANDALONE NOVELS
A Mother's Goodbye
The Secrets We Keep
Not My Daughter
No Time to Say Goodbye
A Hope for Emily
Into the Darkest Day
When You Were Mine
The Girl from Berlin
The Edelweiss Sisters
Beyond the Olive Grove
My Daughter's Mistake
The Child I Never Had
The Angel of Vienna
When We Were Innocent
That Night at the Beach
The Mother's Secret
In the Blink of an Eye

The Other Mother
And Then He Fell
Rainy Day Sisters
Now and Then Friends
A Mother like Mine

KATE HEWITT

The
GIRL WHO
NEVER
GAVE UP

bookouture

Published by Bookouture in 2025

An imprint of Storyfire Ltd.
Carmelite House
50 Victoria Embankment
London EC4Y 0DZ

www.bookouture.com

The authorised representative in the EEA is Hachette Ireland
8 Castlecourt Centre
Dublin 15 D15 XTP3
Ireland
(email: info@hbgi.ie)

Copyright © Kate Hewitt, 2025

Kate Hewitt has asserted her right to be identified as the author of this work.

All rights reserved. No part of this publication may be reproduced, stored in any retrieval system, or transmitted, in any form or by any means, electronic, mechanical, photocopying, recording or otherwise, without the prior written permission of the publishers.

ISBN: 978-1-83525-216-1
eBook ISBN: 978-1-83525-215-4

This book is a work of fiction. Names, characters, businesses, organizations, places and events other than those clearly in the public domain, are either the product of the author's imagination or are used fictitiously. Any resemblance to actual persons, living or dead, events or locales is entirely coincidental.

To Charlotte, whom I love talking about writing with! You're The Girl Who is Going to Write A Novel! And to Anna, who has read more of my books than anyone else. Hope you enjoy this one. Love you, Mom

PROLOGUE

JUNE 1946—PARIS

In a shabby little café in the shadow of the Eiffel Tower, the air felt electric. Three women stared at each other, wide-eyed and wordless with shock. There were meant to be four of them meeting that day, a year after the end of the war, as Paris staggered back to her feet and all of Europe struggled to remember how life used to be.

Four women had met back in 1939 on the doomed ship the SS *St Louis*, bound for Havana, Cuba, from Hamburg but never to dock. The ship, along with all its passengers, had been destined to trawl through the seas, searching for a safe port, rejected by every country they entreated for help. Eventually, those thousand desperate souls had been sent their separate ways—to England, to France, to Belgium, and to the Netherlands. The four friends had been forced to say their heartfelt farewells, but they'd promised to meet here, at Henri's Cafe, on the anniversary of the date they'd first been parted.

And only three had come.

"You said you think she's *alive*?" The woman in the doorway's voice was hoarse, her heart-shaped face pale and drawn, light brown hair pulled back from her wide hazel eyes. "But I *saw* her fall." She gulped, doing her best to hold back tears. "Back at Izieu… when they raided the children's home… Lotte was there…"

"Lotte…" The woman by the bar spoke softly, with deep dismay, her dark blue eyes creased with concern, one hand fluttering by her throat. "Oh, Hannah… did your sister… Lotte… did she…"

"She's alive, thank God." Hannah gulped as she blinked back more tears, swiping one hand across her pale cheek. "She's alive because of that day… because of Sophie."

"She is?" The woman by the bar looked relieved. "Oh, I'm glad…"

Hannah took a step toward the others, her tone turning urgent and plaintive. "Rachel… do you know what happened to Sophie? You said you saw her…"

Rachel, standing by the bar, her chestnut brown hair now streaked faintly with silver, shook her head slowly. "I did, but… I can't say for certain what happened after. But I…" She gulped. "I fear the worst."

"Where did *you* see her?" Rosa, who had spoken very little, now demanded. Tall and proud, her dark hair pulled back into a low bun, her eyes snapped furious denial at the terrible truth that was smacking each one of them in the face. "Rachel, how is it that *you* saw Sophie, too?"

"It was at Auschwitz," Rachel admitted quietly, and a silence fell on the group that felt like grief, thick and heavy, as realization of what their friend had endured settled over them.

"Oh, Rachel…" Hannah shook her head sorrowfully. "Auschwitz? I'm so sorry…"

"Was Sophie…" Rosa began, and then stopped, unable to go on.

The newspapers had been full of condemnation for the camps, with terribly vivid photographs of the heinous crimes that had taken place there—bodies stacked like lumber, gas chambers marked by the desperate scratching of fingernails in a futile bid for freedom, crematoriums with towering smokestacks that had belched the greasy smoke of death up to the sky... it was all so unimaginably evil, and Rachel had been there, as well as Sophie? No one wanted to think of it.

"She made it to the end," Rachel explained, her voice choking with both sorrow and remembrance. She was terribly thin, her face lined and tired, although she was only just a few years past thirty, the oldest of their little group. "Right before the liberation. We knew the Soviets were coming, but the guards... they made us leave the camp. Anyone who could walk had to go... there were thousands of us..." She shook her head slowly, momentarily lost in memory. "It was the middle of winter, utterly freezing... and so many were ill, too weak to go on. If you stumbled or fell, it was a bullet in the head."

"Oh, Rachel." Hannah's voice was soft and sad, yet without any surprise. She had clearly experienced enough Nazi cruelty not to be shocked by such a thing. "I'm so sorry."

"We were both on the march, we started out together, but then... we were separated." Rachel bit her lip, her gaze full of anguish. "I last saw her a few miles from camp. I promised to find her again, but I feared for her. She'd been ill, you see, with a chest cold. A small thing in this life, but there, with no medicine, so little food, in the cold..." Rachel shook her head, her eyes dark with pain. "I feared the worst."

They were all silent again, absorbing this grim reality. Had Sophie fallen in the snow, forgotten as the other prisoners were forced to march on?

"And you?" Hannah asked softly. "What happened to you, Rachel? And to Franz?"

A soft sigh escaped Rachel as she shook her head, and now her dark blue eyes were full of not just pain, but grief. "Too much..." she confessed in a whisper. "Far too much."

CHAPTER 1

MAY 1939—HAMBURG

"Would you look at that, Franz!" Rachel Blau's voice rang out with excitement as she steered her husband toward the dock where the SS *St Louis* waited under a springtime sky of pale blue. "Isn't it magnificent?" she exclaimed.

Franz, walking with slow, shuffling steps, his thinning brown hair brushed back from his forehead, did not reply.

Rachel kept her smile and even widened it, as she had been doing since Franz had been released from Dachau—a camp for political prisoners—with the threat of rearrest and imprisonment—or worse—if he did not leave the country within the month. The *St Louis* was the first ship they'd been able to book passage on, using all their meager savings, pawning every possession they owned, and humbly accepting what relatives had insisted were just loans but Rachel knew in her heart they would never be able to repay. They *had* to leave Germany. This had been the only way, and finally—*finally*—they were about to board.

Franz glanced up at the hulking ship with a disinterested air. "It's quite big," he agreed, not sounding particularly impressed or enthused.

"It certainly is," Rachel replied in the same cheerful tone. It had been two weeks since Franz had returned from Dachau, and in all those days he'd barely spoken, and never with much enthusiasm. Still, it was early days, as her mother had reminded her more than once. She needed to be patient as well as strong, and Rachel was determined, for her husband's sake, to be both.

It was just a matter of time, she told herself—as she had on numerous occasions already—before Franz returned to what he'd been. *Who* he'd been. With her continued love and encouragement, he would regain his courage and flair, his purpose and conviction. She chose to believe that the man she loved was still there, and she acted out that belief every moment of every day, never wavering in it for a second.

It was what her mother had advised, her beloved, lined face full of determination, as she'd pressed the wrinkled Reichsmarks into Rachel's hands, gained from the precious Sabbath silver she'd pawned for their passage, despite Rachel's admittedly feeble protests. "He will come back to you," she had promised, just as she had when Franz had been in Dachau. "Rachel, *Liebling*, he will come back, I know it."

He was right here next to her now, Rachel thought, and he wasn't back yet, but he would be. He would be one day soon, once they were on this ship, sailing to safety...

Slipping her arm more firmly through her husband's, Rachel guided him through the crowds to the back of the line snaking toward the tourist-class gate. The Hamburg harborside was seething with people—men in dusty black frockcoats and wide-brimmed hats, women in worn dresses with demure lace collars and hand-crocheted shawls, as well as the more well-heeled passengers of First class, in satin dresses or sharp suits, tailored overcoats or well-preserved furs.

Jews of every description and demographic were clamoring for passage on this ship, desperate to get out of Germany, where they'd been persecuted for the better part of a decade, many losing not just their jobs, but their property and savings, any attempt at a livelihood and sometimes even their very lives.

And yet Rachel still would have chosen to stay if she could have, simply to be close to her dear mother Ester, who had been such a support to her during Franz's imprisonment. When would she see her again? Ester Stein's own mother was seventy-eight years old, too frail to be moved, as well as too set in her ways, and her daughter wouldn't go without her.

"You know I can't leave her," Ester had stated matter-of-factly when Rachel had, hesitantly at first and then with desperate pleading, asked her mother to accompany her and Franz to Havana. "She's known nothing but this street, Rachel, this very apartment, for more than twenty years. And, in any case, with her heart, I don't think she'd survive the journey. I cannot leave her alone. You know how wrong such a thing would be."

Oma Stein had already had two heart attacks, leaving her as good as bedridden, a martyr to her own suffering. Since Hitler's rise, with Jews limited to which doctors and hospitals they could use, it had been harder to obtain any medication to help her condition. Even when Rachel had suggested that her grandmother might be able to get the pills she needed in Cuba, her mother had not been moved.

"*Liebling*, you know I can't," she'd said, pressing her lips together to keep them from trembling as she'd reached for Rachel's hands. "Please don't ask me again. God goes with you. He directs your steps, as well as mine. Let that be our bond, and an unbreakable one at that."

Her mother's faith, Rachel reflected, was unshakeable, even in the face of so much hardship and heartache—her own husband dying of a stroke in 1936, her mother's ill health, her son-in-law's arrest and imprisonment, and now her daughter leaving for Cuba, maybe forever. What more was in store for her, if she stayed in Germany?

Kristallnacht had been terrible enough, last November, when Jewish stores and businesses had been deliberately destroyed, a wanton rampage of senseless destruction orchestrated by Goebbels, Hitler's minister of propaganda. Many Jews had been arrested and some even killed, and then, to add insult to grievous injury, the Jewish population had been charged a billion Reichsmarks for the pleasure of having so many of their belongings and lives destroyed.

But worse than any of that, *far* worse in Rachel's mind, had been Franz's arrest and imprisonment. Dragged from their apartment in the dead of night, his face bloodied, his eyes wild... Even now she had to suppress a shudder of sick terror at the memory, the way her insides had hollowed out as SS officers had stormed her marital home, tossing her precious Meissen plates—a wedding present from her mother—to the floor, gloating as they'd watched them shatter into beautiful, glittering shards.

They'd gloated too as they'd pulled Franz from bed, punched him full in the face before he'd so much as uttered a word. Rachel still recalled his nose spurting blood as he'd spat out a tooth, still shouting out encouragements and endearments to her as she'd stood in the doorway of their bedroom, too shocked even to weep.

Franz had been a different person then—reckless, defiant, brave. He had worked for a law office that supported socialist workers until 1933, when the Nazi Party had outlawed it, along with all other political parties. After that, he'd continued to work for its causes secretly—and illegally, a fact that had made Rachel feel proud and anxious, and even angry, in turns. She admired her husband's fierce convictions, but she had not always shared them. And, in the end, his courage had cost him —if not his life, then at least his sense of self... for now. Only for now.

Rachel drew a steadying breath, doing her best to put such

troubling memories behind her. For Franz's sake, as well as her own, she wanted to focus on the future. *Their* future, in Havana, Cuba, where once more Franz would find work in a law office, and she as a history teacher, and they would live in a little apartment near the Old Town and make it their own, a safe and cozy haven. They would learn Spanish and drink daiquiris by the Caribbean moonlight; they would walk along the white sand beach and dip their toes in the warm, sultry sea.

It was a dream Rachel held tucked close to her heart, too precious to share with anyone... or maybe just too unlikely. They had no savings, owned little more than the clothes they were wearing and, unlike the first-class passengers parading through their separate gate, she and Franz were slipping onto the SS *St Louis* by what felt like the skin of their teeth. Most Jews who emigrated had to prove their wealth and therefore suitability to set up life elsewhere, but Rachel and Franz had been forced to flee, thanks to his imprisonment, with practically nothing.

But none of that mattered now, she reminded herself, because they had finally made it, they were in line, about to step on board—and into their sparkling new life. It was all going to be all right. It was going to be *wonderful*, and maybe even her mother would be able to join them one day soon.

A sudden shout had her turning in surprise as she craned her neck to see a commotion kicking up in the first-class queue. A glamorous couple had been posing for a photographer, the woman wearing satin and dripping jewels, the man puffing out his chest and looking pompously self-important, when a short, bristle-haired man in Hapag uniform stormed toward them and forcibly ejected the photographer from the line, shouting something about propaganda not happening on his ship.

Bemused, Rachel glanced around at her fellow tourist-class passengers, who seemed as uninterested as Franz in what had been going on, whatever it had been. She supposed no one worried too much about the first-class passengers, who were so obviously wealthy and privileged, with their many steamer trunks and suitcases, their fancy outfits and aura of confidence and entitlement, so certain that this new world would embrace them. Like her and Franz, many of those in tourist class had had to scrape together the money for their fares, and their new life abroad felt like both a precarious and precious thing.

"Some sort of to-do over there," she told Franz, slipping her arm through his once more, and he smiled faintly at her, the barest glint in his eyes reminding Rachel of the man he used to be, and would be again.

An hour crawled past as they slowly shuffled forward in the line. The sunny springtime day turned hot and airless in the embarkation shed, and people removed the shawls and coats over their best Sabbath clothes for the departure from Germany. Rachel kept up a light and cheerful conversation with Franz, remarking on the ship, the weather, the prospect of entertainments that evening that they might enjoy, but, exhausted and overheated, she eventually fell silent, deciding to be content to simply stand and wait, her arm still firmly tucked through his.

Since his release, Rachel thought she could probably count the number of conversations she and Franz had had on one hand, and calling them conversations was, she feared, being generous. But when they were on board, she told herself, and then in their cabin, it would finally be different. Alone together, Franz would take her in his arms, smile at her and say with the rich chuckle she remembered so well, 'At last!' And then he would kiss her...

A sigh escaped her without her meaning it to. It could be dangerous to embroider these fanciful daydreams, Rachel knew, with the gossamer thread of wishful thinking. Franz had not kissed her once since he'd been released two weeks ago. He'd embraced her briefly upon his return, or rather she had embraced *him*, clinging to his thin form while he'd barely clasped her in his arms before moving away.

Since then, he spoke little, touched her even less, and went through his day like a man sleep-walking, retreating into himself, seeming almost as if he were existing somewhere else entirely... and where and what that place was, Rachel couldn't bear to think. He had not said one word about his seven months in Dachau to her, or to anyone else.

When they finally got to their cabin, she knew, the likelihood was he would curl up in bed and fall asleep. Either that, or sit in a chair and stare into space, as he'd done every day since his release, which she found even more troubling.

Enough, she told herself. She was not going to think like this, for she knew that at least one of them had to keep up their spirits, and that had to be her. She returned to the wished-for scenario of Franz taking her into his arms, because one day it would happen, and maybe, God willing, one day soon. She just had to stay strong... and cheerful.

"Almost there now," she murmured, shooting Franz a quick smile. "Won't it be nice to be on the ship?"

"Better than this shed, at any rate," he replied, and looked away.

Fifteen minutes later, they were finally at the gate. Rachel held her breath as the customs officer inspected their papers, including the precious visas that had cost one hundred and fifty American dollars each—an unthinkable sum. And then he was waving them through, and Rachel's breath came out in a grateful rush that ended on something close to a laugh, because they'd made it. They'd finally made it! This was, she promised herself, the beginning of everything.

They followed the stream of passengers onto the ship, and then were directed by a steward to the B deck where the tourist-class cabins were located. Although not as large or elegant as the first-class berths she'd seen in the brochure, Rachel was more than satisfied by their neat cabin, with its two single beds, dresser, and washstand. There was even a dressing table with a mirror and chair. Their two shabby suitcases, all that remained of their worldly possessions, were waiting for them in the cabin, and outside the one porthole, the sea bobbed blue, sparkling with sunlight.

"Isn't this lovely?" she exclaimed, turning to Franz, longing for a response—*any* response—his familiar, crooked smile, the glint in his brown eyes, the way his lids would drop when he was about to kiss her.

He was standing in the middle of the room, one hand in the pocket of his trousers as he gazed vacantly ahead, not even looking at her, the slump of his shoulders and the weariness on his face making him appear so defeated. "Very nice," he agreed tonelessly.

With gentle determination, Rachel took a step toward him. She'd curled her hair that morning and was wearing her second-best dress in pale blue crepe, not that Franz had seemed to notice either, although he'd once remarked, years ago, that this dress brought out the blue in her eyes. "Like forget-me-nots," he'd said, catching her around the waist and kissing her thoroughly.

Right then, she longed for a return, no matter how brief, of his old self, as well as *her* old self. The two of them together, as they once had been, joyous in their love, certain they could weather any storm, even the disapproval of her parents when they'd married. Their love had always been enough. They'd made it so, and they could do so again.

"We made it, Franz," she said softly, and then dared to slip her arms around her husband's waist. The bony feel of him shocked her a little; even through his shirt and jacket she could feel the sharp protrusion of his ribs under his palms. Of course, she'd known he'd grown thin at Dachau; it had been all too obvious since his return, his clothes hanging off him, the skin of his face and neck slack, and yet to *feel* it was more unsettling. Under her questing hands, he felt like someone she didn't know.

She took a step closer as Franz stilled, his body tensing.

"We're free," Rachel whispered, and then, her heart beating hard, she stood on her tiptoes to brush a hopeful kiss against her husband's lips.

His lips remained slack and dry under hers, but at least he gripped her waist with his hands, although whether to embrace her or keep her from getting any closer, Rachel couldn't tell.

After a few seconds of no response, she eased back, managing a smile. "I love you," she whispered, her voice choking just a little, and Franz finally moved his gaze, with seeming reluctance, to look down at her.

His dark eyes drooped with sadness and what Rachel hoped was affection, but he didn't reply. She told herself not to be hurt. It was still early days, as her mother had told her again and again over the last two weeks. "Pfft, no time at all," her mother had insisted, robust in her certainty. "You must be patient, Rachel! You always wanted everything five minutes ago, but it is not to be so."

All she could do now, Rachel knew, was try to wait—and hope.

"Shall we explore the ship?" she asked, injecting a playful note of enthusiasm into her voice, and after a second, Franz nodded.

Rachel smiled as she stepped back. "Let me just freshen up," she said, and was glad there was no audible tremor in her voice. Franz's apparent rejection had stung, more than she knew she should let it, but she pushed the hurt feelings away because they served no purpose.

Lifting her chin, she gazed at her face in the mirror—pretty enough, she supposed, in an unremarkable way, with dark brown hair, deep blue eyes, and a round face kept from looking too girlish by the deep worry line knifing between her brows.

Five years ago, when she'd still been a student, Franz Blau had filled her with awe and longing. She'd watched him from afar, admiring his passionate politics and firebrand personality, as well as his quick wit and cheerful humor. His bright hazel eyes and shock of brown hair had helped too, along with his ready smile. Just looking at him had made her heart skip a hopeful beat. The man standing in the middle of the room now seemed so depressingly different... but he could change. He *would* change, Rachel told herself.

Surveying her reflection, she ran her thumb along the crease in her forehead, doing her best to smooth it away. *No more worries*, she told herself. *No more regrets.*

"Ready?" she called over her shoulder, only to see in the mirror that Franz hadn't moved so much as an inch.

She tucked a stray tendril of hair behind her ear as she turned to her husband with yet another forced smile.

"I can't wait to see all the rooms," she remarked. "A cinema and a library *and* a nightclub...! I heard there was a swimming pool, as well. Fancy that, on a boat! What should we see first, do you think?"

Franz gave a little shrug, his gaze sliding away from hers, and Rachel decided to treat it as a reply.

"The library?" she asked, as if he'd suggested such a thing. "What a good idea." She tucked her arm firmly through Franz's, tilting her head up to his gaze with a sunny smile. "Shall we?"

Franz looked down at her for a moment, his expression torn between sorrow and something Rachel thought was softer, more appealing. It made her breath catch in her chest; there, in his eyes, was a flicker of the man he used to be. Not quite the teasing glint, but almost, a faint echo of it...

"I'm sorry," he said quietly, the words heartfelt and full of grief, and Rachel's heart twisted inside her. She didn't want him to be sorry; she wanted him to be glad, or, better yet, defiant and determined, like the man she'd fallen in love with and married.

She wanted them to fight this—whatever *this* was—together, not her having to drag him along, using all her strength to heave and pull.

Had he sensed those flickers of fear and frustration that flashed through her sometimes, no matter how desperately she tried to suppress them? Rachel vowed to do better. The face Franz saw, that *anyone* saw, would be serene and confident, certain of the future they were forging for themselves, starting today.

The thought steadied her, and made her straighten her shoulders as, smiling, she patted Franz's thin hand. "There's nothing to be sorry for, my darling," she assured him softly. "Nothing at all in the whole world."

And with a deliberate spring in her step, she led her husband out of their cabin, to explore the rest of the ship and start the life she knew could be theirs for the taking, if they simply reached for it—and believed.

CHAPTER 2

The cool night air blew Rachel's hair from its neat French roll as she slowly walked along the deck under a starless sky.

They were a day out from Hamburg, and the passengers on the *St Louis* were starting to relax at last. Last night, many had stood on deck to watch the ship be freed from its moorings, seeming more incredulous than hopeful that it was happening, that the German government was *allowing* it to happen. A few people had muttered darkly under their breath, as if waiting for the government to change its mind and force them back to land.

But the ship had sailed deeper into the placid, moonlit sea, until the shore had disappeared into the darkness and everyone on board had realized they were really, finally *free*. Someone had started singing; others had wept. It had, Rachel thought, felt like a miracle, and for a moment, as she and Franz had stood at the deck, their shoulders brushing, she'd had a glimpse of what their future could be. Then Franz had turned away from the sight of the harbor.

"I'm tired," he'd said, and Rachel had sprung to attention.

"Let's go back to our cabin," she'd murmured, although she

would have rather stayed up on deck, with all the other passengers, enjoying the evening. "I'm tired, too."

Over the last twenty-four hours, there had been glad moments, mere flickers, it was true, of an emotional reawakening in her husband, all of which had heartened her. He'd smiled faintly when a cheer had risen at dinner, and several diners, in their exuberance, had spontaneously started dancing right there at their tables. When they'd walked back to their cabin after watching the ship move away, her fingers had brushed his, and he hadn't pulled away as quickly as he usually did. And this afternoon, when they'd settled themselves in the library with books and cups of coffee, he'd given her a small, grateful smile before turning to his chosen volume.

They were such little things, and yet they *mattered*. Rachel clung to them the way a drowning person clutched at a buoy, anchoring her in this swirling sea of uncertainty—not just about their future in Havana, but as husband and wife. What if the rest of her life were like this? Rachel tried not to wonder, to *fear*, as she walked the deck alone, feeling lonelier than she had in a long while.

Across the ship, everyone was enjoying themselves—a film in the cinema, a dance in the nightclub, all of them reveling in their freedom—and Franz was fast asleep in bed, and she was out here by herself, wondering if, at twenty-six, she'd become as good as a governess to her own husband.

She'd already tucked him up like a child with a kiss on his forehead—the only kind of kiss he didn't resist. When he'd fallen asleep, she'd slipped out of the cabin, needing a few moments of fresh air and freedom, even though she felt guilty for wanting them, and in any case, they weren't making her feel any better.

She ached for the man Franz had used to be—back when she'd met him at university, and he'd been so charming and she'd been so starstruck. He'd worked for the student newspaper, daringly writing stories no one else would print about the Nazi regime, the hope of Communism, as well as the dangers of Stalinism, the utopian ideal he believed they should all struggle for, no matter what the personal cost, raging against corrupt empires.

She had assumed such a man as Franz, so charismatic and dynamic, would never even notice a girl like her—quiet, hardworking, a little shy, more or less unremarkable. But then he *had*, when she'd been reading one of his newspaper articles in the library, poring it over like it was an ancient scroll and, as bold as brass, Franz had sat down across from her and asked her what she'd thought of it. His hair had a been a dark shock that had stood up in places like he'd never met with a comb, and his eyes had snapped with humor and interest as he'd cocked his head, a smile lurking about his lips.

Rachel's mind had gone completely and predictably blank. Fortunately, after a few awful seconds of silence while Franz had waited for what she knew simply *had* to be a witty response, if she were ever to dare to dream of catching his attention, she'd managed to regain her senses and remarked with a shrug that she *supposed* it was adequate, for a student, anyway. Perhaps when he was older, he would be able to do better.

He'd stared at her, his hazel eyes widening in shock for a single second and then he'd let out a shout of laughter, while Rachel had blushed furiously. She'd been flirting without even realizing what she was doing, and it had only taken a laughing look of Franz's to make her feel as if she were floating up by the ceiling, everything in her as light as air, and yet also desperately, breathlessly anxious to keep pleasing him.

He'd asked her out for a coffee there and then, and they'd spent three hours chatting and laughing in a nearby café; every time Franz asked her a question, seeming as if he genuinely wanted to know the answer, Rachel became bolder in her own opinions, as well as her own appeal to this fascinating and funny man. He'd been so clearly *listening* to her, interested and alert, and after a childhood of quiet obedience in a loving but stolid household, Rachel had felt as if she were unfurling like some kind of exotic, tropical flower, all silky petals and sweet fragrance.

Franz didn't mind laughing loudly, or pounding the table with his fist, or debating ideas with passionate intensity. He conceded points as elegantly as he argued them, his mind moving at a lightning speed Rachel struggled to match, but once in a while she succeeded.

When Franz had looked at her, his gaze blazing with intent, her heart had somersaulted in her chest, and she'd felt like the most important person he'd ever met. When he'd kissed her, the whole world had spun until she'd felt dizzy. Falling in love with him had felt like tumbling down a set of stairs, a flight so fast and forceful she hadn't even had a chance to think about whether she wanted to fall.

Her parents, however, had been less than thrilled by the prospective match; the first time she'd brought Franz home for dinner, feeling both proud and more than a little anxious, it hadn't gone well at all. Just remembering that awkward meal had Rachel caught between a wince and a rueful smile. Franz had been at his most passionate, expostulating about politics, while her parents, conservative and deeply, quietly religious, had listened silently, bemused and perhaps even appalled by his careless manner when it came to matters of faith.

A self-declared secularist, Franz had as Jewish a lineage as Rachel, but he certainly hadn't acted like it. When her father had asked him if he observed the Sabbath, he'd dismissed the question with an airy shrug of his shoulders before realizing the inconsiderate insouciance of his gesture and apologizing awkwardly in a way that had only made the situation worse.

"I wasn't *trying* to offend," he'd told Rachel earnestly several days later, catching her hand as they'd strolled through the Tiergarten. "I just didn't even think about it. There's so much good to fight for, and religion has caused all sorts of harms throughout the centuries..."

"And yet it is the Jews who are being harmed now," Rachel had reminded him quietly, "*for* their religion." While she'd always felt her father could be a bit stuffy about such things, she still loved him and she absolutely adored her mother; she hated the thought of either of her parents not loving Franz as much as she did, although she'd always suspected in her heart of hearts that they wouldn't, for the very reasons that they hadn't.

It hadn't stopped *her* from loving Franz, though. He'd taken up all her time, thoughts, air, and she'd given all three gladly. She'd been twenty-one years old, never having had a boyfriend or even been kissed before Franz, and when, a year after he'd first invited her for a coffee, he'd asked her to marry him, she hadn't even had to think about her answer. Never mind her father's disapproval, his blustering threats of her being disinherited or her mother's knitted brow and quiet, anxious sorrow. All she'd wanted was Franz.

They'd married when she was just twenty-two. The wedding ceremony had been small and rushed, at the city hall rather than the synagogue—something she knew her father would never be able to forgive, and which we would have preferred. While her faith sometimes felt like a fragile thing, she still had it, even if Franz did not. Neither of her parents had attended the brief service, although her mother had sent the Meissen plates as a present, along with a letter praying for a blessing upon their marriage. Rachel had felt her parents' absence keenly, but she'd still been dizzy with happiness, simply to be with Franz; her parents' rejection of their love had somehow made everything more romantic and defiant, in true Franz style—them against the world. Just like him, she could be daring and bold. They could be so *together*.

Then her father had died of a stroke six months later, before they'd ever been able to reconcile, and Rachel had been plunged into a sudden, swirling grief. For a few torturous months, she'd questioned—and doubted—just about everything, even her marriage to Franz, and the regret of never reconciling with her father was one she still harbored in her heart. Her mother had insisted that Rachel not let her regret fester, and that her father would have come around to her marriage in time, as she had, if he'd had the chance, and, as proof, she'd given Rachel his pocket watch, a precious heirloom.

Rachel had wanted to believe it all, but she still lamented the fact she and her father had never made up, wishing they had been able to lay aside their petty hurts and prejudices. Now, however, that loss made her all the more determined to fight for those she loved... especially Franz. And that was what she was doing, day by day and hour by hour, sometimes minute by minute... to help Franz find a way back to being the man he used to be.

Rachel stopped to stand at the railing, her fingers curling around the curved wood as she gazed out at the dark expanse of empty sea. *He'll come back to you.* She could almost hear her mother's voice, soft and rich and full of both affection and certainty. *Oh, Mutti.*

Already, Rachel missed her with a sorrow that swamped her and felt closer to grief, as if her mother had died. She longed for her mother's warm arms around her, the comforting smell of her rosewater-scented face powder, the softness of her cheek pressed to Rachel's as she encouraged her to be strong. The thought of never seeing her again felt both agonizing and impossible. Rachel's mind rejected it even as she recognized she would have to learn to live with that truth, or, really, to live without her mother's comforting presence—her steady voice, her calm manner, her unshakeable belief that a cup of coffee and a slice of *Apfelkuchen* at the old, weathered kitchen table in her apartment in Prenzlauer Berg could cure all ills.

Her mother, Rachel knew, would never want her to stew in her own sadness, as much as she was, in her weaker moments, tempted to do just that. Her mother would want her to live for each moment, accepting it for what it was, walking into the next by faith.

Rachel had just taken a deep breath, straightened her shoulders, intent on doing as her mother wanted, when she heard a sound like a sob and saw a man hurtling down the deck, running right past her, his breath coming in tearing gasps as tears streaked his lined face.

"What... sir... can I help?" She stumbled over her words as she took a step toward him, her heart climbing up her throat when she saw him hurl himself at the railing. Was he going to jump off? "*No!*" she cried helplessly, only to fall silent when two women ran past her, one younger and faster, the other tall and thin and elegantly dressed, holding up the folds of her satin skirt with one slender hand.

"Papa!" the younger woman cried, her voice full of fear and distress. "Papa, please! Don't!"

The man was bent over the railing, perilously close to throwing himself into the sea. "I *told* you!" he wept. "I *told* you this ship was doomed, damned. *Damned*! It is not safe. The Gestapo will come for us, they will come and, by God, I won't let them. Not this time! I'll die first!"

The older woman let out a shriek of terror as the man struggled to hoist himself up and then balance with one foot on the railing, his position far too precarious with the sea churning below him.

Rachel stood rooted to the spot, horrified by the scene unspooling in front of her. She wanted to help, but she had no idea how. She was afraid if she moved, she might spur the man to jump.

"Josef!" the older woman cried. "No, please! *Don't!*"

Just then, the younger woman threw herself at her father,

wrapping her arms around his waist. Rachel watched as the two of them fought in a macabre dance, the daughter trying to pull him onto the deck, the man seeming desperate to fling himself overboard.

Why wasn't she *moving*? Rachel thought numbly. Why wasn't she doing something—*anything*? All she could do was stand there, horrified, helpless, wondering if Franz had ever had the same impulse as this man—to end his misery and his life. Was this the sort of agony her husband suffered silently, hiding his pain beneath his blank expression, while she had been trying to jolly him along, as if they were out for a stroll in the park on a rainy day?

The young woman finally won her life-or-death battle, and both she and her father landed heavily on the deck, clearly winded, while the older woman wept quietly into her hands.

Rachel sprang into action at last, and hurried forward, extending a hand to the younger woman. "Let me help you up," she said. It felt like far too little too late, but it was all she could think to do.

The woman, her blond hair disheveled and her blue eyes unfocused, gazed up at her, blinking dazedly, before she took her hand.

"The best thing is a bit of brandy," Rachel continued, instinctively parroting her mother's advice for any kind of shock. "But only a drop or two. Do you know your way back to your cabin?" She glanced at the woman's father; he was curled up into a ball, his knees tucked into his chest, tears trickling silently down his weathered face. Rachel's heart ached with sympathy for him—and also for Franz.

While she knew she could not equate the two men's experiences, at least not without knowing more, this glimpse into another's state of mind had shaken her. She'd wanted Franz back, had thought she could cajole him into his old, assured self, but it was only now that she realized just how difficult, and maybe even impossible, that journey might be. Her husband had no visible scars from his seven months' imprisonment, but like this man, his emotional ones might run deep—and last forever. It was a disturbing thought, and one she knew she needed time to come to grips with.

"Yes," the woman choked out in reply. "But my little brother is sleeping there—"

"The library is empty at this time of night," Rachel inserted quickly. "We can take him there."

Tears pooled in the woman's eyes, and she blinked them away. "I don't know where the library is," she whispered. She sounded wretched, and Rachel's heart ached again, this time for this young woman. She didn't look as if she could be more than twenty, and the confusion and distress Rachel saw on her face mirrored that which she'd felt herself, when Franz had first stumbled home from Dachau, barely speaking, a broken man, starting at sudden noises, staring blank-faced at horrors only he could see.

"You've had a shock," she murmured. She glanced at the older woman, who was struggling to compose herself. "All of you. Let me show you to the library." It was a quiet, peaceful room, used far less than the others, and she and Franz had spent most of the afternoon there.

The next few moments passed in a blur of activity as Rachel guided the little group to the library and arranged for a steward to bring them brandy, which the man drank down quickly before beginning to rock quietly back and forth. Rachel was about to excuse herself and leave them to their sorrow when the young woman turned to her, her unhappy expression replaced by determination and gratitude.

"Thank you," she said in a low voice. "You have been so kind and helpful, and I don't even know your name."

"Rachel Blau," Rachel replied with a small, sympathetic smile. "And it is no trouble." She paused, wanting to say something more, to offer some kind of comfort and encouragement—not just to this woman and her family, but to herself. "Give him time," she said at last, knowing it was what she needed to hear, as well. "We are all hoping for a new life in Havana. If you ever need anything…" She trailed off, wondering what on earth she could give this woman, or anyone. Judging by the cut of their clothes, they were clearly well-to-do, and she and Franz had next to nothing. Besides which, despite her determined cheer, she was struggling enough herself with Franz's condition. How could she possibly offer any hope, any strength, to anyone else? And yet she wanted to… for both their sakes. Gently, she reached out to touch the woman's arm. "God bless you," she whispered, and then, knowing there was nothing else she could say, no more comfort she could give, she slipped through the doors of the library.

Rachel realized she had been gone for the better part of an hour, and a new and alarming anxiety suddenly gripped her as she hurried back to her cabin. What if Franz, like that man, had become distraught? What if he had left the cabin and gone searching for her, or worse, searching for relief from his distress in the same way? She could almost picture it—his thin body hunched over the railing, his blank expression turning wild as he hurled himself overboard…

Her breath hitched and her heart beat hard as she started to run down the corridor. How could she have been so stupid, so *selfish*, as to leave Franz alone for even a minute, never mind nearly an *hour*? Why hadn't she realized the dangers, assuming his silence and seeming indifference hid nothing darker or deeper?

She burst into the cabin, her breath ragged, half expecting to see the bed holding nothing more than rumpled sheets, her husband gone. But as her eyes adjusted to the darkness, she saw that Franz was lying in bed, tucked on his side, his breathing deep and even. Her husband was, thankfully, fast asleep.

Rachel released her pent-up breath in a slow, careful sigh as she closed the door behind her. Her body trembled and she stood there for a moment, her palm flat on the door, as she struggled to compose herself, the waves of fear that had been threatening to crash over now receding.

Quietly, she took off her shoes and undressed, slipping into her nightgown before undoing her hair and quietly brushing her teeth. As she climbed into bed beside Franz, she longed to snuggle into his arms, to feel him pull her close. She craved the comfort of his steady heartbeat beneath her cheek, the sense of safety of being held in his warm embrace, the way he used to stroke her hair, his thumb drifting toward her cheek as his chin settled on top of her head.

But Franz didn't stir, and Rachel didn't want to disturb his slumber by moving any closer. His sleep had been restless enough since his return from Dachau, with him often tossing or turning for much of the night, and she wasn't about to make it any worse.

Yet as she lay in bed, she found her own sleep elusive. The steady hum and rock of the ship should have sent her drifting off, but instead she simply stared at the ceiling, gritty-eyed and full of grief—for Franz, for herself, for the unknown man and his family. Had he been imprisoned in Dachau or somewhere similar? Why was the world so very evil, to allow innocents to be so *tortured*? And was there any hope for either the unknown man or her husband?

Rachel drew a deep breath and then let it out slowly. She was not about to admit defeat or even discouragement now. Strangely, seeing that man in his awful desperation had strengthened her own conviction, not weakened it. She would not feel sorry for herself, to wish futilely for a life she might never have, a husband who was attentive and affectionate, laughing and light and fully *there*.

No, instead she would *fight* for Franz, as that young woman had fought for her father, wrestling him down onto the deck, and back to the land of the living. Rachel might not need to fight in such a physical way, but it was a battle all the same—and one she was, now more than ever, focused on winning—with tenderness and persistence.

Eventually, her eyelids fluttered closed, but it was long after midnight before she finally fell into a fitful sleep.

The next few days passed quietly and peacefully enough. Rachel and Franz spent much of their time in the library or the reading and writing room, either perusing the novels on offer, writing letters, or, in Franz's case, simply sitting and staring into space. Sometimes Rachel read to him from a book of poetry, enjoying the way he'd cock his head as he listened, clearly attentive, even if he didn't say very much. Once, he'd touched her hand, his touch as light as a butterfly's wing, a silent thanks that made her heart sing.

Rachel had tried to compose a letter to her mother to send from Cherbourg, where the ship was due to dock on Monday, but any words she thought seemed stilted. She'd wanted to pour out all her fears, as well as her newly found determination to help her husband, but all she'd written was *Dear Mutti* before the ink dried on the paper and she had not been able to think of how to continue, even as she'd imagined her mother's voice, both soft and stern. *Darling Rachel, you must be patient. You want the world in your hand before a week has passed. You are not God, my girl, although He loves you.*

She'd folded the piece of paper up with just the two words written on it; she would send a letter from Havana, she'd promised herself. By that time, she'd have thought of more to say... and how to say it. And, she'd hoped, by that time she would have more good news—about Franz and their life together.

On Tuesday morning, after picking up passengers in Cherbourg, the *St Louis* steamed westward, its next port of call Havana, in just ten days' time. Only ten short days, Rachel told herself, before they would finally be able to start their lives over again, free from fear. Despite this, the mood on the ship seemed to be caught between fragile hope and a deeper, more persistent anxiety. There had been rumors of the water being poisoned at Cherbourg and also that the *St Louis* firemen were actually members of the Gestapo, placed there to wreak havoc among the passengers on board the ship.

At supper one night, Rachel learned from their fellow diners that a Nazi propaganda reel had been shown before the film on the second night—the same night that poor man had tried to throw himself overboard.

"It could have just been an oversight," Elsa Heglin, a stout woman with a deliberate air, her husband smaller and slighter, remarked darkly as she pressed her lips together, "but it does make one wonder. On a ship of Jews, do we really need *that man* ranting in our faces? And everyone was so looking forward to the film."

"It all sounds so distressing," Rachel murmured. She was very glad Franz had not wanted to go to the cinema.

Overall, Rachel did her best to ignore the other passengers' fearful looks or dark murmurings. She had enough to worry about, and the last thing she wanted to do was make Franz more anxious than he already was.

Although, in truth, Rachel acknowledged as they strolled into the reading and writing room on Tuesday morning, Franz had seemed a little more relaxed these last few days, a fact which heartened her greatly. Every small smile or brush of Franz's fingertips was a balm to her soul, and, she hoped, to his.

"Oh, it's *you!*"

Rachel stopped in surprise to see the young woman from the other evening standing in front of her, her blond hair curling about her heart-shaped face, her blue eyes widening in amazement. She seemed pleased to see her, but as Rachel stood there, she saw the woman's gaze move to Franz, and a look of confusion darkened her eyes.

For a second, Rachel saw her husband through the lens of this young woman's now narrowed gaze—his newly thinning hair, his shabby suit, his shoulders rounded, and his head lowered. He looked like an old man, and yet he was only twenty-eight, and a little over seven months ago he'd been full of fire, passion and wit.

Rachel tucked her arm more firmly through Franz's as she gave the woman a small smile in return. "Hello. I didn't expect to see you here," she remarked. She had assumed the young woman and her family were in first class, simply by the cut of their fashionable clothes.

"I was looking for you, actually," the woman admitted as a blush came to her cheeks. She was very pretty, Rachel thought, and very young.

"You were?" she asked.

"I just... wanted to thank you for your kindness, that night on the deck. I don't know what I would have done without you—"

"You would have managed," Rachel assured her, "if you had to." Despite the woman's youth, she sensed a strength in her, the same kind of strength she wanted to possess in order to help her husband.

"I'm not sure about that." The woman's voice wavered.

"How's your father?" Rachel asked.

"He's—well, he's as best as he can be, I suppose." Her voice cracked as she brushed at her eyes, fighting back tears. "I'm so sorry—"

Rachel's heart twisted with sympathy. "Wait a moment." She turned to Franz, who had been observing this whole exchange with his usual uninterested expression. "Franz, let me get you a seat somewhere comfortable."

Rachel walked him to a quiet corner and gently settled him into a chair.

"Sit here for a moment," she murmured. "I'll get us coffee."

Franz gave a little nod and smile, and Rachel smiled back. They were making progress, she thought.

She turned back to the woman and motioned to take a seat a few tables away from Franz. "Franz will be all right for a bit," she told her. Her husband was, at least, amenable to most things, which was, Rachel supposed, a much-needed mercy. "And I think you could use a cup of coffee, or," she half-teased, "maybe something stronger?"

"Coffee would be wonderful," the woman replied. "But..." She glanced uncertainly at Franz, who was sitting with his hands in his lap as he simply stared into space.

"He'll be all right," Rachel reiterated gently. "He likes being alone, these days. He prefers the quiet." She tried to speak matter-of-factly, not wanting this woman to see how much her husband's emotional absence had the power to hurt her. Not wanting Franz to see it, either, because how would that help?

"Oh, I see..."

Rachel could tell the woman had no idea who Franz was to her, and so she stated quietly, "Franz is my husband."

The woman looked so surprised Rachel would have laughed, except there was nothing remotely funny about it.

"He was in Dachau until two weeks ago," she explained. She kept her voice calm and matter-of-fact, with only a trace of sorrow. "The government told him he had to leave the country within the month, or he would be re-arrested. We were very fortunate to get passage on this ship." Once again, she thought of her mother pawning her precious silver, and a lump formed in her throat, which she resolutely swallowed down.

"I'm so sorry," the woman whispered, clearly appalled.

She sounded so horrified and surprised that Rachel couldn't help but remark carefully, "I assumed, from the other night, your father had experienced something similar."

"He was in protective custody for two weeks," the woman allowed. "I don't know where."

Surely she was not so naïve that she could not have guessed? Rachel did not reply, and the woman let out a little gasp of shock at her silence.

"You don't think he was actually somewhere like Dachau?"

Rachel hesitated for a moment before admitting, "My husband was said to be in protective custody... for seven months."

The woman's eyes widened. "Since *Kristallnacht*?"

Rachel nodded and the woman swallowed hard.

"What does your husband say about his time in Dachau?" she asked in a low voice. "Was it... was it as terrible as they say?"

Rachel shook her head. "He does not speak of it." Franz had not said one word about his seven months there, and Rachel had not wanted to ask him. Now, she wondered if she should.

"Nor does my father," the woman admitted.

"Perhaps it is better that way." Rachel gestured to a steward, who came forward, and she asked him to bring coffee. Once it was poured, she brought a cup to Franz, milky and sweet. His grateful smile warmed her heart, and she stroked his soft hair, savoring the moment, such as it was, and letting it be enough.

As she turned back to her companion, she saw a look on her face that seemed like both pity and admiration, and she quickly looked away, wanting neither emotion. Her marriage felt like a private and sacred thing, not something to be examined and speculated upon, whether for good or for ill.

Rachel poured herself coffee as she sat back down at their table.

"What will you do in Havana?" the woman asked as she sipped her own drink.

"Find a way to make a living, as best as we can," Rachel replied. She glanced at Franz, who had yet to take a sip of his coffee. Could he find work in the law in Havana in his current state? Would he even want to? She straightened as she turned her gaze back to Sophie. "I used to be a history teacher, before the laws changed. I don't know if I will be able to teach in Cuba."

She tried to ignore the fear that cramped her stomach at the thought. She'd loved her work at a girls' school, but she'd been fired two years ago, when Jews had been forbidden to teach gentiles, and the work she'd found in a Jewish school had paid very little. When Franz had been imprisoned, she'd given up their apartment and moved in with her mother to save money. They really had so very little to start their new life with.

"I have a book on the Spanish language," Rachel continued, "but I must admit, it is slow going. I am not a natural when it comes to languages."

"I don't know much Spanish either," her companion replied, "but I do have something of a knack for languages. Well, a bit." She ducked her head, looking shy. "I was hoping to study languages at university, but it never came to pass. But if you'd like some tuition, or to study together...?" She trailed off, seeming uncertain, but Rachel was deeply touched.

"Would you?" she asked as something inside her eased and lightened. She hadn't realized how lonely she'd felt on board ship, with only Franz for company. "That would be marvelous."

"We only have a few days left, but we could make a start. My friends, Hannah and Rosa, might enjoy it, as well. They don't know any Spanish." The woman's eyes lit up. "We could form a little class!"

"Hannah and Rosa?" Rachel repeated, unable to keep from sounding a little wary. "Are they in first class, as well?"

"Yes, but we could have the classes on the sports deck," the woman replied quickly. "That's available to everyone, and it would give Heinrich—my little brother—and Lotte—Hannah's sister—a chance to play." Inadvertently, she glanced at Franz, a question in her eyes. She clearly equated him with these children, someone to care for and *manage*, a thought that Rachel firmly pushed away.

"Franz would enjoy the sunshine," Rachel replied. "Especially now that it is starting to get warmer." Impulsively, she reached over to touch the woman's hand. "Thank you for your kindness. I realize I don't even know your name!"

She let out an embarrassed little laugh. "Sophie. Sophie Weiss."

"Thank you, Sophie," Rachel said quietly. She smiled as she blinked back sudden tears. "I didn't realize until you came to find me how much I could use a friend."

CHAPTER 3

ANTWERP, BELGIUM—SATURDAY, JUNE 17, 1939, ONE MONTH LATER

Rachel stood at the deck, the splinter of emerald glinting in the palm of her hand as she gazed out at the placid harbor, hardly able to believe that, in just one more day, she and Franz would be on land... and in the Netherlands, of all places. Cuba, and their hoped-for life in Havana, was now farther away than ever, a distant dream that had vanished like the morning mist over the sea as the weeks on the Atlantic had stretched on and on.

The cruel twists of fate that had brought them to this moment still had the power to make her bitter and, worse, despairing, if she let them, which she was trying her hardest not to.

It had all started so wonderfully, Rachel acknowledged on a small sigh as her fingers closed around the green jewel in her hand.

Sophie had introduced her to her friends Rosa and Hannah, and the four of them had started a little study group while Lotte and Heinrich—Hannah's sister and Sophie's half-brother—had played together on the sports deck. Franz had been content to sit nearby, and occasionally he'd offered a small, wry remark that reminded Rachel of the cheerful, dry wit she remembered and loved so well.

As the *St Louis* had steamed closer to Cuba, the air had turned warm and sultry, and the children had clamored to play in the pool. Even Franz had dipped his toes in, smiling faintly at the feel of the warm water.

One night, as she'd gotten ready for dinner, he'd kissed her cheek, the brush of his lips so swift and light, Rachel had half wondered if she'd imagined it... but she hadn't, and she tucked the memory close to her heart, like a photograph she could treasure and take out, smooth its creased folds, and do her best to commit to memory.

The night before they had been meant to dock, they had all attended a masquerade ball, although Rachel, in solidarity with Franz, had declined to wear a costume. The other women had seemed so *young* to Rachel, clowning about in their outfits, delighted to be silly, and she'd half-wished that she still possessed that kind of carefree *joie de vivre*. She'd had it once, when she'd first fallen in love with Franz, when life had felt as heady as a glass of champagne, all bubbles and froth, but it felt a very long time ago now.

Still, it had been enjoyable to wear her best dress, to tap her foot in time to the music, to drink champagne, and, most of all, to *hope*. Franz was getting better, she saw signs of it every day, and soon the four friends would all be in Havana. Rosa had mentioned meeting up for cocktails at a fancy hotel. In that moment, Rachel had been able to believe that she would find a job, that Franz would work again, that they would live together as they used to, with love and laughter. She'd even imagined her mother coming out to Cuba when she could; Havana would become her home, too. It had all felt so wonderfully possible, especially when she, Sophie, Rosa, and Hannah had all toasted each other and their brightly shimmering future, which had seemed as if it had been *right there* for the taking. All they had to do was reach for it...

How had it all gone so disastrously wrong?

First had been the Cuban government's refusal to allow the *St Louis* into Havana's port just two days later. The ship had had to moor outside the harbor, the blank walls of the fortress El Murro shimmering under the hot sun in the distance, making the shoreline seem like an impenetrable wall they could not pass. Then there had been the endless days of waiting in the humid heat, having no idea what was going on, as a restless fear had gripped everyone on board. Passengers had become fractious, fretful, and sometimes angry.

Hope fell, rose, and fell again. Rumors swirled and a few fortunate passengers were let off the ship, taken to Cuba. Relatives, including Hannah's father, came in fishing boats, calling up to their beloved family members, making promises that it soon became all too apparent they did not possess the power to keep.

Cuba, it seemed, did not want to accept a thousand Jews.

Rosa, whose father was on a select passenger committee, spoke darkly of the *Abwehr*—the German military intelligence—being on board the ship. According to her father, the whole enterprise, she'd proclaimed bitterly, might have been no more than a Nazi propaganda exercise, to show the world that *nobody* wanted the Jews.

What would become of them? There had been frightened whispers of the refugees being sent back to Germany—a prospect that had caused one man to attempt to take his life. A few passengers had been roughed up by the Gestapo firemen on board, while some female passengers had rushed a ladder, desperate to get off the ship, and been pushed back; one poor woman had broken her arm.

Then Sophie's father, his health already frail, had attempted to kill himself, slitting his wrists and throwing himself overboard. Fortunately, he'd been rescued and had since recovered, in physical if not mental health, but it had made Rachel fear for Franz and his own increasingly precarious state. After those first, small forays into hope that he was getting better, since the ship had anchored outside the harbor, he'd retreated into himself once again, even more so than before—hardly speaking, never looking her in the eye, spending hours simply staring into space.

He was standing right next to her now, but it was as if he wasn't there. What silent torment was he enduring? And what would happen if he snapped?

As the sun rose higher in the bright summer sky, Rachel glanced down once more at the shard of emerald in her palm. It had been given to her by Sophie before she'd left for Washington DC to stay with acquaintances of her family. A precious jewel, split into four pieces, one for each friend, as they'd promised to meet again at Henri's, a café in Paris, when the world was made safe and right again. Rachel could not imagine how any of them could keep such a promise, but she'd made it all the same. She longed to believe in a future where she saw her friends, where Franz was well, where they were happy and in love. The sliver of emerald felt like a talisman, a promise of better things to come, even if right now the whole world seemed both uncertain and so very dark.

It had been over two weeks since they'd split the emerald, and the *St Louis* had been forced by the Cuban government to leave its waters, cruising north to near Miami in the hope that the United States might take them in.

But that was not to be. The United States refused the *St Louis* entry, and after returning to Cuba to anchor off the Isle of Pines, with the vain hope that they might disembark there, the *St Louis* had started cruising east, all the way back to Europe, where Rachel, Rosa, and Hannah had finally learned their fates. England, France, Belgium, and the Netherlands had all agreed to take a quarter share of the passengers, announcing who had been allocated where in turn.

By one of those lamentable twists of fate, the three women were all to be separated. Rosa and her family were to go to England, Hannah and her sister to France, and Rachel and Franz to the Netherlands—a place she'd never been, although Franz had once, to Amsterdam, before they were married. Still, neither of them spoke a single word of Dutch. And how long would they be there, in a strange land, and one so close to the Nazi threat?

Many of the passengers were already talking about rebooking their passage to Cuba or even America, but Rachel knew she and Franz did not have that luxury. There simply wasn't money for another trip, never mind the exorbitant price of visas. It seemed they would have to make the Netherlands their home, at least for a time, a prospect which caused Rachel some trepidation. How would she find work? How would they survive financially? And what if it came to war, as so many were saying it would? The Netherlands was not all that far from Germany; they'd gone halfway around the world and back again, and the Nazi threat felt almost as close as it ever had.

With a sigh, Rachel slipped the shard of emerald into the pocket of her skirt and turned to Franz. "It feels like a holiday," she told him brightly, even though it didn't. "Just to the Netherlands, rather than Havana." She shrugged, smiling. "I've never been there before, but I've heard it's pretty. All windmills and bicycles, isn't that right? Do you remember what it was like, when you went to Amsterdam?" He didn't reply and she continued, a slight edge of desperation creeping into her voice now, "Does it matter where we go, as long as we are together?"

Franz was silent, his gaze on the horizon. "I don't suppose it does," he finally replied, his tone terribly bleak.

"We'll be all right, Franz," she whispered. "We'll find a little apartment, maybe in an attic of a townhouse, with a view of the city." They were meant to travel on to Rotterdam, and Rachel had no idea what that place looked like, but she was determined to dream. "We'll hear the church bells every hour, and we'll watch the stars come out in the sky. And I'll learn to make Dutch food... What do they eat in the Netherlands? Pancakes?" She had no idea.

Franz smiled faintly, although he didn't look at her. "And sausage," he said.

"Pancakes and sausage!" Rachel exclaimed. "Perfect."

"And potatoes," Franz added, the barest lilt of humor to his voice. "And herring. They eat them whole, headfirst." His eyes glinted as he looked down at her. "You don't even like fish."

"I can *learn* to like it," Rachel replied firmly. This was the most they'd spoken in days. "Pancakes and potatoes, herring and sausage." She chanted it like a poem she needed to remember, one that would somehow keep them safe. "How international we shall be!" She smiled up at him, but as he looked down at her, his own faint smile faltered, and then he looked away.

Rachel leaned her head on his thin shoulder and closed her eyes, doing her best to hold onto the hope their few moments of lighthearted banter had given her. It could be so hard to keep dreaming, but she was determined to do it. *Pancakes and potatoes, herring and sausage... in their little attic apartment, looking over the towers and spires of the city, listening to church bells...*

"Good morning," Rosa greeted them, and Rachel opened her eyes to see her friend strolling down the deck, looking somber. She glanced out at the pier where the *St Louis* was meant to berth. "It's hard to believe it's actually happening," she remarked quietly. "Those bound for Belgium will be allowed to disembark this morning. The Weisses are going there, you know."

Rachel had heard as much, although she hadn't spoken to Sophie's family. "How is Sophie's father?" she asked.

Rosa shrugged. "They've all been keeping their distance since Sophie left. I suppose we never knew them, not really." She paused, frowning. "I hope he'll be all right. He seems so fragile."

"He just needs some time to recover." Rachel glanced at Franz, worried that this type of talk might distress him, but once again he'd retreated into his own world, his expression distant.

Rosa looked at Rachel in concerned sympathy. "And you? How do you feel about going to the Netherlands?"

"I was just telling Franz it's like a holiday," Rachel replied as cheerfully as she could. "I've never been there before, you see. I've never even ridden a bicycle, but I hear it's all the fashion there, I suppose because it's so flat. Everyone rides them, so I shall simply have to learn."

Rosa's smile was soft and sad. "You certainly will." Her gaze flicked to Franz. "And you, as well, Franz." She'd gentled her tone, the way you might when speaking to a slow child, and it made Rachel stiffen.

"Oh, Franz already knows how to ride a bicycle," she assured Rosa. She glanced at her husband. "Don't you, darling?"

"I learned some time ago," Franz agreed without expression, and an awkward silence ensued.

"We disembark for the Netherlands tomorrow," Rachel continued in the same cheerful voice. "We're actually very lucky, you know. At dinner, Frau Heglin told me that the Netherlands is only accepting those with U.S. registration cards because they have so many Jewish refugees there already. They don't want anyone to stay longer than they have to." She let out a little laugh that felt and sounded forced, because that didn't seem like much of a welcome. "We don't have such a card," she explained, "but they took us anyway, thank goodness." She hoped it hadn't been an administration error that would cause them trouble later.

"It's good of you to see that as luck," Rosa replied with wry sympathy. "Truth be told, I'd rather have the registration card." She rolled her eyes, and Rachel found a smile.

"Well, you can't have everything," she answered lightly, and then turned to smile at Franz, whose gaze flitted away. Rachel gazed blindly out at the harbor, the early-morning sunlight making the surface of the water shimmer, trying not to show her dismay at her husband's withdrawal.

The summer's day was already turning hot, even though it was only a little past dawn, and her blouse was sticking to her back. At the quayside, sailors and stevedores were starting to move around—hauling crates and calling to each other, the harbor a hive of industry. In the stuffy social hall on board, the two hundred and fourteen passengers selected to go to Belgium were already assembling, even though the ship was not likely to berth for hours yet. Everyone, Rachel thought, wanted to get off this wretched ship—the voyage of the damned, as some had already bitterly called their ill-fated journey.

"No, you can't have everything," Rosa agreed with a sigh as she also stared out at the sea. Rachel knew her friend was anxious about her own future, but surely England was safer than the Netherlands? It was farther from Germany, at any rate, which could only be a good thing. Not that she begrudged Rosa her fate, or Sophie's, or Hannah's. She wouldn't let herself. At least, she told herself, they were all going *somewhere*.

"We shall have to write each other," Rachel said, "through Sophie's address in Washington. I suppose it might take a few months, but soon we'll all be settled and regaling each other with all sorts of tales about the food and customs of the places we've landed. I wonder who will have the strangest story to tell?"

Rosa shook her head slowly, her mouth downturned and her eyes full of sorrow. "How do you keep so cheerful, Rachel?" she asked, and her gaze slid inexorably to Franz before jerking back to her friend.

Rachel stiffened, color flaring into her face as she tried not to feel affronted. Did her situation really invoke that much *pity*? Over the last few weeks, she'd seen her friends look at Franz in a way that made her feel self-conscious and embarrassed, but she'd never asked for their pity, and never would. She didn't need it from Rosa now.

Rosa's parents, Rachel knew, were well-connected and wealthy, and they would probably be living in a luxurious apartment in London within a few days of their arrival in England, a far cry from her and Franz's likely situation. Still, she would not let herself feel envious.

"What should I do instead?" Rachel countered with a touch of uncharacteristic asperity. "None of us has any choice in the matter. I *choose* to make the best of it, and so should you."

Rosa looked abashed. "I know, I'm sorry," she murmured. She glanced out at the harbor again, Antwerp's piers visible in the hazy distance. "I'm just afraid."

"We're all afraid," Franz interjected, his tone turning harsh, surprising both women and silencing them completely, because there seemed to be nothing more to say.

The day passed slowly, a ferment of waiting, until the passengers destined for Belgium finally trooped off the ship at seven o'clock at night. Those bound for Rotterdam were told they would be disembarking in the morning, to be transferred to a small steamer that would take them to the city. From there, Rachel had no idea where they would go. The Dutch representative in charge of the passengers, Alfred Moser, had seemed reluctant to impart any information about their final destination, which made her nervous, even though she tried not to be.

That night was sticky and hot, and Rachel threw off the covers as she quietly slipped out of bed, not wanting to disturb Franz, who had slept even more restlessly since the ship had turned back east. She sat by the porthole, gazing out at the tranquil harbor, everything quiet and still. It would have felt peaceful, save for the uncertainty and anxiety seething in her stomach.

They were now only a few hundred miles from where they'd started out in Hamburg—a fact that seemed both incredible and laughable. Rachel rested her forehead against the beveled glass. In moments like this, when the world was dark and she felt so terribly alone, it was hard not to give into despair. She missed her mother, the cozy apartment she'd shared with Franz, her small circle of friends. She missed her job, teaching in a Jewish school, even though with the further persecutions and restrictions against Jews, it had become more and more challenging—no money for books, sudden raids, soldiers tripping their pupils in the street, or worse. She wanted to believe it would all be better in the Netherlands, that they would find their little apartment and eat pancakes and ride bicycles and be happy.

For Franz, she acted as if she was certain of it. But here, alone in the dark, still night with nothing but her anxious thoughts to keep her company, she couldn't pretend, not to Franz, and not even to herself.

A small, broken sound escaped her, and she sucked in a hard breath, not wanting to succumb to tears. Not now, and not ever. For Franz, Rachel told herself, as she had so many times before, she had to be strong.

Taking a deep breath, she wiped her dry cheeks, pressing her fingertips to her burning eyelids, and then slipped back into bed next to her sleeping husband to wait for the morning... and whatever it might hold.

Just a few hours later, at five o'clock the next morning, a steward thumped on their cabin door, startling Rachel out of a light and uneasy sleep.

"Wake up, wake up! You leave for Rotterdam within the hour!" he called before moving onto the next room.

Rachel clambered out of bed, while Franz simply rolled over, his back to her.

Quickly, she splashed water on her face before slipping into a serviceable dress of pale green cotton she'd had to wash out in the little sink. "Franz, wake up," she urged as she touched his shoulder. "We're leaving now."

Her husband blinked up at her blearily, and for a second Rachel feared he might resist.

"Come on, darling," she cajoled, tugging on his hand. "You know how I'm looking forward to seeing the Netherlands." She pulled a little harder, and reluctantly he came up into a seated position, his hair rumpled, his jaw unshaven. "We never had a honeymoon," she teased. "Maybe this is it?"

For a second, a light flickered in his eyes and a smile tugged at his mouth as he gazed up at her. "Some honeymoon," he remarked dryly.

Rachel wagged a finger at him. "How can you say that, when we haven't even started yet? We'll bicycle by the river, and eat by candlelight, and see the sights..." She scrambled to think of something to see in Rotterdam, but her mind went blank, and to her delight, Franz's mouth kicked up even more at the corner.

"The *sights*?" he prompted, and Rachel rolled her eyes, laughing.

"All right, I don't even know what the sights are," she admitted, "but we'll see them. *All* of them."

To her surprise, Franz tugged her toward him, until she was sitting next to him on the bed. He gazed at her seriously for a moment and Rachel felt as if her heart were suspended in her chest. He had not looked at her so meaningfully since he'd returned from Dachau, and she was afraid to break the moment by so much as taking a breath.

"You are the bravest woman I know," he told her in a low voice that throbbed with feeling, and then, tenderly, he put his arms around her and drew her cheek down to his shoulder, just as she'd longed for all these days and weeks.

"Oh, Franz." Her voice thickened and she closed her eyes against the hot press of tears as she savored the feel of his lean arms around her shoulders, his body warm and solid next to hers. "You're the brave one."

"No." Now he sounded sad, as well as very certain. "No, I am most certainly not brave at all."

Rachel pulled back slightly to look at him, taking in both the affection and somberness in his gaze. "Franz," she began hesitantly, fumbling her way through the words, "whatever happened... in that camp... whatever you might have endured..." She didn't like to think of such things—she knew most prisoners were tortured in some way, either physically or emotionally, or both—but maybe she needed to speak of them now, for Franz's sake. "You can tell me," she urged him, but he was already shaking his head.

"Let's not talk of it," he insisted brusquely. His arms dropped from around her and Rachel felt their loss.

He rose from the bed, raking a hand through his hair, and she wished she hadn't said anything about Dachau. She'd been so afraid to break the moment, and then she'd gone and done it. She could have kicked herself, but there was no point lamenting her mistake now. Franz was getting dressed, and they needed to have breakfast and be on deck in just forty-five minutes.

They'd had the beginning of a conversation, Rachel told herself. And they could have other ones... in time.

. . .

The morning, hot and humid, passed slowly. After breakfast, at six o'clock, the passengers bound for Rotterdam waited in the social hall, wilting in the heat, as hour after hour passed. Hannah and Rosa, who were both due to board another ship headed to France and then England, stopped by to see them, offering them what encouragement they could, little Lotte clinging to Hannah's hand.

"I'm sure it won't be too much longer," Hannah told Rachel. "The *Jan van Arckel* has docked alongside us. You're sure to board it any moment."

"What's taking so long, then?" Rosa demanded. She sounded as impatient as Rachel felt, pacing in front of them, her hands laced tightly together.

"Oh, the usual necessary bureaucracy, I'm sure," Rachel answered with a weak attempt at humor. "Why do something efficiently when you can take half a day to do it?" This whole journey had been filled with such delays, day after day of waiting without knowing anything. She sighed, and then brought herself up short. They were close now, so very close.

Finally, just after nine o'clock in the morning, they were allowed to board the steamer. Rosa flung her arms around Rachel and then Hannah did as well, and Rachel's heart lurched as she realized this really was goodbye. Would they ever see each other again? Their friendship had sparked so quickly and flared so brightly, but just four weeks on from boarding at Hamburg, they were all going their separate ways, to different countries. The promise to meet up at Henri's seemed flimsy at best, wishful thinking at its worst. How on earth would they ever be able to make such a thing happen?

"Godspeed," Rosa murmured as she kissed both of Rachel's cheeks. "It's going to be all right, Rachel, I'm sure of it."

Rachel could only nod as she squeezed Rosa's hands; her throat was too thick with tears for her to manage a word.

"We'll see each other at Henri's," Rosa reminded her. She

slipped her hand out of Rachel's to draw her sliver of emerald from her pocket. With a wan smile, Rachel reached for hers and they touched the two shards together for a brief moment.

"It will happen," Rosa said forcefully, and she hugged Rachel one last time before stepping away, the emerald still clutched in her hand.

Rachel kept hold of her own precious shard as the passengers crowded on the decks of the little steamer left the pier at Antwerp, leaving the *St Louis* behind and beginning its slow and complicated journey through a system of waterways and canals to Rotterdam. River police boats escorted the *Jan van Arckel* on either side, just as they had the *St Louis* upon the departure from Havana, and the sides of the narrow canals were lined with bystanders, many of them calling out their good wishes to the refugees of the ship that had come to be known the whole world over.

"Isn't it nice, Franz?" Rachel exclaimed, her spirits lifting a little at the sight of all those smiling faces. "Look how everyone is wishing us well. It seems the Netherlands is happy to accept a few hundred more Jews, after all."

"Or they're just caught up in the moment," Franz replied as he gazed dispassionately out at the smiling crowds. "After all, it doesn't cost them anything, does it, to wish a stranger well?"

"I don't suppose it does," Rachel agreed after a second's pause, "but they didn't have to come out all this way, did they? I think they do mean it." She waved at a little girl who stood on the shore, standing on her tiptoes to get a better view. "It seems like a good omen," she stated firmly, wanting to believe it. Needing it to be true.

Franz angled himself away from her, hunching his shoulders. "Let's just see what it's like in Rotterdam," he muttered. "That's the important thing."

They didn't discover that until five o'clock that evening, when the *Jan van Arckel* finally arrived at Rotterdam, the city glowing gold under the hazy sun of a summer's afternoon. It had been a pleasant if long journey, as the steamer had traveled slowly and steadily though the different waterways, a maze of narrow canals that wended their way through unrelentingly flat marshlands, the only sound the whisper of wind in the grass, along with the steady chug of the steamer. The bystanders and well-wishers had long since drifted away as Rotterdam's ancient towers and spires had appeared through the summer haze like a ghost city.

Before Rachel could take any of it in, an officer from the dock was shouting up at them, his voice guttural, the German unschooled and abrasive.

"*Raus, Raus!*" he called, sounding angry and impatient as he ordered them off the boat. "*Schnell!*"

Next to her, Franz stiffened, his eyes going wide with what Rachel feared was both shock and remembrance. Other passengers were looking at each other anxiously. The man sounded like a surly prison guard, harshly telling them to get out, and be quick about it. No one had spoken like that to them since they'd left Hamburg, not even some of the less sympathetic members of the crew on the *St Louis*.

"*Raus!*" the guard continued. "Off the ship! You will be taken immediately to a quarantine camp! Off, off! *Schnell*, hurry!"

Everyone began to rush around, grabbing suitcases and children and hats, fumbling in their fear, as the man continued to shout, sounding angrier with every second.

Rachel had no time to be afraid or even to think on what the guard had meant by a quarantine camp. Her whole focus was on Franz, whose face had drained of color, his body stiff and unyielding as if he were gripped by a terror, or maybe a memory. She looped her arm through his as she did her best to propel him forward even as he resisted.

"Franz, Franz," she murmured urgently. "It will be all right,

I promise. But we need to go. It's time to get off this ship, at last! Isn't that good news?"

Her husband did not reply as they were herded along with everyone else, off the steamer and onto one of the waiting trucks. Its back was covered with a tarpaulin, and there were two rough wooden benches running along either side. The refugees stumbled as they hurled themselves up into the truck, and Rachel landed hard on her knees before she scrambled onto a bench, quickly drawing Franz down to sit next to her, his whole body taut with tension. No one spoke, and everyone's face was pale and tense, wide-eyed with dawning realization—and fear.

This wasn't, Rachel thought numbly, anything close to the kind of welcome any of them had hoped for.

CHAPTER 4

JULY 1939—HEIJPLAAT, THE NETHERLANDS

Rachel dumped out the dirty water, watching it seep into the dry, cracked earth, taking this moment alone, outside the crowded barracks, to simply breathe and *be*. The last month at the quarantine camp of Heijplaat had been challenging in so many ways.

The trucks they'd been loaded onto, like so much chattel, from the *Jan van Arckel* had rumbled on for the better part of an hour before they'd all tumbled out to face their future—the barbed wire and snarling guard dogs of Heijplaat, a quarantine camp for the Jews nobody in the Netherlands seemed to want.

At first, everyone had tried to console themselves that this sort of isolating treatment would only be for a few days. A quarantine camp, after all, people said, was just that. A few days to prove they were not dangerously ill and then they would be allowed to settle in Rotterdam, or Amsterdam, or wherever they chose, and live as Dutch citizens, or as good as.

Rachel longed to believe these things and wished desperately for Franz to believe them as well, for his own sake as much as hers, but from the beginning, she sensed they were not to be. The two hundred refugees were herded into the camp that had once been a quarantine station for sailors and, without apology or explanation, the gates locked behind them. They were as good as in prison. But while the accommodation was crowded and the amenities limited, Rachel assured herself it could have been much worse.

Their barracks were divided into two large rooms—one for women, one for men, with wooden bunks lining the walls. They had the use of separate washrooms, a laundry, a small kitchen, and a bare-looking sitting room that held just a few worn armchairs, a handful of tattered books and a single backgammon board. Outside, there was a recreational hall and a playing field, as well as a small beach stretching out to the Maacht River, where they could see ships pass in the distance, a web of cranes from the port stretched against an endless sky.

It was adequate, if only just, but it was hardly the sort of life any of the refugees had imagined for themselves, trapped behind barbed wire, and in yet more limbo. As one elderly gentleman had wryly said, "It's like being on the *St Louis*, but with less food and more flies."

They were given food twice a day—mainly potatoes and herring, which Rachel had tried to joke about, daring Franz to eat one headfirst as he'd described, but he'd remained stony-faced throughout her little pantomime, as he had for much of their time in this place.

The days passed in a stultifying haze of hot weather, short tempers, and no further information. The youngest children were allowed to set up a school of sorts, but the only building suitable was, in a macabre twist, the mortuary. The adults spent most of their waking hours trying to find a way out of the camp, queuing endlessly to speak to the camp administrator, or writing letters to anyone they knew who could possibly help them obtain a visa or, even better, a precious U.S. registration card.

Rachel had no such acquaintances, but she had written to both her mother and Sophie, trying to paint as optimistic a picture as she could, even though she suspected they would see through to the pervading fear seething beneath. *How were they going to get out of here?* It was a question that tormented most of her waking moments because, for Franz's sake, they had to find a way. Being in the prison-like camp was, Rachel feared, too grim a reminder of his seven months in Dachau.

After the first week, a trickle of fortunate people with the U.S. registration card were allowed to leave, heading to America, that promised land with streets of gold and dreams. The lucky ones packed their suitcases hurriedly, with harried looks of apology for those they were happily leaving behind, before they scurried through the gates, not looking back once to see the baleful stares of bitter envy on the faces of the refugees left to molder in the camp.

Since she and Franz had no such card, nor the means to obtain one, Rachel knew their names would never be called. They would never walk through those barbed-wire gates to board a ship for New York or Washington, or even Southampton or Cherbourg, as some had, with thankful embraces and tears of joy. They couldn't even begin to imagine such a thing, and so they needed to think about how they could make a life here, in the Netherlands. Would the Dutch government really insist they stay in such a place as this, penned up like *criminals*? A month on, it seemed all too likely.

Sometimes, as she stood in line for the daily ration of potato and herring, or shook out her thin mattress, or did her best to comb her hair and keep her clothes neat despite the sweltering conditions, Rachel wondered how her dear friends were faring. Was Sophie settled in Washington? Had her family been able to join her from Belgium? Maybe Rosa was living in luxury in London; her father, Rachel had recalled, had talked about renting a house, setting up a medical practice. And Hannah, in France?

Like her, Hannah had been afraid to be so close to the

threat of war, especially with her little sister Lotte to look after. But surely France was safe, Rachel thought as she gazed down at her sliver of emerald, as she had so often, drawing comfort from the promise it held. Everyone spoke of the indomitable strength of the Maginot Line—unlike the Netherlands, with its open land, sixteen thousand square miles of marshy flatlands, so easy for German tanks to roll across, should they so choose... which one day, it seemed, they might.

Not, of course, that she wanted to think like that. Rachel did her best to keep her spirits up, for Franz's sake, as well as her own. Since their arrival at Heijplaat, he had sunk into a worse state. Gone was the blank face, the vague air, replaced by a far more pervading despair, as if he were sinking inside himself, disappearing down into the depths of futility, never to return.

It had started the moment they had arrived, when they'd been herded off the trucks with more shouts of *Raus* and *Schnell*, and he'd seen the barbed wire looming up in front of them, its jagged edges cutting across a hazy gray sky. A German Shepherd on a chain leash had barked and snarled as it had leaped toward them. Rachel had shrunk back, terrified, but Franz had simply stood there, staring at those gates, a look of such bleak resignation coming over his face that Rachel had forced herself to rally, ignoring the slathering dog and insisting to Franz that this was nothing more than a necessary measure, and would be over before they knew it, when they were both given a clean bill of health, as they surely would be.

A month on, she could no longer summon the energy or conviction to participate in that longed-for fantasy. She needed, Rachel knew, to find a solution that was something other than simply hoping for the best, despite all the odds against it.

Bracing the empty basin against her hip, she turned back to the barracks. In the four weeks since the refugees had come to Heijplaat, they'd done their best to turn the long, narrow rooms with their plank bunk beds into something homely, limited as their accommodation so obviously was. Each barracks held fifty people, when really, Rachel reflected, they should only hold thirty, and even that might be considered uncomfortably close quarters.

With fifty, privacy was a pipe dream that the refugees resolutely tried to maintain, hanging sheets or towels between bunks, propping pictures against the walls, and generally trying to make the bare and unfriendly space more welcoming.

"*Guten Tag, Fräulein,*" Elsa Heglin, her neighbor from the next bunk and former dining companion on board the *St Louis*, greeted her with a wan smile as she straightened in front of her bed, one hand bracing her hip. A once-stout woman in her sixties, she seemed to be fading before Rachel's eyes, although not as much as her husband, who had come down with stomach pains while they'd still been on the *St Louis* and was now bedridden and helpless in the men's quarters. He'd been taken to the medical center twice, but they'd insisted there was nothing they could do for him and sent him back each time.

"*Guten Tag,*" Rachel returned with a small smile. "How is Herr Heglin this morning?"

"He's a little better today, I think," Elsa replied, her cheeks pinkening with purpose. "He sat up this morning and took some broth. Truly, I think he is on the mend, thanks be to God."

Rachel pressed the older woman's hands with her own. "I'm so glad," she told her warmly, thinking that she *would* be glad, if this was not the same thing Frau Heglin had said every morning since they'd come to the camp, and her husband's condition had not changed. If anything, it had grown worse.

"And your husband, *Fräulein*?" Elsa asked hopefully, yet with a certain shrewdness in her eyes that Rachel did her best to ignore. "How does he fare?"

"Oh, Franz is well," Rachel replied firmly. "Very well. He is going to take the sun this afternoon. It's such a warm day."

The older woman's faced sagged with sympathy, and really,

naked pity, for while her own husband was clearly ill, he was at least *trying* to get better. Franz was not. They were both fooling themselves, she thought despondently.

Giving Frau Heglin a purposeful smile of farewell, Rachel slipped the basin underneath her bunk, next to her suitcase, and then straightening her dress and tidying her hair, she went in search of her husband.

Although the unspoken rule was that men and women were not allowed in each other's quarters, this was broken so often as to be completely ignored. Most of the refugees were married, and living apart was an indignity they were not willing to suffer. As Rachel tapped on the door and then slipped inside the men's barracks, she was greeted by a few tired smiles and more looks of sympathy than she would wish. Franz, she feared, had not risen from his bunk yet.

Sure enough, she found him lying there, unmoving, on the thin mattress, his face to the wall. He looked, Rachel thought with a necessary dispassion, utterly dreadful. He was pasty-skinned and sickly pale, unshaven, his hair greasy and lank, and, worst of all, he *smelled*.

When they'd first arrived at Heijplaat, he'd tried to rouse himself, spending at least part of the day in the sitting room or outside. Rachel had done her best to entice him to play backgammon, which she knew he'd once enjoyed. When they'd first been married, they'd spent many contented evenings playing the game—Franz had teased her about how hopeless she was at it, and then, with a glinting smile, had let her win—but those days felt far away.

As the weeks had passed, Franz had retreated more and more to his bunk, and now Rachel could barely get him to sit up. She usually managed to get him to eat a little at the two meals they were offered, but it was hardly enough to sustain a child, never mind a grown man, and he'd been gaunt already. Now he was little more than skin and bone.

Franz didn't stir as Rachel scooted next to him on the bed, drawing her knees up to her chest as she ducked her head to avoid hitting the bunk above.

"Herr Heglin seems much the same," she remarked in a chatty tone. "And little Ethel Stein has lost a tooth. She's very proud. She asks her Mutti if *Zahnfee* comes to Heijplaat," she added, referring to the little white mouse in a blue dress that acted as a tooth fairy. "She said of course she does and she's kept aside a coin just for that purpose."

Franz released a tiny sigh, which Rachel chose to take as an encouraging sign.

"There's been some talk of people with certain jobs being allowed to settle in Rotterdam," she continued, although she feared it was no more than baseless rumor and wishful thinking, both of which ran through the camp like wildfire. "Cooks and cleaners and factory workers. Herr Kleinfeld said he'd put his name forward, as he knows how to push a broom, at least." Kleinfeld, Rachel had learned, had managed a bank back in Frankfurt, not that such things mattered here.

Still Franz did not reply.

"I thought perhaps we could do the same," she continued into the silence. "Why not try, at least? Most people want to settle in America, of course, but I think Rotterdam or Amsterdam or Haarlem would do just as well."

Anywhere but here, she thought but did not say.

"Shall I put our names forward?" she asked after a moment when he had not responded. "For such jobs? What would you like to do, if you had a choice? I don't think I'd mind cleaning, myself."

She waited for a response, but Franz only closed his eyes.

Rachel felt the now familiar tide of frustration rising within her, tightening her chest and pricking her eyes. She'd so wanted to be patient with her husband, and she *had* been, for so very long, staying determinedly cheerful in the face of one dispiriting setback after another, but now she needed him to try, just a little. A *very* little, just to give her the meanest crumb of hope. She'd feast on it, Rachel thought, if he would let her. If he just gave her *something*, after a month of nothing—or worse than nothing, a despair so deep she feared she'd never reach him through it. He was sinking deeper every day, and one day she feared he would be gone completely, nothing more than an empty husk of a man rather than the vibrant, laughing man he'd once been, approaching every challenge of life with both joy and passion.

"I thought we could go out to the beach today," she remarked with careful emphasis. "It's not as hot, and the breeze is so refreshing. It's nice to see the boats. And maybe," she added, daring to try for a little levity, "you could venture to the washroom, as well, and wash your neck and ears, at the least. You'll feel better for it, I know you will." Playfully, she nudged him with her foot. "I'm very sorry to say it, Franz, but I think you might smell, just a bit. Perhaps you've noticed. I fear other people might have."

Franz didn't even open his eyes.

Rachel nudged him again, a little harder this time. "*Franz.*" There was a splintering, strident note to her voice that had not been there in the nearly three months since he'd returned from Dachau, and as much as she wanted to stay breezy and good-natured, cheerfully cajoling, she found in that moment she simply couldn't. It was too hot, and she was so tired and dirty and dispirited, and they'd been in this wretched place for a *month* without even the merest flicker of hope—not from the Dutch authorities, and not from her husband. "Franz, please," she said in a low, desperate voice. "Just do that one little thing for me. Wash yourself today, that's all." Her voice wavered, nearly broke, and then she put some steel into it. "What sort of husband refuses to *wash*?" she asked, keeping her voice low so their neighbors did not hear. The last thing she wanted was for the others in the barracks to see her weakness, never mind her husband's, and gossip about it, condemning or gloating or merely offering yet more pity. "What kind of husband just lies here like... a *corpse*?"

Franz opened his eyes, but there was no expression in them at all. "One who is already dead," he told her flatly.

Rachel blinked, recoiling at his harsh tone, the grim certainty of his words.

She pressed her lips together, biting back a sharp retort. "But you're *not* dead," she stated quietly. "And neither am *I*, your wife. Surely you have a duty to me as well as to yourself to try to survive this place? We said *vows*, Franz. Don't you remember what they were?"

She remembered. She remembered feeling so determinedly happy, choosing Franz and love and *life* against all the odds, even though it had cost her. And she'd *kept* doing it, all through Franz's imprisonment, and then his release, which in its own way had been just as awful. But sitting there, squished in that fetid bunk, next to a husband who wouldn't even wash his face, Rachel felt perilously close not to tears, but to rage. She feared she might say something that would push them both over the edge, and then where would they be? Falling into a dark void neither of them might ever climb out of, and that, Rachel knew, would be far worse than this.

In response to her impassioned plea, Franz simply turned his face to the wall once more.

Rachel sat there for a few more seconds and then, not trusting herself to stay cheerful, she rose from the bunk. Heedless of the curious—and somewhat censorious—stares directed her way, she strode away from Franz and out of the barracks, even allowing the door to crash closed behind her, despite knowing it would send tongues wagging for hours, if not days. In that moment, she didn't care.

She walked past the sitting room and laundry, ignoring any

greetings or questioning smiles, heading outside into the hot sun. Her hands opened and closed into fists at her sides as tears blurred her vision. Unfortunately, there was nowhere to go. Besides the barracks, the quarantine camp had only a few other buildings, and most of them were off limits—the kitchen, the administrator's office, the medical center, the mortuary. She walked instead to the little fenced-off beach with its view of the river, jagged rows of barbed wire on the other side, just in case anyone was foolhardy enough to try to swim across. She stared blindly between the wires at the endless flat fields that surrounded the camp as she tried to steady her ragged breathing.

She would apologize to Franz, she told herself. She'd explain how tired she was, how she hadn't meant it. She'd try to jolly him along again, maybe bring the basin and a cloth to his bunk and help him... But in that moment, she didn't want to do any of that. She wanted to grab Franz by his bony shoulders and shake him until his teeth rattled. She was *tired* of being patient. Tired of trying. Tired, she admitted on a defeated sigh, full stop.

Oh Mutti, what do I do now?

If only her mother could answer, although, Rachel acknowledged, she thanked God that her mother had not accompanied them, after all. She could not have borne her mother having to endure the indignity of these conditions, the awful sense of feeling like a criminal, even as she recognized her mother would have accepted her situation with both stoicism and peace.

Could she be the same? Did she have the strength? The *faith*? Not right now she didn't. She didn't even want to summon it.

Rachel slipped her hand into her pocket for the shard of emerald she carried everywhere, gripping it so tightly its jagged edge bit into her skin, hard enough to hurt. Was Sophie swilling champagne in Washington DC? Was Rosa kicking up her heels at some London nightclub? And maybe

Hannah was in gay Paris, tripping the light fantastic beneath a million stars... Surely none of them had been herded into a camp like this, with no future and no hope of ever getting out?

Don't be bitter, she told herself desperately. *Don't be envious. It will poison you and then you won't be able to help Franz...*

"Rachel."

Rachel stiffened in surprise. The gentle voice sounded like her husband's, but Franz had barely risen from his bunk in a month. Could it be...?

Slowly, she turned around. Her husband stood there, stooped over, clearly exhausted from the short walk, one hand pressed to his side as he tried to catch his breath... But he was *there*. He'd tried, and by God, it was enough. She would make sure it was.

Her anger evaporating in an instant, Rachel's voice came out choked as she answered, "Franz?"

"I'm sorry," he said in a low voice. "I'm sorry for being such a—a failure—in so many ways—"

"You're not—"

"And a wretched husband," he continued grimly, cutting across her. "I've been no husband at all to you in nearly a year."

"Franz, none of that matters if you'll just try now," Rachel urged, her voice catching. "Just a little."

He was silent for a long moment, staring at her with agonized eyes. "I don't know if I can," he whispered hoarsely.

"I'll help you," Rachel cried, tears spilling over as she held her hands out to him. "Franz, I promise."

He shook his head, sending her heart plummeting, and yet still she hoped, because this was more than he'd given her since his return from Dachau.

"I will," she promised him. "Franz, I *will*."

She stood there, her hands outstretched, tears streaking down her cheeks, longing with every desperate fiber of her being to have him reach for her hands, take that one small yet so necessary step.

"Herr Blau?"

The unfamiliar voice had them both stilling, and then Rachel dropped her hands and quickly wiped her cheeks. One of the camp officials stood a few feet away, looking both impatient and uncertain.

"I am Herr Blau," Franz said slowly as he turned to face him.

Rachel's heart seemed to leap into her throat. What could a camp official want with Franz? What if they decided he was too ill to stay? A few others had had to leave due to medical conditions and someone could have reported him; it wasn't outside the realm of possibility. Everyone in the camp was deathly afraid, holding their family close, not wanting anything to jeopardize their own safety or that of their loved ones. What if they took him away, just as they had back in Berlin, when he'd been dragged from their apartment, still strong and defiant, and then returned as...

"You're wanted in the camp administrator's office," the man said, and a gasp was torn from Rachel's throat.

"No—" she began, before Franz gave her a strangely quelling look. He almost seemed as if he were relishing this summons, yet how could he be?

"And is there a reason for my attendance?" he asked, his tone formal, his shoulders straightening as he took on the kind of proud stature Rachel hadn't seen in months.

The man looked as if he wanted to say something sharp, but instead he merely admitted in a grumble, "You have a visitor."

A visitor? How was that even possible?

With Rachel still gaping in disbelief, Franz nodded and walked slowly toward the camp administrator's office.

CHAPTER 5

AUGUST 1939—HAARLEM, THE NETHERLANDS

The apartment was a mere two rooms, bedroom and kitchen-cum-sitting-room, cramped and small, in the attic of a townhouse, just as Rachel had dreamed on the ship. It was on a narrow side street off the Grote Markt in Haarlem's Old Town, with a view of the city's gabled roofs and a ceiling so steeped, Franz hit his head every time he went to the kitchen.

It was paradise compared to the quarantine camp at Heijplaat, but at the same time, in some ways it felt worse.

Two weeks after their arrival, Rachel could still hardly believe they were there, in a city teeming with artists and intellectuals, with the freedom to wander among its hidden gardens and peaceful canals. When Franz had been summoned to the administrator's office, she'd assumed the worst—that he would be sent away, due to his broken-down health or some other trumped-up reason. But instead he'd been given their passport to freedom.

The visitor had been Jan van Dijk, a lawyer from Haarlem whom Franz had known in the old days, when he'd visited Amsterdam. He had managed to convince the camp authorities that Franz had a position waiting for him in a law firm in

Amsterdam and that he and Rachel should be released forthwith so he could take it up. He'd spoken with a self-important certainty that had convinced the camp officials, and amazingly, within a few hours of their interview, Rachel and Franz were walking through the gates of the camp, their suitcases banging against their knees, as free as any Dutch citizen to roam the land, work for their living and strive for the best.

Rachel only learned how it had happened in bits and pieces. Jan and Franz had spoken in earnest as they'd taken a bus into Rotterdam, and then a train an hour north to Haarlem, where Jan had arranged their lodgings. Apparently, Franz had written to Jan asking for help when they'd first arrived at Heijplaat—something he'd never told Rachel—and his old friend had come to their rescue.

"I'm owed a few favors," Jan had explained with a wink, and Franz had given a hearty laugh, the likes of which Rachel had not heard for the better part of a year. She did not know what to think of her husband laughing like that now, and with a *stranger*. And she did not know what she thought of the stranger, this *Jan*, who seemed on such good terms with Franz and yet, the rare times he bothered to look at her, regarded her with a certain cool bemusement, as if she were in the way.

It was Jan who had arranged Franz's job as a lowly clerk in a small law office that worked with the Revolutionary Socialist Party, defending political prisoners and dissidents, as well as their little apartment, even their circle of friends—if Rachel could call them that—anti-Stalinist lawyers and journalists who sat in the kitchen smoking and drinking and mostly ignoring Rachel. She tried not to mind; in fact, she *didn't* mind, not really, because the truth was, she'd never been nearly as interested in politics as Franz was, and their impassioned talk went right over her head.

This new group of associates was raucous and assured, constantly holding forth on their opinions on workers' militia, the abolition of the monarchy, and amnesty for political prisoners with a vehement certainty that Rachel had never felt about anything—except for Franz.

And yet, she reminded herself, as she retreated to their bedroom to sit out her evenings alone, it was precisely Franz's certainty about himself and his view of the world that had attracted her to him in the first place.

Had *she* changed, along with her husband?

It was a question she pondered disconsolately as Franz sat with his new friends, often quiet, it was true, but still a far cry from the empty shell of a man he'd been with Rachel. Jan van Dijk had reached Franz in a matter of hours in a way she had not been able to, Rachel acknowledged, in her weeks of patient ministering and gentle cajoling. Maybe, she thought ruefully, she should have taken a bolder approach—waxed passionately about solidarity and conscientious objectors rather than murmuring about their happy future together as husband and wife. Franz now certainly seemed to care more about the former than the latter.

Sometimes, when she dared to venture into the kitchen, the raucous group would fall silent in the middle of one speech or another, glancing at her askance as if she were an interloper rather than a wife, and then bursting into boisterous laughter when she'd slunk back into the bedroom.

It was, Rachel decided after a month, a rather miserable state of affairs, and yet at least Franz was showing more interest in life than he had with her—a fact which gratified her as much as it stung. She wanted him to be better, she'd just wanted to be a *part* of it. But, she told herself more than once, better for him to be taking an interest in life again, even if it had nothing to do with her.

And yet, Rachel acknowledged one evening as she darned another tear in one of her few remaining pairs of stockings, her own unhappiness aside, their life in this little apartment was not a sustainable situation. The job Franz had been promised hadn't quite materialized, at least not in terms of any money. The law office had very little, and while he took the train to Amsterdam to work there a few afternoons a week, he was hardly ever paid, and Rachel herself had no work. The small savings they'd taken with them had already dwindled to nothing, and the guilders Jan van Dijk had lent Franz at the beginning had also disappeared. Fortunately, the little apartment was rent-free, owned by Jan's acquaintances who were working abroad, but they had nothing to eat.

Something had to change.

Putting the stocking aside with determination, she decided to broach the subject with Franz. He was smoking in the kitchen, Jan having just left after spending several hours whiling away the time talking politics. There was, Rachel acknowledged, forcing herself to be fair, certainly plenty to talk about—Germany was becoming more aggressive against its neighbors, and there were rumors swirling about that the Dutch army might soon be mobilized. Meanwhile, a new prime minister had formed a government of the Christian Historical Party that was decidedly anti-revolutionary and caused much impassioned debate in the little kitchen of the apartment off the Grote Markt—most of which Rachel couldn't even begin to understand.

"Shall we have potatoes for supper?" she asked brightly as she came into the room, which was a ridiculous question because potatoes were all they had, and only a few runty ones at that.

Franz flicked his gaze to her and back to the end of his cigarette, giving no more than a little shrug to signal his assent.

"We're almost out," Rachel told him in that same cheerful, matter-of-fact voice that was, she realized, a kind of aggression. With pointed precision, she placed three small potatoes on the worn table of scrubbed pine. She paused, waiting for him to say something, but he didn't speak, and she had to strive to keep her voice even as she stated, "Franz, we need food. We need *money* to buy food."

"I'm going to be paid soon," he replied dismissively, as if her remark was ridiculous, as he flicked the ash off the end of his cigarette.

Rachel had to bite her tongue to keep from saying something sharp, because Franz had been going to be paid since they'd arrived in Haarlem. So far, he had little more than a handful of guilders to show for his afternoons of work.

"You don't believe me," he accused, and she stiffened.

"It's not that I don't believe *you*," Rachel replied carefully, "it's that we have three potatoes, Franz, and we need more food than that before the next few days. I'd even take some herring!" She'd tried to lighten her voice, make it something of a joke even though it wasn't.

Franz still did not reply.

Rachel took a breath, then let it out slowly, trying not to show her anger, her bitterness that they only had three potatoes, and her husband didn't seem to care.

"I thought..." she began, "I thought perhaps *I* should look for work."

She'd picked up a few Dutch phrases since they'd come to Haarlem, but hardly enough to be able to be employed. Still, she was at a loss as to what else she could do. They needed money, and Franz was right, she *didn't* believe him. She certainly didn't believe he was going to make any money working for a law firm that had allied itself with the small, and not always well-regarded, Revolutionary Socialist Party. Looking for a job seemed the only alternative, even if she wasn't sure she'd be hired anywhere.

Franz stared at her for a moment, expressionless, while Rachel held her breath and waited for his verdict. She knew he had no issue with a wife working the way some men did, but she realized how little she understood him now, and she had no idea what his reaction would be... to anything.

A moment passed, seeming to stretch on endlessly, and then, to Rachel's surprise and dismay, his face crumpled. He tossed his cigarette into a tin that served as an ashtray as he covered his face with his hands.

"I'm sorry," he said in a low, choked voice. "I'm acting like a louse. And I'm not providing for you. *Three potatoes*! What sort of husband am I?"

"Oh, Franz." Rachel's voice softened, but her heart only felt weary. She'd had enough of Franz's apologies to know they might be heartfelt, but they never seemed to change anything. And yet... she knew his remorse was real, and she ached for him —as well as for herself. "Who could have guessed we'd end up like this?" she told him. She pictured them back in their apartment in Berlin, which had been almost as shabby as this one, yet somehow it hadn't mattered, because they'd had each other. Franz had had the effortless ability to make a joke or a game out of everything, even their meager paycheck, or the far more alarming threat of Nazi persecutions, and out of love for him— and faith in who he was—Rachel had always laughed along. "It's not your fault," she said. She believed that much, at least.

"Still." He sighed as he lowered his hands from his face to look at her with bleary, pain-filled eyes. "Do you still love me, Rachel, *Schatzie*?" he asked, his voice barely a whisper.

"Oh, Franz, of course I do." Blinking back tears of her own, Rachel hurried over to him and put her arms around him, breathing in his familiar smell of soap and cigarettes. Even in their present situation, that hadn't changed, and she took comfort from it.

He leaned into her, his cheek pressed against her shoulder as she stroked his hair.

"This isn't the kind of life you agreed to," he mumbled against her shoulder. "The kind of marriage."

"We said vows," she reminded him gently as she continued to stroke his hair. "To spend the rest of our lives together, no matter what might happen. Who could have foreseen something like this?"

"Even so." He pushed away from her in an abrupt way that Rachel tried not to mind as he reached for his cigarettes. "Maybe Jan knows of a place you could work? That's the beauty of the Party, Rachel. We all help each other."

"Yes, that's true," she replied after a moment. She was not entirely convinced by the effectiveness of the Revolutionary Socialist Party, although she appreciated their ardor. And she did not particularly welcome the idea of Jan van Dijk providing more for them than he already was. She wasn't sure she trusted the man, as kind as he'd been, and she certainly didn't want to be beholden to him any more than they already were.

The next day, she decided to look for a job herself. In the freshness of the morning, before the heat become too much, she walked the streets around the Grote Markt, peering into shop windows, looking for the *hulp gezocht* cards sometimes propped against the glass—help wanted. There were precious few of those cards, however, and so when she saw one in the window of a bakery, she hesitated, because she had no experience in such a place and the only bread she'd ever made was the *Shabbat challah* with her mother, a memory that was now painful in its poignancy.

Rachel glanced at the fresh loaves filling the display in the window, their rounded tops golden and gleaming, making her mouth water. On a tray next to them were what looked like cinnamon rolls, and next to those were *Ontbijtkoek*, the small gingerbread loaves she'd learned were so popular for breakfast. Everything looked delicious, and when a customer opened the door, a loaf tucked under his arm, the yeasty smell of fresh bread emanating from within made Rachel's stomach growl.

Compelled by her own hunger as much as a need for a job, she stepped inside.

A stout-looking man was behind the counter, a voluminous apron wrapped around his middle, his head completely bald and shiny from the heat. His florid face was not without some kindness, or so Rachel hoped.

She offered a smile and the man nodded at her, his eyes creasing as he waited for her to speak.

"*Goedemorgen,*" Rachel greeted him hesitantly. Her Dutch was still clumsy but hopefully understandable. She paused, struggling to find the words and only came up with a hopeful, "*Hulp gozocht?*"

The man eyed her appraisingly for a moment. "German?" he finally asked, and Rachel swallowed and nodded.

"*Ja.*"

"*Joods?*" he asked. *Jewish?*

After a second's pause, Rachel nodded, bracing herself for an unenthused or even sneering response. So far, people had been kind, or, if not kind, then at least more or less indifferent, but she'd heard from other refugees about the antisemitism, sometimes virulent, that they had encountered in their adopted homeland.

"Have you ever worked in a bakery before?" the man asked, surprising Rachel by switching to decent-sounding German.

She shook her head and replied in Dutch, "*Nee.*"

The man pursed his lips.

Words clambered up Rachel's throat. She wanted to tell him she was trustworthy, that she wasn't afraid of long hours or hard work, that she needed money and she desperately wanted to eat. But something in the man's expression made her stay silent, because she had a sense that when it came to making a decision, none of that would matter.

After a long pause, the man gave a brisk nod. "You can start tomorrow," he said brusquely. "Working in the back, with the ovens. It's hot work and hard hours. You'll have to be here at four in the morning. The pay is fair, but it won't make you rich."

Rachel gaped at him, stunned that it had been easy, or, really, that this man, whose name she didn't even know, had been that kind. "*Danke*," she whispered in German. "Tomorrow. Four o'clock. Yes."

"My name is Willem Smit," the man told her. "My wife, Annemie, and I run this bakery. We're God-fearing people and we do our duty."

Rachel nodded. "*Ja*. Yes. *Danke*."

The man raised his eyebrows. "And your name?"

"Rachel Blau."

"Then I will see you tomorrow before dawn breaks, *Mevrouw* Blau."

Rachel walked back to the apartment as if on air. *She had a job!* They would have money and food, and they would *eat*. She could hardly wait to tell Franz, but when she came into the apartment, she saw Jan van Dijk was in the kitchen with him, and her heart sank a little. She would have rather spoken to her husband alone.

"Where have you been?" Jan asked in the same dry tone he always used with her, which Rachel tried not to resent. He sounded as if he found her amusing, or perhaps just provincial, simply because she did not have the same fiery politics as he did.

"I was looking for a job," she replied, directing her remark to Franz, who was sitting at the table, silently smoking. "And I got one, at a bakery. I start tomorrow morning, bright and early."

"At a bakery!" Jan repeated in surprise while Franz merely nodded. "Which one?"

"It's run by Willem Smit."

"Smit, that old *ezel*," Jan scoffed. "He's so stuck in his ways you'd think it was the last century. And he's antirevolutionary. Big in the Christian Historical Party—I don't suppose you mentioned where your husband works?" He smirked as he lit another cigarette.

"Such matters did not arise in our conversation," Rachel replied shortly. "And in any case, it's a job."

Jan leaned back in his chair as he eyed her speculatively. "What will they have you doing? Taking bread out of the oven?" He blew a ring of smoke up to the ceiling. "It shouldn't be too arduous. Although, if they get you kneading the dough, who knows? Smit's wife has arms like sides of beef. The woman's built like a Panzer."

Rachel, determinedly ignoring Jan's rudeness, turned to Franz. "Isn't that good news?" she remarked, and Franz finally looked her in the eye, if only just.

"Yes," he agreed, his tone expressionless. "That's very good news."

The next morning, Rachel stepped outside into the darkness of early morning, the sky barely starting to lighten at its edges as mist swirled up from the Spaarne River in ghostly, gossamer strands.

She pulled her coat more closely around her, for at this time of the day there was a chill in the air, as she started walking toward the Grote Markt, Haarlem's largest and most imposing square, with the spire of the magnificent St Bavo's Church piercing the predawn sky. She had no real idea what to expect from the day's work, and she felt equal parts excitement and apprehension. She could surely learn how to take bread out of an oven, but as for the rest…?

"Well," she said to herself under her breath, determined to be cheerful, "it's always good to learn something new."

After the unspoken tension that had been flaring up

between her and her husband recently, it felt more important than ever to focus on the good things in their life and their marriage. And really, Rachel told herself, there was much to be thankful for. They had a roof over their head and food on their table—at least they would, after today—and she had work, and so did Franz, of a kind. Haarlem was a beautiful city, with its canals and gardens and hidden courtyards, and the Dutch, for the most part, were welcoming.

Deliberately, she put a spring in her step as she walked through the Grote Markt that was waking up as dawn pinked the sky. A grocer's boy rattled by on his bicycle—the Dutch were all so competent with their cycles, but Rachel had yet to try one—doffing his cap as he gave her a cheeky grin, which had her smiling back, her heart ever lighter. Today, she decided, was going to be a *good* day. At last.

The Smit bakery was on the ground floor of a tall, narrow building, with a single bow window where fresh loaves of bread and trays of pastries would be laid out when it opened. As Rachel stepped inside, she was greeted with a blast of warm, yeasty air, just as she had been yesterday, and a woman who had arms like Jan had said looked up at her, squinting.

"Are you the German girl?" she asked in respectable German.

Rachel nodded.

"There's an apron in the back."

Rachel didn't mind the rather terse welcome; she felt a wave of relief that this woman, like her husband, spoke German, and that she was ready to work.

"*Dank u wel*," she murmured. Thank you was at least one phrase she'd learned in Dutch.

The woman gave a brisk nod and Rachel slipped around the wide, wooden counter to the kitchen in the back, which was hotter still, the big bread ovens already fired up and going full blast.

It was going to be a hot, sweaty sort of day, but at least they would eat tonight.

The next few hours passed in a blur of activity and heat. Rachel was given the job of taking the loaves out of the oven with a long wooden paddle—an unwieldy instrument that took her some time to get the measure of. Once they were cool, she was to stack them carefully on the shelves behind the counter. And she was not to speak to customers, since she was German.

"I'm sure you understand," Annemie Smit told her rather brusquely, although her smile was a grimace of sympathy. "We speak German, yes, but you *are* German. And at the moment, with war on the horizon, we Dutch are not all that fond of Germans."

"Do you think it really will come to war?" Rachel asked, a tremor to her voice. So many talked of it with such certainty now, a matter of when rather than if.

Annemie Smit snorted. "It practically already has! What with Hitler agreeing with the wretched Soviets..." She shook her head, lapsing back into Dutch as she muttered darkly to herself.

War. The word was like a curtain drawn across the world, a shadow blotting out the sky. Rachel had known it was a possibility, of course; there had been plenty of anxious talk about it on the *St Louis*. But back then it had felt strangely and even comfortingly distant, as she had thought she and Franz would be far away in Cuba, and she'd dared to entertain daydreams that she would be able to convince her mother to join her before any fighting actually began.

Yet now, with the specter of war looming greater still, she was a mere few hundred kilometers from the German border, and her mother would never leave Berlin or her own mother behind. And, in any case, she no longer had anywhere else to go, or any safe haven to offer. War felt far more frightening and *real* here in Haarlem than it ever had on the *St Louis*, or even back in Berlin.

Rachel did her best to push such worries from her mind as she went about her work. By the end of the day, she felt exhausted, grimy with sweat, her arms aching from lifting the heavy paddles.

As she was leaving, Annemie bundled two slightly burned loaves that hadn't sold into her arms. Rachel stared at her in amazement.

"You mean I can have them—" she whispered in awe.

"They'll go stale," Annemie replied in her brusque way. "They wouldn't have sold, even as day-old. Take them."

Rachel was deeply moved by this simple kindness. "Thank you," she said, meaning it utterly.

"It's a hard world, *schatje*," the older woman said gruffly. "We do what we can to make it a little softer."

Rachel walked home slowly in the soft, mellow light of the late afternoon, the warm bread in her arms and her heart full of gratitude. She had a job, she would soon have money, and she had bread! Sweet, soft white bread, the likes of which she and Franz never could have afforded.

She let herself in to their building, climbing up the steep, narrow stairs to the top floor, already looking forward to showing Franz the bread and then eating it together. She hoped Jan wasn't there, or any of his other friends.

Rachel came up short as she stepped into their apartment. Evening sunlight streamed through the windows and gilded their little kitchen table in gold. It was set like a fancy restaurant, a scarf draped over its rough service to serve as a tablecloth, and even a few flowers Franz must have purloined from a garden somewhere placed in a pickle jar.

Franz stepped toward her, his arms outstretched, his whole face softened in a way Rachel hadn't seen in months, if not longer. "Welcome home, darling," he said, smiling with a tentative tenderness that both tore at and filled Rachel's heart. In that moment, all her worries and fears fell away, and she was reminded—fiercely—of just how much she loved her husband.

"It's good to be back," she said as she walked into his arms. "And look, Franz, *bread*!" She brandished the loaves.

"Aren't you clever?" he told her, and then gently he kissed her, and in that moment Rachel just *knew* everything was going to be all right.

CHAPTER 6

⌘

Over the next few weeks, Rachel fell into a rhythm of work and sleep and not very much else.

Waking up at three in the morning to be at the bakery on time had her struggling not to fall asleep over her soup in the evening, and she went to bed soon after. After that first night, when Franz had made their supper and been so tender, she'd hoped for more closeness, but he'd slipped back into his usual remoteness, as if the effort of that one evening had exhausted him. Rachel had tried to get it back, kissing him hello when she returned in the evening, but his responses had been cool and so she'd stopped, feeling both hurt and disappointed.

Meanwhile, Franz seemed determined to spend as little time with her as he could. He was either at the law office, working for very little money, or going out with Jan and his other friends. After a long day at work, Rachel was usually too tired to be of much use anyway, but she still felt lonely, even when Franz was right there with her.

Had she *done* something, she wondered, to make him seem almost as if he resented her presence? She'd tried to ask him about it once, haltingly, embarrassed by her own need, but Franz had shut the conversation down.

"I'm tired from work," he'd said briefly. "As are you, I might add."

Although the work at the bakery *was* hot and tiring, Rachel found she enjoyed being busy, and after her first week, she was given additional duties, including kneading the dough—she'd laughingly flexed her biceps at Franz after a day of arm-aching work and been given, to her quiet delight, a small smile in return—and fashioning *Zeeuwse bolus*, the sweet cinnamon rolls, into their neat spirals. Sometimes she even chatted with customers, or at least smiled or said hello. Her Dutch was coming on very slowly, but she had gained a few more phrases, and Annemie had grudgingly told her that perhaps it wasn't so bad, her being German, after all.

"It's not like you're a Nazi," she'd added, muttering under her breath the way she so often did, "like some of my *own* countrymen!"

Rachel had come to realize that a worryingly significant portion of the Dutch population sympathized with the Nazi party—and hated Jews. Fortunately, she had yet to come across any in person, but she heard about it from fellow Jewish refugees when she decided, to Franz's surprise, to attend evening prayers at the synagogue one Friday night after she'd started at the bakery.

"You haven't observed Shabbat once since we were married," he remarked wryly, his eyebrows raised as he glanced at her speculatively. She was standing in front of the little age-spotted mirror, pinning her hat to her hair.

"I know, but I did so as a child, and I want to again," Rachel replied, her gaze fixed on her reflection. "And thank God for all He has done for us."

Franz's lips twisted as he glanced around their small, shabby apartment. "All?" he repeated. "You have very low expectations, then," he remarked dryly. "I think your God might have turned His back on us Jews."

"Franz, please don't." They rarely spoke of matters of faith; Rachel knew how little Franz had, and the truth was, she'd never felt she had very much of her own, and what she had, she needed to guard as something precious. That day, when she had so much to be thankful for, she felt not just the desire but the *need* to attend. And she also hoped it might make her feel closer to her mother. She'd had a letter from her the day before, full of love and wisdom, its warmth making Rachel long to talk to her again in person, hear her dry, firm voice, full of affection, offering advice.

"All right, I won't," Franz said after a moment. "If you want to go, go. It hardly matters to me."

Rachel gazed at him for a moment, trying not to feel hurt by his seemingly deliberate indifference. While Franz was certainly more talkative than he had been either at Heijplaat or on the *St Louis*, she felt there was a hardness to him now, and she had been tiptoeing around him without even realizing she was doing it, for fear of what might erupt.

Did every marriage face these trials? she wondered. She and Franz had been married for four years. Their honeymoon was long over. And yet... as Rachel looked at the faint challenge in his dark eyes, she realized she did not want to start a fight, and certainly not about Shabbat prayers, of all things. She didn't want to fight at all, and yet it wasn't until that moment that she recognized just how much had remained unsaid between them.

"I'll be back in an hour or so," she told him briefly, and walked out the door, wishing her heart wasn't so heavy. Already she could imagine her mother's gentle scoffing—*"You've got all you wanted, and now you want more, my girl? What next? The moon?"*

"No, *Mutti*," she whispered out loud. "Just a few stars, maybe. Or even one."

A sigh escaped her. She straightened and starting walking toward the synagogue that had been formed recently, with the influx of German Jews into the Netherlands. The evening was balmy and warm, and people were strolling along the canal, looking relaxed, despite the tension that had seemed to shimmer in the air for the last few weeks with the talk of war on everyone's lips.

Just a few days ago, Hitler had threatened to invade Poland. Great Britain was determined to keep such a disaster from happening, but many feared they would be unsuccessful. Rachel only scanned the headlines of the papers festooning the kiosks as she hurried home from work, but she heard enough political talk around her own kitchen table to know—and fear— what was going on. She did not want to think of it now, on a warm August evening, when she was going to pray.

She slipped into the woman's section of the synagogue, taking comfort in the familiarity of the setting and the words, even as the city and culture around her remained so strange. This, at least, she thought, would never change.

Blessed are You, Adonai, who sanctifies Shabbat. Baruch atah, Adonai Eloheinu, Melech ha-olam, haMotzi lechem min ha-aretz. Blessed are You, Adonai our God, Sovereign of all, who brings forth bread from the earth. One God, the Eternal One, honored, glorified and praised.

Rachel closed her eyes, her lips moving soundlessly as she prayed, the words falling over her like a comforting rain. To her surprise, halfway through the prayer, she felt a gnarled hand on her own and, startled, she opened her eyes to see an elderly woman, her face wizened and seamed with deep wrinkles beneath her *tichel*, or headscarf, smiling at her with a gentle kindness.

"You are recently arrived?" the woman guessed quietly in German.

Rachel nodded. "How did you know?"

"The new ones come to prayer like a starving man to a feast. It is always possible to tell." She squeezed her hand. "It will get better."

After the service, the woman introduced herself as Frieda Aronbach. She'd been living in Haarlem for two years; her husband had died a year ago.

"Not much fun, to be a widow in a strange place," the woman said with a good-natured grimace. "And some of the people here... well, they're not always so friendly to us Jews. Others, though, aren't so bad. My son is still in Germany. He couldn't get away."

"I'm sorry," Rachel replied. "That must be hard."

"And you? Who have you left behind?"

Rachel let out an uncertain laugh. "How do you know that I have?"

"It's in the *eyes*, always in the eyes." Frieda gestured to her own faded brown eyes. "The pain. Someone important?" she guessed.

Rachel swallowed and nodded. "My mother."

The older woman's expression softened. "Ah, poor girl. To lose your mother. She couldn't get a visa?"

"She couldn't leave her own mother, my *Oma*. She was too ill to travel."

Frieda nodded. "Your mother sounds like a wise woman. We must take care of each other always, because as God in His heaven knows, no one else is going to do it for us—not in Germany, and not even here." She sighed and then gave a little shake of her head. "You're here alone?"

"In Haarlem, you mean? I'm with my husband." Rachel hesitated. "He didn't come tonight."

Frieda nodded sagely. "It's hard for the men. They feel so powerless. They shake their fists at God, whereas we women can still see His goodness, the light coming through the cracks."

"I try," Rachel whispered. She'd been trying so hard for so

long, and yet it still didn't feel enough. Frieda must have seen something of that in her face, for her eyes were full of sympathy as she wagged a finger at her.

"It's hard, to keep trying," she said, "but it's the only way. If you don't try, what else is there? Curl up and die?" She shook her head as she squeezed Rachel's hand in farewell. "Come visit me sometime. I'm on Zoestraat, number 32." She gave one last squeeze before she let her hand go. "You can always find me there."

"Thank you," Rachel whispered, her throat turning tight.

Frieda reminded her of her own dear mother, and talking to her, she realized, had made her feel less alone. The future still loomed in front of her, full of uncertainty, and she had no idea what it held… But right then, she was glad to have made an unexpected friend.

CHAPTER 7

SEPTEMBER 1939

When war came, it felt strangely distant.

The declaration of war on Germany by Great Britain was like a ripple on the surface of a pond, rather than the cataclysmic thunderstorm Rachel had been expecting as the storm clouds gathered on the horizon and the newspaper and radio reports filled with mobilizing armies and talks and treaties. Sometimes, she and Franz were able to get a German transmission on their little set in the apartment, and Hitler's screeching voice would come over the airwaves, making Rachel jump as she hurried to turn it off, while Franz stiffened where he sat, a look of dread coming over his face before he'd try to shrug it off.

As the fears of war had grown, Rachel had noticed how Franz had retreated more into himself, spending less time at the law office and lapsing into dark silences that no amount of cajoling or jollying could draw him out of. Jan continued to come around, although some of the others dropped off, which Rachel found to be a relief. At the end of a long day of work, she preferred a quieter home to return to, even if sometimes it was *too* quiet. Despite the tension that had sometimes flared between her and Franz, she didn't want to lose him to the bleak despair he'd struggled with for so long, and yet she feared there was little she could do to stop his descent into that all-too-familiar darkness.

Her cheerful running commentaries over supper seemed to exhaust them both and elicited no response. At night, he rolled away from her, his back like a brick wall. When he roused himself to go to the law office, she was encouraged, but he came back seeming exhausted and as silent as ever, while her own days were long and left her aching from hard work.

On the first of September, after they had, in quiet trepidation, listened to a broadcast on Germany's invasion of Poland that morning, he reached over and gave the knob of the radio one savage twist, plunging the room into a sudden silence, before lighting a cigarette, his gaze on the rooftops of the Old Town visible from the window. For several minutes, neither of them spoke.

"Do you think Great Britain really will declare war on Germany if they don't withdraw?" Rachel finally asked hesitantly.

Franz's parents and sister were still in Berlin, although he wasn't particularly close to them. As secular Jews, they'd assumed they would be able to rise above the Nazi persecutions and restrictions, but they'd been subject to the same rules and forbidden from the same establishments as Rachel and every other Jew had, no matter the strength—or weakness—of their religious conviction. Was Franz afraid for them, as she was for her own dear mother?

"I don't suppose it matters," Franz replied. "Hitler will do what he likes, regardless."

Rachel hated it when he spoke like this, with a listlessness that bordered on indifference to life itself, as well as to her. It both scared and frustrated her, and it felt impossible to fight against.

"Surely it *matters*, Franz," she replied, trying to gentle her voice. "If the English declare war, Hitler might be defeated, and Germany would be free again."

He turned to glance at her, a look of bleak cynicism in his eyes. "Rachel, you saw the parades of Panzers down the Unter den Linden nearly every week. Do you really think Great Britain is any match for the Nazi might?"

"They... they might be," she faltered. "And if others join..."

Franz shook his head, resolute. "No."

How could he sound so certain, Rachel wondered, even as she feared she knew the answer. Franz had seen the Nazi might firsthand, and if they'd taken his strength and courage... would they steal the whole world's? Was such a thing really possible?

"Evil must be fought against," Franz declared wearily as he stubbed out his cigarette, "but that doesn't mean it will be *defeated*."

And then he rose from his seat and left the room, without looking back at her once.

Just two days later, Great Britain declared war on Germany, followed almost immediately by France, and then South Africa, Australia, New Zealand, and Canada. The next day, the Netherlands and Belgium declared their neutrality in the whole matter, and life in Haarlem, for the most part, went on, untroubled.

"Cowards," Jan had sneered as he'd paced their kitchen, smoking furiously as Franz had sat at the table and simply watched. "Cowards and traitors."

When Rachel had gone to work the next day, everyone had acted airily assured that life would go on as normal. "Just like the last war," they'd said sagely, nodding their heads. "It's nothing to do with us."

The prime minister had insisted on a radio broadcast that the Netherlands would not get involved. It wasn't their fight, he said, and never need be. It was what everyone recited, repeating it like a prayer, and Rachel kept her mouth shut, partly because she didn't want to draw attention to the fact that she was German, but also because she didn't truly know how she felt.

She didn't want to get embroiled in a war here in their new life, such as it was, but like Jan and Franz's other friends, she didn't want to be a coward. Just as she'd said, Hitler's regime was one that had to be fought—and defeated, even if Franz didn't think that was possible. How could that happen if everyone, the Dutch included, kept their heads down and insisted it wasn't their business?

And yet life continued on as it always had, despite the newspapers full of war—people queued for bread, and chatted about the weather, and strolled by the canals under the September sunshine. Rachel felt as if she were living in some kind of strange dream. *War*, she wanted to cry. *War with Germany*! What would it mean for her mother? For everyone she'd left behind in Berlin?

And, she wondered bleakly, what would it mean for her friends? Sophie, far away in the States, was surely safe—but what about Rosa and Hannah? They were both now living in countries that were at war. In the papers, there were reports of expected air raids in England, people wearing gas masks in the street, bomb shelters already being built in preparation for what was to come. Was it true? Was Rosa afraid? Rachel had no idea. And what of Hannah? She was surely even closer to the threat of invasion. Did she and little Lotte fear for their lives?

Rachel had yet to hear from any of her friends, although she'd written Sophie when they'd been released from Heijplaat and given her new address. She'd also written her mother, pouring out some of her fears and disappointments in this new life, although in the end she hadn't been able to bring herself to send such a letter full of self-pity and complaining. Writing all her frustrations down had been a relief, a kind of emotional bloodletting, but it had also left her feeling emptier than ever. She wouldn't, she knew, show the letter to anyone, and certainly not to her mother. She'd tucked it underneath her stockings and underwear, a reminder of what she had to fight against in herself... for Franz's sake.

She still hoped to receive letters from *someone* soon, whether her friends or her mother, but she had no idea if hers to Sophie had even able to get through. The world, already unfamiliar, had become an even stranger place, and yet her own days remained the same—work, eat, sleep, and little else. At least, Rachel thought, determined as ever to remain cheerful, *eat* was part of her mundane schedule. She brought home bread every day from the bakery, and there was enough money for food. Things could have, she knew, been much worse. She was choosing to be grateful.

Two weeks after the declaration of war, Rachel came home to Franz, Jan, and several others all talking loudly in the kitchen, the air thick with cigarette smoke, and several half-drunk glasses of beer on the table. It had been a day filled with dire news; the Soviets had invaded Poland, Lublin was about to fall, and the total defeat of Poland seemed imminent. In their little apartment, there was a sense of dread and expectation that strangely almost felt like excitement, lending a kind of electricity to the air.

Her heart sank at the sight of them crowded in her kitchen. It had been a long day, her feet ached, and she had a painful blister on her hand from where she'd burned herself on the hot oven. She wanted only to sit in the quiet, and eat her evening meal with Franz, and then go to bed.

"Ah, our little *baker*," Jan greeted Rachel as she came, reluctantly, into the kitchen. "How is the good Meneer Smit? Spouting his prayers, as pious as ever?" His mouth twisted up in a sneer as his eyes glinted mockery, and Rachel stiffened.

"He is baking bread," she replied evenly. "And he is a good

man." She could not fault Willem Smit; he had hired her even though he'd had no need to, and he'd always been fair.

"Ah, the little mouse finally squeaks!" someone else remarked with a laugh, and the others guffawed, eyeing her in amusement while Rachel's cheeks burned. *A mouse, indeed!*

"Squeak, squeak," someone else said, tauntingly, their eyes glinting malice, and a hush fell over the kitchen and tautened the air as they waited gleefully for her response.

Furious and humiliated, Rachel glanced at Franz, longing for him to say something in her defense, but he wasn't even looking at her. She realized she might as well be a stranger to him, and in that moment it felt like the very last straw—and the worst betrayal. She was his *wife*. Why was he not treating her as such? Why was he not defending her to his mocking friends, especially when she was trying so hard in so many ways? He hadn't, she realized, acted like she was his wife since they'd come to this country, save for that one brief evening after she'd started at the bakery, and she'd so hoped things would become better... but they hadn't. She kept trying and trying, and meanwhile Franz behaved as if he didn't care one way or another about anything, including her. In that moment, she couldn't take another second of his damning silence.

Without a word, Rachel turned around and walked out of the apartment, and then out of the building, right onto the street. She didn't even know where she was going; it would be dusk soon, and she was so very tired. Tears blurred her vision, and she blinked them back angrily. She'd shed enough tears, surely, over Franz and his silences? She didn't want to waste any more now, not when she felt so angry as well as hurt. Did he not care for her *at all*?

Her fury carried her all the way to De Bolwerken, the park on the other side of the train station that she and Franz had, on happier days, strolled through, enjoying its paths that followed the old city wall. She came to the Spaarne that cut through the park and stopped suddenly, exhausted and emotionally spent. Her anger drained away, leaving her with nothing but despair that felt as bleak as her husband's. Slowly, she walked to a bench and slumped on it as she stared unseeingly at the placid river in front of her.

When had it started to go wrong between them? she wondered dully. Had it been Dachau, or Franz's release from that wretched place... or before? *Far* before? It was an uncomfortable and dispiriting thought, because she was terribly afraid that she already knew the answer.

She'd married Franz in a haze of happiness, at just twenty-two years old, a whirlwind of fairytale romance, caught up in his charisma and the excitement of being wanted and loved. She'd ignored her parents' disapproval, and the fact that she didn't share the strength of her new husband's convictions and had simply *loved* him. And she loved him still, she *did*... but was it the sort of love that carried and sustained you through the invariably hard times of life—the suffering and the struggle, the doubt and the fear? Did Franz have that love for her?

In this moment, as dusk settled on the park and the shadows grew long, Rachel had a terrible, creeping fear that he didn't.

A sigh escaped her, long and low and weary. Franz felt more a stranger to her now than he had even when he'd first returned from Dachau, emaciated and blank-faced. And maybe, Rachel acknowledged, he'd *always* been a stranger to her in some way... more than she'd ever been willing to admit, even to herself. She'd loved his passion and humor and spark, and most of all, she'd loved how he'd loved *her*. But when that had gone? When he looked at her like he didn't care whether she was there or not, or maybe even preferred if she wasn't? When his friends filled their rooms and mocked her to her face, and he didn't even meet her gaze, never mind speak in her defense?

What was left then, that was worth keeping?

Before Dachau, Rachel acknowledged, Franz would have

snatched her onto his lap and buried his face in her hair. He would have laughingly told whatever obnoxious friend had made such a remark to kindly shut up and then insisted that Rachel was the best of everyone in the room, the best of himself. And Rachel would have blushed and laughed and felt loved and accepted and *treasured* in a way she hadn't, she realized, in a very long time.

But that's not what marriage is, Schnecke, Rachel could hear her mother say, her voice full of love but also impatience as she called her that old endearment—snail, a joke between them because Rachel had once been so slow getting ready for school. *Marriage is a promise, a sacred vow. It's not just for sunny days or moonlit nights, far from it!*

She would not be a fair-weather wife, Rachel told herself sternly, and yet it was so *hard*. Her temples throbbed and her feet ached and the blister on her hand was weeping and raw. She wanted a husband who would take her in his arms and tell her how much he loved her. Who held her at night and stroked her hair and kissed and touched her in a way she felt she could barely remember. She wanted a husband who insisted they were in this *together*, and together they would triumph or fail, it didn't matter which, because they would never be alone.

That was not, she acknowledged bleakly, the husband she had, at least not right now.

A voice behind her, full of humor, had her lurching around to stare blankly at a man standing behind the bench. He was nattily dressed in a three-piece suit, his coat tossed over his shoulders, and a smile lurking about his mobile mouth. He had curly brown hair and warm brown eyes, and he was speaking in Dutch, which she couldn't understand.

He must have registered her blank expression for he said "*Duits?*" which Rachel knew meant German. Before she could reply, he switched to German. "*Deutsch?*"

Wordlessly, she nodded.

"I was saying," he said in respectable German, "that you looked as if you were about to throw yourself in." He nodded toward the river. "I hope you were not in fact contemplating such a drastic thing."

"No." Rachel's voice and smile were both shaky. "I wasn't."

The man cocked his head, his expression friendly, but also concerned. "Is everything all right? You look as if you've just lost your best friend."

For a second, Rachel could only stare, because she realized that was *exactly* how she felt. Like she'd lost her best friend, her *husband*.

The man's expression became alarmed, his dark eyebrows drawing together as he started toward her. "I'm so sorry! I fear I've made you more upset—"

"No." Rachel brushed hurriedly at her eyes. "No, you didn't." She angled her face away, both to hide her threatening tears and because she was not used to being addressed by a strange man in a park, kind as he seemed. Surely men did not normally speak to women in this way in the Netherlands, just as they never would in Germany?

The man took another step toward her. "Are you newly arrived?"

Rachel kept her head slightly averted. "A few months ago."

"I imagine it's very difficult." His voice was soft and sad, turning the seemingly trite sentiment into something heartfelt and genuine.

"Yes, it has been," Rachel replied rather shortly. She could not, in good conscience, continue this conversation, and besides, it was getting dark. She rose from the bench, straightening her skirt as she looked slightly to the left of him, not wanting to meet his eye. "I should go. My husband will be wondering where I am."

"And my wife will be wondering where *I* am," the man returned, his tone both wry and knowing, and Rachel knew he'd seen through her obvious ploy in mentioning Franz. "But I wish you well, *Fraülein*." He doffed his hat, offering her one last rueful smile, before he continued walking down the path.

Rachel watched him go, feeling both regretful at having ended their conversation so abruptly, and relieved that she had.

CHAPTER 8

Rachel knocked on the door of number 32 Zoestraat with some trepidation, as she wasn't entirely sure she had the right address.

It was Sunday afternoon, her only day off, and it had been several weeks since she'd met Frieda Aronbach at Shabbat prayers, and she hoped that the older woman remembered her from their brief conversation. She'd invited her to visit, but had she really *meant* it? Assuming she really was at the right place, Rachel would soon find out.

She was just about to knock again when the door suddenly opened, and Frieda stood there, a shawl draped around her bony shoulders, her wrinkled face creased into a welcoming smile. "Ah, my little exile! Rachel, is it not? Come in, come in. I'm so glad you came."

"I wasn't sure you'd remember me," Rachel admitted as she stepped into the small apartment. Much like her own, it was shabby and bare, decorated with a few pieces of mismatched furniture, but with several clearly precious items from Germany placed around to give it a homely air—a fringed shawl draped over a table, a faded, sepia-tinted photograph of Frieda as a young bride, a brass menorah over the fireplace.

"*Pah*! Of course I remembered you!" Frieda exclaimed. "I am not so old to forget a face, or a conversation. Now, coffee." Frieda lifted a kettle off the stove and went to fill it. "You have not returned for prayers, though," she added. "I worried."

"I'm sorry," Rachel replied as she came into the kitchen. "I've..." She was about to say 'been busy', but realized it wasn't entirely true. "I just haven't," she admitted with a shrug, and Frieda nodded knowingly.

"When life is hard, you either turn to God or away from Him," Frieda told her gently. "Choose wisely, my dear."

"Sometimes I feel as if I'm not choosing anything at all," Rachel blurted. "Life feels..." She paused, her throat working. "Out of my control."

"Of course it does," Frieda replied robustly, clearly unfazed. "The only thing in your control is your own response to whatever befalls you. Remember that."

Rachel swallowed and nodded. Frieda's voice was kind, but the words were stern. "Yes," she murmured, slightly chastened. "I will."

"Now. Coffee. Cake." Frieda uncovered a golden *Apfelkuchen,* brushed with melted butter and sugar. It looked delectable, and just like her mother might have made, back in the old apartment in Prenzlauer Berg. Rachel's mouth watered at the sight, and she could almost taste the apples on her tongue already.

"You're very kind," Rachel whispered.

"Cake cures many ills," Frieda told her with a smile. "Come. Sit."

Soon, they were both seated at the table, with cups of coffee and thick slices of cake in front of them, September sunlight streaming through the window. Frieda kept the conversation light at first, cheerfully telling Rachel where she could find the freshest fruit, the fairest butcher, regaling her with tales of daily life as a refugee in Haarlem, without touching on any deeper or darker subjects.

"Casper ten Boom is a good man," she stated definitively. "A watchmaker on Barteljorisstraat. An honest man, and a friend to Jews. Many go to him for advice or help. And he is clever with watches, of course, if you have one!" She let out a raspy laugh.

"I have my father's pocket watch," Rachel replied with a small smile. "My mother gave it to me when he died." It was in her chest of drawers, wrapped in a handkerchief. Even when they'd been at their poorest, she had not considered pawning it —or her sliver of emerald. The two were her most precious treasures.

"There you are, then." Frieda's face softened as she took a sip of her coffee. "And your husband?" she asked gently, almost as if she already knew the answer.

Rachel stared down at the crumbs of her slice of cake, compelled to a painful honesty. "It's been... difficult," she admitted wretchedly. "He was in Dachau for seven months, after Kristallnacht. He came back a changed man."

Frieda nodded in understanding, waiting for more.

"At first," Rachel continued haltingly, part of her longing to pour out her woes and troubles even as she strove to be fair, "he was just so *silent*. It was almost as if he wasn't there. And I thought that was hard enough. I wanted him back, not even the way he was, but just at all."

She stopped, her throat tightening, and after a moment Frieda prompted gently, "And then?"

"And then we came to Haarlem," Rachel resumed. "We were in the quarantine camp at Heijplaat for a month, and it was dreadful. Not the conditions, not so much, although I certainly got tired of eating potatoes and herring." She tried for a smile and was rewarded with a small smile of understanding back. "It's that in that place, with the dogs and the barbed wire… he was almost like a dead man. I suppose it reminded him of Dachau, and for a while it seemed as if we might never get out. But then an acquaintance of his arranged our release, as well as a position for Franz at a law firm in Amsterdam. But…" Rachel bit her lip before finishing in an aggrieved rush, "Franz hadn't even told me he'd written to him! And when we came here to Haarlem, and he had some work even though it didn't pay very much, if anything… well, he became someone entirely different, almost a stranger to me."

She felt a flash of guilt for betraying Franz in this way, and yet she knew she needed to talk to someone, and Frieda seemed a willing and kindly listener.

"We've had moments of happiness over the last few months," she amended, "but that's all they've been, just *moments*." So fleeting, Rachel thought painfully, and over so soon, making her wonder if they were even real. She'd mere flashes of the man Franz used to be—tender, funny, loving. They were gone before she had a chance even to enjoy them. "And more recently," she added, swallowing hard, "it's been even harder. Sometimes I feel he barely looks at me," she confessed, her gaze back on her plate. "He talks with Jan—that's the acquaintance—and his friends, but not with me. Not like he used to." Although had Franz ever talked about politics with her, really? She hadn't even wanted him to. She'd wanted his attention, and that was something she hadn't felt she'd had in a long time. "I almost wonder if he *resents* me," she told Frieda. "If he'd rather be free of me. Maybe he wants to start this new life on his own?"

Until she said the words, Rachel hadn't realized the fear that had been lurking in her mind, like some creature deep in dark water. Saying it out loud only made her feel worse.

"Have you said such things to him?" Frieda asked after a moment.

"No." Rachel shook her head. "I… I wouldn't. And in any

case, we hardly talk, it seems. Like I said, there have been moments... flashes... where I felt things might be all right again, or could be, in time, but then things go back to the way it feels they've always been. And it makes me so tired..." She trailed off, her voice wobbling, before she confessed quietly, "I don't know how to be a good wife to him anymore."

A silence fell on the room that felt heavy. As relieved as Rachel had been to admit all that, she also felt terribly guilty, and wondered if she should have said any of it. She had no idea what Frieda thought; maybe the older woman thought she was whining about nothing. Finally, she dared to look up, only to see Frieda looking at her with an expression that was both compassionate and uncomfortably shrewd.

"Is that *truly* what you are asking me?" she countered quietly. "How to be a good wife to your husband?"

Rachel stared down at her plate again as she took a few deep breaths in an effort to compose herself. "Yes," she said when she trusted her voice to be steady, if not quite firm. "Yes, that is what I am asking. That is what I want... to be a good wife to my husband." She took another breath and then looked up to see Frieda nodding slowly.

"It's not easy, but then so much in life rarely is. But you must love him, *Schatzie*, even when it's hard. *Especially* when it's hard. Darn his socks and make his supper and hold him in your arms at night and, God willing, he will come back to you one day," she said. "But even if he doesn't... well, we all have our burdens to bear. Perhaps this is yours."

Rachel stared at her, feeling heartened and dispirited at the same time. Such simple, seemingly easy advice, the kind of sensible advice her mother would give... and yet it came with no guarantees or promises. Frieda was sympathetic, but she certainly had no intention of letting Rachel wallow in self-pity, just as her own dear mother hadn't. She'd needed the reminder.

With a grateful smile, Rachel heaved herself from her seat. She needed to get back to Franz and start following the older woman's advice. "Thank you," she said, and Frieda nodded and smiled back.

"Keep trying," Frieda told her as she patted her hand. "That is all you can do."

It was late afternoon as Rachel headed back to their apartment, wearily determined to do what she'd told Frieda she would, and be a good wife to her husband. *Darn his socks and make his supper and hold him in your arms at night...*

If that was all it took, Rachel reflected, perhaps it would be easy... but what about Franz being a good husband to *her*?

The apartment was quiet as she opened the door, and she breathed a sigh of relief. She didn't think she could have coped with Jan and the others just then. Slowly, she walked inside, running a hand along the blanket folded over the armchair, the photograph of her mother on the mantle. Small signs that this was her home, *their* home, and she took comfort from them, drew much-needed strength. They'd had a life together, she reminded herself. They could do so again.

"Franz?" she called into the silence.

There was no answer.

Anxiety fluttered in her stomach, and she walked into to the kitchen to see Franz sitting alone at the table, silent and unmoving, his head averted. He didn't move as she came into the room, and Rachel's heart felt as if it were somersaulting in her chest as her trepidation grew. "Franz?" she asked again, uncertainly.

Finally, he glanced at her, and now he didn't look blank, he looked angry. His eyes were narrowed, flashing fire, his lips pursed. She had not seen this kind of fury from him since before Dachau, and certainly not directed at her.

"Franz..." Rachel faltered, alarmed. "Is everything all right?"

Wordlessly, he lifted a piece of paper from the table and held it out to her. Even from across the room, Rachel could see what it was—the letter she'd written to her mother and never sent, hidden beneath her underclothes.

Her stomach felt as if it had hollowed out, her heart still thumping madly. "Did you... did you read my letter?" she asked faintly. She couldn't remember everything she'd written—she'd kept herself from the worst, at least—but she knew there were thoughts and feelings in that letter that she would never, ever have wanted Franz to read, not in the state he'd been in, at any rate. "Franz..." she began, and then stopped, because she had no idea what to say.

He dropped the letter back onto the table and lit a cigarette, his face angled away from her.

"I didn't send it," she said after a moment, her tone turning pleading. "No one read it but me—"

"And *me*," he observed coldly. "But I gather you didn't want me to read it. At least, that is my assumption, considering its contents."

Briefly, she closed her eyes. "It was just... a moment of weakness. I wasn't—"

"Do you *really* feel this way?" Franz demanded. He snatched the letter up again and read aloud, "'Sometimes the days feel so endless, *Mutti*, and so very dreary. There's nothing to look forward to, just more of the same—work, sleep, hoping Franz might be different, but he never is...'" He stopped to stare at her, his gaze penetrating and full of fury. "So, *this* is what you really think of me?"

"No, Franz," Rachel began, and then suddenly stopped. Maybe she needed to be more honest. "Sometimes, yes," she admitted quietly. "Franz, these last few months—you've been so distant, so *different*. It's been hard for me. Surely you can understand that?"

He pressed his hand flat against the table. "And you don't think they've been hard for *me*?"

Rachel drew herself up. "I didn't say that!" she protested. "Of course they've been hard for you. But, Franz, sometimes it seems as if you—you *resent* me!"

"*I* resent *you*?" he repeated incredulously. "*I* didn't write this letter!" He flung it onto the table in disgust.

"I only wrote it to sort out my feelings," Rachel explained miserably. "If you would just talk to me, Franz. Tell me... tell me what it was like, back at the camp. Tell me anything. Just please don't—don't shut me out the way you have been—first with so much silence, and then with your *friends*." She spat the word, unable to keep herself from it. "It's like you can't stand to be alone with me! That's what I don't like. *That's* what I was railing against in that letter—"

Franz stood up and whirled away from her, his shoulders hunched. "If I shut you out, it's because you treat me like a child and that's what *I* don't like, not that *you* even care," he snapped. "'*Franz, wash your ears! Franz, eat your supper. Don't worry, Franz, things will get better.*'" His voice was a high, cruel falsetto that made Rachel flinch. Was *that* how she'd sounded to him? He turned back to face her, his eyes flashing anger, his whole body taut with it. "Does any man want to be spoken to like that, and by his *wife*? You've unmanned me, Rachel, more than I ever did myself—and I did, I *know* I did. At that damned camp..." He trailed off, his voice breaking as he shook his head in bitter memory.

Rachel took a step toward him, hating that her behavior might have caused such anguish as well as anger. "Tell me," she pleaded softly. "*Please*, Franz. Whatever it is... whatever still torments you... *tell* me. Share the burden. I want to help you..."

He shook his head, his lips twisting. "Why, so you can run to your dear *Mutti* and tell her all about what a pathetic weakling your husband is? The husband she never even wanted you to marry? No thank you."

"I wouldn't," Rachel whispered, blinking back tears of hurt. "Franz, I would never do something like that."

"I can't trust you," he stated flatly. "And now that I know you dread spending so much as a single second with me, I can't bear to be near you, just as you can't bear to be near me—"

"I never said that!" she cried. It all felt so unfair, and yet she knew he was hurling accusations from a place of deep hurt. She never should have written that letter. She certainly shouldn't have kept it.

"You didn't need to," he replied, and then he pushed past her, out of the kitchen.

Rachel heard the door of their apartment slam, and in wearied sorrow she closed her eyes. She'd come back from Frieda's full of purpose, if not quite hope, and now things between her and Franz were, incredibly and dispiritingly, worse than ever.

Sinking onto a chair, she dropped her head into her hands as the slam of the door continued to reverberate through her, the sound so grimly final. Where had Franz gone—and when would he be back? And, more importantly, what could she possibly do to make things better?

Rachel lifted her head from her hands as she drew a ragged breath. Sitting here awash with regrets and feeling sorry for herself would not accomplish anything, she knew. She rose from the table and reached for her apron. She'd make a meal, a lovely meal, in the hopes that when Franz returned, they could eat and talk properly. He had always been a reactive sort of person, every emotion felt so passionately. It was what she'd loved about him, but it did mean accepting the lows along with the highs, which she *would*.

There were potatoes, as ever, to make potato schalet, and a little bit of old beef to make some *Sauerbraten*. Rachel set to work, chopping and slicing, frying and stirring as if her life depended on it, and maybe it did. Her marriage did, anyway, she feared.

Darn his socks and make his supper and hold him in your arms...

She could do at least one of those.

She'd had a moment—or more—of weakness over these last months, Rachel acknowledged, but she'd meant what she'd said to Frieda, and she felt it now. She would work harder, do whatever it took, to make sure she and Franz weathered this storm. *Together.*

Night had drawn in and Rachel had to turn up the lamp as the sauerbraten simmered and the potatoes lay covered and then congealing on top of the stove, but Franz still did not come home. By ten o'clock, Rachel feared he might stay out all night. Where was he—with Jan, or wandering the streets? She worried, and yet there was nothing she could do. She had to be up early for the bakery, and she knew she could not wait up any longer, although she feared she would not sleep.

She put the meal she'd made away, too heartsick to eat herself, and undressed for bed. Slipping beneath the sheets, she lay there gritty-eyed and listened for Franz's footsteps on the stairs, the creak of the door opening, but all was silence as the moon rose in the sky and she waited out the lonely hours of the night, one by one.

CHAPTER 9

NOVEMBER 1939

Rain streaked the window of the bakery as Rachel stood behind the counter, wrapping a fresh loaf for a customer. Recently, Annemie and Willem had decided she could serve customers; her Dutch was now good enough, and perhaps being a German Jew wasn't so bad after all, considering the way Hitler was carrying on.

It had been over two months since the war had begun, and sometimes it felt like nothing had happened—at least nothing decisive. The Soviets had invaded Finland, and the Germans were wreaking havoc in Czechoslovakia, but life in Haarlem continued as ever, as it seemed to in both England and France, according to the reports on the radio. There had been no air raids, and in England, people were starting to call it "the Phoney War" because it seemed as if nothing was happening anywhere.

Rachel's days continued much the same, but she plodded through them with a heavy heart. Since the night Franz had stormed out of their apartment, they'd barely spoken, moving around each other like polite strangers. That first night, he'd come home in the early hours of the morning, just as Rachel was dressing for work, and for a long moment they'd simply stared at each other through the predawn darkness, a tension as well as a sorrow heavy between them, the silence turning oppressive, a burden Rachel couldn't bear. She'd opened her mouth to say something, *anything*, but then Franz had turned away and Rachel had continued to button her dress. In the end, there seemed to be nothing *to* say.

The silence had continued as the days and weeks had stretched on. Franz did more work for the law office and went out with Jan and his other friends. Rachel spent many evenings alone, going to sleep by herself, only to wake up when Franz slipped in silently to their bed, always with his back to her.

Her loneliness was punctuated by brief moments of companionship and joy—she'd visited Frieda a few more times, although she had not been brave enough to be honest and admit things with Franz had grown worse. Rachel suspected the older woman guessed anyway, but she still kept up the pretense that she and Franz were muddling along well enough, more out of shame than pride. She didn't want to tell Frieda about the letter to her mother she'd never sent. After Franz had stormed out that night, she'd ripped it into a dozen pieces and tossed them all into the fire, wishing bitterly that she'd done so in the first place.

She'd heard from her mother again, a long letter full of affection and assurances.

> *Things remain much the same, although there have been whispers and rumors that the Jews in Poland and Czechoslovakia do not fare so well. I pray for them, and for you, but be assured, my darling, that I am well and cheerful, trusting as ever in God's mercy. As are you, I hope, for I know things must be difficult. It is hard to make a home out of a strange place, but you have always been determined to find the best in everything*

and everyone, Rachel, so I pray you will do it now, in this place.

Rachel prayed so, as well, although she had not been very successful in finding the best in Franz so far.

She bid good day to the housewife leaving the bakery with her wrapped loaf, and turned to tidy the display of loaves, their tops burnished and golden brown. Outside, a gray fog smothered the Spaarne, and a steady, icy drizzle turned the autumn day cold and dreary, but inside the bakery was cozy and warm. Rachel had come to enjoy her work there; Annemie was slowly teaching her how to make some of the more complicated Dutch breads—*Krentenbollen*, sticky-sweet with currants and raisins, *Kerststol*, with candied fruit and sprinkled with sugar, and, of course, the much-loved *Ontbitjkoek*, a rye bread spiced with ginger, nutmeg, cinnamon, honey, and cloves.

Sometimes, when she was alone in the front of the shop, she liked to imagine it was hers and Franz's. In her mind, they had a little apartment upstairs that was always warm from the ovens below. There were gingham curtains on the kitchen window, and a pot of *Eintopf*, a stew of potatoes and carrots, bubbling on the stove. Sometimes, Rachel dared to embroider this fantasy with more delicate threads, and pictured a baby, round-cheeked and dark-haired, sleeping in a cradle. Franz would be sitting at the kitchen table, reading the newspaper and rocking the cradle with his foot. Every once in a while, he would look up and smile lovingly at Rachel, who moved around the kitchen full of gladhearted purpose, the cheerful mistress of her little domain.

It was dangerous thinking like that, Rachel knew. While it comforted and encouraged her for a few minutes, it made returning to reality so much harder—the empty apartment, Franz's cold silences, a future that stretched out in front of her in an unrelenting line, and the grim possibility that with the threat of war things might get worse.

"It's *you*!"

Rachel looked up, blinking away the ephemeral trappings of her longed-for life to see a man standing in the middle of the bakery, looking happily flummoxed. For a second, she didn't recognize him, with his hat pulled low down against the rain, but then he removed it, and his brown hair sprang up in curls, his mouth curving into a delighted smile, and she realized he was the man who had teased her in the park about throwing herself into the river, months ago now.

"I..." Her mind swam as she struggled to think of something to say. "Yes, it's me," she finally said, feeling both silly and discomfited.

The man chuckled, his warm brown eyes glinting with humor. "And who is *me*, may I ask? But let me introduce myself so it's all good and proper. My name is Emiel de Vries, resident of Haarlem and manager of a lightbulb factory." He made a laughing grimace. "The family business, I'm afraid. I'd much rather be a violinist, but there you are." He cocked his head, waiting for her to reply, but Rachel felt as if her mind were moving slowly. This man's easy charm was so different from the cool silence she was normally met with when talking to a man... that was, her husband. It felt both welcome and strange, as well as overwhelming. "And *you* are?" he prompted when she still hadn't spoken.

"Rachel Blau." It also, Rachel realized, felt inappropriate to be having this kind of conversation with a man who was still a stranger, and so she straightened, placing her palms flat on the counter as if to bring some much-needed formality to their conversation. "May I help you?"

Just as in their last meeting, the man—Emiel de Vries—seemed to know exactly why she had said what she had. "Yes, you may, Miss Blau," he replied, his expression turning serious as he spoke with even more formality than she had. "One

Ontbitjkoek loaf, please. My daughters cannot go a morning without their gingerbread."

Daughters, Rachel thought, *as well as wife*. A family man. She felt reassured; his familiar manner had to be just common friendliness. She was foolish to be so unsettled and suspicious. It had been too long since she'd had a normal interaction with anyone, save for the Smits, and they were her employers.

"Where are you from in Germany?" he asked as she fetched his loaf. He was resting one elbow on the counter, lounging against it as if he were chatting at a party. The shoulders of his coat were damp with rain, and a wet stray curl rested against his forehead.

Rachel reached for a sheet of brown paper to wrap the bread in. "Berlin," she answered.

"And what did you do there?" he asked.

She hesitated, although she wasn't sure why. "I was a history teacher," she said finally.

"A history teacher!" He sounded impressed. "An educated woman."

She shrugged, embarrassed, and handed him his loaf.

He gave her a few coins in return and she put them in the till, closing it with a snap that was meant to punctuate the conversation.

Emiel de Vries, however, did not seem to notice the firmness of her gesture.

"Will you teach here in Haarlem?" he asked, and she let out a short laugh as she shook her head.

"I shouldn't think so, considering the state of my Dutch."

"I'm sure you're getting better all the time."

"Fortunately, the languages are similar. But sometimes that actually makes it harder."

"I can imagine." He looked as if he wanted to say something more, but Annemie Smit suddenly bore down on them like a ship in full sail, her apron billowing out about her, her face full of disapproval.

"Ah, Meneer de Vries. Is everything well? How are your wife and lovely daughters?"

Emiel straightened from where he'd been leaning, a look of amusement on his face. He glanced at Rachel as if to share the joke, and she looked away quickly. Bowing to Mevrouw Smit and then Rachel, he replaced his hat on his head and, with his loaf tucked under his arm, walked out of the shop.

Rachel quickly busied herself tidying, feeling Annemie's shrewd gaze on her. A few uncomfortable minutes ticked past before the baker's wife finally spoke.

"You want to watch that one, my girl," she said at last. "He's harmless, really, and certainly friendly, but tongues wag in a place like this. Haarlem might be a city, but it feels like a village. Everyone talks."

"He—he was just asking me about Germany," Rachel stammered, a blush rising to her cheeks. She felt both embarrassed and guilty, although she told herself she'd done nothing wrong— and neither had Emiel de Vries. He had been friendly, nothing more. Annemie Smit had said so herself.

"So he was," Annemie agreed. "And that's all there is to it, and ever will be. He's a kind man stuck in a job he hates, so he chats with everyone to make life better. His wife, would you believe, was a ballerina in Amsterdam. A *beautiful* woman. Their daughters are like angels." She paused and Rachel tensed, bracing herself for something more. "It's only, my dear," Annemie continued more gently, "that you seem to me to be... *unhappy*." She held up a hand to forestall any objections, although Rachel was too shocked to say a word.

She hardly ever spoke to the baker's wife beyond what her daily duties were, or how to make sure the spiral of a *Zeeuwse bolus* curved just right, yet she'd seen through Rachel's cheerful manner. Just as Franz had, and Frieda too, and everyone, it seemed. It made Rachel feel like a failure. All along, she'd tried so hard to have a cheerful manner, let no one see beneath her smile, but apparently everyone had. No wonder Franz was so frustrated with her.

"You never complain," Annemie continued, "I am not saying that, not at all. You work hard and you do right. You're a good girl." She paused, her expression soft even as her voice hardened, just a little. "But a man like Emil de Vries... you need to be careful. He won't mean anything by it, but *you* might."

Rachel's cheeks felt red hot as she stared at the older woman, horrified by the obvious and unsettling implication. "I would never," she said in a low voice that throbbed with feeling. "*Never.*"

Annemie nodded, seemingly satisfied. She patted Rachel gently on her shoulder before turning away. "Good girl," she murmured. "Good girl."

It was twilight by the time Rachel left the bakery that evening, buttoning up her coat and wrapping her scarf firmly about her neck, for the misty drizzle had continued steadily all afternoon, and the wind off the Spaarne was frigid. She'd just started down Houtstraat when a shadowy figure suddenly loomed in front of her, making her let out a little yelp of surprise and fear.

"I am so sorry!" a voice exclaimed as a hand gripped her elbow to steady her. "I did not mean to startle you. It's Emiel de Vries, Miss Blau, from before." In the weak light of a streetlamp, Rachel could make out his face, see the flash of his white teeth as he gave her a whimsical smile. "You remember?" he asked, still holding her arm.

"Of course I remember." As politely as she could, Rachel pulled her arm away from his grip. "What are you doing here, Meneer de Vries?"

"Waiting for you, of course," he replied as his smile

widened. "But it's a dreadful evening. I'm turning to ice myself! Do you have time for a cup of solace?"

Rachel stared at him blankly. "A cup of solace?"

Emiel laughed. "Coffee, of course. Do you not know that turn of phrase? Already I see how it is. You shall teach me German, and I shall teach you Dutch."

Rachel shook her head slowly, uncomprehending. She felt as if she'd missed a conversation, or maybe three, with this man. His level of familiarity, the way he spoke to her as if they were old friends, was jarring, and yet some part of her yearned for it, because it felt so easy, like slipping underneath a blanket, or into a pair of comfortable shoes.

"I have a business proposition to put to you," Emiel explained, clearly seeing, or at least sensing, her confusion. "Completely respectable, of course, so there is no need for you to worry on that account. But I can't talk in this needling rain. There's a coffeehouse nearby. Please let me buy you a cup of coffee so we can discuss my idea."

"You mean a cup of *solace*," Rachel quipped with a small smile, and he laughed.

"Indeed, yes." He smiled charmingly, his head cocked in inquiry, waiting for her reply.

She should refuse, Rachel knew, especially considering Annemie's well-meant warning, and yet, to her own surprise, she found she wasn't quite willing to. She was too intrigued by the idea of a business proposition to say no, and, in truth, the thought of having a coffee and conversation with a man who seemed to hang on her every word was much more appealing than returning to her apartment with Franz either out or ignoring her so she would have to spend another lonely evening by herself. That didn't make it wrong... or dangerous, did it?

"Very well," she said, tightening her scarf a little more. "But only for a moment. I must get back to my husband."

He made a gallant, little bow. "Of course."

"Thank you," she said, rather belatedly, and he smiled.

"It is, I assure you, Frau Blau, my pleasure."

There was no opportunity to talk with the rain, so, in silence, Rachel followed Emiel to the promised coffeehouse, stepping inside its warm, smoky interior with a small sigh of relief—as well as a ripple of trepidation. What was she doing here, really? What sort of business proposition could a man like Emiel de Vries possibly have?

"Have you tried our *koffie verkeerd*?" he asked once they were settled in their seats.

Rachel glanced around, uncomfortably aware that there were few women in the café; coffeehouses, it seemed, were still mainly a masculine establishment in the Netherlands.

"It is called 'wrong coffee,' because it is half coffee, half milk, and usually you only have a *wolkje* amount of milk in your coffee—that is, a small cloud."

Wordlessly, Rachel shook her head. She had not had either kind of coffee.

"And of course," Emiel continued, "you must have a cookie with your coffee! It is a Dutch tradition, quite sacrosanct." He motioned to a waiter, who came over to take their order. Emiel glanced at Rachel, his eyebrows raised. "Would you like to try the *koffee verkeerd*?"

"Thank you, that would be very kind," Rachel murmured. She was already starting to regret her acceptance of his invitation; it felt now that it had been too forward. She would end this conversation as quickly as she could, she decided; she would drink her coffee and go.

"It is done." He placed the order in Dutch, and as the waiter left, he turned to face her with a more businesslike expression on his handsome face—and he *was* handsome, Rachel acknowledged uncomfortably, with his twinkling eyes and curly hair. He had high cheekbones and a mouth that always seemed poised to quirk into a smile. She pushed such thoughts away as she tried to match his serious expression. "My proposition is this," he began, his hands folded on the table in front of him. "My two daughters, Evi and Beatrix, are six and eight years old. Little Evi goes to *kleuterschool*, that is, kindergarten, and Beatrix is in the *lagere*, or lower, school. They are happy there, but I am not entirely satisfied with their education. I would like them to learn German, as I did, but the school does not teach it at this age. And so, I propose you become their German teacher. You could teach them after school several times a week. They need the tuition, and they would enjoy the company. And, I might add, it would help my wife, who has had trouble engaging a governess who suits her, as well as the children. What do you think?"

Rachel stared at him, blinking in surprise. Perhaps she should have expected something like this, considering how admiring he'd been of the fact she'd been a teacher, but she hadn't. "Thank you kindly," she finally managed, "but I have my work at the bakery—"

Emiel waved a hand, airily dismissive. "But surely you want to use your education and skills, and work as a teacher instead of a... a skivvy?"

Rachel flinched a little at that, and he made a moue of apology.

"I'm sorry, I mean no offense. It is good, honest work. But..." He paused, cocking his head thoughtfully. "My hope is that you could teach them some history, as well. It is so important to remember our past in these turbulent times, wouldn't you agree? And whatever you are earning at Smit's bakery, I will pay it again by half." He sat back in his chair, completely at ease. "Money, I assure you, is not an issue."

Again by half? Rachel was stunned. "But it would only be for a few hours a week," she protested, feeling the need to point out what surely had to be obvious; the work would be so much less.

"Shall we say three afternoons, from three until six?" Emiel sounded as if they had already agreed.

Once again, Rachel felt she should refuse, although she couldn't have entirely said why. Was it that Emiel de Vries was too handsome and sure of himself? With Annemie Smit's warning still running through her mind, accepting a job such as this seemed suspect, maybe even dangerous. And what would Franz think of it?

And yet... to do something she actually enjoyed, and to earn even more money! She wouldn't have to get up at three o'clock in the morning; she would have more time to make a home for her and Franz, to spend time with him, reconcile and learn to love each other again... And she would certainly not lose her head, much less her heart, to the charming man in front of her. Absolutely not.

"Well?" Emiel asked. "What do you say?"

Still Rachel hesitated. "Have you spoken to your wife about this idea?" she asked after a moment. The waiter had returned with their coffees, foaming with rich milk, a small, waffle-shaped cookie on the saucer.

"Indeed, she is quite amenable," Emiel replied easily. "She speaks German, as well, and sees the importance of it."

"Your German is more than adequate," Rachel felt compelled to protest. "Why not teach them yourself?"

Emiel laughed and shook his head. "I am no teacher, and besides, I have my work." His mouth twisted ironically. "Light-bulb factories must be managed, you know."

Rachel recalled Annemie telling her Emiel hated his job. He certainly didn't seem to be at work very much, considering he'd had the time to come to the bakery in the morning, and then wait for her to finish work in the afternoon.

"Well?" he asked again, the very faintest edge of impatience to his voice.

It was a generous idea, Rachel thought. There was no doubt about that, and yet...

She opened her mouth to thank him for the kind offer, but explain it was not one she could take up at present. Her job at the bakery was too important, and she didn't want to let the Smits down. And there were other considerations, as well... The words were there in her mind, forming on the tip of her tongue, when she heard herself say something else instead.

"Thank you, that is very kind. I am pleased to accept."

CHAPTER 10

The de Vries family lived in a tall, narrow townhouse on Leidsestraat—an elegant street not far from the river. The following Monday afternoon, Rachel presented herself at the front door, wearing the blue crepe she'd donned to board the *St Louis*, her hair back in a neat French roll, her heart thumping madly, although she did her best to keep her expression composed. She still wasn't sure if she'd made a terrible mistake by accepting this position.

Annemie Smit certainly thought she had. The day after her coffee with Emiel, Rachel had spoken to the baker's wife about leaving work early three days a week so she could tutor the de Vries girls. She'd come up with the happy solution after she'd left Emiel; why not keep both jobs, at least for now? She and Franz needed the money and then she would not be burning her bridges quite so drastically, by casting her lot entirely with Emiel de Vries, whom she was not entirely sure of.

Annemie, however, was not having it. "Tutoring the de Vries girls? As if they need it," she'd scoffed. "They go to a very good school, and they can learn German when they are older."

"Meneer de Vries wishes it…" Rachel had begun, and Annemie had clucked her tongue.

"I'm *sure* he does! A pretty young woman in the house, blushing and simpering at him? He'd like nothing better."

Rachel had blushed right then, both in shame and indignation. She was hardly going to *simper* at her new employer. The suggestion was distasteful in the extreme.

"It is good work," she'd told Annemie with as much dignity as she'd been able to muster. "That is all. I trained as a teacher, back in Berlin. I would like to use my knowledge—"

"Of course you would," Annemie had responded on a sigh as she'd wearily shaken her head. "But, Rachel, my girl, you must know as well as I do that it is not wise. Emiel de Vries… he's a good man, a kind man, but he is also a *weak* man. And I cannot hold your job for you here." She spoke resolutely, although her eyes were kind. "This isn't a charity, you know, and we need someone who can work the hours we ask them, not when they pick and choose to suit themselves."

Rachel had bristled slightly at that; she had worked hard for the Smits for three long months, never asking for a moment off, but with steel in her spine, she'd accepted the older woman's decision. "Very well, then, I understand," she'd told her with stiff politeness. "Then I am sorry to have to leave you."

At this announcement, Annemie had looked both annoyed and regretful; perhaps she'd thought Rachel would reconsider, with such an ultimatum thrown at her, and maybe she should have… but the tutoring position had felt too good an opportunity to pass up, and she was alert to the dangers, even if Annemie didn't think she was.

While the baker's wife had been decidedly disapproving, Franz's attitude toward her new work had been as indifferent as she might have expected, considering the state of their marriage. He'd simply shrugged and remarked that she should do as she liked, but it was a pity they would no longer have fresh bread.

Now, as she knocked on the door, Rachel pushed such thoughts from her mind, wanting only to focus on the present... and all she hoped it might offer.

A housemaid, elderly and seeming disapproving, answered the door, dressed in dusty black, a mob cap covering her stiff gray curls. Rachel's bright smile dimmed slightly as the woman narrowed her eyes and sniffed at her when she explained who she was, before standing aside to let her in.

"You can wait in the front parlor," the maid said in Dutch that Rachel managed to get the gist of, "until Mevrouw de Vries is ready to see you."

"*Dank u wel*," she murmured.

Rachel was relieved that it would be the mistress of the house, rather than its master, who would be her point of contact, although she felt some trepidation at meeting this unknown woman. Had Emiel's wife been as keen for her appointment as her husband? She could only hope.

The maid ushered her to an elegant room, its long windows overlooking the street. Its furnishings were mainly heavy, solid pieces of dark wood, interspersed with the occasional newer piece, jarring in its modernity. Rachel stood in front of a painting of abstract rectangles bisected by thick, dark lines, positioned above a heavy dresser that looked as if it hadn't been moved in a hundred years.

She was still studying it when the door opened and a light, laughing voice inquired in German, "It's a striking piece, is it not? Piet Mondrian. My husband is a champion of Dutch artists, especially those who are seen as avant-garde. He fancies himself a bit of a collector."

Rachel whirled around to see a slender, waif-like woman, graceful and lithe, standing in the doorway, her expression friendly, but also appraising. She looked to be in her early thirties, her blond hair pulled back into an elegant chignon, laugh lines fanning out from her pale blue eyes. Her clothes were carelessly sophisticated—a pair of wide-legged trousers and a turtleneck sweater, its sleeves hiding her hands. In her presence, Rachel immediately felt ungainly, old-fashioned, and gauche.

"I've never seen its like," she replied after a moment, nodding toward the painting. "Although I believe a Mondrian was shown at the Degenerate Art Exhibition in Berlin a few years ago. My husband and I went to see it—many more people, I heard, wanted to see the so-called degenerate art rather than its counterpart, the Great German Art Exhibition." She gave a small, rueful laugh, and the woman cocked her head, her eyes lighting with interest.

"Out of curiosity, do you think," she asked, "or solidarity?"

Rachel spread her hands. "Both, perhaps. If I'm honest, Franz and I went for those two reasons. We were hoping to be shocked."

The woman laughed, a sparkling sound. "And were you?"

"I was," Rachel replied wryly, remembering her blushes and how Franz had lovingly teased her. "I'm not sure about Franz."

The woman glided forward, one hand outstretched. "Your candor is refreshing. I am Amalia de Vries."

"Rachel Blau."

They shook hands, the woman's small and slender, everything about her fine-boned and elegant. Rachel wasn't particularly tall or stout, but she felt both in this elfin woman's presence.

"So," Amalia said as she took a cigarette from a small silver box resting on a marble-topped table, "my husband hired you as a tutor for dear Evi and Beatrix."

Rachel bowed her head. "That is so, Mevrouw de Vries."

"You may call me Amalia." The words were kind enough, but the tone was slightly imperious. Rachel was not entirely sure what to make of this woman; her kindness was tempered with what seemed like a kind of calculating confidence. "Well, I suppose it's a good enough idea," she continued as she lit her cigarette and then drew on it sharply. "Although they are rather young to learn German. And history? They learn history at school."

"I don't have to teach them history—" Rachel began uncertainly.

"No, no, you must do what you like," Amalia cut her off, her tone decisive. "It will occupy them, at any rate, which can only be for the good." She paused to level Rachel with a look that was cooler than any she'd given her before. "I should tell you that my husband likes to have his little pet projects, Miss Blau. *You* are one of them."

Rachel did her best to keep her expression composed as she tried to think of how to reply. Finally, she decided honesty was the best way forward.

"I don't particularly care to be anyone's *pet project*, Mevrouw—Amalia. As a former teacher, I was gratified that Meneer de Vries wished to hire me. However, if it's no more than an idle notion of his, and not one you support, I can leave right now. Indeed, I would feel a duty to do so." She lifted her chin slightly, trembling inwardly at the thought. Would the Smits take her back at the bakery if this all ended before it began? And yet what else could she have said in the circumstances?

Amalia de Vries' mouth curved in a small, approving smile. "You have spirit, I see, but don't worry, there's no need to get yourself in a snit. As I said, it is good for the girls to be occupied and if they learn something along the way, so much the better." Her expression softened, just a little. "You seem a kind woman, Miss Blau. I am not threatened by you, so do not be concerned on my account. I just wanted to warn you, for your own sake."

Rachel nodded stiffly, both embarrassed and gratified by the older woman's plain speaking. "I understand."

"Good." Amalia stubbed out her cigarette. "Then let me introduce you to Evi and Beatrix."

Rachel's hands were clammy, her heart still thumping as she followed Amalia de Vries up two flights of narrow stairs to the nursery on the top floor. As they climbed, she caught glimpses of other rooms—a heavy Turkish carpet, a fringed tablecloth, an antique vase. The house had the feel of a museum with flashes of a home—another modern painting, a violin case, a book left open on a table.

Amalia tapped once on the door of the nursery before throwing it open and stepping into the long, narrow room that ran the length of the house, with steep eaves and white-painted walls. Two girls, still in their school uniforms, were sitting at a long, oak table in the center of the room. Evi, the younger one, was coloring, and Beatrix was reading a book of fairy tales.

"Hello, my darlings!" Amalia cried, kissing her daughters on their cheeks before she flung a hand out toward Rachel. "Here is your new language tutor, Miss Blau. Won't you welcome her, girls?"

Rather dutifully, the girls murmured their hellos. Evi had a head of blond ringlets, and Beatrix had freckles across her nose and a bright blue bow in her shining brown hair, the color and curl so like her father's.

"Good afternoon," Rachel greeted them in careful Dutch as she offered a smile. "I'm so pleased to meet you."

"I'll leave it to you, then," Amalia said, and without further ado, she left the room, closing the door on Rachel and her two charges, who were eyeing her with a doleful sort of curiosity.

"Are you German?" Beatrix asked abruptly in Dutch. "And Jewish?"

"Yes to both," Rachel replied, and the girls stared at her dumbly. She'd spoken in German, and clearly, unlike their parents, they didn't know a word. Rachel realized belatedly that she had not considered the language barrier when it came to teaching two little girls German. "I don't know many words in Dutch," she stated carefully, reverting back to her limited knowledge of the language; the girls giggled at her clumsy attempt at speaking it. "Maybe I can teach you German, and you can teach me Dutch?" she suggested. "It will be a game."

Evi's eyes brightened at the word game—it was very similar to the German—but Beatrix looked unconvinced.

"A game?" she repeated.

"Yes, a game," Rachel assured her cheerfully. "Let's see." She glanced around the nursery, which was decorated lavishly —a comfortable sofa and chairs at one end, and all sorts of toys at the other, including a magnificent dollhouse that had to be as tall as Evi and just as wide. She pointed to the sofa. "What is that?" she asked in Dutch.

Evi and Beatrix glanced at each other, and then Evi piped up, her voice high and lilting, "*Zitbank.*"

"And in German it is *Das Sofa,*" Rachel replied. "Isn't that interesting? What about this?" She pointed to a chair.

"*Stoel,*" Evi cried, getting into the spirit of the game.

"And in German it's *Stuhl.*"

"My turn!" Beatrix cried, and Rachel pointed to her book of fairy tales.

"*Boek,*" the little girl cried triumphantly.

"And in German, *Buch,*" Rachel told her. "Another?"

For the next hour, they played the game, taking turns pointing and saying the names in both German and Dutch until they'd named nearly every object in the room. Then Rachel had them do it again, repeating the German, until they'd learned most of the words by heart. The girls were eager pupils, but by the time an hour had passed, she could tell they were both tired; Beatrix was becoming reticent, Evi a little fractious.

"And now it's time for a rest, I think," she said in German. The languages were close enough that she thought her charges would be able to get the gist of what she meant. "You can only learn so much in one go." She glanced around the room. "Evi and Beatrix, will you show me the dollhouse?" She used the

Dutch word she'd learned—*poppenhuis*—which was very similar to the German, *Puppenhaus*.

"Oh yes!" Evi cried, scrambling off her chair. She grabbed Rachel by the hand, making her laugh as she tugged her along. "Papa had it made it for us. Come see, come see."

The three of them sat down in front of the dollhouse, and Rachel gazed at its interior in admiring wonder. Every room was decorated just as a grand house might be, with furniture, wallpaper, even ornaments and lamps. The dining-room table was set with little porcelain dishes and tiny knives and forks, like minute slivers of silver. The music room had a tiny piano and an even tinier violin. Gently, Rachel picked it up and plucked one string with the very tip of her finger, and a little twanging sound emerged from the miniscule instrument.

"Marvelous!" she exclaimed, and the girls both grinned; her amazement needed no translation.

They spent a pleasant half-hour exploring the intricacies of the dollhouse together, with Beatrix and Evi offering the Dutch for the items Rachel pointed to, and Rachel giving them the German. Outside, the sky had darkened to violet and then indigo, and the first stars glimmered on the horizon. Rachel glanced at the clock, amazed it was already after five o'clock; the time had flown by.

Just then, the door to the nursery opened, and Evi cried, "Papa!"

Rachel scrambled up to her feet as she turned to face Emiel de Vries, who was swinging Evi up into his arms, his face split into a wide smile, his dark, rumpled hair springing out in curls that fell over his forehead. He was wearing a fashionable pinstriped suit, complete with waistcoat, and he looked every inch the well-heeled man of business.

"Ah, my beautiful girls!" he said in German before switching to Dutch to talk to his children.

Rachel stood with her hands hidden in her skirt as the two girls jabbered at him in Dutch, far too fast for her to understand.

Over their heads, Emiel gave her a humorous look. "They are telling me how much fun you've had together," he told her in German. "It seems you are a complete success, Miss Blau."

"They are charming girls," Rachel replied, ducking her head, embarrassed by his praise.

"You must come downstairs and sit with us," Emiel said. He caressed Evi's curls as he added, "I am sure you are all quite famished."

Rachel hesitated, uncertain how to reply. She really should get back home to Franz, but, according to their agreement, she had another half-hour of tutoring time with Evi and Beatrix. She didn't want to ask to leave early, and yet...

Emiel must have seen her glance at the clock because he laughed and wagged a finger at her. "Now, now, we cannot let go of you yet, Miss Blau! Come join us." He spoke firmly, inviting no argument, and Beatrix caught her hand.

"*Ja*, Miss Blau," she said. "*Kom.*"

It was the same in German, and so Rachel understood readily enough, and knowing she really had no choice, she gave the little girl a wider smile and then followed Emiel and his daughters downstairs.

He led them to the back parlor, which was a far cozier room than the front, with no heavy, dark furniture or muddy-looking oil paintings. Wide windows overlooked the back garden, and several lamps were lit, along with a fire, to make the room even more cozy. A piano was tucked into one corner, and a violin was propped next to a music stand. Books were piled on tables, and pillows lined the sofa, giving the room an air of both industry and entertainment. It had been a long time, Rachel thought, since she had been in such a comfortable and welcoming room.

"Ah, our governess," Amalia said as she swept into the parlor.

Beatrix threw her arms around her mother, and she laughed as she stroked her daughter's hair, asking her something in Dutch that Rachel didn't understand. Beatrix answered back, and Amalia lifted her gaze to look at Rachel.

"It seems my daughters enjoyed themselves, Frau Blau," she remarked. "Well done." Her manner, Rachel thought, was friendly, if slightly reserved, which she supposed she understood. Emiel acted in a familiar enough way for both of them—a fact Rachel was trying to get used to.

"I enjoyed myself, as well," she replied, before feeling compelled to add, "but if our tutoring is now finished, perhaps I should take my leave? You will want to be together as a family, and I have my own husband to return to."

She thought she saw a gleam of something like approval in Amalia's eyes, but before she could reply, Emiel interjected cheerfully, "But, no! You must stay with us. Cook has made *bitterballen*, and I insist you have a drink after several hours with these two terrors." He glanced at Amalia. "Don't you agree, my darling?"

Amalia paused, her lips pursed, before she gave a nod. "Yes, of course, you must stay."

"*Sta op, sta op,*" Beatrix entreated, which Rachel knew meant "stay."

Still, she hesitated. As cheerful and comfortable as this room was, she was not part of this family and never would be, and she had her own home to return to.

"I—" she began, only to be cut off by Emiel.

"It's decided," he stated, putting down Evi and taking Rachel rather firmly by the elbow. "Come, sit, and tell us about your German lesson."

Rachel allowed herself to be propelled to a sofa, where she sat down, Evi scrambling up next to her. "The girls can tell you themselves," she said. "Evi, Beatrix. Do you remember your German?" She smiled at them encouragingly and the girls began to chatter excitedly to their parents, leaving Rachel to sit back and simply observe.

Emiel and Amalia were clearly doting parents, enjoying their daughters' excitement, caressing their heads, or pressing laughing kisses to their plump cheeks. They were also, Rachel noticed, affectionate with each other; Emiel draped an arm around Amalia as they all chatted, and she smiled up at him, entirely at ease. It made Rachel feel both reassured in terms of her employer's intentions—or lack thereof—toward her, and melancholy at the state of her own marriage. When was the last time Franz had held her? Kissed her? Before Dachau, they'd shared the same easy affection as Emiel and Amalia—a quick kiss, a draped arm, a squeeze. Rachel had relished those little touches, but when she thought now of what awaited her that evening—Franz sitting silently, glowering at her, that was if he was looking at her at all, or an otherwise empty apartment—she was inclined to stay in this warm and cozy room just a little bit longer, and keep hold of the memories that were so bittersweet.

The maid, whose name Rachel learned was Gerda, brought in the *bitterballen*—deep-fried meatballs they ate with sharp mustard and which were utterly delicious. Emiel insisted she have a drink with them, pressing a tulip-shaped glass of Dutch-made jenever into her hands.

Rachel took one sip and nearly choked; the spirit was stronger than any she'd had before. At her sputtering response, Emiel roared with laughter and even Amalia smiled, and she was compelled by them both to drink the entire, albeit tiny, glass, until her head was swimming. The girls were getting tired and fractious by that point, and realizing it was well after six o'clock, Rachel decided it was time to go.

On embarrassingly unsteady feet, she rose from her chair. "This has been delightful," she told her hosts, "but I really must go. My husband will be wondering where I am." Or not, but she was not about to admit that to them.

"I will walk you home," Emiel pronounced, and Rachel drew back, horrified by the notion. From the corner of her eye, she saw Amalia press her lips together.

"Oh, no!" she said quickly. "I wouldn't dream of so imposing. I will be quite safe, I assure you. I walk alone often."

"Nonsense," Emiel insisted, lumbering to his feet with a smile. He'd had two glasses of jenever himself, and his face was flushed. "I insist."

"As do I," Rachel replied, smiling to take any sting from her words. "Stay here with your family." She looked around for her coat, and Amalia called for Gerda to bring it.

Emiel made a few more protests, but they were halfhearted, and Rachel was both relieved and a little sorry to leave the cheerful family and the warm, comfortable room and head outside on her own.

As the door closed on the happy home, Rachel felt the cold and darkness all around her. Buttoning up her coat, she hurried down the street, back to her apartment, the silent husband and the unhappy home that awaited her.

CHAPTER 11

The next few months fell into a comfortable and even pleasing routine as Rachel continued to visit the de Vries household three times a week.

Amalia had warmed to her—or so she hoped—as had Beatrix and Evi, and Rachel had become confident enough in both her teaching and her Dutch to discipline them gently when necessary. Over the weeks and months, she'd discovered that Evi could sometimes be spoiled, and Beatrix liked to sulk, but on the whole, the girls were delightful, and Rachel reveled in being able to teach again.

The hours she spent in the cheerful nursery were the highlight of her week; with Evi often on her lap and Beatrix sitting by her elbow, she worked through their lessons, enjoying their childish pleasure in getting a word right, or how they would tug her hand to show her the latest toy or treasure their dear Papa had bought them.

What she had come to like even more than the lessons, to her own disquiet, was the pleasant half-hour afterwards, when Amalia or Emiel beckoned her downstairs to the back parlor with its cozy fire and comfortable armchairs, a fire blazing away in the hearth. Gerda would bring in some delicacy or other, and sometimes Amalia would play the piano, or Emiel the violin. The girls would get up and dance, and Emiel would swing them around while Amalia clapped her hands and laughter rang through the room. Rachel watched them all enjoying themselves and an ache of longing would overwhelm her, for a similar home to return to, the same kind of life to have and to savor. Even children one day, when the world was at peace and such things could be considered.

She'd had hopes, at the start of her teaching Evi and Beatrix, that the free time she now had during the week would help her to make more of a welcoming home for her and Franz. She'd even cherished fragile dreams that they might spend more time together, and rediscover their love for each other, but as the weeks passed, she realized it was not to be.

Franz remained as cool and distant as ever, involving himself with the law office or visiting with his friends; when he was home, he simply sat and smoked or listened to the radio, ignoring Rachel. More than once, Rachel had returned to find him tuned into a German station, listening to one of Hitler's ranting speeches, much to her dismay.

"Why do you listen to such stuff?" she exclaimed, reaching to turn the set off, but Franz stayed her with one hand.

"Better to know and accept than to live in delusion," he stated flatly, and Rachel could only shake her head. She felt as if they were spinning in separate orbits, and she had no idea how to bring them into each other's universe again. When they were in the apartment together, they barely spoke; sometimes it felt as if Franz could hardly bring himself to look at her. At night, they lay side by side in bed, never touching or speaking.

How, she wondered despondently more than once, had it come to this? Had it really just been over the letter she'd never sent to her mother, or had the seeds of dissension been there all along, perhaps even before they'd married, sown in the soil of her own naiveté? She'd been so in love with Franz's ebullience and conviction, his passion and his joy, but now she wondered if she'd ever truly known her husband at all.

In January, Rachel received a letter from Sophie, remarking how glad she was that Rachel was well settled. Rachel had winced to realize how pretty a picture she'd painted of their lives here in Haarlem in the letter to her friend, touching on very few of the hardships that had befallen them. Sophie wrote that she was working at a Jewish Center in Washington DC and living in a boardinghouse. She'd heard from Hannah and Rosa, and enclosed their addresses, which Rachel was grateful for. Now she could be in touch with all her friends—but could she bear to tell any of them the hard truth of her situation?

On board the *St Louis*, Rachel had suspected that they'd all looked up to her a little, the oldest and married one of their group of four, supposedly wise in her ways. They had admired her determined cheerfulness in light of the challenges they all faced, and hers in particular, with Franz the way he was. How could she admit to them what a mess she'd made of her life here in Haarlem, with a husband who now seemed as if he couldn't stand her, and her own heart feeling so wounded and unhappy?

A sigh escaped her at the thought, and she slipped Sophie's letter back into its envelope. She would write later, when she could think of what she wanted to say... and how honest she was willing to be, to all her friends.

With a pang of bittersweet nostalgia, Rachel opened her drawer and reached for the shard of emerald she kept wrapped in a handkerchief beneath her clothes, unfolding it and letting it rest in the palm of her hand. For a second, she pictured them all as they'd been, toasting each other on board the *St Louis*, so excited for the future they'd believe had awaited them.

As she closed her fingers around the jewel, she hoped Sophie, Rosa, and Hannah had all found more happiness in their new homelands than she had.

. . .

In the middle of January, the coldest in Europe for over fifty years, with the canals frozen and the air absolutely frigid, "a state of readiness" was announced by the prime minister, with all army leave canceled.

The news, although it should have been expected considering the continued mobilization of the Germany army, as well as the Winter War raging on in Finland, came as an almighty shock to all the Dutch citizens who had been so smugly certain they would not get involved in the conflict setting Europe ablaze.

For Rachel and Franz, however, there arose a more immediately pressing problem. One Monday evening toward the end of the month, Rachel returned from the de Vries' home to find Franz smoking in the kitchen, a glass of beer half-drunk on the table in front of him, his expression grimmer than ever.

"Franz...?" she asked uncertainly as she took off her coat. The apartment was icy as they did not have the money for coal to heat it properly, and with the freezing temperatures, it had made Rachel even more reluctant to return home to such an unwelcome space. "Is... is something wrong?" She was almost afraid to ask the question, for fear of what the answer might be: *Everything.*

When was the last time they'd spoken to each other properly? She couldn't even remember.

"Jan came by this afternoon," Franz replied flatly. "We have to leave this apartment by the end of the week."

Rachel gaped at him. "The end of the *week*!" How on earth would they find suitable, and more importantly, affordable, lodgings in such a short amount of time? She didn't even know where to begin to look.

Franz shrugged in reply. "The journalist who lives here is returning from France, because of the threat of war. Not that

Haarlem is much safer." He pressed his lips together. "The Germans are going to march through all of Europe, mark my words, and set it on fire." His fingers holding the cigarette trembled, and ash fell on his trousers. He didn't bother brushing it away.

Rachel stared at him, her heart both racing with anxiety and aching with sorrow. Sometimes, in the light of Franz's coolness, she forgot how much he'd endured, how scarred he still was, even if those wounds were invisible. If she was a better woman, Rachel thought, a better *wife*, she would always remember. She never would let herself forget for a second.

"They've mobilized the Dutch army. They're not unprepared," she ventured after a moment, and Franz let out a humorless laugh.

"The Dutch army will last five minutes, if that."

A ripple of fear went through Rachel as she looked out at the night sky and imagined, for a few awful seconds, it being lit up by fighter planes and exploding bombs, the air full of gunfire and death, Nazi stormtroopers flooding the streets and field-gray lines of Wehrmacht soldiers goosestepping through the Grote Markt...

No. She shook her head to clear the image and turned back to her husband. "Surely it won't come to that," she protested, trying to inject a note of optimism into her wavering voice. "*All* of Europe? Even Hitler must be reasonable at some point—"

"Hitler? Reasonable?" He shook his head vehemently as he stubbed out his cigarette, only to quickly light another. "Do you know what they're doing to the Jews in Poland?" he demanded, a tremor to his voice. "They're herding them into ghettos—thousands upon thousands in a space only fit for a tenth of that amount. They're surrounded by high walls topped with broken glass and barbed wire, and if anyone says so much as a word in protest about anything, they're *shot*. And that's not even accounting for the dirty water, the whole place rife with disease... the Nazis have compared us to *rats*," he stated, his voice rising, "and now they're treating us as such, and that is how they will have us die. Like filthy, desperate creatures!"

"*Franz*." Rachel hated when he spoke in such a dark and despairing way. How could she possibly keep up any sense of hope herself, when he said such things? "Surely it can't be as bad as all that," she argued. "In any case, how could we possibly know what is going on in Poland?"

"Jan tells me. He has connections."

She would take a large pinch of salt with anything Jan van Dijk had to say, Rachel thought darkly. "Those must be exaggerations, surely—"

"Rachel, don't be so damned *naïve*!" Franz cried, his voice now a ragged roar. "Don't you think *I* know what Hitler is capable of?" He dropped his head into his hands, mindless of his burning cigarette, as his shoulders began to shake.

"Franz, oh Franz..." Swiftly, Rachel removed his cigarette and stubbed it out before dropping onto her knees in front of him. "Franz..." Tentatively, she put her arms around him, mindful that they hadn't hugged or even touched in months. The feel of him now in her arms was both familiar and strange, and only lasted a moment before he roughly threw her arms off him, causing her to fall back hard onto the floor, winded.

"But what do *you* care?" he demanded as he wiped his face with his sleeve. "If it comes to war, you can just hole up with your precious *vriendje* and his family, can't you?" He'd used the Dutch diminutive for boyfriend, a word Rachel hadn't even realized he'd known—and horrified, she knew just whom he meant by it.

"Franz—" she began as she scrambled up to a sitting position, but he cut her off, his voice hardening, turning ugly.

"Do you really think I don't know?" he asked as he glared at her. "Everyone in Haarlem is talking about it! How that useless *dummkopf* has turned your head. He's always got a pretty girl dangling on the line—you aren't the first, you know, and you won't be the last."

"Franz, I am the de Vries' girls' *tutor*," Rachel insisted, deeply shaken by the accusations he was hurling at her. "That is *all*—"

"You must truly take me for a fool!" he scoffed in return. "Do you think seven months at Dachau has addled me that much, that I can't see when my own wife is falling in love with another man?"

"I am not!" Rachel declared hotly, a flush rising to her face. "But if you would be more of a husband to me at home, perhaps such a thought wouldn't cross *your* mind!"

As soon as she'd said the words, Rachel regretted them.

Franz's face drained of color as he stared at her in disbelief. "You would use such a thing against me? *Unman* me—"

"Franz, please." She flung her hands out toward him, instantly apologetic. "I don't want to fight with you. I've never wanted to fight with you. I only want to be your wife, your *devoted* wife—"

"Such devotion," he sneered. "When you've been seen at a coffeehouse with another man—"

"That was months ago!" Rachel cried. "And I told you, it was only to discuss the tutoring position—"

"You come home *smelling* of him," Franz declared flatly, and she stared at him, shocked into a second's silence by the ugliness of the implied accusation.

"I do not," she insisted after a moment, her voice low. Admittedly, Emiel daubed himself liberally with a sharp-scented cologne, but the implication of her husband's words was distressingly clear. "I do not," she said again, quietly. "You do me a great disservice, Franz, to suggest such a thing."

"It's what everyone else is suggesting," he muttered, swinging away from her.

"But you are my husband," she persisted. "We're meant to

love and trust and support one another." And yet, how long had it been since Franz had shown her any of those emotions, Rachel thought despondently. "What can I do, Franz?" Her voice rose, broke. "What can I do to make things better between us again?"

The words fell into the silence, rippled out, and still there was no reply. Rachel stared at her husband's taut back, too weary to summon yet more supplications. She was too tired to keep trying, she thought, no matter what Frieda had advised. A marriage took two people. She could not do this on her own. Not anymore.

"There's nothing you can do," Franz said in a low voice. "There's nothing *anyone* can do." And then he pushed past her into their bedroom, leaving Rachel alone again.

Rachel spent the next few mornings tramping the streets of the Old Town, looking for a new place for her and Franz to live.

They had not spoken since their argument—a fact which brought as much relief as it did distress. In truth, she did not know what she would say to him now, and she was too tired to try. The uncertainty of their living situation was, in any case, more pressing; after several mornings looking for somewhere suitable, it became depressingly clear that they'd been fortunate indeed to have two whole rooms to themselves.

The best she was able to find on their wages was a single room on the top floor of a boarding house, freezing in winter and no doubt stifling in summer. It possessed a bed, a chair, and a single gas ring for cooking, and that was all. The landlady had asked if she was Jewish, and pressed her lips together in a grimace of disapproval when Rachel had admitted she was, but still agreed to let them rent the room. Rachel hoped they would not have to be there very long, although she could not see a way forward to anything else.

As winter melted into spring, her afternoons at the de Vries home felt like the only bright spots in her otherwise bleak days, and yet they were often dogged by guilt, for preferring that happy household to her own, as Franz had accused, although she made sure there was not so much as a hint of impropriety in her conduct with Emiel de Vries, who remained as expansively charming and familiar as ever.

Each evening as Rachel walked home, she found herself more and more reluctant to return to the single room, cold and drafty, she now shared with Franz, to spend the evening in a silence colder still. She hadn't realized how being with another person could sometimes make you feel lonelier than if you were by yourself.

And meanwhile, the news of war was becoming more and more ominous. There had been reports of German troops near the Maginot Line, and Finland was losing against the Soviets. In February, the commander of the Dutch army had resigned due to its lack of preparedness. No one seemed to believe the prime minister's soothing assurances that there would still be no war, and yet at the same time, it seemed no one could bring themselves to believe it could ever really happen. They were all, Rachel reflected, existing in a state of limbo that surely couldn't last.

Then, in early April, just before dawn, the Germans attacked Denmark; the country fell in the space of six hours, with the Danish government surrendering by breakfast. Rachel and Franz listened to it over the radio, silent and shaken; she didn't think even Franz had thought they would capitulate that quickly.

"The Netherlands will be next," he remarked tonelessly as he turned the radio off. "And they'll come for the Jews first. Who knows, maybe we'll last longer than the Danes. Maybe all the way to lunch!" He let out a sound that was half laugh, half sob as he reached for his cigarettes.

Rachel gazed out at the spring morning, the cherry blossoms just starting to bud, the air full of birdsong. It seemed far too beautiful a day for war.

"What should we do?" she asked after a moment. There was no point arguing about the what-ifs anymore. The Dutch might still stubbornly hold onto their prime minister's assurances, but Rachel knew she and Franz no longer had that luxury, as foreign-born Jews.

"What *can* we do?" Franz replied as he lit a cigarette. "There's nowhere to go in this godforsaken country. Nothing but flat fields in every direction. And they aren't giving out any more visas, which hardly matters, as we don't have the money in the first place."

That much certainly was true. Now that they had to pay for their accommodation, money was scarcer than ever.

Rachel gazed down at her cup of coffee, made from leftover grounds, little more than a cup of brown water, as she tried to think practically.

"It feels wrong," she said quietly, "to simply sit here and wait for the worst."

"Isn't that what all of life is?" Franz retorted. "The worst certainly seems to happen more often than not. But don't worry," he threw at her, his tone turning into a sneer, "you can always turn to your precious de Vries if things get really desperate. I'm sure they'd be willing to help you. *I*, however, might be another matter."

"Franz, please." It had been months since they'd argued about Emiel de Vries, but the wounds were still raw and fresh for both of them. "Perhaps... I could ask them for help?" Rachel suggested tentatively. "For both of us, I mean. They have connections. They might be able to—"

"Over my dead body." Franz's voice was a low growl as he ground his cigarette out. "And frankly, that's all too likely, considering our future."

Rachel flinched at his words, the sardonic savagery of them. "I hate when you talk like this," she said in a low voice. "If we lose all hope, then what is there left for us? Please, Franz. There must be something we can do."

"*What?*" he demanded, glaring at her, his expression caught between anger and despair. "What, Rachel?" His voice rang out, unrelenting. "The Germans will invade. The Netherlands will fall. I am as sure of those two facts as I am of the sun rising or setting—and trust me, it's setting now, because when this country does fall, they will come for the Jews, and most likely those who aren't Dutch, first. It will be *Kristallnacht* all over again, but worse." His voice rose, trembling with both terror and fury. "They will take us all to camps or ghettos or whatever hellish prison they can devise," he continued, pounding the table with his fist. "They will kill us one by one and *relish* doing it—"

"*Don't!*" Rachel cried, the words torn from her as she threw her hands out toward him. The picture he painted was horrifying in its bleakness. "Please, please, don't—"

"Hitler said he wanted to *annihilate* all the Jews of Europe," Franz continued relentlessly. "All of them! What do you think that means, Rachel? *Annihilating* an entire people." His eyes were wild, his breath coming in ragged pants. Rachel had never seen him so worked up, as if he were reliving some personal horror, and perhaps he was. "How do you think he will do it? They might be devising ways right now, the cruelest kind of torture. I'd rather take my own life." He thrust his chin out, a new gleam of defiance entering his eyes, firing them with sudden purpose. "Maybe I will."

"Franz!" Rachel half rose from the table, truly alarmed now. "Franz, *please*—"

"It would be better for you if I did," Franz cut across her. "Then you wouldn't have to worry about me anymore. There would be no need to feel guilty, and the de Vries family would most likely take you in. With their connections, you might be safe." He spoke with a detached calm that was, in its own way, just as disturbing as the defiance that had come before. "You could survive, Rachel, whatever happened. Without me, you might have a chance."

"Franz..." Rachel lowered her hands from her face to stare at him in pleading concern. *What was he saying?*

"It makes sense," he stated, and with a strange new vigor to his voice that Rachel didn't understand until she saw him heading toward the window that overlooked the street three floors below, a determination in his step, in the set of his face.

For a second, all she could do was stare, and it was as if she was back on the *St Louis*, watching Sophie Weiss' father fight to die.

Franz was raising the old window with a protesting squeak before Rachel had the wherewithal to spring out of her chair.

"*No!*" she screamed, tackling her husband and wrapping her arms around his waist, doing her best to pull him back as they struggled against one another, the balmy spring breeze blowing over them from the open window.

Franz lunged forward and Rachel dug in her heels and heaved back, sobbing and panting with the effort. He couldn't take his life. She wouldn't let him, not after all they'd endured and fought for...

Then Franz finally stopped resisting, his body going slack, and unprepared, Rachel fell backward, just as Sophie had on the ship, landing flat on her back as she blinked up at the ceiling, dazed and breathless, Franz lying heavily next to her.

For a long moment, neither of them spoke. Rachel's body ached and her ears rang from her fall. She could hardly believe how close they'd come to utter disaster.

Franz raised his arm and flung it over his face. "I won't," he said, his voice muffled. "I won't do it, for your sake, I promise, but by God, Rachel, one day you might wish I had."

CHAPTER 12

MAY 10, 1940

In the predawn darkness of the spring morning, an explosion lit up the sky, and the bed Rachel shared with Franz shook from the force of it. She jerked awake, gasping with shock, as outside, the sky glowed red and another explosion sounded, followed by another, too steady and regular to be thunder.

The Germans were invading.

Just a few hours before, on his evening broadcast, the prime minister had once more assured his faithful listeners that "Holland's neutrality would be respected." He'd insisted there was nothing to fear, and Dutchmen were urged to remain calm and go about their business as usual.

And now bombs were dropping on Haarlem, and the sky was like a livid red scar. Even though they'd been bracing themselves for war for months, Rachel could not grasp the enormity of it. The Germans in Holland. In *Haarlem*. The future, always uncertain, had, in an instant, become something only to dread and fear.

Next to her, Franz rose from bed, his hair rumpled as he blinked the sleep out of his eyes, realization already dawning in his dark eyes. In the last month, since he'd tried to fling himself from their window, they'd reached an uneasy stasis of sorts, a truce born more of weariness than conviction.

Rachel continued to work for the de Vries family, coming home each night with her heart in her mouth, afraid of what she might find, and Franz continued to keep his promise... so far. Their marriage didn't seem to be in any better a state, but at least the hostility was gone. There were far bigger things to be worrying about... like war. What would this mean for them? For their very lives?

The explosions outside cast a crimson glow over Franz's face as he blinked the sleep from his eyes. "It's coming from the airport," he said, just as the wail of fire alarms rose up in their street.

Rachel clambered out of bed to go to the window and look down. Far below, the hose trucks were clattering over the cobbles, and in the distance, she could see smoke billowing up in thick, dark clouds. Even then, with the destruction right in front of her, it all seemed terribly unreal.

"We won't sleep, with all that noise," Franz stated matter-of-factly. When Rachel turned to look at him, she saw his face was haggard, with a fatality in his expression that she didn't like. She might find this all so difficult to believe, but Franz did not. What would that mean for him... and his promise?

"I'll make coffee," she said, and went to use their old grounds for a third time.

Over the next few days, the news trickled in slowly.

That first morning, they listened to a broadcast that advised everyone to tape their ground-floor windows to keep them from shattering from the expected bombing. For a brief time, there was a sense almost of camaraderie as neighbors shared both rolls of adhesive and stories of how they'd endured the night of bombing; there was almost an excitement in the air, that this was happening at all, along with a sense of unreality.

It reminded Rachel of those first few days on the *St Louis*, when they'd been denied entry to Havana, and there had been the feeling that somehow they could fight, even prevail, if they just put their minds to it. It hadn't lasted then, and she doubted it would last now. Sure enough, with the windows taped, everyone went back to their own business, and to wait and see if their country held out.

The bombing had moved on, at least, from Haarlem, and the next night was quiet, although Rachel still didn't sleep. She lay next to Franz and wondered what the next few days and weeks would hold. How long would the Dutch hold out against the relentless might of the Wehrmacht? And what would happen when they surrendered, which they surely would?

Franz was fatalistically accepting of the inevitable surrender and occupation by the Germans and whatever suffering it brought, but Rachel longed to do something—*anything*. She hated the thought of simply waiting for the inevitable—and awful—to happen. Perhaps if she asked the de Vries for help, as Franz had suggested... for *both* of them. And yet what help could they offer? Everyone was existing in a state of suspension, simply waiting to see what happened next.

The next afternoon, Rachel headed to the house on Leidsestraat, through the streets of the Old Town that were mostly empty. People were staying inside, their windows taped, the very air seeming muted. Rachel had heard on the radio that there had been bombing in Rotterdam, and she wondered how the Jews left at nearby Heijplaat had fared.

She had yet to decide if she would ask the de Vries for help, but in any case, she wasn't given the opportunity. When she arrived at the townhouse, she found their door locked, the windows shuttered.

"They've gone to his father's house in the country," a

neighbor told her, poking her gray head out of the window suspiciously as she stood on their doorstep and knocked. "Until the war's over."

And when would that be? Rachel wondered. Days, weeks, months, *years*? Would she ever see Evi and Beatrix again?

"*Dank u wel*," she murmured to the neighbor, and then, disconsolately, she turned from the door. She was disappointed that neither Emiel nor Amalia had thought to get word to her, although she supposed they must have been acting in frantic fear. She was also sorry not to have said goodbye to the girls, and even sorrier that, at least for the foreseeable future, she would no longer be making a wage. How would she and Franz survive?

It was a question that was on everyone's lips as the days passed and the news grew bleaker. First, they heard on the radio that Queen Wilhelmina had fled the country, and then, the continued, relentless blitz of nearby Rotterdam, with the Nazi planes targeting civilian areas, and over twenty-five thousand homes destroyed.

On the fifteenth of May, just five days after the first bombing, Rachel and Franz listened to the news on the radio that the entirety of the Dutch government had fled, and German tanks were already rolling across their borders.

"That's that, then," Franz stated flatly, and turned off the radio, plunging the room into a silence that felt thick and oppressive, the beginning of the end.

From outside, Rachel heard the murmuring of crowds, and she rose to go to the window and look out. To her surprise she saw the street below was thronged with people. It seemed everyone had heard the news and was now joining together to witness the end of their beloved country—and, it seemed, to draw strength from each other's presence.

"Franz, look!" she said quietly and nodded to the scene below.

Franz came to the window and gazed down at the crowds impassively. Some of them had tears rolling down their cheeks, their arms around each other as they commiserated and wept together, grieving their homeland and the life that they had known.

"Poor fools," he remarked. "But it won't be nearly as bad for them as it will be for us."

The grim finality of his tone sent a shiver down Rachel's spine. "It's their country," she pointed out quietly. "To lose it must be very hard."

"It's one thing to lose your country," Franz replied, "another to lose your life... or worse, your *soul*." His gaze roved over the crowded street. "In the end, they might lose both. And so might we." He let out a hard huff of humorless laughter. "In any case, I've already lost my soul. Losing my life surely won't be as painful as that."

Before Rachel could reply, someone flung open a window in the building across the street. "It's official, we've surrendered!" they called out, and a stunned hush fell over the crowd below, as if even now, when they'd been mourning the loss of their homeland with tearful embraces, they still couldn't quite believe it had actually come to pass.

In the days that followed, life both changed entirely and stayed strangely the same.

The first time Rachel saw a German soldier in his field-gray uniform in the Grote Markt, on a sunny May morning, she faltered in her step, shocked to her core by the simple sight of him sauntering down the pavement like a young man on holiday, taking in the sights. That one soldier was soon followed by dozens of others, and then there were German tanks and trucks in the streets, and German spoken in shops, soldiers crowding the parks like tourists, taking pictures and buying mementoes for their mothers and wives, their sisters and sweethearts.

And yet despite all this, so much seemed unchanged. After the Netherlands' surrender, the de Vries family came back to Haarlem, and Rachel resumed her tutoring of Evi and Beatrix as if they'd simply gone on a holiday like any other, and had returned, full of stories of springtime at their grandparents' estate in Heemstede, south of the city.

"There were geese *and* ducks!" Evi exclaimed, her face flushed with excitement. "And Papa let us swim in the river. Sometimes we saw planes go by. They flew so low—*zoom, zoom*!" She and Evi both flung out their arms and careened around the nursery, giggling madly as they pretended to be planes while Rachel tried to smile.

To these innocent children, the occupation was nothing more than a source of excitement; the Germans now marching through the Old Town, the swastikas flying from every public building, the laws that were already being enacted one by one... None of it would affect or bother them the way it undoubtedly would her and Franz, as well as every other Jew in this country.

"I am glad you have returned to us," Amalia told her, as if Rachel had been the one to go away rather than the de Vrieses. "It's now more important than ever for them to learn German," she added with a wry grimace. "Although, God willing, not for long." She looked sympathetic, laying a hand on Rachel's arm. "Are you keeping all right? It hasn't been too difficult?"

"We're fine," Rachel replied firmly. "Nothing much has changed, really." Now that she was employed again, they could eat, and as long as the German army busied itself with buying trinkets and not persecuting Jews, maybe, just maybe, they could keep their heads down and survive whatever came next. She clung to that hope, naïve as she feared it might turn out to be, and as the months passed and little changed, it felt easier to believe it, even though more restrictions were inevitably put in place.

Several months after the occupation, all Jews were required to register with the Population Registration Office, and receive a black J stamped on their identity papers. It seemed more of a formality than anything else, and yet still caused Rachel a sense of unease, for now they were *known*, marked out and set apart... But for what purpose?

The German soldier who had taken down her name had been as officious as any other bureaucrat, cold-eyed and uncaring, but, Rachel told herself staunchly, it could have been worse. At least she was still allowed to work, although Franz had lost his job. Jews were still allowed to work in the law—for now—but all political parties and their affiliated organizations had been banned, and the law office that had given him work had been put out of business due to its association with the Revolutionary Socialist Party. Jan had lost his job, as well, and was now working as a janitor in a school.

The new Nazi government had, to many Dutch people's dismay, implemented a policy of *Gleichschaltung*, or conformity, which systematically eliminated all non-Nazi organizations, including political organizations and religious groups; there was nothing, Rachel soon realized, but the NSDP, and everyone was encouraged to join its ranks, save, of course, for Jews.

Despite this, the new civil government, headed by the Austrian Nazi Arthur Seyss-Inquart, was taking what was considered a "velvet glove" approach, by treating the Dutch, considered by Hitler to be "of good Germanic stock," not as a people to be oppressed but rather one to work with. Instead of extracting what they could economically from the country, leaving it wrung out and bone-dry, Dutch businesses were allowed to export to Germany and enjoy the profits. Emiel de Vries, Rachel discovered, quickly became pragmatically and even cheerfully resigned to his factory's lightbulbs being used to power the country of his oppressors.

"What is one to do?" he told Rachel one afternoon in October, when he'd come up for his usual visit to the nursery. Beatrix and Evi had been dismissed from their lessons and were curled up on the sofa with a book, and Emiel sat down at the table across from Rachel, one arm flung out along another chair's back. Outside, the leaves were turning russet and gold, and the canal glinted under the autumn sunshine. "As long as the Germans need lightbulbs," he continued with a smiling shrug, "I don't suppose it matters who is in charge. Life will go on much the same, and truly, the Germans and the Dutch are not so very different. You know yourself how similar our languages are!"

The remark was so breathtakingly thoughtless that Rachel found she could not hold her tongue. "Perhaps it does not matter to *you*," she replied carefully, "but it might to me and my husband, as well as all the other Jews in Europe who will surely suffer under Hitler's rule, and already have."

Along with Denmark and the Netherlands, France and Belgium had both fallen, and Hitler seemed poised to sweep across the whole of Europe and enact his restrictive regime. Already, in addition to having to register with the Population Registration Office, Jews had been forbidden from owning their own businesses or practicing in certain professions. What would be next? How long would she and Franz, and all the other Jews, be able to live as they liked, or even at all?

Emiel reached for both her hands and clasped them tightly. "My dear, forgive me, I was being insensitive," he exclaimed. "Of course it matters to you who is in charge! How thoughtless of me, to think for a moment that it doesn't. How are you faring?" He cocked his head, his eyes and smile warm. "Is there any way we can help?"

Rachel opened her mouth to say, as she always did, that

there wasn't, when she hesitated. Emiel was clearly profiting from the occupation, and meanwhile, without the money Franz had earned, admittedly sporadically, from his work at the law office, they were struggling to eat and pay their rent.

"There is a way you could help," she told Emiel slowly. His hands were still clasped in hers, and carefully she slipped them out, clenching them together tightly in her lap. "My husband Franz trained as a lawyer, but he cannot find work here. Is there something he could do in your factory? It doesn't matter what..." She trailed off, wondering at the wisdom of her suggestion. Franz would surely balk at the notion of working for Emiel de Vries, of all people, and yet he needed work, they needed the money, and Rachel hoped his spirits might improve if he was more profitably engaged. At the moment, he spent most days sitting at their kitchen table, smoking and staring into space. It was no way for any man to live.

"Work in the factory?" Emiel repeated, frowning a little. Rachel's heart sank; he sounded hesitant. She shouldn't have asked. Then Emiel gave one of his usual wide, warm smiles. "Of course, I would be *delighted* to find a position for him!" he exclaimed. "Nothing that is prohibited, of course, but if he doesn't mind something a bit humbler? He's not a proud man?"

The teasing note in Emiel's voice made Rachel stiffen, just a little. He almost made it sound as if a man like Franz, a Jew, did not have the luxury or even the right to be proud of anything.

"He is a proud man," she replied, "but he is also a practical one. Thank you for your kindness."

To Rachel's surprise, Franz agreed to work in the de Vries factory, although he was far from enthused.

"You are right, we need to eat," he told her. "And what does it matter where I work, or who for? I'll sweep floors for that pompous prat if it earns me a few guilders. The end will come soon enough, anyway."

Rachel ignored his last remark, as she had so many others. Since the occupation, Franz had descended into a fatalistic indifference that she found even more wearing than his previous despair or fury, yet which, in its own way, was easier to bear. At least they no longer argued, she told herself, although sometimes she almost wished they did. Whatever spark Franz had once possessed, the fire and wit that she'd once reveled in that had then turned to derision and fury, seemed to have winked out completely. He was just waiting through the days, enduring each one, but perhaps that was all any of them were doing, or could do. What more really was there, at least for now?

"One day this will all be over," Frieda had remarked in her placid, pragmatic way when Rachel spared an afternoon to visit her. "Until then, we must do our best to hold on. We Jews are good at surviving. Look at how we have thrived wherever we have gone—from Babylon to Berlin, eh? They keep trying to destroy us, and we keep rising again, much to their annoyance." She smiled whimsically, although her eyes were troubled. Rachel knew she hadn't heard from her son for several months, just as she hadn't heard from her mother. What was happening to their families back in Germany?

If the Jews in the Netherlands were experiencing these hardships, what, Rachel wondered more than once, were the Jews there enduring?

As autumn sank into winter and then melted into spring, Rachel and Franz continued to struggle on, earning enough to keep body and soul together, if only just. Her afternoons in the de Vries home remained the one pleasure in the midst of troubling times. In the cheerful comfort of the nursery or the back parlor, she could lose herself in her teaching, the simple pleasures of food and music with convivial people and forget the troubles that swirled and grew outside with every day.

In November, all Jewish civil servants had been dismissed from their posts. Shortly after, they were removed from all teaching positions. Meanwhile, Rachel noticed more and more signs in various shop windows—"No Jews Will Be Served." A placard appeared on the gate to De Bolwerken, "No Jews." Entire neighborhoods had painted signs declaring *"Joden Niet Gewenst"*— Jews Not Wanted. Although legally Jews were still allowed in such places, it seemed the Dutch had decided they weren't welcome. Rachel was not brave enough to enter anywhere she saw such a sign, and the places where she was able to buy food and other necessities had become depressingly few.

She spent hours queuing for bread at every bakery she could find, including the Smits', and wrote Sophie a humorous letter about the joy of finally finding a single, small loaf, but in reality, it was far from funny. It had become harder and harder to find anyone willing to sell them food, and what food Rachel was able to buy was lamentably poor— the potatoes often black, the bread hard, the flour full of weevils. Meanwhile, she still hadn't heard from any of her friends or her mother, and Rachel feared for them all, especially as it was so difficult to find any news that wasn't tainted by Nazi propaganda.

She and Franz had been forced to turn in their radio soon after the occupation, as had all Dutch citizens, although she knew some people had kept a hidden set. Indeed, the de Vries had a small set they kept in the back parlor, and occasionally they brought it out and listened to the BBC's broadcast to the Netherlands, Radio *Oranje*, but as her Dutch was still limited, she didn't always understand it all, although it was heartening to hear of those who were fighting for the Allies, and therefore, for the Jews. As alone as Rachel sometimes felt, listening to the radio reminded her that she wasn't.

One evening in the May of 1941, however, when they had been living under the occupation for a long, weary year, the radio disappeared.

"Papa put it away," Beatrix said matter-of-factly when Rachel asked her about it. "He said we shouldn't have things the government doesn't want us to, and the programs on the radio are full of nonsense anyway."

"Did he?" Rachel replied, the childish remark giving her a deep unease. She knew well enough that Emiel's lightbulb factory was now exporting entirely to Germany. Did he really think the BBC broadcasts were nonsense, or was he feeling the pressure to toe the party line? And if so, what would that mean for her... and Franz?

She found out just a short while later. By October, the nights were drawing in and the air had turned damp and chilly, the mist hovering over the Spaarne. As Rachel knocked on the de Vries' door, she was ushered by Gerda not upstairs to the cheerful nursery and her two young charges, but to the front parlor with its heavy furniture and thick velvet curtains, where she'd had her first meeting with Amalia, nearly two years earlier, and not stepped inside since.

This afternoon, Emiel stood there, looking somber, his hands clasped behind him, his shoulders thrust back.

"Frau Blau," he greeted her, more formally than he ever had.

Rachel faltered in her step, registering his tone, the look of remote resolve on his handsome face. His hair no longer curled over his forehead but was swept back and flattened with cream. It made him look less approachable, Rachel thought, and more like a Nazi bureaucrat.

"Is something wrong?" she asked, her hands clasped tightly in front of her.

Emiel's gaze flicked away from her. "I'm sorry," he stated, his voice toneless, his gaze still averted, "but I'm afraid we have to let you go."

For a second, Rachel could only stare. She knew what was happening—and why—yet she could hardly believe it. Emiel had always been so kind to her, so warm and encouraging. She thought of the pleasant evenings spent in the back parlor, listening to music, and feeling part of this family. Although, admittedly, in recent months, those happy times had been less frequent. Rachel had tried not to notice, but the truth of it was staring her right in the face now. Emiel wasn't even looking at her.

"Is it because I'm Jewish?" she asked numbly.

"You have to understand my position," Emiel replied, his gaze firmly fixed on the window. "Soon enough, the government is going to pass a decree forbidding Jews from working for non-Jews. I can hardly be seen to flaunt such a regulation. I am a prominent man of business in this city, after all." His chest swelled a little. "The de Vries family have been making light-bulbs for as long as there has been electricity!"

Rachel almost laughed at that, as it was the first she'd ever heard him sound proud of what he did for a living. "I understand," she said, knowing she did all too well. Emiel de Vries had to look out for his own interests, his own family, before hers. She understood the sentiment, and yet she still felt hurt. She'd thought Emiel de Vries was a better man than this.

"I'm sorry," Emiel told her. "I wish it could be another way." For the first time since she'd come into the room, he looked at her. His expression was sympathetic but also resolute, and Rachel thought she saw a new hardness in his eyes.

She nodded slowly, accepting, because what else could she do? This, along with so much else, was utterly out of her power. And yet for a moment she saw the future just as Franz surely saw it—bleak and unrelenting because the people around them were either too cowardly or indifferent to fight for things to be a different way. *What is happening to the Jews*, she'd read in a newspaper, *is a Jewish problem*. It was a sentiment she suspected was shared by many, including now Emiel de Vries.

"I see," she said at last. She pulled her coat more closely around her. "May I say goodbye to Beatrix and Evi?"

Emiel pressed his lips together. "I don't think that would be a good idea."

So it was like that, then. He was cutting off all ties with complete finality, as if wielding a pair of ruthlessly sharp scissors.

Rachel shook her head slowly. She should have heeded Annemie Smit's warning, and realized just how weak a man Emiel de Vries was—not just in matters of the heart, but in ones of courage. "I see," she said again.

The moment spun out into a tense awkwardness; there seemed to be nothing more to say. Emiel shifted where he stood, clearly wanting her to go. He must have fired Franz at his factory, as well, Rachel realized, and with a plunging sensation, she wondered how her husband had taken the news.

With both of their jobs gone, she and Franz would have no money, no way to pay their rent or put food on the table. Would anyone else hire them, especially with this new law in place? Her stomach hollowed out at the thought, but she refused to show Emiel de Vries just how much pain he'd caused her. She'd thought they were friends, of a sort, and that he was a kind and good man. She'd felt part of his family, even if she'd reminded herself repeatedly that she wasn't. Now she knew the cold, hard truth.

"*Auf Wiedersehen*," she bid him with as much dignity as she could muster, and Emiel gave a tight nod in reply.

Rachel turned and left the room.

She walked back to their boarding house in a blind fog of shock. For the first time since they'd boarded the *St Louis*, she really could see no way forward at all. At least at Heijplaat, they'd been fed. In their little apartment off the Grote Markt, they'd had a roof over their heads, and the possibility of work. Now, with the restrictions against the Jews getting more stringent every day, and the prospect of finding any work at all looking bleak indeed, if not downright impossible, the future felt more frightening than ever.

How on earth were she and Franz meant to survive now?

CHAPTER 13

APRIL 1942

The watchmaker's shop on Barteljorisstraat was on the ground floor of a tall, narrow townhouse, two small, dark rooms—the first full of glass cases of watches, the other behind a workroom. Frieda had told her about Casper ten Boom when they'd first visited, and how he was a good man who helped Jews. Now Rachel hoped he would help her by buying her father's precious pocket watch.

A bell tinkled as Rachel stepped into the interior, blinking in the gloom. Half a dozen wall clocks measured the time in steady ticks as she carefully shut the door behind her. At least there hadn't been a "No Jews" sign in the window, only a dusty placard that had simply read "Ten Boom Watches."

It had been six months since Emiel de Vries had let her and Franz both go, leaving them as good as penniless. When Rachel had returned to their room, Franz had been in his usual place at the table, seeming almost unconcerned that neither of them had a job.

"What does it matter? It was going to happen sooner or later," he'd remarked with a shrug.

"Well, it matters to *me*," Rachel had replied, trying to smile.

"I want to eat!" She'd gazed at her husband, full of a weary compassion for him. He'd changed so much since *Kristallnacht*, when he'd been dragged from their apartment, determined and defiant. He'd changed even from the ghost-like figure he'd been back on the *St Louis*, drifting through his days. Then, Rachel realized, he'd been healing, taking small steps toward recovery, each one giving her so much hope.

There had been hope, even, when he'd been angry at her for those long and difficult months; at least then he'd had a spark of defiance, of feeling. Since the occupation, it had all gone, replaced by this weary fatalism. Gazing at his face so blank and haggard, she'd feared there was no longer any hope; there was just this indifference, this waiting.

She'd wanted more for both of them, and she'd been determined to make sure they both survived the occupation... whatever came next.

Over the next few weeks, they'd managed to cobble together enough money to pay their rent and keep some food on the table. Jan van Dijk had lent them some money—Rachel had regretted every unkind thought she'd had about the man—and the Smits had, in their goodness, set aside a loaf of day-old bread for them on most days, at least for a while. Somehow, they'd managed to lurch from day to day, week to week, surviving, if only just.

In January, Rachel had come face to face with Emiel in the street. He'd looked well, with a new coat and hat and a spring in his step. Clearly, he was prospering under German rule. Rachel had been ashamed of her shabby coat, twice patched, her shoes with a hole in the sole, lined with cardboard, but she'd held her head high as she'd greeted him with cool politeness. Emiel had looked abject at the sight of her—two months of barely enough to keep body and soul together had taken their unfortunate toll; she'd become thinner, with a deeper line between her brows and a streak of gray in her hair, even though she was only twenty-nine.

"Rachel..." he'd said wretchedly. "Are you... are you well?"

"As well as can be expected, Meneer de Vries, but perhaps you shouldn't be seen talking to a Jew such as me in the street." She'd spoken matter-of-factly, without either antipathy or warmth, and a flash of something like irritation had passed across her old employer's face.

"There's no need..." he'd begun, before hurriedly taking out his billfold and pressing a few notes into her hand. "With my best wishes," he'd said, and strode away before Rachel had had a chance to give him back his money—which she couldn't have afforded to do, anyway, as much as she hated having to take anything from him. At least it meant they could eat for another week.

They could not, however, afford their room in the boarding house. In February, unable to pay their rent, they were turned out, and Frieda, in great kindness, had offered for them to live with her. Having no choice but to accept her friend's generosity, Rachel did, with gratitude. Frieda split her bedroom in half, with a bedsheet making a curtain, and Rachel and Franz slept on a mattress on the floor.

"It's more comfortable than Heijplaat, at any rate," Rachel had teased, still trying to find the good where she could.

Whenever she managed to find a few guilders, she tried to give them to Frieda, but the older woman refused all offers of rent, insisting she liked their company. Franz, at least, had found work in a Jewish-owned bakery several nights a week, cleaning, and Rachel, despite being only an adequate seamstress, managed to take in some sewing, although she suspected that no one needed much hemmed or darned, and the people who approached her were doing so out of charity.

Where it would all end, she had no idea. A few months earlier, several hundred Jews had been arrested and deported to labor camps. The Dutch had gone on strike in response, something which would have heartened Rachel, except the result was their occupiers came down even more fiercely on Dutch and Jew alike and made matters worse for everyone, especially the Jews.

In recent months, law after law had been rolled out; Frieda had joked that it was a strange day if there wasn't a new restriction put in place. Jews could no longer go to public parks, libraries, or many non-Jewish shops. They could not marry, or drive cars, or travel without a permit. Foreign-born Jews had been encouraged to "emigrate voluntarily" and Franz had let out a bark of hard laughter at that.

"And I wonder *where* they would take us. Straight back to Dachau, or worse?" He'd shaken his head in despair.

Rachel had wanted to argue that it might not be that bad, but reality had forced her to acknowledge that it would probably be worse. The Germans were determined to squeeze the Jews in every way that they could. Already in Amsterdam, the authorities had erected walls around the *Jodenbuurt*, creating a ghetto like the kind Franz had spoken of in Poland. A fence had been erected around the entire quarter, with armed guards at every bridge. How long would it be until such a place was built in Haarlem? And would they even be allowed in it, as foreign-born Jews, or would they be forced to "voluntarily emigrate" to a camp first, as Franz believed?

And, more distressingly, Rachel wondered, how would Franz survive such a thing? As the months had passed, he'd become even more fatalistic, spending his days sitting at the table and staring into space, with Frieda keeping a kindly eye on him. There was no money for cigarettes, so he was denied even that dubious comfort. Rachel's sole focus now was simply to put food on the table for both of them—as well as Frieda—and keep her husband alive. Hence, her attempt to sell her father's pocket watch, and gain a few guilders.

At the sound of the bell, an elderly man with kind, twinkling blue eyes and a white beard, like cotton wool, emerged from the back workroom of the little shop.

"May I help you?" he asked in Dutch.

"*Ja*... I would like to sell this pocket watch, if I may." Rachel spoke careful Dutch—she'd learned a lot in the nearly three years since she'd come to this country—as she laid her father's watch on the wooden counter.

The man frowned and put a monocle to his eye as he studied the watch. "This is a fine piece," he said after a moment. "Golay Fils and Stahl is a reputable company. And the case is eighteen carat gold, if I'm not mistaken..." He glanced up at her as he lowered the monocle. "A family piece?"

Rachel nodded. "My father's."

"You are German."

Again, she nodded.

"And Jewish." It was not a question.

Rachel tensed. Frieda had told her Casper ten Boom was a good man and a friend to Jews, but times had changed, and maybe the old man's views had, as well. Plenty of good people had decided it was safer simply to turn a blind eye to all that was going on around them. Rachel had seen it in a thousand different ways since the start of the occupation. Why should Casper ten Boom be any different? "Yes," she admitted quietly, knowing there was no point in denying it. "I am."

Casper ten Boom smiled at her. "My dear," he said, "will you come upstairs and take tea with my daughters and me?"

For a second, Rachel could only gape. It was just about the last thing she'd expected.

"We would be so pleased to have you," he added, smiling in a way that strangely made her want to cry. She couldn't remember the last time someone had been so kind; even the Smits, in the last few months, had stopped giving her their old loaves, and she couldn't even blame them. Why should they risk their very lives over day-old bread? "It is time for tea," Casper ten Boom announced as he took off his apron. "Corrie!" he called. "Come, we have a visitor."

Rachel was still struggling to frame a reply as a woman who looked to be about fifty, wearing glasses with her dark, silver-streaked hair pulled back from her lined, friendly-looking face, came from the workroom. Her expression of cautious curiosity was replaced with a quick smile as she caught sight of Rachel.

"Betsie will be delighted to welcome visitors, I am sure," she said with a smile, and reached out to shake Rachel's hand. "She can usually magic a cake from somewhere, as well. I am Corrie ten Boom. I work with my father."

"Rachel Blau," Rachel said as she shook the other woman's hand. She felt as if she'd stumbled into a dream. Tea and cake...! When had she last had such things? She glanced at her father's pocket watch lying on top of the counter. "But my father's watch..."

"Ah, yes." Casper picked up the watch and showed it to his daughter, who nodded approvingly at its workmanship. "It's a remarkable piece, is it not?" He handed it back to Rachel. "Please keep it, at least for now."

Rachel slipped the watch into her pocket, trying not to show her disappointment that it seemed he wasn't going to buy it, after all. Tea and cake were all very well, and kindly meant, she was sure, but she needed money, and proper food to bring home to Frieda and Franz.

When Rachel thought how she'd lamented Franz's moods when they'd first arrived in Haarlem, she almost wanted to laugh. She certainly wanted to shake a finger at herself, to wonder how she could have been so silly and lovesick, so *childish*, as to be sorry that her husband didn't pay her more attention, or that he seemed angry or remote. Now she simply hoped he was alive when she returned home in the evening. Jan van Dijk had, she knew, been arrested, as had many of the others who had once frequented their kitchen, full of their views. It was a wonder, really, that she and Franz had not, that they were still *here*, as hard as it was.

"Thank you," she said as she followed the ten Booms from the shop up the stairs to the house above. "You're very kind."

"The Beje is a funny house," Corrie told her as she led her up a short set of stairs and down a narrow hallway to the back of the house. "It was two houses once, but sometime in its long history it was made into one, with a staircase like a corkscrew connecting them, so there are all sorts of strange rooms and hiding places." She opened the door to a dining room, which was comfortably furnished if looking rather worn, a brick fireplace in the corner. "Jesus is the Victor" had been carved into the tile above the hearth. "Betsie!" she called. "We have a visitor!"

"A visitor?" A woman emerged from the tiny kitchen, little more than a closet in the back of the dining room, wiping her hands on her apron. She was smiling and slender, with a natural beauty and grace even though she had to be in her late fifties. She came toward Rachel, her hands outstretched. "How pleased I am to meet you," she said warmly. "I am Betsie ten Boom."

"Rachel Blau," Rachel whispered. Her hands were clasped in the other woman's and again, bizarrely, she had the urge to cry. She had never expected these people to be so kind.

"Come sit," Betsie urged. "This has always been the heart of the house. I will make tea. Corrie, there is bread in the sideboard. Won't you have some?" She turned back to Rachel with another warm smile.

"Th—thank you," Rachel stammered.

She sat at the table with Casper ten Boom while Corrie took a loaf of bread from a drawer in the sideboard, and cut several slices, slathering them with margarine, and giving Rachel the thickest one. With another murmured thanks, Rachel bit into it, her eyes fluttering closed at the taste of soft, fresh bread. Her stomach growled in response, and her eyes flew open as she let out an embarrassed laugh. Corrie laughed too and started cutting her another slice, as Betsie brought in a tray with a teapot and cups.

"How long have you been in Haarlem?" Casper asked in fluent German as Betsie poured them all tea, clearly made from old leaves, but fresher and more fragrant than any Rachel had had in a long while.

"Nearly three years," Rachel replied, swallowing. "My husband Franz and I were on the *St Louis*, meant for Havana."

"We read about that in the papers," Corrie remarked with a nod. She spoke as fluent German as her father. "A terrible tragedy that all the passengers were denied entry to Cuba. How can people be so unkind?"

"Yes, it was difficult." Rachel took a sip of coffee.

Her time on the *St Louis* seemed so far away in light of her current reality, the cares she'd had then so small and petty compared to those that dogged her now, and yet she still thought of her friends often, although she had not received a letter from either Sophie, Rosa, or Hannah in nearly a year. No matter how desperate her and Franz's situation became, she had vowed never to sell her precious shard of emerald. One day, she told herself, she would meet her friends in Paris and the emerald would be whole again. *One day...*

"And how have you been finding Haarlem?" Casper asked. His voice was gentle, full of warmth and wry kindness, as if he already knew just how difficult everything had been.

"Since the occupation..." Rachel replied carefully, "it has been challenging."

Corrie nodded, frowning. "To us, it has seemed to happen slowly. The signs in the shops, the park, the library... every day there are more places you are forbidden to go, things you are not allowed to do. It is a terrible thing."

"It is more than a terrible thing," Casper replied, the gentleness dropping from his voice as he drew himself up, a deep frown between his faded eyes. "It is a great *evil*, one of the worst known to man. These Germans... they have harmed the very apple of God's eye, His chosen people. I fear for the state of their souls, and moreover, I am concerned for *you*." He turned back to Rachel, his voice becoming gentle once more as his mouth turned up in a small, compassionate smile. "You must tell us how we can help you."

"Oh..." Rachel began, having no idea what to say. Her and Franz's need felt so great, yet she could hardly ask these people for money, for food, for a roof over their heads! "You are very kind," she finally said, glancing down at her half-drunk cup of tea. "Very kind."

"It is no trouble," Casper replied firmly.

"Indeed, it is no trouble at all," Betsie exclaimed. Rachel looked up to see the other woman's face was suffused with what looked like genuine joy. "It is our honor and pleasure," Betsie declared, her voice as firm as her father's. "Of course we will help you. You said you have a husband? You must both come to supper." She glanced at Corrie, then her father. "Tomorrow night?" she asked them, and Corrie laughed.

"You know the state of our larder better than I do, Betsie," she said before turning to Rachel and explaining, "I used to manage the household and Betsie helped Father in the shop, until we realized we had it the wrong way round! Betsie does much better as hostess and housekeeper, and I prefer my work with watches." Her smile was full of humor, her eyes of understanding. "Sometimes it takes more time than we would like to find our place in the world. Will you come to dinner tomorrow evening? Shall we say six o'clock?"

"Yes, thank you," Rachel replied, still stunned by this family's innate generosity and kindness. "That would be wonderful."

"Then it is settled." Betsie reached for the teapot. "Now, let me fill your cup."

Rachel stayed for over an hour, chatting with the ten Booms, learning about their lives. The little watchmaker shop had been on the Barteljorisstraat for over a hundred years, with the ten Booms living above, in the topsy-turvy house with its poky little rooms and narrow hallways, known as the Beje.

"We've always had people living with us," Corrie told Rachel. "Tante Jans and Tante Bep and Tante Anna... those were our dear mother's sisters. But after they exchanged this world for eternity, the house felt too quiet, and Papa has always liked children around him. There have been eleven that have lived with us so far, and they are like family to us still. Betsie is very good at feeding everyone," Corrie finished with a smile for her sister. "She can make magic with three potatoes and a pound of mutton!"

Rachel thought of the three potatoes she had once placed on the table in front of Franz, like an accusation. "That is a skill indeed," she remarked quietly. It was only in seeing these sisters' simple joy, and their father's quiet certainty, that Rachel was able to acknowledge just how much bitterness she'd stored up in her heart without realizing it, all the while pretending to be so cheerful. It was a deeply humbling thought that Franz had seen through her in a way she had not.

By the time she finally tore herself away from the ten Booms and their comfortable dining room, the rest of the loaf wrapped in a cloth and pressed into her hands to take away, it was afternoon, and Rachel knew she needed to get back. Franz would be setting off for work, and she needed to help Frieda with supper, paltry as it was sure to be. She thanked the ten Booms, grateful they'd given her so much of their time, as well as the bread, and promised to bring Franz for supper the following night.

The warmth and friendliness of their little house seemed to follow her all the way back to the boarding house, down streets lined with shops proclaiming they did not serve Jews, and soldiers swaggering by, hands on their holsters. The world was as hard a place as ever, and yet still Rachel kept hold of the hope that the ten Booms had given her—that there were kind people in this world, *good* people.

And with their help, maybe, just maybe, she and Franz would survive after all.

CHAPTER 14

Rachel hadn't been sure if Franz would be willing to come to the ten Booms' for supper or not, but to her relief he'd shruggingly agreed, as seemingly docile as he'd once been back on the *St Louis*. The fight, Rachel feared, had gone right out of her husband, along with any conviction or desire to survive the occupation. He went through his days in a weary haze, neither railing against nor caring about what happened, but at least he'd agreed to come with her when she asked.

"I'm sorry to leave you for the evening," Rachel told Frieda as she put on her old blue crepe—now shiny with wear and loose through the bodice—for the meal. "I should have asked if you could come with us, I'm sure they would have said yes."

"Nonsense, you two must go out and enjoy your evening," Frieda insisted. "God knows, we must find our pleasures where we can."

The evening was balmy and warm, the cherry blossoms in their pink, puffed glory as she and Franz walked along the canal. There had been rumors that soon Jews would be under a curfew from eight o'clock in the evening to six in the morning, so Rachel was glad they were going out while they could, even as inwardly she shrank against further restrictions.

"Isn't it lovely out?" she remarked to Franz. "The cherry blossoms are so beautiful." She squeezed his arm. "There are things they will never be able to take away from us, Franz."

"There was a cherry tree at Dachau," Franz remarked, shocking Rachel into silence because he never spoke about his time at the labor camp. "It had just begun to bloom when I was released."

She squeezed his arm again, in encouragement. "Was it a beautiful tree?" she asked softly.

"It reminded me of what I'd sold my soul for," Franz replied flatly. He stopped suddenly, forcing Rachel to, as well, for a van had pulled up to a house across the street, with a loud squeal of brakes. Several men in the unforgiving black of the SS uniform jumped out of the truck and began to pound on the door before one of them kicked it in and they raced inside, shouting in German.

Beneath Rachel's hand, Franz's arm was like iron.

"We should go..." she whispered as she tried to tug him along.

"No," he replied, resolute and immovable. "Let's see what happens."

It was not the first time Rachel had witnessed such a scene, although each occasion held the power to both terrify and grieve her. She already knew what was coming next—the SS would herd out some poor man or woman, maybe even a child, and bundle them into the van to take them to who-knew-where. There would be tears, and feeble protests, and then, as the van disappeared down the street, an awful, endless silence.

"Franz..." she whispered. He knew as well as she did that it wasn't safe to be here.

"Look." He nodded toward the house, and, sure enough, a couple was being marched to the van. They were in their sixties, dazed, the man's lip bleeding, the woman's face pale with shock. They were pushed into the van, hard enough that they both fell, and then the doors were locked, and the van sped away.

No one in the street stirred, and not one neighbor so much as twitched a curtain. Still, Franz did not move.

"Franz... we should go," Rachel urged him. Her heart was beating hard as her gaze moved around the empty street. "You know it's not safe to be out here when something like this has happened."

"What do you suppose that man did?" Franz mused. "Did he go into a forbidden shop, or maybe the park? Did he speak up against some injustice? Did he fight for what he believed in?"

Rachel stared at him in uneasy confusion. "He probably did nothing," she pointed out quietly. "You know they don't need a reason to arrest people anymore."

"Nothing," Franz repeated as he nodded slowly. "He did *nothing*." He slipped his arm from hers as he continued to stare at the house, its door left ajar, the hallway dark and empty. "Once, that would give you your freedom. Now it's a reason for them to arrest you."

Rachel had no idea what to make of that. She reached for his arm again.

"Come," she urged. "The ten Booms will be waiting for us."

Corrie ten Boom was at the door as Rachel and Franz came down the Barteljorisstraat, her lined face wreathed with worry.

"We heard there had been trouble," she explained as she ushered them in and upstairs to the living quarters above. "We were worried for you."

"A couple was arrested down by the canal," Rachel

explained, still shaken by what they'd witnessed. "We saw it happen."

Corrie shook her head. "So terrible. A few months ago, our dear neighbors received the same treatment. The Weils, they ran the furrier down the street. The Nazis came and took all their furs—armfuls and armfuls. We managed to get Mr. Weil away, and his poor wife was in Amsterdam, with no idea what had gone on."

"Dear man," Casper murmured as he came into the room. "Such a trial for him. But I am so pleased to see you both!" He shook both their hands as Betsie came in from the dining room, bearing a tray of stew and bread.

"Corrie took the train to Amsterdam and met his wife on the platform," she continued, taking up the story of the Weils. "The poor woman was so startled! But at least she was safe." She turned to Franz with a smile. "You must be Franz, Rachel's husband," she said, as if they were old friends. "We are so pleased to meet you."

Franz looked as startled as Rachel had been, to receive such easy, open-hearted kindness. "I am pleased to meet you, as well," he replied after a moment.

"Come, sit down and eat. No one goes hungry here at the Beje."

For the next hour, they ate and drank with the three ten Booms, enjoying their friendliness and warmth. It felt so normal, and yet so strange, to listen and laugh, to eat and talk. Even Franz became a bit more animated, especially when Corrie brought out their hidden radio so they could listen to Radio *Oranje*.

"It is our guilty secret," she confessed with a small, impish smile. "Father likes to listen to the music. I prefer the news."

They listened to a song performed by Jetty Paerl, making fun of the Nazi regime, so even Franz smiled, and then a short broadcast about the state of the war—the United States had attacked the Japanese mainland, and the Finnish had had a victory against the Soviets. The tone of the presenter, den Doolard, was bracing, full of determination and encouraging the Dutch people to resistance. Hearing it heartened Rachel, as it meant she and Franz really weren't alone. She glanced around at the ten Booms and when Betsie caught her eye and smiled, Rachel smiled back. In that moment, full of good food and bonhomie, she felt almost certain that she and Franz would make it through.

After the broadcast ended, Corrie switched off the radio and returned it to its hiding place under the stairs. "Peter devised that for us," she explained. "One of our foster children. He's so clever! And such a musician too." She let out a little sigh before she came and sat down with them again in the little dining room. "But we must talk more practically," she told them, her expression turning serious.

"Practically?" Rachel repeated, uncertain.

"How we can help you?" Betsie chimed in, her lovely face as full of purpose as her sister's. "We fear things are only going to get worse here for you and other Jews, and we are determined to be of use. What do you need?"

Rachel stared at her blankly, shocked by the simple question.

After a second's pause, Franz said slowly, "You are putting yourselves in grave danger simply by asking that question."

Betsie and Corrie exchanged looks that seemed almost humorous and then Betsie replied, "We know we are. That is not of concern to us. Our eternal future is secure, and that is all that matters." She sounded both peaceful and confident, but Rachel noticed that Corrie's expression had become just a little drawn.

"Do you feel the same?" Franz asked her, and she glanced up with a wry smile.

"I do, although I fear I sometimes lack my sister's joyful

conviction." She gave a wry grimace before continuing quietly, "Right at the start of the occupation, I had a dream—or really, a vision. I saw a farm wagon, the old kind, out of place in the city —in the Grote Markt, drawn by four big, black horses." She paused, her throat working, seemingly transfixed by the terrible image. "I was sitting in its wagon, as was Betsie and my father, my brother Willem, as well. We couldn't get off—there was no way, and we were being drawn by those great big horses, out, out of the city, far from here..." Her hand fluttered by her throat. "I didn't want to go, but I knew I had to, I had no choice, those dark horses would take us wherever they would..." Her voice, sounding faraway, trailed off, and Rachel had to suppress a shiver as an icy unease crawled up her spine. The image was a dreadful one.

"Sometimes," Betsie chimed in quietly, "God shows us things to assure us that they are in His hands. So do not worry yourselves on our account, please. We know the cost, and we are more than willing to pay it."

It was dark by the time Rachel and Franz left the ten Booms, with promises to return soon, and a loaf of bread and a packet of tea to take home, as well.

"We have friends in the ration card office," Corrie whispered as she pressed the precious gifts into Rachel's hands. "Somehow he finds us a hundred extra ration cards a month!" Her eyes danced with humor, and Rachel stared at her in surprise.

The ten Booms really were risking all they had to help their Jewish friends, she realized. That kind of activity could get them imprisoned, or worse. She thought of the other woman's dream of the dark horses, and she wondered whether it truly had been a vision from God, as fanciful a notion as that seemed.

She hoped not, simply because she did not want such good people to suffer.

"Thank you," Rachel whispered, and pressed Corrie's hand before heading down the Barteljorisstraat with Franz.

"I didn't realize such people existed," Franz remarked as they walked quickly and quietly toward Frieda's apartment on Zoestraat, doing their best to avoid attracting attention. "If there were more such people, perhaps things wouldn't go as badly as they will for the Jews."

"There might be more," Rachel replied, "and we simply don't know about them." She reached for her husband's hand. "We mustn't give up, Franz."

Franz stared out in the darkness as a gusty sigh escaped him. "I gave up a long time ago, Rachel," he said quietly. "Long before you have even realized."

"Franz—"

He shook his head, and she fell silent. "No, let me say it. Perhaps I should have told you before, long before, but I was so ashamed, and I couldn't bear for you to be ashamed of me, as well."

Rachel held her breath, realizing that now perhaps he was finally going to talk about his time at Dachau. Had their time with the ten Booms unlocked something inside him? What secret had he been keeping, that had tormented him so? And did she truly want to know it?

"When I was arrested, I feared the worst," he began, his gaze still on the darkened street. "Many don't come back from Dachau, you know. I'd heard that they sent prisoners' ashes in little, lacquered boxes to their families—or sometimes just their spectacles. A perverse kind of torture, but then that's what they like, isn't it? To induce as much pain as they can—emotional as well as physical. I thought I could have withstood both. I was sure I could. I was, dare I say it, even arrogant." He shook his head, his mouth turning down. "Part of me almost relished it, which is so *stupid*." A savage note entered his voice. "But others had been arrested, and I wanted to show my mettle. What I was made of! What a *joke*."

"Franz..." Rachel began, although she had no idea what she could possibly say.

"No, let me tell you. I want to, now. After seeing that family..." He glanced down the street, toward the Beje. "They're risking everything. *Everything*! And they know it. They're not like me. They're not like me at all."

"Franz," Rachel protested, "you were brave, in continuing to work and write as you did. To speak out against the Nazi regime, to endure a place like Dachau—"

"And the moment it cost me something," he cut her off, "I stopped." He threw his arm over his eyes as a shudder racked him. "I am so ashamed of myself," he confessed in a low, aching voice. "When I first came back, I couldn't bear to look you in the eye. And then it became easier to simply... *sink* into a sort of oblivion. To not feel, think, want, *anything*. I know it confused and hurt you, I know it, but I just couldn't..."

"I can understand that," Rachel whispered.

"And when we came to Heijplaat..." he continued, his arm still over his eyes, "it felt like Dachau all over again, in so many ways, and I couldn't bear it. I couldn't bear to be the man I'd been at Dachau there, as well, and I couldn't explain that to you, I *couldn't*..." His voice rose, his words running into one another as he continued to explain, "And then Jan rescued us, and when I was with him, I could pretend to be the man I used to be. I knew you'd see through it, though. I'm sorry, I know I shut you out, I was angry, so angry at everything..."

"Oh, Franz." Rachel shook her head, full of sorrow. If only they'd spoken like this before, instead of enduring years of silence and hostility, which now seemed such a waste. "Whatever happened when you were at that camp, I wouldn't have blamed you. I just wanted you back."

Finally, he dropped his arm, his expression so terribly bleak. "But nothing happened, Rachel, that's the true shame of it. Oh, the conditions were primitive, it was true, and they kept me isolated much of the time, and I had little food... but they didn't *hurt* me. They didn't even have to hurt me. After six months of... of nothing more than boredom, they showed me Erich Lieser. Do you remember him? He came to our house once, for dinner. A staunch communist and a musician."

Vaguely, Rachel recalled a fair, slight man with glasses and a shy smile. "Yes, I remember him," she whispered.

"They'd ruined him," Franz stated flatly. "Completely ruined him. His *hands*... the nails pulled out, every finger broken, and not just broken, but smashed to bits. He couldn't even hold a pencil, and he used to be a violinist."

"Oh, no..." Her stomach roiled and she pressed a hand to her mouth as she tried to blink the awful image away. "How dreadful..."

"He was a completely shattered man. A gibbering wreck... he couldn't even *speak*. He could barely stand up. I can't imagine he would ever recover. And I thought then, I *can't*. I can't face that, I *won't*. And when they brought me in for questioning the next day, I told them everything. *Everything*, Rachel!" He gave her a look that was half anger, half agony. "I gave them names, addresses, facts and figures... God only knows how many people were arrested or worse because of me. *Me!* They would have been tortured, even killed... and it's all *my* fault. *Only* my fault. I have blood on my hands, Rachel." His voice caught on a sob as he flung out his hands as if to show her their bloodstains. "I have so much *blood*."

"Oh, Franz. *Franz.*" Rachel put her arms around him as her husband started to cry in earnest, his body shuddering with the force of his sobs. She felt only compassion for him then, a deep, sorrowful pity. How could she judge or disdain how he'd acted under such duress? How could anyone, unless they'd been in such a situation themselves? God alone knew how much courage she would have had if faced with the like.

"How can you even bear to touch me?" he wept. "Or look at me? I've been hating myself since they told me I could walk out a free man. They handed me my papers and I wanted to tear them up, throw them in their smirking faces... but I didn't, Rachel, I *didn't*. I walked out of those gates a free man, and yet one who felt he should have died. It would have been better if I had. I've kept myself alive for your sake, because I didn't want you to feel guilty, but, my God, I've wished I was dead every day since I left Dachau."

"Oh, Franz." Tears slipped silently down Rachel's cheeks as she held him. There was nothing more she could say, nothing to help or absolve him, not when he'd condemned himself so long ago. All she could do was hold him and accept him for who he was... and what he *hadn't* done.

They remained that way, Franz clasped in Rachel's arms, for several more moments until the sound of a car in the distance had them springing apart in alarm, for it was only Gestapo or Nazi bureaucrats who had cars these days. In any case, it was getting late, and the curfew for all under occupation was ten o'clock. They needed to get back to Frieda.

Rachel didn't know if things were now better or worse between her and Franz. They walked in a silence that felt more exhausted than defeated, which she hoped was a good thing. Had Franz experienced any sense of relief in finally telling her? Would it change anything?

She didn't have much time to reflect on such matters because when they arrived at the apartment building in Zoestraat, she saw, with her heart lurching against her ribs, that the front door to the front building had been flung open and a few people were huddled by it, shoulders hunched as they talked in low, frightened voices. There were several Jewish families in the building, and whatever was going on had clearly shaken them all.

"Something's happened..." Rachel murmured as she started walking more quickly. "Do you think there has there been an arrest?"

It didn't take her long to find out; she hadn't even reached the door before a neighbor who had been kind to them over the last few months grabbed her arm, her expression still full of fear, as well as foreboding. "They stormed in just a short while ago..." she told Rachel. "They kicked in the door, they were shouting..."

Rachel stared at her in dawning realization. "Not..."

The woman nodded. "They arrested Frieda, took her away in the van. I'm so sorry, Rachel."

CHAPTER 15

JUNE 1942

Rachel pursed her lips in concentration as she carefully threaded the needle. The yellow fabric spread across her lap was bright, a color she normally would have liked, save for what it signified. Just last week, a decree had come through—yet another restriction, Frieda would have said with a roll of her eyes, if she had been there—that all Jews had to wear a yellow star sewn to their clothes. It was a badge of shame, not honor, to mark them out—and for what? Yet more persecution.

In the two months since Frieda had been arrested, things had grown even worse for Jews. They were no longer allowed to buy fruit or vegetables from non-Jewish shops, and all Jewish butchers had been shut down. They could not ride bicycles or travel without permission; they could not play sports or use public telephones; they could not enter any non-Jewish shop, save for between the hours of three and five p.m., and then only if the shopkeeper allowed it. Most recently, they had not been allowed to be out after eight o'clock at night, and now, this star of David, to signify their status. What would be next?

After hearing of their friend's arrest, Rachel and Franz had mounted the stairs to Frieda's apartment with growing dread.

Rachel had gasped out loud when she'd seen the state of her friend's cozy little sitting room—her precious wedding picture smashed, some callous soldier's jackboot having ground the glass down into dust and ruined the photograph. Dishes had been hurled to the floor, the table and chairs upturned, Frieda's brass menorah bent and twisted.

"She didn't fight," their neighbor had explained in a hushed voice. "They just did it because they could, the fiends."

"But why?" Rachel had turned slowly in a circle to survey the awful damage, while Franz had simply stood by the door, taking it all in. "Why Frieda? She was an old woman. Harmless, surely."

"We're all harmless, aren't we?" Franz had pointed out dryly.

"That's true," Rachel had agreed. She felt deeply shaken; this was the first person she'd known who had been arrested. She hadn't quite realized until that moment how, despite all the dangers and restrictions, this kind of situation had still felt at a distance, something that happened to other people. "But *Frieda...*" she had persisted helplessly. She picked up a chair and righted it, just for want of something to do. Something to make everything, no matter how dreadful and hopeless, a tiny bit better. "It makes no sense." Rachel would have understood it better if Franz, with his revolutionary activities and his time in Dachau, had been arrested and imprisoned, *again*. But Frieda?

"It was something to do with her son, back in Germany," their neighbor had said mournfully. "That's what they were shouting about. I don't know what he did, though. Frieda didn't even put up a fuss, she just went."

"Poor Frieda." A lump had formed in Rachel's throat, and she'd resolutely swallowed it down. "Will she come back?" she'd asked, but no one had replied.

Frieda hadn't come back. At Rachel's hesitant suggestion, Corrie ten Boom had inquired of the authorities on her behalf, and then sorrowfully informed Rachel that her friend was being held at the prison Scheveningen, in the Hague. She was not able to get any more information than that, and in the two months since the arrest, Rachel had learned no more about Frieda's whereabouts, or the potential for her release.

Meanwhile, she and Franz had been living in a state of near-constant fear and dread-filled anticipation. Every motor in the distance, every heavy footfall on the stair... when would the Gestapo come for them? In her darker moments, Rachel thought it was surely only a matter of time. If Frieda could be arrested and imprisoned because of her son's activities—whatever they had been—back in Germany, then she and Franz certainly could be, for his own defiant history, or even simply for being Jewish. Although, he'd remarked with a sardonic twist of his lips, perhaps the Nazis didn't see him as a threat, since he'd sung like a canary for them.

"That's in the past, Franz," Rachel had said, and he'd given her a smile full of sudden tenderness.

"So you keep reminding me," he'd replied, and then, to her surprise, he'd put his arms around her and gently kissed her.

His confession after the evening with the ten Booms, as heart-wrenching and painful as it had been, had released something from inside Franz. While he still seemed fatalistic about their prospects, he was showing her more kindness. And now that she understood his experience at Dachau, Rachel found she had far more patience and compassion—and yes, love—for him than she'd had before. The man she'd so admired, and even idolized, back at university was as weak and fallible as any other. That man, she'd come to realize, was someone who needed her—and her love, now more than ever.

And yet despite these heartening encouragements, the world was becoming a darker and grimmer place. As the weeks had gone on, more and more people were taken away; Rachel heard of an arrest nearly every day, often people she knew, if only as acquaintances.

"I'm sorry I've brought you into this," Franz had told her one night in May as they lay in bed facing each other, the windows opened to the warm night air. His face was somber and full of regret. "If not for me..."

Rachel had rested her hand against his cheek, grateful for this moment of intimacy; they shared so few. "Franz, I'd still be Jewish," she'd reminded him gently. "As you said yourself, we're all harmless. This is not your fault, or mine, or any Jew's. Only Hitler and his evil regime bears responsibility, surely. There's no reason, no excuse, for how they act, save for their own evil."

"That's true, I suppose." He had let out a long, low sigh as he'd rested his hand over her own, keeping it on his cheek. In the darkness, Rachel had just been able to make out the glint of his hazel eyes as he looked at her. "But I don't want to be someone who does nothing, Rachel. Not again."

His words had caused a leap of alarm low in her belly; surely now was not the time for bravery, and yet she knew Franz still deeply regretted what he saw as his own faithless cowardice while at Dachau, and she understood it... even if she didn't want to.

"We are doing something simply by surviving," she had said quietly, and yet she wondered if that would ever be enough for Franz.

One highlight of their bleak days was visiting the ten Booms at least once a week, to listen to a Radio *Oranje* broadcast as well as share a meal. Although food was now scarce for everyone, thanks to the increase in rationing, the ten Booms were always generous with what they had, and Rachel never left without a parcel of tea or bread or jam that Betsie had bottled, pressed into her hands with joyful insistence.

The broadcasts they listened to were always deliberately encouraging, entreating the Dutch to stay strong and practice acts of resistance. They also gleefully related the recent defeats of the Wehrmacht against the relentless Soviet might—surely a sign that the tide was slowly yet inexorably turning against Germany.

"It will be the end of them, mark my words," Peter, one of the ten Booms' foster children, now a young man, had insisted one evening in May as they'd all sat in the dining room, listening to Radio *Oranje* on the lowest volume. He'd already been arrested once, Corrie had told Rachel, but remained defiant. "One day, it will be," he'd declared, half-rising from his chair, "and we'll banish the Nazis from our land *forever!*"

"One day," Corrie had agreed with a small, weary smile of understanding for Rachel, who had wanted to be encouraged by the young man's rash certainty but could not quite find it in herself. "One day."

Yes, she'd thought then, but one day *when?*

No matter how many encouraging broadcasts she listened to, the reality, day in and day out, was a life more and more limited by their occupiers' restrictions and baseless cruelty. Now, as Rachel gazed down at the star sewn to the left breast of her coat, with the word '*Jood*' printed starkly on it, she wondered what would come next. She had always been proud of her Jewish identity, felt it as a deeply held part of herself, and yet now it seemed a source of shame. Had the Nazis taken even her own faith from her?

No, she wouldn't let them. She would wear this star proudly, she told herself, even if it became a source of humiliation, ridicule, or worse.

In reality, the reaction to the star on her coat—as well as on every other Jewish person's—was inevitably mixed. Some people gave her smiles of solidarity, or even pressed her hand in comfort and encouragement, while others tossed their heads and sneered. And the German soldiers who strolled down Zoestraat or through the Grote Markt either ignored or insulted her, thankfully often seeming too bored to do much more.

One afternoon in July, however, a soldier held out his boot to trip her. Rachel, her head tucked low, quickly stepped over it, only to have him push her hard on her back so she went flying, falling on her hands and knees, the breath knocked out of her.

"That's where you belong, Jew," he sneered in German. "And don't you forget it." He kicked her for good measure, a halfhearted blow to her stomach that still had Rachel gasping out loud in pain.

As the soldier sauntered off, she stayed there for a moment, her hands and knees both bloodied, her stomach aching, too dazed to cry, amazed that it had come to this, that any human being could act in such a way to another, for no reason at all.

"Let me help you up." The voice was kind and girlish.

Still dazed, Rachel looked up toward the hand that was extended down to her, only to let out a gasp when she saw who it was. Beatrix de Vries, looking grown up at twelve years old, her dark hair held back with a barrette.

"*Rachel...*" The girl's eyes widened in realization as she grasped Rachel's hand. Rachel winced, for the palms of both her hands were bloodied and stinging, the scraped skin embedded with bits of gravel. "I'm so sorry." Beatrix dropped her hand to take her handkerchief out of her pocket and hand it to her.

"*Dank u wel*," Rachel murmured as she dabbed at her hands. "I'm afraid it will be ruined."

"I don't mind, I've got others."

Slowly, every muscle aching, Rachel got to her feet. She dabbed ineffectually again at her hands before folding the handkerchief in half to cover the bloodstains. She had no idea what to say to Beatrix.

"I've wondered how you were," Beatrix blurted. "Evi and I have both missed you. We were cross with Papa, that he let you go." A hint of her old sulkiness came through her voice, almost making Rachel smile.

"Well, you see the difficulties, I'm sure," she replied half-heartedly. She did not have any great desire to defend Emiel, but neither did she want to speak badly of him to his daughter.

"It was wrong," Beatrix insisted staunchly. "Mama said so."

"Did she?" Rachel was glad Amalia had spoken on her behalf, not that it had made any difference. "These are strange times," she told Beatrix. "But I hope you are keeping well?" She glanced at the girl with a smile, only to realize with a jolt that Beatrix was wearing the dark skirt and military-style blouse of the *Nationale Jeugdstorm*—the Nazi organization for youth in this country. The insignia for her age group—*meeuwke*, or gull—was sewn to her blouse, along with several badges for her achievements. Rachel's stomach twisted at the sight.

"Papa made me," Beatrix said quickly, seeing Rachel's gaze move over her uniform. "I don't like it."

"It doesn't matter," Rachel replied, a little brusquely. Had Emiel truly become such a Nazi stooge as that? It made her feel both sad and angry. He really was a weak man, and in these times, weakness was as destructive as true evil; the end result was the same. She thrust the bloodied handkerchief back toward the girl, and reluctantly Beatrix took it.

"Rachel..." she began.

"It was good to see you," Rachel cut her off. "Take care of yourself, Beatrix." She started walking past, her hands and knees still aching, along with her stomach, but then Beatrix called after her.

"*Wait!*" She hurried up to Rachel, fumbling with her purse and then taking out a few guilders and pushing them toward her. "Please, take these..."

"No." Rachel desperately needed the money, but she would not appease another person's conscience again, the way she had

THE GIRL WHO NEVER GAVE UP 181

Emiel's. Not any longer. "No, thank you," she said firmly, and walked on.

In early July, Jews were forbidden from visiting non-Jews. Rachel feared their evenings with the ten Booms would come to an end, but when she risked heading to the Beje, ostensibly to bid them farewell, Corrie only laughed at her.

"Do you suppose we will follow that rule?" she demanded, her hands on her hips as Rachel stood in the crowded front room of the watchmaker's. "Why, we wouldn't even dream of it!"

"I cannot allow myself to put you at risk—" Rachel protested.

"Rachel, my dear, my sister, Father and I are so much at risk already that your visits hardly matter!" Corrie exclaimed. "And you are not the only Jewish person to grace our house with your presence," she added, her mouth twitching into a smile. "Admittedly, we need to be careful. There are always people coming and going, and not everyone is as kindly disposed to us or our views as we might like. Besides which, we are less than half a block from the police quarters! But God watches over us, and you." Impulsively, she grasped Rachel's hands. "You have more friends than perhaps you realize," she told her with a smile. "As long as *you* feel safe enough to do so, you must continue to visit with us. I insist upon it."

Once again, Rachel was both humbled and overwhelmed by the ten Booms' kindness. "Thank you," she murmured. "Franz and I would like nothing better."

"You must take care, though," Corrie told her, her tone turning serious as she released her hands. "These times become more dangerous by the day, even by the hour. I have heard a rumor just today that a new camp has been established—the old refugee camp, Westerbork. But it is not to keep refugees safe anymore. It is to send them on."

Rachel stared at the other woman's grave expression, an icy fingertip of unease trailing up her spine. For a second, she recalled the vision Corrie had shared, of the four black horses, taking her and her family away. "Send them on where?" she asked, instinctively dropping her voice to a hushed whisper.

Corrie shook her head, her expression turning even more troubled. "I don't know," she admitted. "East, someone said. But wherever it is... surely it can't be anywhere good?" She reached for Rachel's hands once more, giving them a squeeze. "Do bring Franz and visit us again soon. But mind the curfew!"

Rachel was still ruminating over Corrie's words as she headed back to their apartment. It had been nearly three months since Frieda's arrest, and she still missed her friend and worried greatly for her. Moreover, she had no idea how long she and Franz would be able to stay in Frieda's home; the money from his job sweeping floors and her bit of sewing was not going to last them much longer. What would happen then? And if the rumor Corrie had heard about Westerbork was true... what did it even mean? Where would they send the Jews on to? What more could they possibly do to them?

She'd just reached her door and was turning the key when a clatter on the stairs behind her had her whirling around, her heart climbing toward her throat. A thud of footsteps, the ragged, tearing breath of someone in a hurry. Was it a Gestapo officer?

Rachel knew she should lose no time in getting inside her apartment, locking the door, and praying for deliverance, but she was frozen to the spot, too terrified to move.

Another gasp, then a sob. Her fear began to turn to a terrible concern, and she took an instinctive step forward, only to gasp herself as Franz rounded the corner.

His face was bloodied, his nose broken, and he was cradling his right hand against his chest.

"*Franz...*" Rachel hurried toward him, her arms outstretched. "What happened?" she asked, although she could already guess.

Franz shook his head, still struggling for breath. His face was a mess of blood; besides his broken nose, both his lips were split, and he'd lost a tooth. "Help me inside," he choked out, and with her arm around him, Rachel guided him into the apartment, sitting him down at the table before she went to wet a rag to clean him up as best as she could. They had nothing to help with his healing, she realized—no bandages, no medicine, no antiseptic, and certainly no money for a doctor. She would simply have to do the best she could with what little they had.

She straightened her shoulders and turned back to him, only to draw a shocked breath when she saw the state of his hand—all the fingers of his right hand were broken and twisted, his whole hand purple and swollen.

"Oh, Franz..." she whispered, her face draining of color. "Your *hand*..."

He grimaced, flinching with pain, his own face gray and beaded with sweat. "Ironic, isn't it? It was Erich's hands that undid me, back at Dachau. I couldn't bear the thought of something like that happening to me, and yet here I am." He let out a ragged laugh, almost sounding proud.

"You need a doctor," Rachel murmured. The sight of his hand made her stomach churn; his fingers were so mangled that she didn't even know if a doctor would be able to help him. "To look at your hand," she continued more firmly. "If the bones aren't set properly, you'll never be able to use it again."

"I don't care," Franz replied recklessly, his head thrown back and eyes clenched shut against the pain. "I really don't."

This wasn't the fatalistic attitude from before that Rachel had so dreaded, she realized, but rather a new and different kind of defiance. Franz might have had no use for their religion, but it seemed he'd needed atonement all the same, and perhaps he'd found at least a little of it here.

"Even so, it must be seen to," Rachel stated. "You cannot work with a hand like that, and you'll just be an easy target for the Nazis. You know how they can't stand any weakness or disability in anyone, and certainly not in a Jew."

Franz regarded her with something like humor, even though he was still grimacing with pain. "And where will we find a doctor?"

"I don't know," Rachel admitted, although already she was thinking of the ten Booms. Surely they could help, and yet they'd already given them so much. "I'll go ask at the Beje."

"They have enough troubles—" Franz protested.

"You know they are always willing and eager to help," Rachel reproved gently. "But first, let me clean you up a bit." She dabbed carefully at the dried blood on his ruined face while he gazed up at her.

"They were beating up a boy," he told her in a low voice. "He couldn't have been more than twelve or thirteen, just a child. Everyone was hurrying by, even other Jews." He paused, closing his eyes as he grimaced in pain. "I almost did the same myself."

And she almost wished he had, Rachel thought sadly, although she knew she didn't mean it. Just like she had had to by refusing Beatrix's money, Franz had needed to make a stand. His, however, had been far costlier.

"But you didn't," she told him gently. "And they beat you for it." Practically to a pulp.

"Worse than that," Franz admitted. He drew a ragged breath, wincing again with the pain of it. "They threatened me.

They said they'd come and find me, make sure I made it onto a train, whatever that means. It can't be good."

Rachel thought of Westerbork, and her hand stilled over Franz's face as dread pooled icily in her stomach. "Corrie said she had heard rumors they were sending Jews on trains, somewhere east," she told him in a low voice. "Somewhere that couldn't be good."

"No." Franz was silent for a moment, his breathing still ragged from the pain of his injuries. "I don't suppose it could be. I'm sorry, Rachel," he said at last. "Maybe my courage, such as it was, will cost you... again."

"You don't need to be sorry," Rachel told him. "Certainly not for something like that."

"I think they meant what they said," Franz said. "I think they'll come find me. *Us*."

"They might forget about it," Rachel replied, unconvincingly. She already knew it was too great a risk to take, to depend on the laziness of a German soldier. She dabbed at his face once more as she tried to order her thoughts. "I suppose we'll have to find new accommodation somehow." Could she prevail on the ten Booms not just for a doctor, but for a place to stay? It felt like far too much to ask, and yet she didn't know what else to do. She did not know anyone else who could help them.

"I suppose we will," Franz agreed soberly. "But where?"

"I'll ask the ten Booms. They've helped other people. They might know something or someone." Rachel gazed out the window at the summer afternoon, the sky a hazy blue, the day hot and still. From the street below, she heard the squeak of a bicycle, the peal of a child's laughter, both such simple, easy joys that felt a million miles from what she and Franz were facing now.

From her window, the world looked at peace, but right then, Rachel felt as if those four dark horses weren't coming just for Corrie and her family, but for her and Franz, as well.

CHAPTER 16

SEPTEMBER 1942—HILVERSUM, THE NETHERLANDS

The room was ten feet by ten feet, with whitewashed walls and a bare wooden floor, the only furniture an iron bedstead with a lumpy mattress, and a washstand with a chipped bowl and pitcher. It had been Franz and Rachel's home for the last three months, since she'd rushed over to the Beje to ask for the ten Booms' help once again.

Casper had answered the door, his friendly smile replaced by a look of concern as Rachel had haltingly explained what had happened.

"It is monstrous," Casper had said quietly, his expression turning grave. "*Monstrous.*" He'd paused before shaking himself out of a reverie, and then turned to Rachel with a gentle yet determined smile. "Come in and we will make arrangements."

The ten Booms had, in their graciousness, taken care of everything. They had found a doctor to see to Franz's injuries and set his hand, although two of his fingers had been damaged beyond repair, and remained bent and twisted, virtually useless. The ten Booms had also found them a place to stay.

"My brother Willem knows people in the countryside," Corrie had explained. "It's safest there, and there is more food, although everyone is feeling the pinch. They used to take people without ration cards, but now they won't."

"But we don't have ration cards," Rachel had replied uncertainly. Jews were forbidden from having them, which had made finding food all the more difficult.

"Oh, I know that," Corrie had assured her. "But I have them."

Rachel had stared at her blankly. "We can't take your ration cards..."

"Oh, we have extra," she'd assured her. "Remember what I told you? Just don't flash them around! Now, is it safe to return to your apartment?" She and Franz had gone to the Beje with the doctor and Rachel had no idea if the Gestapo had already stormed their apartment, or if it really had been an idle threat on the part of the nameless soldier.

"I—I don't know," she admitted.

"Then it is not worth the risk," Corrie declared. "We'll send Peter to get your things. If it can be arranged, you will leave tonight."

And so they had—slipping out the back of the Beje with their single suitcase of possessions, the shard of emerald feeling heavy in Rachel's pocket. Part of her was still amazed that she'd been able to hold onto it for this long. How long she'd be able to keep it, she didn't know. Did her friends still have theirs? It had been so long since she'd heard from them, and it would be longer still, she feared, before they saw each other again. Yet it was the hope of Henri's, of that joyous reunion by the Eiffel Tower one day, that often kept her putting one weary foot in front of another.

A truck was waiting in the alleyway behind the house, belonging to a farmer who was still allowed to drive a vehicle. Rachel had clambered into the back before helping Franz up, his arm in a sling, his jaw taut with pain. Corrie had wished them both Godspeed, her kindly face wreathed in concern.

"Remember, God goes with you," she'd entreated as she'd clasped Rachel's hand. "He ordains every moment. Nothing takes Him by surprise!"

Rachel had nodded dumbly. She wanted to believe that, and she thought she probably did, but considering their current situation, fleeing for their very lives, the thought did not provide much comfort.

For over an hour, they'd rattled through the night, hidden under some old potato sacks, barely daring to take a breath in case they were stopped.

But they'd made it, emerging into the moonlit night outside a farm, flat fields stretching endlessly to the darkened horizon. The wide-open space had taken Rachel's breath away. For three years now, she had not left the narrow streets of Haarlem's Old Town, and while she had enjoyed the beauty of the buildings, she now realized just how small and cramped her world had been.

The farmer's wife, Nora Visser, had greeted them at the door, looking friendly but also guarded. She was taking an enormous risk in hiding them, Rachel knew, and she had no way to repay the woman's kindness.

The kindness, she and Franz discovered, however, had only extended so far. They were required to stay in their small room all day, coming out only at night to sit in the kitchen for a brief hour of respite, watched over anxiously by Nora and her husband Hendrik. She and Franz were never allowed outside, and they were not to make any noise when they were in their room. Twice a day, Nora brought them food—bread with a thin smear of margarine in the morning, and soup with vegetables and occasionally a chunk of sausage in the evening. Rachel knew food was becoming scarce for everyone, but it wasn't much more than what they'd been eating back with Frieda in Zoestraat.

The hours passed slowly, so slowly, that sometimes Rachel

thought she would go mad. Sometimes she had the urge to scream, or claw the walls, or even hurl herself out the window, just to alleviate the endless tedium. She'd stand by the one window for hours at a time, viewing the flat farm fields under a hard blue sky, taking some solace in all the space and air, although their small room was unbearably stuffy and hot.

Sometimes she would think about the past—her childhood in Prenzlauer Berg, with her mother and father. She pictured her mother humming in the kitchen as she made the challah for Shabbat dinner, her father coming in after work, looking weary but always with a smile for them both. She thought about when she'd first met Franz, and how he'd set her world alight. How, even with the restrictions against the Jews that had already started, she'd felt as if her future had been shimmering with possibility.

And she thought of her three friends from the *St Louis*, and tried to imagine where they might be now. Was Sophie still working for the Jewish refugee center in Washington? The last she'd heard from Rosa, she'd been doing some kind of war work outside London. And Hannah... she hadn't heard from Hannah in so long, but she'd been in Paris, working as a secretary, with Lotte being cared for at a children's home. Was she still safe? As a Jew in a German-occupied country, perhaps her situation was as precarious as Rachel's. Although, Rachel recalled, Hannah was only half-Jewish. Perhaps that would save her?

But what would save her and Franz? Could they really wait out the war in this one room? Would the Vissers even let them?

After three months, Rachel feared their hosts were becoming weary of living in a constant state of caution and fear, and she could hardly blame them. Every day felt both endless and exhausting, and yet they were doing nothing. Nothing but waiting.

Sometimes she and Franz would talk, although he was more content than she was simply to while away the hours.

He'd learned the hard school of patience in Dachau, Rachel realized, when he'd been in solitary confinement for six months.

"The room was half again as small as this one," he'd told her once with a faint smile. "And no window."

Rachel had shaken her head slowly. "I don't know how you coped."

His expression had become shuttered then, and she knew he was thinking of Erich Lieser. "It wasn't so hard," he'd said quietly.

The only books they had belonged to the Vissers—a copy of the Bible and another of nineteenth-century poetry, by the Dutch writer Everhardus Johannes Potgieter. Both books were, of course, in Dutch, and Rachel read them cover to cover more than once, simply for something to do. Franz read them as well, poring over passages in the Bible, somewhat to Rachel's surprise. Would her husband find God in these difficult times? She could scarcely credit it, and yet she had taken some comfort in reading the psalms herself, the familiar words, even in Dutch, possessing a sacred kind of power.

God is our refuge and strength, an ever-present help in trouble. Therefore we will not fear, though the earth give way and the mountains fall into the heart of the sea...

It felt as if the very earth were giving way right now, Rachel reflected, the entire world in desperate upheaval as the fight against Hitler's relentless evil surged on. She thought of what Corrie had told her when she'd said goodbye—how God ordained every moment. Was it truly possible to see His hand even in this? Perhaps that was where real faith came in— believing even when nothing, absolutely nothing, in the world around you encouraged you to do so.

"I can understand," Franz had remarked once, as he'd flipped through the gospel of John, "how faith can sustain and strengthen you, when all else fails." Slowly he had closed the

Bible, resting his palm on the worn leather cover. "I wasn't strong enough on my own, at Dachau."

"No one would be, Franz—" Rachel had begun, but he had shaken his head, making her fall silent.

"Some were. Some were far stronger than I was. They held out, even against the most unthinkable torture. Erich Lieser never gave anything away." He'd given her a crooked smile, his eyes dark with sorrow. "Maybe I should have asked God for the strength to resist."

Rachel wasn't sure if he was joking or not, but it made her think about her own life, and all the things she'd tried to do in her own strength. Helping Franz. Being so relentlessly cheerful for so long, despite all the obstacles. Loving her husband the way she knew she should. In the end, she'd failed, just as Franz had failed at Dachau. She hadn't had the strength, or even the will. But did God? Had she been doing it all wrong, trying to drag herself and Franz along, straining and heaving, rather than letting them be directed by a far stronger and gentler hand? It was a question she could not answer, and yet she had plenty of time to reflect as the days passed, and one month slid dreamlike into another.

From the window, Rachel watched the seasons change—the hot, dry days of August were replaced by cooler nights and some welcome rain, mists rising above the wheat in silvery, ephemeral clouds. She wondered what her friends were doing, as well as her mother. Were they safe? What was it even like in Germany now, for Jews? Or France, or Belgium, where Sophie's family had gone? And beyond her small circle of loved ones, Rachel wondered what was going on in the world, and if the Allies were prevailing. She had absolutely no way of knowing. Her hosts did not listen to Radio *Oranje*, and they did not share any news with her or Franz. They were clearly good, God-fearing people who did their duty, and not much more.

In October, Franz's seemingly endless patience finally

began to fray. "I want to *do* something!" he exclaimed, pacing the confines of their room like a caged lion. He pounded his left fist into his right palm; the fingers on his right hand were still too twisted to make a fist at all. "How long are we meant to hide in here, like the rats they think we are?" He shook his head, derisively self-condemning. "It's cowardice, Rachel, it's nothing but *cowardice*."

"And what," Rachel asked, keeping her voice reasonable, "would be the good of walking out of here? We'd be arrested and deported, or worse. We'd have caused no good to anybody, least of all ourselves."

"Still…" He braced his shoulder against the window frame as he gazed out at the fields, now mowed and barren, the hard earth touched with frost. "There must be something we can do. We're useless vessels, clanging cymbals, up here."

"Clanging cymbals? I should hope not," Rachel replied with a laugh. "That would make too much noise!" A sudden thought assailed her; the words had sounded familiar. "That's from the Bible," she exclaimed. "Why, have you memorized the whole thing, Franz?"

He smiled a little shamefacedly as he shrugged. "What else is there to do?"

"'If I speak in the tongues of men and of angels,'" Rachel quoted slowly as she recalled the verse, "'but have not love, I am a noisy gong or a clanging cymbal.'"

"Yes, something like that."

"But don't you see, Franz?" Rachel exclaimed, rising from the bed to join her husband at the window. "What we need is *love*. We are choosing love in a world that chooses hatred. Isn't that another kind of courage?"

He turned to her, a small smile softening his features as the frustration drained from him. "How is it," he asked her with an ache in his voice, "that even after all this, you can speak of love? And to *me*?"

Rachel knew instantly what he was talking about, and it made her heart twist inside her. "I love you," she replied, a little unsteadily. "I always have."

He touched her cheek, tucking a tendril of hair behind her ear and letting his fingers skim her jaw. "Even when I've given you very little reason to do so."

"That's not how love works. Not how marriage works," she told him, catching his hand with her own and pressing it against her cheek.

He gazed down at her, his hazel eyes full of warmth and memory.

"We said vows," he agreed, parroting her words of so many years ago.

Rachel nodded, a lump in her throat. "Yes, we did." They'd been through some incredibly difficult experiences, and sometimes she'd wished, desperately, that things had been different, that *Franz* had been, but right now Rachel was simply grateful that they'd made it to this moment, together. Whatever the future held, and it was unlikely to be anything good, at least they'd made it here, to this.

"I love you," she said again, and gently Franz kissed her lips.

That night, when they crept down to the kitchen to sit and drink tea—made with leaves used three times over already— with Nora and Hendrik Visser, the mood was palpably tense. It was a tension that had, Rachel acknowledged uneasily, been growing over the last few weeks, although she hadn't wanted to acknowledge it. Now, with Hendrik sitting in a glowering silence and Nora flitting about as if she didn't know what to do with herself, Rachel felt it like a thickness in the air.

She glanced at Franz, wondering if they should go back to their room. Their hosts, it seemed, had truly grown tired of them.

"Things have been difficult," Hendrik finally said into the silence, his voice low, the words a stark pronouncement.

Rachel tensed and glanced again at Franz, who raised his eyebrows.

"Things are very difficult," her husband agreed, and she heard the slightest edge to his voice. The implication, she feared, was clear; things were much more difficult for them than the Vissers, and their hosts shouldn't forget it.

"What's been going on?" Rachel asked in as placating a tone as she could manage. "I can only imagine how hard it has been. We are very grateful—"

"There have been raids," Hendrik stated abruptly, cutting her off. "Raids on the homes of good, honest Christian people, who have been arrested as a result, and some even sent to prison."

"Good, honest Christian people?" Franz echoed, his mouth taking on a sardonic twist. "Do you mean, as opposed to Jews?"

"*Franz*," Rachel murmured, putting a restraining hand on his arm. This was hardly the time to start an argument, although it seemed one had been brewing before they'd even come downstairs.

"Yes, as opposed to Jews," Hendrik replied, his voice rising to an aggrieved rumble. "We could live our lives as decent people, without any danger, if—"

"Is that what your Jesus said you should do?" Franz shot back, while Rachel let out a little whimper of dismay. She really did not want to argue with their hosts, especially when they were risking their lives to shelter them. "'Then the righteous will answer him, 'Lord, when did we see you hungry and feed you, or thirsty and give you something to drink?'" Franz quoted ruthlessly, while Hendrik Visser's jaw dropped in shock at a Jew reciting the New Testament. "'When did we see you a stranger and invite you in, or needing clothes and clothe you?'" Franz continued, his voice rising while the Vissers simply stared at him in silence. "'When did we see you sick or in prison and go to visit you?'" He paused, seeming to wait for their reply, but they had nothing to say.

Rachel watched, her breath caught in her chest, as Franz dropped his voice to a soft, almost tender murmur.

"'The King will reply,'" he quoted quietly. "'Truly I tell you, whatever you did for one of the least of these brothers and sisters of mine, you did for me.'"

For a long moment, no one spoke. Hendrik stared at Franz, caught between admiration and deep annoyance. Nora twisted her hands in her apron.

"It's only," Nora said finally, quietly, like a confession, her voice trembling with emotion, "that we are so afraid."

"Of course you are," Rachel cried. "And we are so very grateful to you for sheltering us." She glanced at Franz, who gave a small, grimacing smile of apology for his uncomfortably pointed use of the Bible. "It might be your Christian duty," she continued, "but there are many who are not willing to do it, because it is indeed so dangerous. Thank you. Truly, thank you."

Hendrik gave a brief nod, seemingly placated by her gratitude. "It's just the farmhouse down the way was raided," he said in his rumbling voice. "It wouldn't be good for any of us if that came to pass."

No, it certainly wouldn't, Rachel thought. Then they would be sent to Westerbork, or wherever it was they were now taking Jews, to put them on the mysterious trains that headed east. As for the Vissers? They would be arrested, most certainly, perhaps held in prison.

"We will be more careful," she said, although she wasn't sure how they could be, and after a moment's hesitation, the Vissers both nodded, reluctantly appeased.

. . .

Being careful, however, wasn't enough. Two weeks later, when the nights were freezing and Rachel and Franz had to huddle together for warmth, a knock sounded on their door, rapid and urgent.

"Get up, get up!" Nora hissed through the door. "The Gestapo—they're coming! It's a raid, just as we feared."

CHAPTER 17

Rachel lurched out of bed, her heart beating wildly as she reached blindly for clothes and scrambled into them. Next to her, Franz was doing the same, as Nora continued to talk urgently through the door.

"Hurry, hurry! A neighbor alerted us that they were coming, they'll be here any moment. You must go out the back, into the fields."

Rachel grabbed her coat, pulling it around her, her fingers instinctively reaching for the emerald in her pocket, wrapped in a handkerchief. She clutched it tightly for a single second, drawing strength from its promise, and then turned to help Franz, who still struggled with his right hand, into his coat.

They had only been awake for thirty seconds, if that, but as they raced down the stairs, they heard the rumble of a truck pulling up to the front door, its squeal of brakes, and then the inevitable thunderous hammering on the front door.

"*Hurry!*" Nora entreated, her face pale and pinched as she took them through the kitchen, out the back door and into the night.

Rachel gazed out at the endlessly black fields, rimed with

frost, the air icy with cold, and hesitated. "Where are we to go?" she asked uncertainly.

"Out into the fields," Nora said impatient. "Out, out, before they catch you and us!" She gave Rachel a little push in the back. "You can't come back here," she stated definitively. "The house will be watched."

They could hear voices from the hall, and with no other choice, Rachel and Franz took off running into the darkness. The earth was hard and uneven under her feet as Rachel ran unsteadily along, the cold air burning her lungs. From behind them, they heard voices rising sharply, the sound of breaking glass. They kept running until Rachel's head was swimming, her legs aching, her lungs burning. Finally, when all was darkness around them and they couldn't hear a single sound but that of their own ragged breathing, they stopped, collapsing to the ground, utterly exhausted.

They lay on the frozen ground for several moments, catching their breaths, as the cold seeped through Rachel's coat and right into her skin. Eventually, she forced herself to sit up, staring out at the starry sky.

"What do we do now?" she wondered aloud.

Franz remained lying down, his good arm thrown over his face. "God only knows," he muttered.

Rachel kept staring at the sky, as if she could find inspiration from the stars that littered the endless night like a thousand diamond pinpricks. They had left all their possessions behind, including her father's pocket watch; they had nothing but the clothes on their backs. Where could they go? Who could they trust? She could only think of the ten Booms, but they were at least thirty miles from Haarlem. The chance of being able to walk such a distance undetected was depressingly slim, and that was if they didn't collapse from cold or hunger along the way.

"We need to make it to a road," she said at last. "I can only think of trying to make it back to Haarlem."

"And don't you think the Gestapo will stop a shabby couple like us walking along the road?" Franz gestured to their clothes. "Not to mention the yellow stars on our coats."

Rachel knew it was true. They would most likely be found out before they'd gone so much as a mile.

"What else can we do?" she asked.

In the darkness, Franz's teeth gleamed as he gave her a crooked smile. "Take a step of faith. Knock on someone's door and ask them for help."

"*What*!" Rachel stared at him in dismay. "More people than not are sympathetic to the regime," she told him. "That's taking an awfully big risk."

He shrugged. "Our fate has never been in our own hands."

He ordains every moment. Corrie's words floated through Rachel's mind, and she took a deep breath of frigid air as she steeled herself.

"All right, then," she said with a nod. "But I don't see any houses here."

"Come on, then." Franz scrambled up to standing and then reached for Rachel with his good hand. "Let's find one."

She took his hand, letting him draw her up, and for a second, they simply stood there together, the empty fields stretching darkly all around them. Perhaps this was the beginning of the end, Rachel thought. They might knock on someone's house, and they would send for the Gestapo. They might not even make it to someone's house; the raid on the Vissers would have shown they'd been hiding there. Soldiers might be combing the fields for them, sending out dogs to hunt them down...

A shiver went through her, and Franz put his arm around her.

"Come on," he said. "Let's go."

They walked for three hours in the cold, the sky lit only by the stars and a pale sliver of moon. Dawn was just starting to lighten the horizon with gray when they came upon a farmhouse, made of weathered brick with a steeply sloping roof, a couple of shabby-looking barns nearby. As they ventured nearer, a dog started barking, the sound making them both jump.

Franz glanced at Rachel, his mouth curving wryly. "They know about us now," he said.

A moment later, the back door opened, and a farmer came out into the courtyard, dressed in a nightshirt and a pair of muddy boots, and holding a hunting rifle. A hound hurled itself from behind him, barking madly. Franz and Rachel stayed in the shadows, waiting to see what happened next.

"Who's there?" the farmer demanded. "Show yourselves."

If Rachel had hoped they might learn something of his sympathies from the way he spoke, she was disappointed. She could tell nothing of what manner of man he was, save for that he was understandably suspicious of a nighttime visitor.

"Show yourselves!" he called again, and then, his voice gentler, "There's no need to be afraid."

It was enough to have Franz walking forward, into the farmyard, his hands up in the air as the farmer swung his rifle toward him.

"Please, sir," he said in Dutch. "We are Jews. We were in hiding, but there was a raid. We need to get back to Haarlem."

The farmer's rifle was still pointed at Franz; Rachel was too far away to see the expression on the stranger's face. She prayed he wouldn't shoot.

Then the man lowered his gun. "Come inside and warm yourself," he said gruffly. "Are you alone?"

"No, my wife, as well." Franz motioned to Rachel, and hesitantly she came forward.

"Come inside," the farmer said again. "And we'll see what we can do."

. . .

They were at the Beje by the following evening. Rachel sat in the ten Booms' dining room, nursing a cup of tea, amazed that she was there at all. The farmer had been more than sympathetic; he'd known the ten Booms and been able to contact them and arrange their transportation back. He'd also managed to bring back their few possessions from the Vissers, even her father's precious pocket watch. It had all felt too good to be true, an overwhelming justification for their hesitant step of faith.

"You see," Corrie had said as she'd kissed her on both cheeks in welcome while Franz had gone to greet Casper, "you have more friends than you realize."

"I must," Rachel had agreed shakily. The events of the last twenty-four hours still made her feel wobbly inside. They had come so close to being arrested. How long would they be able to stay hidden? And where were they to go next?

"You won't go *anywhere*," Corrie said when Rachel posed the question to her that night. "I admit, the Beje is not the best hiding place, with the police so close, and people coming and going at all hours. But since you left, we have improved things remarkably!" Her smile was full of impish delight. "We have several others staying with us now. Let me show you my bedroom."

Mystified, Rachel followed Corrie up to the tiny closet she called a bedroom. "What do you see?" the older woman demanded as she presented her modest room with a flourish.

"A bed?" Rachel guessed. "And a wardrobe?" The little room did not hold much else.

"Ah, yes, very good," Corrie replied with a nod. "But nothing else?"

Rachel let out an uncertain laugh. "Nothing else," she agreed. She had no idea what Corrie was trying to show her. "I'm sorry," she added, and Corrie laughed.

"Don't be sorry! I'm so pleased. If you cannot see anything amiss, then the Gestapo surely won't, either."

Rachel frowned, not understanding. "The Gestapo?"

"Look." Corrie went to the far wall, stained by damp and the smoke of coal fires, looking as old as the rest of the house. Sagging bookshelves of old, weathered wood ran across it. In the lefthand corner, beneath the bottom shelf, Corrie pulled a panel up. It slid smoothly, without a sound, revealing a darkness on the other side.

"What..." Rachel breathed.

"Our secret room!" Corrie cried jubilantly. "With space enough for several people, at the very least. Come see!"

Tentatively, Rachel followed Corrie on her hands and knees through the open panel, only about two feet high, to find herself in a cupboard-sized space, a single mattress on the floor. A jug of water, a bottle of vitamins, and a stack of hardtack biscuits were next to the bed.

"If there's a raid," Corrie explained, "several people could hide in here, even for as long as three or four days. Look, there's even a vent for fresh air."

"It's amazing," Rachel told her sincerely. "And what trouble you've gone to!"

Corrie grasped her hand, and even in the dim light, Rachel could see tears sparkling in her eyes. "It's no trouble," she said in a low voice. "No trouble at all."

Over the next few weeks and months, Rachel and Franz fell into a surprisingly pleasant pattern of life. The ten Boom household was a busy one, and indeed as Corrie had said, people were constantly coming and going, most of them friends and supporters of their activities, but not always, and so they'd adopted measures to be careful.

A curtain had been hung in the dining-room window, which at five steps above the street, could be seen into. "There's only meant to be three of us here," Corrie explained with a smile, "and most nights there's at least seven! Just in case someone takes it into their head to peek through the windows."

"They'd have to be awfully tall," Betsie had pointed out, "but it's good to be careful."

"The Lord will take care of us all," Casper had proclaimed, and Corrie and Betsie had exchanged knowing looks.

"Of course He will, Father," Corrie had said, kissing Casper's wrinkled cheek.

Perhaps the most ingenious part of their planning was a buzzer under the dining-room windowsill that sent an alarm clanging at the top of the stairs. It was to be pressed if there was danger, and the occupants of the household had practiced gathering all their belongings and crawling into the secret room as soon as it was sounded.

"When we started a few weeks before you came," Corrie told Rachel and Franz, "we were lamentably slow—four minutes, and we'd left all sorts of things about. Now we're down to seventy seconds, and you wouldn't suspect a thing. We have drills every week—and Betsie makes cream puffs for a treat when we're finished! We use all our sugar ration for it."

Soon, Rachel and Franz were participating in these drills, clambering into the crowded space with the Bejes' other Jewish occupants, who had arrived in their absence—Meyer Mossel, a former cantor from Amsterdam known as Eusie; Thea Dacosta, Meta Monsanto, and Mary Itallie, who at seventy-six, was the oldest resident. They'd all been misfits of some sort, with others unwilling to take them in—Eusie was thought to look "too Jewish," and Mary had asthma, with her loud wheezing compromising any hiding place. Meta was Italian, and Thea an accomplished pianist. Neither of them had been able to find another place to hide.

All in all, it was a surprisingly happy household; Betsie and Corrie, despite their many cares, always seemed full of joy, while their father's quiet and contented faith felt like a rock upon which they could all stand. Eusie's wry humor often had even Franz smiling, and Mary and Meta, although quiet, were kindly. Betsie insisted on everyone enjoying themselves; every evening they would gather in the sitting room for a concert or a reading. One night, they even put on a play by Vondel—"the Dutch Shakespeare"—with Betsie assigning the parts.

Amidst the entertainments, there was always danger. The ten Booms had had a telephone—forbidden for all Dutch—installed, and Corrie was often answering calls, talking about watches in a way Rachel suspected was not about watches at all. They listened to Dutch *Oranje* every night on the secret radio, and Rachel lost count of the number of lost souls, looking as frightened and weary as she knew she once had, who moved through the house like shadows, onto somewhere else, somewhere hopefully safe. There was no more room at the Beje; with Eusie, Meta, Mary, as well as Rachel and Franz the house was dangerously full. Rachel worried someone would suspect something, but Corrie insisted they were safe.

"In any case," Betsie proclaimed, "we are all immortal until our Father calls us home."

Despite the pleasantness of life at the Beje, the war continued on, and with it grimmer and grimmer news. Jews were regularly being deported to Westerbork, and then onto trains heading east. Rumors swirled about their destinations—camps like Dachau, but worse. It was January 1944, and this had been going on for a year and a half. It felt as if it might never end.

Meanwhile, the Allies continued their assault on their enemies—they had invaded Italy in September, and the RAF were relentlessly bombing Berlin, which made Rachel fear for her mother—that was, if her mother was even still in Berlin. Perhaps she had already been arrested, put on one of those dreadful trains like so many others...

It was a dark spiral of fear that could swallow Rachel up if she let it.

"It's the *not* knowing that feels hardest," she confessed to Corrie one night. They were in the sitting room, everyone huddled in front of a rather pitiful fire, for the winter was cold and all the Dutch were running low on fuel. The trees along the canal, Corrie had told them, had all been cut down for people's woodstoves and fireplaces. "If I knew they were all right, or even that they weren't, I think perhaps I could find some peace. But I don't know, and maybe I never will." Rachel pulled her worn cardigan more closely around her. "I most likely will never see my mother again," she said bleakly.

Corrie rested her hand on top of Rachel's. "God gives us what knowledge we need," she said quietly. "Because He knows that more might break us."

Rachel swallowed hard; she already felt broken, and yet she knew there could very well be worse to come.

Corrie gave her a small, playful little smile. "Do you know what my father once told me?" she said, casting a fond glance at Casper, who was smiling and nodding as he listened to Eusie across the room.

Rachel shook her head, and Corrie continued, "I was worried about something once, when I was a child, and he asked me—when did he give me the ticket for the train? Was it days before?" She let out a soft laugh. "No, of course not. It was right before, the moment that I needed it. And God is the same," Corrie explained as she leaned forward, her face flushed and her eyes sparkling. "He gives us what we need—whether it is knowledge or strength or patience—*when* we need it, not before. We don't store it up to deplete it at some later date—it is His gift, in the moment, and only in the moment!" She squeezed Rachel's hand. "Take the gift, Rachel. I know how burdened you are with fear, with worry, with the not knowing.

But give it all to God—He will take your burdens, and He will give you what you need when you need it. I am sure of it."

"Thank you," Rachel replied, moved by the other woman's passionate conviction. With trepidation, she wondered how much strength she would one day need—and what for.

"You were talking rather earnestly with Corrie," Franz remarked when they headed up to bed later that evening. Corrie had given them one of the old bedrooms of her aunts—a narrow room that faced the back courtyard, the curtain always drawn across. It was small and dark with just enough room for a bed, but it was theirs and it felt safe.

"She was telling me a story," Rachel replied. "About train tickets and strength and God." She let out a little laugh. "I do admire their conviction," she told Franz. "I've never known people to be so sure of themselves in their faith."

"It is admirable," Franz agreed, "although I'm sure they would be quick to give any praise to God!"

Rachel laughed softly. "Yes, they would."

Franz turned to her with a small smile. "It's strange," he murmured, "but I've been happy here. Happier than I ever expected to be, all things considered."

"Yes, I know what you mean." She'd been happy too, despite the constant presence of both danger and fear.

Franz drew her into his arms and Rachel rested her cheek against his shoulder.

In the last few months, they'd been closer than ever before in many ways, and yet they had not been as husband and wife. The years of hostility, the constant dangers, the presence of others... all three and more besides had conspired to keep them apart. For months, Rachel had felt as if they'd been living as a loving brother and sister rather than husband and wife, and yet now as Franz put his finger under her chin and tilted her head up toward his, she felt a leap low in her belly that she hadn't in a long, long time.

"Franz..." she murmured, before he kissed her, his lips soft and sweet as they moved over hers.

Rachel gave herself over to the kiss, to the shy pleasure of it, her eyes fluttering closed as Franz drew her more tightly to him.

"Whatever happens," he murmured against her mouth, "we have this. No one can take it from us."

The words, Rachel thought just a few weeks later, had proved to be painfully prescient—and haunted her later, along with Corrie's advice, when she realized just how much she would need it.

But for now, in Franz's arms, the taste of his lips on hers, Rachel could forget all that and simply live for this moment, ordained as every other had been, and love her husband.

CHAPTER 18

FEBRUARY 28, 1944—THE BEJE

It was late morning at the end of February, the barest hint of spring in the air. Rachel was smiling at her reflection in the mirror, Franz stretched out on the bed behind her, when the sound of the alarm rang through the hallway. Their gazes met in the mirror, held for a single second before they both sprang into action. There had been no warning, so this most likely wasn't a drill.

Had it really come to this? Rachel wondered frantically as she bundled her clothes into a case while Franz straightened the bed. They glanced around the little room wildly before they sped toward Corrie's bedroom. She'd been ill with the flu for the last few days, and was still in bed, gazing at them blearily as they dove for the panel.

Eusie, Thea, and Meta were already inside, their faces white and frightened. Franz and Rachel clambered in; the space seemed much smaller with so many people crowded into it. Poor old Mary climbed in after them, wheezing heavily, followed by two Dutch resistance workers who were in the house at the time. Although they weren't Jewish, their lives were in just as much danger.

Finally, and just in time, the panel was slid shut, only to be quickly opened again, and Corrie herself hurled a briefcase that Rachel knew held damning papers inside before slamming the panel shut once more. Just seconds later, they heard a man speaking. Everyone held their breath.

"What's your name?" he demanded, and then came Corrie's sleepy reply.

"What...?"

"Your name!"

"Cornelia ten Boom."

"Get up," he told her roughly. "Get dressed."

A pause, and they could hear Corrie starting to move about.

"So *you're* the ringleader," the man remarked, and now he sounded smug. "So tell me, where are you hiding the Jews?"

In the darkness of the cupboard, everyone's eyes glittered with fear. Mary's breath rattled in her chest, and she put her hand over her mouth. Rachel's heart was beating so loudly, she feared the German outside would be able to hear it. Silently Franz took her hand and held it tightly in his.

Where are you hiding the Jews?

"I don't know what you're talking about," Corrie replied. She sounded, incredibly, genuinely confused.

The man laughed, an ugly sound. "And you don't know anything about the underground ring, either! We'll see about that." The words sounded like a threat. "Let me see your papers."

A scuffle sounded as Corrie showed him her papers, all else was silent. Mary wasn't, Rachel realized, even wheezing as she normally did. She turned to look at the older woman, who slowly lowered her hand from her mouth, amazed at the fact that for once she was not struggling to breathe.

"Hurry up!" the man commanded, and a few seconds later, they heard the thud of the man's boots, and Corrie's following footsteps, heading down the hall and then downstairs.

They hadn't been discovered. Yet.

The next few hours passed torturously slowly. Rachel's legs cramped and her back ached as everyone strove to find a comfortable place in the small space. Meanwhile, they heard all sorts of distressing noises from outside—books being thrown to the floor, furniture being moved. Downstairs, a Gestapo agent was shouting. They were searching for a secret room, Rachel knew, but would they find it?

Then—silence. The slam of a door, the sound of an engine. The Gestapo had gone. Still, no one dared to speak.

"We mustn't go out yet," Eusie finally said after several tense minutes of complete silence. "It could be a trap."

Everyone else nodded, too fearful to say another word. How long, Rachel wondered, would they have to stay in there? There was food and water, but not enough to sustain so many people for more than a day or two. What if the Gestapo watched the house for weeks? When could they dare to open the panel and see?

She leaned her head against the wall, her eyes gritty with fatigue, her body aching. Eusie took one of the pieces of hardtack and split it into pieces, silently handing them around. It felt like a Passover meal, or even a Christian eucharist. Everyone ate as quietly as they could, nibbling at the rations, swallowing dryly.

When would this end, Rachel thought, and more importantly, *how*? The thought of starving to death in this dark, cramped space was almost as unendurable as being arrested. And yet... they simply couldn't take the chance of coming out. Corrie and her family had risked their lives for the poor souls hiding in this space—"the Angel's Den" as some had called it. It would be a poor repayment indeed to throw their sacrifice away.

Corrie...

Rachel's thoughts drifted to the woman who had been so very kind to her. And Casper and Betsie too, their selflessness had profoundly touched everyone they had met. What had happened to them? Were they in prison... or worse? There was no way to know, and there probably would be no way to ever find out. Whenever they did emerge from this angel's den, Rachel realized, it would be only to go into hiding somewhere else, if such a place could be found.

At some point, people slept, although no one could be sure it was night. When they woke again, they took turns moving around, to ease their cramped limbs. Eusie shared out another piece of hardtack, as well as some much-needed water. But still, no one dared to open the panel.

"When it is safe," Eusie declared in a whisper, his voice full of desperate conviction, "someone will come for us. They know we are here. They won't let us die here alone."

It was the only hope they had, and they all clung to it. But as the days passed, one after the other, so stultifyingly slow, it was hard not to doubt. To fear the very worst. At one point, Rachel wondered, would it be worth the risk to venture out into the rest of the Beje? Mary, in particular, struggled with her asthma in the small space and little fresh air, and Rachel worried whether her rattling breaths might be heard by anyone on patrol outside.

Sleep was the only respite, and then only an uneasy doze; Rachel usually awoke suddenly, with a crick in her neck, her eyes straining in the darkness, wondering if she'd heard a footfall on the stair. In the darkness, Franz would find her hand, or she would find his; their clasped fingers felt as if they were the only thing tethering her to both sanity and hope.

Rachel lost track of the hours, and then of the days; the water ran out, along with the hardtack, and as their bellies grew empty and they longed for water, they wondered if they should risk sliding open the panel. They took a vote, and no one voted to open it. Fear, Rachel knew, was a powerful force. The thought of sliding that small panel open only to have a Gestapo agent gleefully pounce on them was too horrifying—and possible—to risk.

And then one evening, after they'd heard footsteps, held their breaths, and feared the worst, the panel opened from the outside, and a face peered in, lit behind by a lamp. Everyone froze, too terrified to speak or even move.

"Greetings, my friends," a man said softly in Dutch. "Are you all right?"

Mary let out a sob of relief and Eusie laughed out loud. Rachel reached for Franz's hand and squeezed it hard; she could hardly believe that after so many days of struggle and suffering and terror, they had been saved.

"It was four days before they put me on shift," their savior explained as he helped them one by one clamber out of the hiding place, many of them falling to their hands and knees with cramp and exhaustion. "The Gestapo gave the job to the Dutch police, thank God."

As she slowly straightened, Rachel recognized Rolf, a police officer who was friendly to their cause.

"We have new places for you all," he told them in a low voice. "You will have to go out quickly from the back. The house is still being watched. Take your possessions with you. Quickly, now."

"The ten Booms—" Rachel asked, and Rolf shook his head.

"In prison."

"Oh no," Rachel said softly. She was not surprised, but the news was still devastating. The cart with its dark horses had come for Corrie just as she'd dreamed.

Rolf gave a commiserating nod. "Quickly, now."

Franz went back to their room and grabbed their one bag, while Rachel slipped her hand into her pocket, curling her fingers tightly around the emerald she had kept all these years. Safe, they were really safe. For now.

Rolf guided them down to the kitchen, and then out to the

back alleyway, where a man was waiting to spirit them away to their various safe places.

Rachel followed blindly, holding tightly to Franz's hand, biting her lips to keep the sobs of sheer emotion from escaping.

Several hours later, all seven of them had been found new hiding places. Rachel and Franz were in a house just a few blocks away, holed up in a windowless cupboard in the back. It wasn't as secure as the Beje, with its ingenious hiding place, but it would have to do. The couple who lived there were kindly and plied them with tea and soup before sending them to bed and then effectively walling them in with a heavy wardrobe dragged across the door.

"I'm sorry," the wife, Ruth, said apologetically. "But it is so dangerous these days. The Gestapo go from house to house, searching at a moment's notice... they are determined to take every Jew from Haarlem. We will let you come out when we can, if it is safe."

Lying together in the narrow bed, Rachel and Franz wrapped their arms around each other, too exhausted and overwhelmed to utter so much as a word. It was enough that they were together, alive and safe... for now.

As the days passed, they did not leave the little room once, which was, all told, barely bigger than the hiding place they'd languished in for four long days. It was less than half the size, Rachel reflected ruefully, of their room at the Vissers' farmhouse. She'd resented the confinement then, but their accommodation had been a palace compared to now. Once a day, the wardrobe was moved so food could be brought in and their chamber pot emptied, and Ruth or her husband, Peter, would whisper what encouragements they could.

"They say it won't be long now, that the Allies are sure to invade soon—they say in France, but no one knows." Ruth grasped Rachel's hand. "But it *will* end," she told her. "I am sure of it! You just need to hold on a little longer."

"The Allies won't invade until spring," Franz remarked one evening, his tone matter-of-fact. They were speaking in whispers, lying close together on the bed, as there was no real room to stand. "How long will that be? Another month, two? Too long."

"It's the end of March now," Rachel replied, trying to rally. "Surely not as long as that?"

"They need to make sure it's dry, I imagine," Franz told her as he shook his head, his arms tightened around her. "Remember the stories of the endless mud from the last war? For all their tanks and Jeeps to get across Europe... it simply must be dry."

Rachel's heart sank as she tried to hold onto her small, encouraging smile. Two more months until a possible invasion, and even then, it would surely be months more before Haarlem and the rest of the Netherlands was liberated. Haarlem was in the north of the country, far from France. Maybe it would even be years.

And yet... there was hope. Hope that this suffering at last would finally end, that the reign of terror and evil would be stopped. If only they could hold on.

In April, Ruth told them that she'd had news of the ten Booms. Corrie and Betsie had been taken to the prison Scheveningen, where Frieda had gone, and then transported to a camp. Casper, the "Old Man" of Haarlem, had died in prison after just a few days, his body thrown carelessly out on a heap outside his cell. The other ten Booms, including Corrie and Betsie's siblings Willem and Nollie, had thankfully been released.

"Poor Casper," Rachel murmured. "Poor Corrie and

Betsie… at a *camp*. And they're not young, and Betsie's health isn't good…" She shook her head in true distress, feeling both gratified and guilty that this family had given so much for the sake of others.

In May, when the air in the little cupboard was becoming stifling, their hosts decided that Rachel and Franz could come out for a few short hours, to get some air.

"It cannot be healthy, to be in such a small space in this heat," Ruth remarked, looking unhappy. "I am so sorry for it."

Sitting in their kitchen, drinking tea that tasted like no more than hot water, felt like the greatest luxury Rachel had ever known. They spoke in whispers with Ruth and Peter, learning all the news they could. The Germans were becoming more fearsome occupiers, savage in their cruelty; in some areas, they were shooting people in the street.

"And not just Jews," Peter put in. "Anyone they don't like the look of. Being Dutch no longer seems to mean anything."

"And there is no food," Ruth chimed in on a sigh. "A ration card gives you nothing. How long can this last?"

"The Germans are losing the war," Peter declared. "The writing is surely on the wall. That is why they are acting as they are. They're afraid."

"What a world to bring a little one into!" Ruth remarked on an embarrassed laugh. With both embarrassment and pride, she touched one hand to the gentle swell of her middle and, with a jolt, Rachel realized the other woman was pregnant. She hadn't known. "I pray we'll be liberated by the time this blessed child makes an appearance," Ruth said shyly.

"Yes…" Rachel stared at her, dazed with dawning suspicion. It had not occurred to her until that very moment, but she had not had her monthly courses since before they'd been in the ten Booms' hiding place. She'd been feeling nauseous but had put it down to how little food she had. And despite her thinness, thanks to their sparse diet, she now realized her own middle had a tiny, telling swell...

Was she pregnant?

"Congratulations," she said belatedly, her mind still spinning from this revelation. A *baby*, a beautiful baby, a son or a daughter. She thrilled at the thought until reality was brought back to her with a terrible thud. To bring a baby into this world, such as it was! She felt both appalled and deeply hopeful, because no matter what the world was like, a baby—her and Franz's baby—was a beautiful thing. "I pray it will be a new world your little one enters into," she told Ruth, a throb of emotion roughening her voice. And hers too, if she was indeed pregnant. God help them all, if it wasn't. The last thing she could ever want was to bring a child into the world as it was.

Ruth smiled in return, and Rachel and Franz were just rising to return to their room, their arms around each other, when there was a squeal of brakes outside, and before anyone could so much as take a breath, a pounding on the door.

Horrified realization flashed across all their faces as they froze where they stood, and then Franz grabbed Rachel's hand and they began racing for the stairs. They had only made it to the first step when the Gestapo burst into the room.

CHAPTER 19

MAY 1944—WESTERBORK TRANSIT CAMP, THE NETHERLANDS

The camp was heaving with people, with rumors, with disease and despair. Thousands of prisoners were crowded behind its barbed wire, all waiting to be put on one of the many trains headed east. No one stayed at Westerbork, Rachel soon learned; everyone was forced onto a train sooner or later.

She and Franz had been there for three days. It had all happened so fast, Rachel could only remember it in snatches—a Gestapo agent slapping her hard across the face, Franz lunging for her before he was wrenched back. A teacup knocked from the table and shattering on the floor; Ruth crying quietly as she and Peter were led out. Their hosts were bundled into a police van, while she and Franz were thrown into the back of a truck crowded with other Jews who had been pulled from their hiding places. Some were weeping, others stoic and silent. No one spoke.

They had spent the night in a prison cell, all crowded together, no one able to sleep, before they were herded onto a bus, the windows painted over, and the seats taken out so more people could be crammed on. Even then, people had tried to find a way forward. Rachel had listened to the rumors, heard the desperation.

"They want to resettle us in the east," someone had insisted. "In towns. It'll be all right, you wait and see."

Others were not so optimistic. "Look at how they've treated us so far," Rachel had heard someone mutter. "And you think they want to settle us in *towns*?"

Several exhausting hours later, they had arrived at Westerbork and Rachel had started to fully understand just how terribly the Nazis saw the Jews—as no more than chattel, and cumbersome chattel at that. Something to be dealt with, and worse, to get rid of. It struck a terror in her heart at what was ahead, especially when she considered bringing a baby into this horrific world. And she'd thought the cramped cupboard would be hard! What about a transit camp, a train, a prison, a death factory?

The rumors that swirled through Westerbork were terribly ominous. Names were bandied about—Bergen-Belsen, Theresienstadt, Auschwitz. Camps where you were worked to death, and that was if you were lucky. The unlucky never even made it that far. Rachel didn't know what to believe. What she could bear to believe.

Were some of these camps better than others? Some spoke about Theresienstadt with hope. The German Red Cross had visited it, apparently, and while it was overcrowded, it wasn't *so* terrible. Auschwitz, they said, with a shake of their heads, was the worst. No one came out of there. No one at all.

Rachel existed in a daze, hardly able to believe what they were talking about, and in such pragmatic terms. Camps for killing people the way a man might gut a fish or skin a rabbit, a job to do, nothing else! The utter *inhumanity* of it, even after all they'd experienced, still had the power to shock her.

At least she and Franz were still together. God willing, they would remain so wherever they went. And, against all odds, she still had her emerald. It had been in the pocket of her skirt when they'd been raided, and so far they had not been searched. How long Rachel could keep it, she had no idea, but she drew solace from it now, clung to the promise it held.

The mood in their quarters was somber and hopeful in turns. Some people insisted they could hold out until the invasion, while others simply shook their heads. Those who had been able to bring their belongings kindly shared them out, and soon Rachel was the recipient of a fresh skirt and blouse, Franz a shirt and a pair of trousers that were a good two inches too short. The days passed slowly in the heat as the flies rose in dark clouds and hovered above the parched earth.

It was June, and Rachel estimated she was at least three months pregnant. She hadn't told Franz, for fear it would only alarm him, for she could see no way forward for having a baby in this world. The mothers who did have little ones feared for them terribly, weeping and praying over them as they held them in their arms. What would the Nazis do with such tender, innocent ones in a camp? What would they do with her child?

She would have to tell Franz soon enough, she realized, when she began to show. But until then, it was a beautiful and fearful secret she felt compelled to keep.

Then, one morning when it was still dark and thankfully cool, they were roused from their bare wooden bunks with shouts. The *Ordnungsdienst*—the Jewish police used by the Nazis to do their bidding and despised by everyone else— stormed through the building, pulling people out of their bunks as they shouted at them roughly.

"Up, up! Move now! Don't take your suitcases! Go! *Go!*"

Rachel stumbled, along with Franz and dozens of other people, a steady stream of sleep-dazed humanity, toward the endless line of train cars—cattle cars, she saw, made of wooden slats, their sliding doors open to reveal the yawning darkness within. *That* was how they were getting to wherever they were going? As if they were truly no better than animals?

Alsatians on chains jumped and snarled to keep everyone moving as people shouted and called to each other, couples and families desperate to stay together. Rachel gripped Franz's hand tightly; they could not be separated. Not now, after all this time.

From a distance, the camp commander, Albert Gemmeker, watched the proceedings with a look of boredom on his face, although his eyes were narrowed, and Rachel had no doubt he would order anyone who resisted to be shot on the spot.

The train stretched under the dawn sky seemingly all the way to the horizon. Soldiers prodded people into the cars, sometimes giving a push hard enough to send someone sprawling into the darkness. People did their best to help others clamber onto the train, and Franz hauled himself with his good hand before pulling Rachel up behind him.

As they scrambled into the car, blinking in the darkness, a sour stench of unwashed humanity, feces, and death itself rose up, making Rachel choke, her stomach swirling with nausea. They were forced to the back of the car as more and more people clambered in behind them, until there wasn't even enough room to sit. Everyone was wedged so close together, Rachel could barely breathe; someone's elbow was poking against her hip, and she and Franz were pressed so closely together, it was as if their bodies were fused. How long were they meant to travel like this?

People did their best to shuffle and shift, trying to give each other space that simply did not exist. Then the door to the car slid shut with a creak and a slam, plunging them into a darkness that was relieved only by the gray dawn light filtering through the cracks between the wooden slats. The sound of an iron bar sliding into place sealed them in this living tomb—for how long?

Hours? Days? *Longer?* How on earth were they meant to survive?

Maybe, Rachel thought with a rising terror, greater than anything she'd felt before, they weren't.

All around her, children cried, mothers wept, men murmured what comfort they could. Rachel's head felt light, and her vision swam. She pressed against Franz, closing her eyes as she tried to even her panicked breathing.

"Rachel..." he began, but she didn't hear anymore as she slumped forward, unconscious, into his arms.

She awoke sometime later to the train moving steadily beneath her. Franz was sitting hunched against the side, Rachel curled on his lap. Most people were still standing, but a few of the elderly and children had been given a space on the floor, Rachel included. She blinked up at Franz, too dazed to speak. For a second, she'd thought it had all been a nightmare, but as the train continued to chug down the track, she realized it was real. This was really happening. They were on a train fit for cattle, heading east to a fate Rachel could not bear to think about.

"How..." She tried to speak, although her mouth was unbearably dry. "How long have I been unconscious?"

"Maybe half an hour." He smoothed her sweat-damped hair back from her forehead. "I was worried about you, *Schatzie*."

Rachel let out a choked laugh of horror as she looked around the crowded train car. The smell was even worse than before; someone must have vomited. Children who had been weeping now stared vacantly ahead, too shocked to cry. Elderly people swayed where they stood; some were crumpled on the floor, their faces gray with exhaustion. Was there even any food or water?

"And so you should be," she quipped wearily before she rested her head against his shoulder and closed her eyes.

The train continued on throughout the day, heading east. At first, everyone tried to be kind and considerate, making room for those who were struggling, passing the one bucket of grimy-looking water around so everyone could at least wet their lips.

It didn't last. Human nature, or perhaps just terror, prevailed; someone spilled the bucket, and a fight broke out. Another bucket was knocked over, this one meant for people to relieve themselves in. No one but children had used it so far, but now the stench rolled out as urine and feces spread across the floor, and people scrambled up from where they had been sitting in disgust.

Murmurs rippled through the car as people wondered where they were going, what would happen when they got there.

"Theresienstadt. Pray to God that it's Theresienstadt."

"Do you really think one is better than another? You think the Nazis are sending some to a good place, some bad? They'll all be *hell*."

"Auschwitz is only death. They kill you as soon as you get off the train."

"Where did you hear that?"

"Everyone knows."

Rachel burrowed into Franz's chest, trying to drown out the frightened murmurs. She could not bear to think about what would happen when they got off the train. She still couldn't believe she was *on* the train, treated worse than any animal would be. But that was how the Nazis had always thought of Jews... as worse than animals.

How could they survive it? And what would it mean for their baby, if they were sent to Auschwitz? It was, she realized, something she and Franz needed to face together.

She took a deep breath, and then wished she hadn't because the air was so fetid. "Franz..." she whispered. "*Franz.*"

He stirred from his uneasy doze. "What is it?"

Wordlessly, she took his hand and pressed it against the slight, telling swell of her middle. For a few seconds, he didn't understand. He stared down at her, his face barely visible in the darkness of the train car, and then realization dawned. He looked shocked, and then, to Rachel's relief, moved.

"Do you mean it?" he asked in a low voice. "You're having a baby?"

She nodded. She was sure now; she had all the symptoms and her stomach had a gentle bump to it.

"Oh, Rachel." Franz spread his fingers across her belly. "A baby, in such a place as this."

Her throat thickened with tears she was too spent to shed. "I know."

"If only..." He shook his head as he let out a small, sad sigh. "It doesn't matter. This baby is life, and we must do what we can to protect it. God knows."

She was surprised to hear him talk about God; perhaps Franz did have a faith after all. Perhaps you needed one in a place such as this.

Corrie's words came back to her, full of wry affection. *When did he give me the ticket to the train? Was it days before? No, of course not. It was right before, the moment I needed it. And God is the same... He gives us what we need—whether it is knowledge or strength or patience—when we need it, not before. We don't store it up to deplete it at some later date—it is His gift, in the moment, and only in the moment.*

Even this moment?

She closed her eyes and whispered a prayer as the train rumbled east.

They'd been traveling for a full day and night, judging by the light that had come through the cracks of the train's siding, when, to everyone's amazement, the train lurched to a stop and the door was unbolted and slid open, letting in hard, bright sunlight that caused them to wince and blink, as blind as moles.

"*Raus, raus!*" the SS officer on the platform shouted. Out, out. He held a whip that whistled through the air, and it was clear he didn't care who it landed on. "*Schnell! Raus!*"

Franz helped Rachel up and the two of them stumbled after others, off the train and onto the platform. The fresh air felt like a balm after the stale and fetid atmosphere of the car, and Rachel breathed in lungfuls gladly as Franz put his arm around her waist, supporting her. The look of tenderness on his face almost made her smile; already he'd become the proud papa. If only things were different... She clamped down on the thought before she'd finished it. There was no point in thinking otherwise. They were here now and they had to find a way to survive. Together.

It was clear they hadn't reached their destination; this was merely a stop to get fresh food and water, such as it was. The officer gave terse instructions for one of the prisoners to fill the water barrel, another to empty the waste. He tossed several loaves of stale bread into the train car, where a few poor souls, too weak to get out, were lying, clearly not caring who got the food. Rachel watched from the platform as several desperate prisoners scrabbled for the bread among the dirt and detritus coating the train car's floor, the officer laughing mockingly at the way they crawled about on all fours, with no shame or dignity.

Someone called from the platform, insisting they must share it out, and defiantly, a woman in her twenties shoved an entire hunk in her mouth. A few people nearby hissed or clucked in disapproval. Rachel shook her head wearily. How had it come to this?

"It didn't look very good anyway," Franz murmured in her ear, and from somewhere she found a smile.

"I wasn't hungry," she told him, which was true. Her nausea had at least kept her from feeling the familiar pangs of hunger, but when would they be given bread again? And how long would this journey be?

A few minutes later, the SS officer was shouting at them to get back on the train, his whip hurtling through the air once more, even though everyone was moving as fast as they could. They were like lambs to the slaughter, as she scrambled into the car after Franz. What if everyone resisted, rebelled? What if they all refused to get on the train?

Then, Rachel suspected, the SS would shoot them all. There might be a thousand Jews or more on this endless train to hell, but they had no power. No choice, but to keep going, and hope for the best.

Back on the train, Franz managed to find a space by the side for them to sit, with Rachel leaning against him, his arm around her. He'd even procured a crust of bread, which they took turns nibbling.

"How long have we been on this train?" Rachel wondered aloud.

He shrugged. "Twenty-four hours, maybe?"

"Where are we going, do you think?"

"Poland, perhaps."

Rachel tensed. "You mean Auschwitz."

"I don't think it matters, Rachel." His voice was gentle. "All the camps will be the same."

"Franz…" She twisted around to look at him. "Do you think…" She could barely make herself say the words. "Do you think they will kill us, when we get there?" Even now, she found it hard to believe, although considering all she'd endured, she supposed it shouldn't be. And yet to be killed, for no reason save that she was Jewish. It was so shocking, and yet it had become something to expect.

He gazed down at her gravely, his former fatalism replaced by a weary grief. "I don't know," he admitted. "It might be better if they do."

A soft cry escaped her as her hand crept toward her middle. "Don't *say* that."

"I'm sorry." He put his hand over hers. "I don't wish it so, God knows I don't, especially now that..." He put his hand over hers. "I want to live now more than I ever did before," he confessed, a throb of emotion in his voice. "For this little one, and for you." His voice choked and he steadied himself. "I just... don't know if it will be in our power."

"Nothing is in our power," Rachel reminded him sadly.

Franz squeezed her hand again and they sat in silence as the train rattled on its hellish journey.

They traveled for three days, with only one more stop for water and bread on a platform in the middle of the countryside.

It had been impossible to tell where they were, everyone blinking dazedly in the harsh sunlight, nothing around them but trees. Then, roughly seventy-two hours after they'd first boarded back in Westerbork, the train finally came to a stop and the doors were unbarred with the usual shouts of *Raus* and *Schnell*.

"Are we here?" Rachel asked in an uncertain whisper. She felt weak from hunger and dehydration, filthy and exhausted as well, and yet part of her would rather stay on this awful train than clamber out and face whatever was out there.

"It appears so." Franz put his arm around her. "We'll be all right," he told her with a small smile, although his eyes were dark with sorrow. "No matter what happens. I love you, Rachel."

It sounded terrifyingly like goodbye.

"I love you," she whispered back. She hugged him briefly as people began to push past them to clamber down off the train car while soldiers shouted for everyone to hurry.

We'll be all right. It didn't make sense, it probably wasn't true, and yet she clung to Franz's words, felt them like a promise, as she followed the rest of the passengers, the press of unwashed bodies making her dizzy, the tang of fear thick in the air, into the bright light of a beautiful summer's morning—and whatever fresh horror awaited them.

CHAPTER 20

JUNE 1944—AUSCHWITZ-BIRKENAU CONCENTRATION CAMP, POLAND

The train station's ramp was a crowded throng of confused and frightened humanity—people crying, clutching their children, calling out names of loved ones, or cringing beneath the shouts and whips of the SS guards.

For a second, Rachel's senses swam, and she was afraid she might pass out. Franz held her hand tightly as they tried to move down the platform, people pressing them on every side, and SS guards in black uniforms and gleaming boots shouting for everyone to move forward as Alsatians lunged on their leashes, snarling and slavering.

In the distance, Rachel saw a high fence of electrified barbed wire cutting off the horizon. Wooden watchtowers were positioned at either end, with armed guards standing on their platforms, rifles at the ready. It was clear there would be no escaping from a place such as this.

"*Schneller, schneller!*" *Faster, faster.*

The guards' voices were a guttural roar as Rachel and Franz were pushed forward by the crowd, everyone dirty and dazed from their three days on the train. "Leave your suitcases!" they shouted. "Throw them in the ditch!"

Rachel watched as those who had managed to bring their most precious possessions were forced, disconsolate, to simply throw them away. An elderly man was clutching the Torah scrolls he must have brought from his synagogue, adamantly refusing to throw the precious documents into the ditch. To let them touch the ground, Rachel knew, was considered a sin. The guard, shouting in his face, began to beat him about the head and shoulders with a truncheon, while the man swayed on his feet, blood trickling from his temple as he kept clutching the scrolls to him, until, exasperated more than angry, the guard pushed the man hard, so he fell back into the ditch, taking his scrolls with him. Rachel watched, horrified, as more suitcases were thrown on top of him; within a few seconds, he was buried beneath them.

"Rachel..." Franz's voice was low and insistent. "We need to keep going."

"*Schnell, schnell!*" another guard snapped out. "Those who can't walk, get on a truck. It will take you to the camp."

A *truck*... Exhausted from the journey, Rachel looked around for it, but Franz propelled her forward. "You don't want to get on a truck," he hissed.

"How do you know—"

"Because if you can't walk, you can't *work*." Grimly, he nodded toward the gates of black iron in the distance; *Arbeit Macht Frei* was visible worked into the iron above. *Work Makes You Free.* "It might not make us free," Franz told her, "but they must want us to work. We have to be healthy, Rachel, if we're going to survive this place."

Rachel's hand fluttered to her middle before she dropped it to her side. Was a pregnant woman considered healthy? And what about Franz's hand, two fingers still hopelessly twisted? Did they have any chance here at all?

She glanced back at the train, but Franz pushed her forward again.

"Don't look back," he commanded in a whisper.

But it was too late. She'd seen prisoners in shapeless, striped shirts and trousers standing in the train cars, tossing bodies out. Rachel swallowed a cry of shocked despair. How many people had died on that train?

And what if they were the lucky ones?

"Children must go on the trucks," a guard shouted in German. He held an Alsatian on a leash that kept lunging forward at the prisoners. One poor woman was savaged by the beast and the guard simply smirked. "Elderly people on the trucks as well. Quickly!" He pointed at the woman who had just been mauled by the dog, now clutching her bloodied arm, too shocked to weep. "You, on the truck. You won't be able to work like that."

It seemed that what Franz had suspected was true. They needed to be able to work.

"As long as we can stay together," Rachel whispered, watching, with tears gathering in her throat, as a toddler was ripped from a mother's arms and tossed carelessly onto a truck, hitting her head hard against the side. She lay there, unconscious, maybe even lifeless, as the mother screamed and wept, lunging forward to reach her child. As calmly as if he were lighting a cigarette, the SS officer withdrew his pistol from its holster and shot the woman in the head.

The crack of the gun echoed down the ramp, momentarily plunging everyone nearby into a hushed, horrified silence. Rachel watched, too shocked to move, as the woman fell to the ground, lifeless, until Franz squeezed her arm hard.

"Come on."

Numb with the sheer horror of it, Rachel let herself be propelled past the dead woman, toward the gates of the camp. What kind of place was this, what kind of *monsters* were these people, to shoot a mother in the head for simply wanting her child?

A choked sound escaped her, and she sucked in a hard breath. They'd entered hell, but they still needed to survive it. Somehow, some way, she needed to survive... for the sake of her unborn baby.

Inexorably, they were pushed by the crowd closer to the gates. Fear was like a living thing inside Rachel, creeping down her spine and crawling up her throat. How could they willingly go through those gates, into whatever horrors lay beyond?

Except, of course, they weren't willing.

They had no choice.

Feeling as if she were being sealed in a tomb, Rachel walked with Franz through the gates.

A guard inside was shouting more instructions. "Men to the left, women and children to the right. *Schneller, Schneller!*"

Rachel clutched Franz's arm. "Franz—"

"It's fine," he assured her. "We'll meet up on the other side."

He tried to move away but she clung to him, unable to bear the thought of letting him go now. They'd been through so much together, and now to be wrenched apart in a place such as this? It was too much; she simply couldn't let it happen. She *wouldn't*—and yet, as with everything else, she had no choice.

Quickly, Franz kissed her cheek. "Don't worry," he told her, his voice sounding strong and confident, the voice of the man she'd known and loved before Dachau, before the *St Louis*, before the occupation and beatings and having to hide. "I love you, Rachel."

He squeezed her arm and then strode toward the men's line.

Why, Rachel thought numbly as she watched him go, had that once more sounded like goodbye? Goodbye *forever*?

She watched as Franz moved up in the line of men; he had his right hand in his pocket, no doubt to hide his twisted fingers. *Oh God*, Rachel prayed, *Keep him safe...*

Someone prodded her from behind and she walked forward to join the line of women and children who had remained; the smaller children had already been taken on the truck… but to where? What was going to happen to them, to everyone?

Moments later, Rachel stood in front of a stern-faced doctor who sat behind a wooden table, a bored-looking SS officer standing smoking next to him.

"Name?" the doctor barked out.

Rachel licked her lips; her mouth was bone-dry, and her heart was thundering. "Rachel Blau."

"Age?"

She swallowed. "Thirty-one."

He glanced at her in cold-eyed assessment, his gaze raking over her body. Rachel stood up straight, her shoulders thrown back, her stomach sucked in. She prayed the man could not see that she was pregnant.

"What was your profession?" the SS officer barked.

She opened her mouth to say teacher and then, by some instinct, she thought of her time at the Smits' bakery and she changed it. "Baker," she told him as firmly as she could.

The man raised his eyebrows but said nothing as he threw his cigarette onto the yard and ground it with his heel. "To the right."

On shaky legs, Rachel walked to the right. Behind her, she saw a woman in her fifties who was silently weeping step up, shaking, to the table. The doctor didn't even ask her name.

"To the left," he snapped.

Rachel released a long, low breath. Had she been saved—yet for what? Dear God, for what?

"Line up, line up!" someone shouted. "Quickly! *Schneller!*"

It was, Rachel saw with some shock, a prisoner—a woman in a gray shapeless dress, but she held a truncheon in one hand, and she had the bored, bossy voice of a guard. How could this be?

"Get into rows of five," she snapped out. "And march!"

Hurriedly, women assembled themselves, while several other women prisoners watched over them, acting as guards.

"What is happening?" one woman asked in German, but the prisoner guard simply shook her head.

"Get in line."

In lines of five, the women began to march right back out the gates. Rachel threw a look behind her, but the line of men had moved on, and she could no longer see Franz. She glanced at the woman next to her, but she was staring straight ahead. No one spoke. No one, Rachel thought, dared.

They walked along the train ramp, now empty save for prisoners who were piling suitcases onto the open beds of several trucks. Rachel swallowed hard and looked away from the stack of dead bodies by one of the train cars. Her stomach churned and her head felt light. She hadn't eaten anything but a crust of black bread in three days. Above her, the sky was a deep blue, and tall evergreens fringed the horizon. The sun beat down relentlessly and sweat prickled between her shoulder blades. Her vision danced and she took a deep breath.

She could not pass out, she could *not*...

They walked on, past the ramp and down a dirt road lined with trees; in the distance, a bird trilled sweetly, the sound so incongruous with the reality of what was happening. Where were they going? Why had they left the camp?

After they'd walked about two miles, fear warring with exhaustion, another set of gates came into view. Wooden watchtowers framed a high fence of barbed wire. It was another camp.

They were ushered through the gates and into the hall of a large brick building. Several wooden tables had been set at the front, with women dressed in the dark jacket and skirt uniform of the SS-*Gefolge*—the women's branch of the SS—behind each one. Rachel had the strange sense of being a student again, ushered into an exam hall. But this exam, she feared, would be a matter of life and death.

At the first table, she was asked her name, age, and occupation again, and then a woman commanded her to strip.

"Leave all your clothes, including undergarments and shoes," she ordered. "It is a matter of hygiene."

Rachel looked around at the other women. Some were simply staring blankly ahead, while others were already starting to undress, fingers fumbling with buttons.

One of the prisoner guards landed a truncheon blow on a young woman's shoulder who hadn't moved.

"Start moving," she snapped, and the woman quickly began to undo the buttons of her dress.

Rachel followed suit, her fingers trembling so much it took three tries to undo the first button. Some women, she saw, were already naked. Everyone was pitifully thin, their ribs visible under their skin as they halfheartedly tried to shield themselves with their hands.

Rachel hurried to undo the rest of her buttons. As she slipped off her skirt, she felt the shard of emerald in her pocket and quickly she took it out, clasping it tightly between her fingers. Some of the women who had undressed quickly had moved onto the next table, where they were getting their heads shaved. She was not going to be able to keep anything, Rachel realized numbly—not her hair, not her clothes, and certainly not a valuable jewel, no matter how small. Yet to lose the one thing she had left that anchored her to her friends, to her sense of self, and most importantly, a flicker of hope in a place where surely none existed? She couldn't do it, no matter how foolhardy it might be to try to hold onto the precious emerald.

She glanced around and saw no one was looking at her; then, pretending to cough, she quickly slipped the sliver of emerald under her tongue, pushing it as far back into her mouth as she dared. God only knew what would happen to her if anyone found out what she had done.

She finished undressing and moved to the next table, taking

her hair from its bun, and bowing her head as a prisoner attacked it roughly with a razor, leaving her scalp stubbly and bare.

It was a strange feeling, to have no hair, a lightness that made her feel heavy inside. Her scalp stung from where the razor had gone too close and the air felt cool on the bare, chafed skin. Franz, she reflected, had always loved her hair—its chestnut color, the heaviness of it. Where was he now? No doubt he was suffering the same sort of indignities, but none of it mattered, she wouldn't let it, as long as he was *alive*.

At the next table, she was wiped down with antiseptic, the smell of it stinging her nostrils, its astringency burning her skin. Some part of Rachel became distant and numb to all these indignities; walking naked and shaven in front of smirking or bored guards was an experience too humiliating to endure, and so she'd removed herself from it, thinking instead of other, happier things. Her mother's *Apfelkuchen*. Dancing with Franz at a club in Berlin. The cherry blossoms along the Spaarne back in Haarlem...

Anything, anything but this.

At the next table, she was asked to hold out her arm. Rachel didn't realize what the woman was about to do until she saw the two needles, connected by a piece of wood. She gasped out loud from the pain as a number was tattooed into her skin—653126.

Rachel ran her fingers over it, the skin already red and swollen. She'd been marked forever, a fact that she felt, with a sudden ferocity that burned like the ink on her skin, shamed her captors, not her. Not a single one of the women here suffering these abuses so clearly designed to humiliate them was lessened by the Nazis' actions, Rachel decided. She would not allow them to be—not, at least, in the sanctity of her own mind.

With her head held high, Rachel walked onto the next and final table, where she was given a shapeless gray dress with buttons up the front, a pair of rough wooden clogs, and two yellow triangles to be sewn onto her dress with her new number written beneath. In this place, she no longer had a name.

Rachel put the dress on quickly, grateful at least to have something to wear. The fabric was rough and chafed her skin, already tender from the disinfectant, and the shoes were ill-fitting; she knew she would get blisters. There were no undergarments provided.

Once they were dressed, the women were ordered to form rows of five and they were marched from the building into the camp proper, past other buildings that looked like long, low sheds that had been hastily erected; there were gaps in the wood big enough in some cases for a cat or dog to get through. Rachel thought she saw a black cat slip between the boards like a shadow, only to realize when she'd glimpsed its bald tail that it was actually an enormous rat.

As discreetly as she could, she removed the sliver of emerald from under her tongue and slipped it into the toe of her shoe. Where she would hide it, how she would keep hold of it, she had no idea, but at least she'd got this far.

In front of one of the buildings, their prisoner guard ordered the women inside. Everyone went silently, dazed but also the tiniest bit hopeful, Rachel thought—if hope could even be found in a place like this. They were alive; they'd been given clothes; they had a place to sleep. Surely they weren't going to be killed now?

It was both wonderful and deeply dispiriting to think how little could give her hope now. How much she was willing to accept.

Inside the barracks, it was dark and gloomy, the air rank with the smell of human sweat. Rachel had to blink several times before her eyes adjusted to the lack of light—when they finally did, she saw bays with bunks built inside, three high, damp brick walls surrounding each one, so she imagined it felt, when you lay down, as if you had climbed into a coffin. A single, small wood stove heated the entire room; in summer, it was stifling, but in winter, she imagined it would be deathly cold. The barracks were empty now, save for the women who had been ordered inside. Everyone else, Rachel supposed, was working, although she had no idea what that entailed.

She took a deep breath and then wished she hadn't; the air was truly rank, catching in her throat and making her empty stomach heave. She pressed a hand to her middle and then dropped it, afraid of giving anything away, although, in the gloom of barracks, she didn't think anyone could even see her.

"I suppose we find a bunk," a woman standing near her said after a moment. She spoke Dutch, and she glanced at a few other women huddling together close by. "They're Hungarian, I think," she told Rachel. "They look like they've had a hard time. They cleared out all the cities there in one fell swoop." She shook her head, grimacing. "Still, they're lucky to be here. They usually just send the Hungarians straight through." She had a worldly air, and despite the fact her head was shaven, and she was wearing the same shapeless gray dress Rachel was, she could imagine her in silk and furs, tossing her head as diamonds glinted in her ears.

"Straight through..." Rachel repeated. She was starting to feel stupid.

The woman gave her a look that was part exasperation, part pity. "Didn't you learn anything on the train? To the gas chambers."

"Gas chambers?" Rachel stared at her blankly. Yes, she'd heard whispers of Jews of being sent east and never coming back, of even being killed en masse, but in *gas chambers*? "Do you mean..." She found she couldn't go on.

"This is a *killing* station," the woman replied matter-of-factly. "A death camp. They'll work us for a while, and then when we've been wrung out and ceased being useful, they'll kill us. Most of the people on that train have probably already died."

Rachel's stomach hollowed out. "How do you know all this?"

The woman gave her a hard-eyed look. "Because I listen, and I take note. And I put two and two together and come up with a very dispiriting four." She sighed. "I mean, what did you *think* they are doing here? Throwing a garden party?"

"No, no, of course not." Rachel passed a shaky hand over her face. *Gas chambers...* Had Franz been chosen for that grim fate? Was he already dead?

"Did you come with someone?" the woman asked, her tone softening only a little.

Rachel gulped and nodded. "My husband."

"A young man? He should be all right... for now."

The room swam and Rachel stumbled over to a bunk and sat down hard on it, dropping her head into her hands. Suddenly, it was all too much. She couldn't take anything more, not one single thing. She simply couldn't.

God will give you the strength in the moment. Where was her strength? she wondered despondently. What was the point of even having any, if they were all going to be killed anyway, sooner or later, like this woman said?

A sob escaped her, and she sucked in a breath, determined not to reveal her weakness. She might not be strong, but she didn't want to be that weak.

She lifted her head from her hands to look at the woman standing before her. The other women had moved further into the barracks and were huddled together, choosing bunks. "Did you come with anyone?" Rachel asked.

The woman tossed her head. "No. Everyone I've loved has already died. My mother and father in the *Jodenbuurt*, from typhoid." Her lips firmed into a hard, unforgiving line. "My fiancé beaten to death in front of my eyes two years ago, when he caught the eye of an SS officer who didn't like the look of him."

Rachel pressed her fist to her lips. "I'm sorry."

The woman shrugged. "Everyone has a story." She met Rachel's weary gaze with something close to a glare. "And the truth is, *no one* is getting out of here alive."

"The war will be over soon," Rachel protested feebly. She wanted to believe that, but in a place like this it felt almost impossible. They were deep within Nazi territory; the Allies might be liberating France or Belgium right now, but that was a thousand miles away, and it felt as if it might as well be a million.

The woman let out a hard laugh. "Do you really think they'll let us just walk out of here? Once the Germans accept they're losing the war, they'll burn this place to the ground, and us with it." She shook her head slowly. "We're really the unlucky ones, I'm afraid."

Rachel tried to summon a tired laugh but only managed a huff of sound. "And who are the lucky ones?" she asked.

"The dead," the woman replied bleakly. "At least they're not suffering any more." She glanced out the doorway, from which the only light filtered in, barely piercing the gloom. "Death, when it comes, might be a relief."

With her toe, Rachel nudged the sliver of emerald in her shoe, letting its presence imbue her with strength. For the sake of the little life beating inside her, she did not want to die. Somehow, some way, she would find a way to survive this dark and evil place.

Somehow—even if right then she could not imagine how.

CHAPTER 21

AUGUST 1944—AUSCHWITZ-BIRKENAU

The bakehouse of the Auschwitz camp was sweltering from the ovens that baked fresh, white loaves for the SS guards and officers every day. Rachel had been working there since her second day, and she knew she was fortunate to be doing so, even if life in Birkenau was bleaker and more dire than she ever could have imagined.

Eva, the Dutch woman she'd spoken to in the barracks on that first day, had warned her well enough, but even so, Rachel had not quite been able to believe, or grasp, the extent of the horrors that their Nazi guards would soon visit on them. That evening, the rest of the women in their barracks had tramped back, gray-faced with exhaustion, few able to summon so much as a smile for the newcomers, although Rebekah, an older woman from Dresden, gave them some advice.

"Best not to have a lower bunk... the rats will get at you. Bread is everything... We're all honest." She'd glanced darkly at the bunks at the far end of the barracks, the worst place in winter, she'd already told them because it was so far from the barracks' small stove. "Maybe not the Russians," she muttered.

"God knows what any of them think. They can't speak German, and they live like beasts."

"Surely not..." Rachel had begun, only to fall silent at the woman's quelling look. It was not for her to challenge the hierarchy of the prisoners' system, and she soon learned that there was one, with Soviets at the bottom, Poles and Hungarians just above, and Germans and other Western Europeans at the top. But, at the end of the day, Rachel thought sadly, they were all Jews. Surely they didn't need to sow more division when their Nazi tormentors were doing it for them?

Because, she soon learned, the guards delighted in creating division between the prisoners. They'd assigned fellow Jews to be their guards, known as kapos, and many of them were even more savage than the Nazis themselves, something Rachel thought she would never understand. For their cruelty, they received perks from their Nazi superiors—cigarettes, alcohol, civilian clothes taken from the transports. Some of them tried to be kind, while others relished their pathetic modicum of power.

At roll call every morning, standing for up to an hour or more in the predawn mist, the SS and kapos sometimes liked to pick out one poor soul for torment, and encouraged others to join in whatever punishment was being meted out—blows from a truncheon or the butt of a pistol, a savaging by one of the cruel Alsatians. If someone didn't, they were as likely to be given the same punishment—or worse.

And yet, amidst these sufferings, there was solidarity. Eva, despite her cold-hearted cynicism, had become something of a friend. Rebekah was like a mother, if a wearied, sometimes callous one, and the evenings in the barracks or out in the yard, the only free time they ever had, were, Rachel felt, a time when peace could not quite be grasped but could almost be seen, somewhere in the distance, as ephemeral as a will-o'-the-wisp but still *there*.

She often found herself thinking of Corrie and Betsie ten

Boom, and wondering if they were suffering in a camp like this. Maybe they were in Birkenau itself, for it was a camp only for women, while the men remained at Auschwitz, two miles away. Sometimes, during roll call, when all the women were called to stand in the central yard like an army of shapeless, ghost-like skeletons, Rachel searched the rows for a familiar face, but she never saw one. And even if she did, she wondered if she would even recognize them now. Her own mother might be in Birkenau, God help her, but Rachel wasn't sure if she'd recognize her in a shapeless dress, her head shaven, her face hollowed out to the bare bones of her skull. No one looked entirely human in this place, and yet their humanity was all they had to hold onto.

As the weeks and then months had passed, Rachel longed for news of Franz. Every morning she, with the other workers of the kitchen kommando, walked the two miles to the Auschwitz camp, and she searched the gangs of men she saw heading out to their own work, digging ditches or building roads, all of them with slumped shoulders and shuffling steps. She never caught sight of Franz.

Once through the camp's gates, she did her best to peer into barracks, squinting into the distance, holding her breath, *hoping*... but she never got so much as a glimpse. Still, she refused to entertain the torturous suspicion that she did not see him because he wasn't there.

He *had* to be alive, Rachel told herself, because she *felt* it, just as Eva had felt when her own fiancé had died. If Franz had died, she would know. Somehow, she told herself, she would know.

Her work in the bakehouse was, she soon discovered, seen as a sort of privilege, as it was considered easier work than in a factory or on a farm, but working in such terrifying proximity to her captors filled Rachel with a heavy, dragging dread. These were not people who were kindly, or reasonable, or even sane.

They acted out of boredom, they tortured for pleasure, they killed for sport.

She'd seen it far too many times already—the lazy lifting of a pistol, pulling the trigger to end some poor soul's life with a sigh of no greater feeling than exasperation. The gleam in their eyes when they unleashed one of their horrible dogs or dragged someone out of line to be beaten to death. The idle conversation she overheard in the canteen when she'd had to deliver the bread, how they complained about the stink of the dead bodies or how ugly the prisoners were to look at, with their shaved heads and starving bodies, told her enough.

She did her best to stay in the bakehouse, kneading dough and manning the ovens, rather than be sent out to the administrators' canteen, where the guards and officers of the SS lounged, chatting and laughing like any other men at work, yet with eyes, Rachel thought, that looked as dead as the bodies they complained about, pulled from the gas chambers and shoved into crematoria, the systematic disposal of hundreds or even thousands every day. Although she hadn't seen such things herself, everyone at camp knew about them, and the bakehouse was close enough to the crematoria that the greasy smoke from their evil chimneys stayed in her lungs and coated her hair and skin.

Once, when Rachel had delivered some fresh loaves to the canteen, she'd seen one of the servers trip. The poor woman had nearly spilled hot coffee into the lap of an officer. A few drops had landed on his boots, and without a second's hesitation or thought, he'd whipped out his pistol and pressed it to the poor woman's temple. She'd stood there, shaking, her own hands scalded and already blistering from the spilled coffee, before he'd burst into laughter and put his pistol away. Then he'd made her kneel on all fours and lick the coffee up from the floor with her tongue like a dog.

No, Rachel did not want to catch the eye of a man like that.

Every night, before she headed back to her barracks at Birkenau, she and the others in the bakehouse were searched for stolen bread. If they had so much as a single stale crust hidden on them, they were likely to be whipped or worse. Rachel had seen no one risk it, although she knew some did. Bread was the currency of camp, and people traded it for information, for cigarettes, sometimes even for medicine or other unheard-of luxuries like chocolate. Rachel had no idea how or where people procured such things; she ate her small, hard roll with her bowl of watery soup with a few rotten vegetables swimming in it and kept her head down. She could not afford to risk any undue attention, not with this baby growing steadily inside her.

Two months on from her arrival, Rachel's bump had swelled noticeably. At night, she lay in her bunk—four of them shared the single mattress draped over a wooden board, its straw filling having long ago disintegrated to dust—and cradled it, silently praying over the blessed life within her. By day, she did her best to hide her shape underneath the loose dress, turning away from any prying eyes when she could. So far, thank God, no one had noticed.

When they did...

Rachel could not bear to think about that.

There was a so-called maternity ward at Birkenau, although to call it such was a travesty. The babies born there were either taken away to be adopted by Germans if they looked Aryan enough; otherwise, they were drowned in a bucket of dirty water outside the barracks.

"Why would they keep Jewish babies?" Eva had demanded when Rachel had expressed distress at learning such gruesome news. "They can't work."

"But *babies*..."

"The sooner you realize how evil these people are, the better off you'll be," Eva had told her shortly. "Hope is a dangerous thing, Rachel."

"Hope," Rachel had replied quietly, "is all we have."

And she *did* hope—stubbornly, desperately, clinging to it like her only anchor in a drowning sea. Whispers had traveled through the camp that the Allies had landed in France—when, no one knew, but they were marching eastward. The Soviets too, were making progress, although everyone expressed trepidation at the notorious Red Army arriving at the walls of the camp.

"Surely," Eva had remarked with a shrug, "they can't treat us worse than the Nazis have?"

And yet, as Rachel stood at morning call, doing her best not to sway with exhaustion, or sat on her bunk in the evening listening to others chat, some women filled with hope, others with despair, she wondered when their liberation would come. Would it ever happen? Auschwitz-Birkenau seemed so far from everything. There was a village nearby, she'd heard, but nobody there seemed to want to know about what was happening at the camp. All else was endless forest beneath a bright blue sky, not a soul in sight save for the guards in the watchtowers, tracking their every move.

"Inspection!" a guard barked, and quickly Rachel stepped away from the oven for the nightly search of the kitchen kommando. She'd come to dread this daily pat-down, for fear her pregnancy would be revealed. She was now, she suspected, five months gone. How long until one of the guards noticed?

Please God, she prayed, as she did every evening. *Let this day pass*.

The guard stood in front of her, her eyes narrowed as she patted Rachel down before turning out her pockets. Rachel stood as tall and straight as she could, doing her best to suck in her stomach. She could see her bump herself, outlined underneath the rough gray fabric, but plenty of women had stomachs swollen from starvation or disease, and she wasn't that big.

"All right. Move on."

Quietly, she released a sigh of relief as she moved past. She'd made it through another day.

Of course, she knew that one day she wouldn't. One day she would be discovered, and marched to the maternity ward, and then she would have to give birth to this child in its squalid confines, and when her darling child was only a few hours, or even just minutes old, he or she would be ripped away from her —either to be given to another family, or far worse, drowned. How could she bear it?

God gives you strength in the moment.

And that moment, thankfully, had not yet come to pass.

Slowly, her feet aching in the wooden clogs—they had given her blisters, just as she'd feared—she walked with her fellow workers back to Birkenau. It was a beautiful summer's day, the relentless heat of the sun beginning to lessen as it sank toward the horizon. What would it be like to walk these two miles in winter? Rachel wondered. She had heard the Polish winters were bitter, especially as she knew they would not be given any proper winter's clothing.

By winter, she would have had the baby. By winter, God willing, the war might be over. That was her hope, her only hope... that this wretched war would end before she had to give birth.

Twilight was settling on the trees, turning the sky violet, with vivid orange streaks of sunset, when the women lined up for their evening roll call. Sometimes, simply for the sheer perversity of it, their guards would force them to stand there unmoving for hours. Once, they'd had to stand all night; when someone had swayed, those next to her had done their best to hold them up. It had been a long, painful night, with work the next morning as always; Rachel had existed in a haze of exhaustion and burned herself badly on one of the ovens as a result.

Now she did her best to enjoy the balmy air, the first stars glimmering on the violet horizon. There was beauty even at

Birkenau, she reflected—although, admittedly, precious little of it.

She scanned the rows of women, looking, as always, for someone she recognized. Frieda, Corrie, Betsie, her dear mother. She prayed both that they were there and not there, for heaven knew she would spare them this life if she could, and yet she longed to see a familiar face.

Her gaze settled on a woman across the courtyard—her head shaven, her body shapeless beneath the dress. Was there something familiar about her heart-shaped face, that pointed chin? Rachel narrowed her eyes, wishing she could see better in the fading light.

She must be mad, she thought, mentally shaking her head at herself. She'd almost thought she'd seen Sophie. Sophie Weiss, who was the last person she knew who would be in Birkenau. Her friend was safe, four thousand miles away in Washington DC, working for a Jewish aid society. She *couldn't* be here...

The woman she'd been staring at straightened, her own gaze moving across the rows and Rachel caught her breath as their eyes met and the woman frowned, her jaw dropping before she snapped it shut. Realization flared through Rachel, a wave of joyful incredulity. It *was* Sophie! Sophie, *here*, but dear God, how...?

It was another twenty minutes before roll call finally ended, and the night had drawn in as the women headed back to their barracks for their precious few hours of free time. Rachel pushed through the crowds, hurrying to find Sophie from across the courtyard, heedless of the attention she might draw to herself. Their guards had wandered away to their own quarters, thankfully. She was safe, for now.

"*Rachel!*"

Rachel whirled around and there was Sophie hurrying toward her, tears pouring down her cheeks as she held out her arms. Rachel ran to her, and both laughing and weeping, the two women embraced.

"I can't believe it's *you!*" Sophie exclaimed, hugging her tightly. "Dear heaven, but it's good to see a friend in this place."

"How is it that you are in this dreadful place?" Rachel asked in wonder. "You're meant to be in America..."

"It's a long story." Sophie took her by the arm. "Come, let's find some quiet place to sit and talk where we won't be overheard. I have so much to tell you."

The evening was warm enough to stay outside; Sophie led her to the side of her barracks, a sheltered spot away from any prying eyes or listening ears.

"I'm sorry you're here," Sophie said somberly once they were seated, taking Rachel's hand in her own. "As glad as I am to see you, I wouldn't wish this place on anyone, not even my enemy. And, heaven knows, we have a great deal of enemies now." She sighed as she brushed the last of her tears from her cheeks. "How long have you been here?"

"About two months, I think. I've lost track of time, but we were arrested in June."

"You and Franz?"

Rachel nodded. "I haven't had any word of him since we were separated on the first day."

"He's young and strong, he could be all right," Sophie said, and Rachel just nodded, not wanting to explain about his ruined hand.

"What about you?" she asked. "How on earth did you get to be here?"

"Oh, well..." Sophie sighed. "I'm here as a Jew, the same as you, which is a good thing for me, because if they knew who I really was I'd be tortured and killed."

"*What?*" Rachel breathed, not understanding.

"I was a spy," Sophie confessed in a low whisper. "For the OSS—the United States' Office of Strategic Services. I was working undercover in France, out of Lyon. I met Hannah there—"

"*Hannah!*" Rachel exclaimed, amazed. "How is that even possible?"

"We were both dumbstruck when we saw each other," Sophie agreed with a small, sad laugh. "But Hannah's sister, Lotte, was in a home for Jewish children, and it was raided by the Gestapo. We went to warn them, but we were caught as we were running away." Her eyes darkened with remembered pain. "Hannah managed to escape, but Lotte didn't, and I was shot and captured." She pulled her dress away from her collarbone to reveal a patch of lumpy, pinkened scar tissue on her shoulder. "They arrested me and sent me to the transit camp at Drancy, as they assumed I was just another Jew. I had papers that said I was a French gentile—false, but they were good forgeries—but, in any case, they didn't care. I was put with all the other Jews and sent onto here... I arrived last month." A sigh escaped her, long and low. "I can't bear to think what happened to Lotte. I looked for her in Drancy, but someone told me that the children from Izieu only stayed there for a few hours. They were put onto the first train to Auschwitz and marched straight to the gas chambers."

"Oh, Sophie." Rachel pictured little Lotte with her blond braids and shy smile, and her heart ached. "Are you sure?"

"I can't be sure of anything, but God knows these monsters don't have need of children."

A soft gasp escaped Rachel before she could hold it in, and she rested one hand on her middle. "Don't say that," she whispered, and shocked realization flashed across Sophie's face.

"Rachel... are you *pregnant?*"

Rachel nodded. "I've kept it secret so far, but I'm nearly five months, now. I won't be able to for much longer."

"Oh, *Rachel.*" Sophie's face twisted with pity. It was clear she knew as well as Rachel what happened to babies born at Birkenau. "I'm sorry."

"I'm not," Rachel replied fiercely, her hand curving around the shape of her child. "This baby is a blessing, and I will never think otherwise. Franz feels the same."

"He knows?"

"I told him on the train here."

Sophie sighed and rested her head back against the barracks wall. "Maybe the war will end before you give birth," she said, although she did not sound too hopeful. "When I was at Drancy, I heard that the Allies had invaded through Normandy. By the time I'd left, they'd taken most of northern France and were on their way to Paris."

"They were?" Rachel exclaimed. "We heard rumors, but... no one knows anything for sure." For the first time in a long while, her spirits lifted. "But isn't that such good news?" she cried. "They could be here in a few weeks—"

"It's a thousand miles from Normandy to Poland," Sophie reminded her quietly.

"But the Germans will have to give up!" Rachel insisted. "Now that they've started losing ground."

Sophie shrugged. "God only knows what they'll do. Hitler's mad, they say. He'll let every last German be bombed or shot or starved to death before he surrenders."

"Including us," Rachel replied softly. She pushed the thought away; such doom mongering wouldn't help her, or her baby. "But maybe not," she insisted staunchly.

A tired smile flickered across Sophie's face. Rachel recalled how young she'd thought Sophie was, back on the *St Louis*. Young and pretty and more than a little naïve. Looking at the lines etched deeply on Sophie's face, the weary knowledge in her eyes, Rachel knew her friend had been forever changed... just as she had.

Impulsively, Sophie leaned forward and caught Rachel's

hand. "You're right, a baby is something to celebrate," she said. "And even if the war isn't over by the time he or she makes his arrival, maybe we can make another plan. But first we need to see if we can find out what's happened to Franz."

Rachel's gaze widened in surprise. "You know how to do that?"

Sophie gave her an impish smile, a ghostly reminder of the girl she used to be. Teasingly, she tapped the side of her nose. "I have my ways." She squeezed Rachel's hand. "It's so good to see you, Rachel."

"And you," Rachel replied fervently. Especially if Sophie could help her find Franz...

God *had* given her the strength for this moment, Rachel thought with a ripple of wonder. He'd given her Sophie.

CHAPTER 22

SEPTEMBER 1944—AUSCHWITZ-BIRKENAU

"Be behind the bakehouse at seven, right at the end of your shift."

"What—" Rachel whirled around, but the man who had hissed her the message had walked on, as if oblivious. He was one of the few prisoners who walked freely between the camps; he wore his own clothes, and he had his own hair. Compared to the army of workers with their shapeless clothes and shaved heads, he looked unsettlingly human, almost like one of the guards.

Rachel was walking between the camps on her way to work with the rest of the bakehouse and kitchen kommando. Mist hovered over the ground in gossamer strands and the leaves of the trees lining the road were just beginning to turn to gleaming shades of russet and ochre. It was a beautiful day, and Rachel had been trying her best to enjoy it, but now her mind whirled with new thoughts, lurching between wild hope and deep fear.

Be behind the bakehouse at seven.

For what? What if it was some kind of trap?

Since she'd first seen Sophie, her friend had been trying to get news of Franz. She had her ways, she'd said, and Rachel had known better than to inquire about them. It seemed Sophie, thanks to her resistance work, had some sort of connections at camp. Rachel was simply glad she was willing to use them to help. And if she could find out about Franz...

Her heart leapt at the thought. She already knew she would do whatever it took to be behind the bakehouse at the end of her shift.

The day passed slowly, every minute feeling like an age, as Rachel mixed and kneaded and baked, her face flushed from the heat, her mind racing all the time, wondering, hoping...

Finally, it was almost time to leave. The other women were tidying up, getting the bakehouse ready for the next day. Rachel took a bucket of rubbish and slipped outside to empty it behind the bakehouse. As she rounded the corner, she glimpsed a man with his back to her. He wore a civilian jacket over his prisoner's uniform, and he still had his hair. Was it a kapo? Had this been a trap, after all?

Rachel faltered in her step and then the man turned, and she gasped out loud.

"Franz!"

He rushed toward her, pulling her into his arms.

Dazed with incredulity, Rachel wrapped her arms around him. He felt the same and yet he smelled different—a strange, sweetish odor clinging to his clothes and skin.

He pulled back first, his hands framing her face as he gazed hungrily down at her. "You're all right? The baby, too?"

"Yes, so far. They haven't discovered I'm pregnant." She swallowed, not wanting to explain her fears of what would happen if they did. "I can't believe it's *you*," she whispered. "You've survived. I was so afraid—"

"I've survived," Franz agreed, but he sounded so grim that inside Rachel quailed.

"Franz..."

"Don't ask me," he told her roughly. "I'll... I'll tell you, but don't ask me. I just need to know that you're all right."

She nodded, troubled by the bleakness of his voice, the anguish in his eyes, reminding her of those days after Dachau. "I'm all right."

"Good." Slowly, he released her and then fumbled in his pocket, withdrawing a crumpled packet of cigarettes, shocking her. How, she wondered numbly, did Franz have cigarettes, a jacket, his own *hair*? The only Jews who had those things were kapos or collaborators.

"Franz, what—" she began, and then stopped abruptly. Did she really want to know?

"I know what you're wondering," he said, gesturing to his jacket. He lit his cigarette and inhaled deeply before blowing out a plume of smoke. "When I left you, they pulled me aside right away. I thought that was it for me, right then. It was over." He took another tense drag of his cigarette. "But then I saw they'd pulled a few of us aside—all young men, healthy looking, strong. I thought, they aren't going to kill young men. They hadn't seen my hand." He paused, his gaze distant and unfocused, the way it had been when he'd first been released from Dachau.

A different kind of terror struck at Rachel's heart. She'd been so afraid that Franz might have been killed in Auschwitz, but she hadn't considered the other option—the far more terrible one that he'd so bleakly told her about back in Haarlem. *It's one thing to lose your country, another to lose your life, or worse... your soul.*

Franz, Rachel thought numbly, looked as if he'd lost his soul.

"They pulled us aside," he continued after a moment, his voice flat and toneless, his gaze still distant. "Gave us separate accommodation, away from everyone else. Better food, better clothes, cigarettes, even alcohol."

Rachel shook her head slowly. Considering her own experience, she could not understand such a thing. The SS did not give such unimaginable boons to Jews for no reason. "But why..." she whispered.

"Because of what they wanted us to do." He turned his gaze back to her, now full of bleak horror. "They call us *Hilflinge*. Helpers. Because that is what we are."

Rachel swallowed dryly. "Tell me," she whispered.

"The bodies," he explained in the same lifeless tone. "We take care of the bodies. We drag them out of the gas chambers, and then we stuff them into the crematoria. Day after day after day." His voice choked and he passed a hand over his face before he hurled his cigarette to the ground, grinding it beneath his heel. "There are so many, Rachel. Men. Women. Children. The elderly... *babies*..." He glanced at her bump meaningfully, and she tasted the acid tang of bile as she shook her head in instinctive denial.

"*No...*"

"The babies, they die in their mothers' arms. Some of the adults' fingers are bloody from scratching at the walls, trying to get out. We stand outside and we hear their moans, their sobs. When I go to sleep at night, when I *can* sleep, I still hear them."

Rachel felt as if her insides had hollowed out. She could not think of anything to say. She swallowed hard before making herself speak. "You had no choice, Franz," she whispered. "If you'd refused, you know you would have been killed."

"I'd rather be killed," he told her. "At least, that is what I tell myself, and yet here I am."

"Someone else would have to do it, if you didn't," she argued, knowing how unconvinced she sounded. The job he was talking about was truly hideous. His only choice *would* be death… but was that the right choice, or at least the nobler one, than being so complicit in such atrocities?

"I've come to realize it's a fitting punishment," he told her as he flicked his cigarette butt to the ground and stamped on it. "My penance, in a way—my own personal hell. I tormented myself for selling out my comrades and friends, so this is the logical conclusion of what happened back in Dachau." He gave her a grim smile, his eyes dark with torment. "I'm just following through."

"Oh, Franz." Rachel brushed at the tears spilling down her cheeks. "The war is going to be over soon. Everyone is saying so."

"Rachel…" He paused, his throat working, and then he reached for her hand with his good one. His fingers were icily cold. "Rachel, it won't end for me. They won't let it."

"Don't say that—"

"We are *Geheimnisträger*—the bearers of secrets. They won't let us live, because then we could tell the rest of the world the truly evil acts they have committed."

"We could all tell them that!" Rachel argued.

"Yes, but I've *seen* it." His voice throbbed as he squeezed her hand. "I've *tasted* it, Rachel. The smell clinging to my skin— I saw how you noticed it, when you first embraced me. That is the smell of death, of burning flesh. It will never leave me."

"This will be over," Rachel insisted, clutching at his hand, her voice rising almost querulously. "It will be over, and you will forget. You will heal. Franz—"

"I'd like to believe so," he said quietly as he released her hand. "But the truth is, I don't. We're not the first *Sonderkommando* unit, you know. Some say there is a new one every two months. Well, it has been over two months, so my time has to be running out."

"Franz, *don't*," Rachel implored, and now she sounded shrill. "Don't," she said again, more quietly. The way he spoke reminded her so much of being back in Heijplaat, when he'd been so despairing, or at the start of the occupation, when he'd practically seen their graves. But it was worse now, *far* worse, because she feared he was right. He was standing in the valley of the shadow of death. She could feel it, and she knew he could, too, like a cloud passing over them, blocking out all the light. "*Please,*" she whispered.

"I love you," he told her. "That's what matters. Remember that."

Rachel stared at him, memorizing the lines of his face, the fullness of his lips, the glint of his hazel eyes that had now so dimmed. "I will always remember," she whispered.

"And stay alive, Rachel, for the sake of our baby."

"I will, Franz. I promise. And you too—"

He gave a little shake of his head as he reached out a hand and rested it gently on the swell of her bump, his eyes closed. "Can you feel the baby kick?" he asked in a low, aching voice.

Tears thickened in Rachel's throat as she nodded. "Sometimes," she whispered.

"That's good. She's strong."

Rachel tried to smile. "You think it's a girl?"

Franz opened his eyes. "I hope so. Like you."

"Oh, Franz..." She didn't know what to say. She didn't want this to feel so much like goodbye all over again, and one that felt even more final. "The war will be over soon," she said again, brokenly.

He smiled and dropped his hand from her bump. "Yes," he said. "It will. Stay strong, Rachel. You can survive."

"You can too," she insisted, more fiercely now. She wouldn't let him give into the fatalism that had once dogged him back in Haarlem, when the war had first started. Not now, when its end was finally so close.

"I have to go."

"No—" And yet Rachel knew she needed to, as well. She had been gone too long already; she couldn't be missed.

Franz stepped towards her, his hands sliding around her waist. He brushed a kiss against her lips, and she closed her eyes. In that moment, a thousand memories tumbled through her mind in a painfully bittersweet kaleidoscope—that first day, when Franz had asked her about his article and captured her heart; when they'd run out of the registry office, newly married and laughing like children; when he'd come back from Dachau blank-eyed and broken; when he'd nearly flung himself out of a window and ended his life. When they'd clung to each other on the train to this hellish place, before they'd been torn apart.

They'd been through so much, and they'd endured it all. In some ways, their marriage was stronger now than it had ever been, for they *knew* the depths of each other, both the shameful and the honorable, the strengths and the weaknesses. It was a good marriage, a solid one, but it also felt, terrifyingly, as if it was about to be over.

Franz broke the kiss and stepped away from her. Dusk was falling, the shadows lengthening and the air growing chilly as he gave her one last sorrowful smile and then turned around and walked quickly away before she could find the strength to say goodbye.

Rachel remained there for a moment, struggling to compose herself even as part of her felt strangely, horribly numb. Then she turned and walked back into the bakehouse, where the other women were assembling for their nightly search. For once, Rachel didn't feel the usual heightened fear as the kapo patted her down. She was thinking only of Franz, her unfocused gaze on the memory of him standing in front of her, when the kapo gave a short gasp and Rachel returned her gaze to the other woman's surprised face. Her hands were cradling Rachel's bump.

For a taut second, they simply stared at each other. Something like pity flashed across the woman's face and Rachel held her breath. She'd been discovered. Moments ago, she'd promised Franz she would stay strong and survive, and now...

"Move along," the woman said roughly, dropping her hands. She jerked her head. "Next."

Rachel stared at her in blank shock before she did as she'd said and moved along, her mind reeling. Had the kapo just kept her secret? *Protected* her?

And how long would it last?

Later that evening, Rachel went in search of Sophie.

"I don't know how you did it, but I saw Franz," she told her friend as she found her in the courtyard by her barracks. She grasped her hands. "Thank you."

Sophie squeezed her hands in return, her face softened with a sympathy that made Rachel realize she probably knew already what Franz had to do to survive. "He's all right?" she asked.

Rachel swallowed. "I don't know," she admitted. "He..." She shook her head.

"It's hard," Sophie said softly. "The Nazis... they make us do the most terrible things."

"I just want him to survive," Rachel whispered. "But..."

"It won't be long now," Sophie told her with another squeeze. "The Soviets have crossed into Hungary, and the Americans into Germany. The German army is being cut off in both directions."

"They have?" Rachel's stomach did a little flip of hopeful wonder. Could their rescuers really be that close? "Sophie," she asked, "how do you know these things?"

Sophie gave a small, secretive smile. "I have my ways."

"So you say," Rachel conceded, "and you must, but... is it *dangerous*, Sophie?" She reached out to grasp her friend's hand. "To get that information?" It surely had to be.

"It's always good to be careful," Sophie answered with another quick squeeze of Rachel's fingers. "But I am careful. You don't need to worry about that."

Rachel nodded. "I won't, then," she promised with a shaky smile. There was certainly enough to worry about already.

September drifted into October. The days became cold, the nights colder. Rachel soon learned how little heat the potbellied stove in the center of their barracks produced, and she was glad for the warmth of her shared bunk, cramped as it was with four of them pressed together.

As the weeks passed, the mood in the camp became taut with expectation, fraught with fear. The guards and officers turned tetchy, as likely to shoot a prisoner in the head as snap at them. Whispers ran through both Auschwitz and Birkenau of camps further east that were already being emptied as the Eastern Front collapsed, and the Germany army was forced into retreat.

Jubilation warred with terror. "It's almost over," one prisoner would whisper gleefully, while another would shake their head in sorrow, muttering how the Nazis would never let them go.

Through it all, Rachel did her best to hold onto her hope, for as she'd told Eva back at the beginning, it was the only thing she had. She was over six months pregnant, and she'd managed to avoid scrutiny. For whatever reason, the kapo in the bakehouse was willing to keep her secret. If the Soviets really were already marching through Poland... surely it was only a matter of time, and not much time at that?

And then, at the end of October, time ran out.

CHAPTER 23

OCTOBER 1944—AUSCHWITZ-BIRKENAU

"Behind the bakehouse, at the end of your shift. Tonight."

This time it was a woman who whispered it, as she passed Rachel in roll call. How did she know? *What* did she know?

Was she going to be able to see Franz again?

Rachel's heart leaped with both hope and fear as she went about her business. It was late October, and the very air seemed to snap with tension. Everyone knew the Germans were losing more and more ground, but no one wanted to admit it—not the Nazi guards, and not the prisoners, who feared retribution for so much as a single look askance. Everyone was keeping their head down, scurrying to and fro, trying not to be noticed.

If only they could hold out to the end of the war, Rachel thought over and over again. It was coming. It surely had to be coming? And yet the days marched on.

But now, she thought, at least she'd be able to see Franz...

Once again, Rachel used the pretext of taking out trash to slip behind the bakehouse. It was already dark, shadows hiding the rats that nosed about, and so she walked carefully.

A man was waiting, his back to her, his hands in her pockets. Rachel started forward. "Franz..."

The man turned around. But it wasn't Franz.

Rachel's breath came out in a quick, shocked rush. The man in front of her was tall and lanky, his hair darker than Franz's, with soulful eyes and full lips that were now curved downward in a grimace of sympathy.

Rachel pressed a hand to her heart. "*No...*" she whispered, for she already knew.

"I'm sorry," the man told her. His German was accented; she thought he was probably Polish. "I promised Franz I would tell you if—if anything happened to him."

For a second, Rachel swayed where she stood. She flung a hand out to the rough brick wall of the building to steady herself, breathing slowly in and out. She shook her head, an instinctive denial, even though the truth was staring her right in the face; it was reflected in the dark sorrow of this stranger's eyes.

"What happened?" she whispered.

"He was brave," the stranger told her. "You must understand that."

"Brave?"

"There was a revolt," the man explained in a low voice. "Franz was part of organizing it—a few dozen of the other *Sonderkommando* attacked the SS and the kapos. They had axes, knives, a few guns and grenades they'd smuggled in. They managed to kill three and injure a dozen more." He let out a small, resigned sigh. "Of course, it would never come to anything. We all knew that, and yet... you have to try, sometimes, don't you? Even when..." He trailed off, shaking his head, his eyes dark with sorrow.

"A revolt," Rachel repeated, dazed. Of course it would come to nothing. A few weakened prisoners with a couple of smuggled weapons, against the Nazi might, the Nazi *hatred*? It was the definition of futility. And yet, even now, her mind was still reeling, still trying to force some way through this man's words to the hope that surely she could find if she just looked for it.

He's been injured, he's in the infirmary... he couldn't come himself this time...

She so wanted those words to be true.

"They were brave," the man continued. "Some of them even managed to escape, although they were recaptured."

"And Franz?" Rachel whispered. She knew, of course she knew, but she needed to hear it.

"He was killed," the man confirmed quietly. "I'm sorry."

"How? In the fight?" Rachel suspected the details would hurt more, and yet she needed to hear them. To make it real, she had to be able to imagine it.

The man hesitated, and she knew then, with a churning certainty, that he hadn't been killed in the fight. Somehow, it was worse.

"Tell me," she whispered. "*Please.*"

"After the revolt was subdued," the man explained reluctantly, "they executed the rest of the *Sonderkommando* of Crematorium IV. Over four hundred were killed that day."

"How were they executed?" she asked, and the man shook his head.

"It doesn't matter—"

"It does." Rachel balled her fists, her voice fierce as she took a step toward him. "I *need* to know."

"The men were forced to strip and lie face down in the dirt," the man told her, clearly hating having to say it out loud. "They were all shot in the back of the head."

Rachel put her hands to her mouth as a broken cry escaped her. She wished then that she hadn't asked. She would never be able to erase the image from her mind of Franz lying naked in some muddy ditch, being shot like a wounded dog. His last moments on earth, to pass in such a terrible way.

The man took a step toward her, one hand outstretched as if

he would comfort her, but then he dropped it and they both stood there in silence as the shadows lengthened and a rat scuttled among the rubbish.

"He was a brave man," he said again.

Rachel nodded. She understood why Franz had done it—not simply to make a stand, but to save himself. The ultimate sacrifice. The necessary atonement. A sigh escaped her, long and low and weary. Yes, she understood why he'd done it, and she could not begrudge him his chance for redemption, but, *oh Franz, it cost you your life. My life with you. Our child knowing you...*

Biting her lips to keep from letting out another cry, Rachel closed her eyes.

"I'm sorry," the man said. "I'm sorry to have brought you such news. To have told you such things."

"It is not your fault, and you took a risk in coming to tell me." She opened her eyes and gazed at the man; he looked about her age, perhaps a little older. "You are doing the same work as he did?"

The man nodded. "I don't know why we were chosen. Sometimes I fear they saw something in my eyes, in my soul... that they would think I could do such things..." He broke off, shaking his head. "Forgive me. That is not important now."

"They can't take your soul," Rachel told him. "They can take everything else, but not that."

He smiled faintly, although his eyes were still dark and sad.

"What is your name?" Rachel asked.

"Jakob."

"Did you come here with anyone?"

He paused, his eyes growing even darker, before he replied, "I came with everyone I ever loved. My mother, my father, my two sisters, my wife." She didn't have to ask, she already knew, but he supplied the grim truth anyway. "All dead, everyone, save for my father, within hours of arrival. Maybe even minutes, in the gas chambers. My father, they killed a week later. I pulled his body out myself."

"*Oh...*" Rachel shook her head. She thought she'd had no more tears, that she was dry and empty inside, but this man's bleak explanation filled her with grief. Eva was right; everyone had a story, and many were far harder than hers. "I'm so sorry," she said.

He gave a little shrug as his lips wobbled into a smile. "So am I."

They remained there, standing in a silence that felt like sorrowful solidarity, before Rachel finally stirred herself. "I must get back."

Jakob nodded. "I, as well."

"Thank you." She reached out and grasped his hand with both of her own. "Thank you, for coming to tell me."

"I made a promise," he told her, "and if it had been me and my wife, I would have wanted her to know." He squeezed her hand before stepping back and then melting into the shadows.

Rachel walked slowly back into the bakehouse. Franz was dead, she told herself, but the words felt hollow and empty. Unreal. *He's dead, dead...* Still, she struggled to believe it.

The other women were already lined up for the nightly search. Rachel quickly joined, only to have her heart fall as she saw the kapo patting them down was a different one, and her face looked hard, the twist of her thin lips cruel. She, Rachel feared, was not going to pretend she hadn't noticed anything when her hands found her bump.

Her mind raced for solutions, but she was seconds away from her own search and she couldn't think of anything. And what was the point, anyway? Franz was dead. She would be discovered at some point. And when her baby was born...

No. She couldn't let herself think like that. She had to hold onto hope. She would do anything to keep this child, *Franz's* child, safe.

"Well, well, what have we here?" The woman's voice was full of malice as she forcefully patted the swell of Rachel's baby bump. "A Jewish sow about to have another squealing piglet."

Rachel flinched, her stomach roiling, but said nothing.

"It's off to the maternity ward for you," the kapo continued, shoving her in the back. She let out a hard laugh. "And then we'll see that baby at the bottom of a barrel."

"*No!*" The word was torn from Rachel, before she could keep herself from it, and in response, the kapo's face twisted with a gleeful malice as she landed a blow with her truncheon across Rachel's shoulders that sent her, gasping, to her knees.

"Next time I'll hit you in the stomach," the woman snarled. "Then we'll see that brat come out. I don't want to see you here again."

Rachel forced herself to her feet, even though her shoulders were throbbing with pain and spots danced before her eyes. She stayed silent as she shuffled unsteadily toward the row of women, to walk back to Birkenau, and the fate that awaited her there.

That night, Rachel found herself in the maternity ward, a barracks built like her former one, but filled with fear, despair, and terrible illness. She stood in the doorway, the thick, cloying smell of blood, urine, and infection assaulting her nostrils as she looked around in the gloom. There was a long trough in the center of the room, with stoves at either end but no fire, for coal and wood had long since become scarce. Women lay on their bunks—some heavily pregnant, others simply ill. A rat, as bold as brass, waddled across the room and disappeared beneath a bunk.

And this, Rachel thought numbly, was where she was meant to give birth.

"And how far along are you?" the attending midwife asked

indifferently. She had a hard look about her, her hair scraped back from a work- and drink-roughened face. Rachel could smell the vodka on her breath and did her best not to flinch.

"A little over seven months, I think," she said quietly.

"And they sent you here already?" the midwife demanded. "Couldn't you work?"

"I don't know why they did," Rachel replied. If she hadn't angered the kapo, perhaps she would have been allowed to continue in the bakehouse for another month or two. Now she would have to wait out her days amidst the vermin and filth; it was no respite at all.

"Find a bunk," the midwife replied. "While you're healthy, you can help. Why should I do all the work, especially for a bunch of filthy Jews, and the brats are going to be drowned anyway?" She let out a raspy chuckle, before, muttering, she shuffled off to her room adjoining the barracks.

Rachel took a deep breath and then moved carefully into the building, blinking in the dim light, her gaze skating over the women who lay in their bunks, their bodies wasted, their eyes vacant. A few of them had babies clutched to their pitifully thin chests; one baby looked barely alive. When Rachel stepped closer, she saw that the woman was hardly breathing; were they *both* dead?

Then the woman blinked, her cracked lips parting soundlessly as she tried to speak, but only a rasping breath came out. Rachel gazed at her, full of both pity and horror. Was this her fate? Her baby's fate?

Releasing a shaky breath, she stepped away to find her own bunk. A rat scurried in front of her, and she moved quickly out of the way before she found an empty bunk—no more than a scrap of old sacking, whatever straw had filled it long since crumbled away to dust, tossed over a few rough boards. She sank onto it, dropping her head into her hands.

Franz was dead. *Dead.* And in a few weeks, maybe months,

so their child would be, as well. So might she—giving birth in a place like this seemed like a death sentence, never mind what her Nazi captors had planned. Liberation felt farther away than ever, an impossible, beautiful dream. What was the point of anything—of trying, of hope—if the result was the same?

A sound escaped her, too tired to be a sob. There was no point to *anything*... why not simply die now, before she had to suffer the loss of her child? Surely that would be a better fate?

God gives you strength in the moment. For a second, she could picture Corrie's kindly face, the way her blue eyes creased at the corners as she smiled.

Rachel took a deep breath, and then another, doing her best to inch away from the abyss of her own despair. After a moment, she lifted her head from her hands and then reached down to take the sliver of emerald from her shoe, clasping it tightly between her fingers.

She'd kept it all this time, hidden in a hollow in the board of her bunk. Every night her fingers found it, clutched it like the talisman it had become. As long as she had her emerald, she could believe in the future. She could picture herself meeting Sophie, Rosa, and Hannah at Henri's, toasting each other with champagne, her baby in her arms... and Sophie was *here*, she reminded herself. She was not alone, even if she felt so in this moment.

"Rachel!" As if called from the depths of her memory, Sophie emerged out of the gloom of the barracks, hurrying toward her. Rachel slipped the emerald back in her shoe. "Thank God I've found you," Sophie exclaimed in a low voice. "Eva told me you'd been moved to the maternity ward."

"They found out I was pregnant," Rachel explained dully. "Sophie, Franz is dead."

"I know, I heard." Sophie sat down next to her on the bunk, clasping her limp hands in hers. "Rachel, I'm so sorry."

Rachel shook her head slowly. "He didn't have to do it. It

was such a *stupid* sacrifice." The words burst out of her, full of resentment. Why couldn't Franz have held on, for her? For their baby? She wanted to understand, she *did* understand, really, and yet...

Everything felt so *futile*.

"Sacrifice is a choice," Sophie said quietly. "And one we can make when all other choices have been taken away from us. In that moment, Rachel, it might have felt like the only thing he could have done. But I know it's hard. We've lost so many."

Rachel knew Sophie had lost the man she'd loved at Pearl Harbor. Her own family had been sent to Belgium; they could be here at Auschwitz, or at another camp, or already dead. Sophie had not had word of them in over four years.

"I know," Rachel whispered. She closed her eyes against the press of tears she felt too weary to shed. "I know."

"Listen." Sophie dropped her voice as she leaned forward. "I was hoping you wouldn't be discovered for some time yet, but we need to work with what we have. I won't let them kill your baby, Rachel. We'll find a way."

Rachel's eyes flew open as she stared at Sophie in incomprehension, too incredulous to hope. "*How?*"

"There are ways." Sophie's voice dropped lower. "One of the midwives is sympathetic."

"Not the one I met," Rachel returned with a shudder. "She seems like she *relishes* killing these poor infants."

Sophie gave a swift nod. "That would be Klara, and her assistant Pfani. But they can be fooled. It's been done before, and we can do it again."

"How?" Rachel whispered again. She wanted to believe such a thing, heaven knew she did more than anything in the whole world, but when she considered her circumstances, how could she?

"Let me worry about that," Sophie replied. "And you worry about staying healthy." She glanced around the barracks with a grimace. "God knows how any woman manages to give birth in such a place as this. Eva and I can bring you some more food. It won't be long, I promise it won't. You must keep your strength up."

Rachel stared at her friend as she felt the first flicker of hope lick her insides, a flame beginning to kindle and burn against all the odds, all the darkness.

"Promise me," Sophie commanded her. "Promise me you will?"

The despair Rachel had felt only moments before began to ebb away, its shadows replaced by the new light of determination. *God gives you strength in the moment...* and He *had*, through Sophie. She could hold on, Rachel told herself. She felt a new ferocity and took strength from it. For the sake of her baby, her baby's precious life, she could hold on. She *would*.

"I promise," Rachel whispered, and Sophie smiled.

CHAPTER 24

NOVEMBER 1944—AUSCHWITZ-BIRKENAU

The next month passed in a haze of work and exhaustion. Klara, the midwife Rachel had met on her first day in the maternity ward, was as good as her word and commanded her help doing the most menial jobs—collecting what scraps of firewood she could, hauling pails of fresh water—a half-hour walk each way in the freezing cold—and cleaning the dirty bandages and cloths from the laboring or ill women. While Rachel was glad to be of some use, the unimaginable—and unendurable—conditions these poor women had to labor under were too dispiriting to bear, and even more so considering she herself would be doing the same in just a few weeks.

At night, Rachel lay in her bunk and cradled her bump, praying soundlessly over her child. Praying, too, for the Allied soldiers who were steadily making their way through Poland. According to camp rumors, relayed to her by Sophie, the Allied armies had liberated both Belgium and Paris, and the Russian army was marching through Poland. Rachel's heart leapt at the news, even as she feared she would never live to see those gates flung open wide. With every passing day, their Nazi guards became more tense, more fearful, and more likely to pull the trigger.

They would not let their Jewish prisoners go easily, Rachel knew. Like the *Sonderkommando*, the inmates were the bearers of secrets. Secrets their Nazi captors would want them to take to their grave.

And yet still she hoped, because hope was all she had. She hoped that her baby would be born safely, despite the grim conditions suggesting otherwise. Another midwife, the kindly Stanisława Leszczyńska, a Polish Catholic, had overseen three births since Rachel's arrival. Her tenderness and competence as she'd helped the laboring women with nothing more than a few dirty bandages and a couple of aspirin had humbled, comforted, and frightened Rachel all at once.

The older woman must have seen the fear on Rachel's face for after a particularly long birth, she'd patted her arm and told her, "I have been here for two years and, in that time, I have delivered over three thousand babies. I have not lost a single one."

Rachel had gaped at her. "Not *one*? Surely that must be a miracle."

"Indeed it is," Stanisława had replied placidly, unruffled by the idea of a such a thing. "Every child is in God's hands, including yours. Even in this place."

It would have been comforting, Rachel had thought, if not for the fact that almost every child, and certainly every Jewish child, was drowned in a barrel by Klara or Pfani just minutes after the poor creature was born. Stanisława had refused to participate in this cold-blooded murder, and did her utmost to make sure each mother had at least a few minutes with her precious baby before the evil act was done... But was that all Rachel could hope for? How could she possibly bear it?

"I think there might be a way," Sophie told her in a low voice one evening when she had come to visit her. Her friend had been as good as her word, and had come often, sometimes with Eva, to give Rachel news and whatever food she managed to find—an extra ration of bread, a mug of soup, and once, incredibly, a piece of sausage.

"How?" Rachel asked, the yearning she felt making her voice tremble.

"If Stanisława delivers your baby," Sophie explained, dropping her voice to a whisper even though Klara and Pfani were, as they often were, in Klara's office drinking vodka, "she can tattoo the child with your number." Rachel gave a small cry of protest and Sophie placed a placating hand on her arm. "I know it sounds dreadful, but it means you will be able to find your baby again, one day when this is all over. And Eva might know someone who can take your baby out of the camp... There is a farmer's wife nearby who is willing to take a child." Sophie let out a soft sigh as she looked around the barracks. "If only she could do it for all these poor souls."

Guilt warred with hope, for Rachel knew she was no more special or privileged than any of the other women lying wretchedly on their bunks, praying for deliverance not for themselves, but for their children. Why should she be singled out for such treatment? And yet she was, and she would accept it gladly, with both hands.

But would this plan, as tenuous and impossible as it seemed, actually *work*?

By the end of November, Rachel knew her time must be close. Her bump felt enormous, especially considering how thin her arms and legs had become.

"You're nothing but baby!" Sophie exclaimed during one of her visits and somehow this made them both laugh, as if she'd told the most outrageous joke.

"He's getting crowded in there," Rachel replied, rubbing the taut skin of her belly. "He used to move all the time, but now he just squirms."

Sophie raised an eyebrow, amused. "You hope it's a boy?"

Rachel ducked her head. "I would be pleased with a girl or a boy, God knows, as long as they're healthy. But I like to think of a boy... a boy like Franz." Her throat thickened and she glanced down at her lap, blinking back tears.

Sophie rested her hand over hers. "You miss him," she stated quietly.

Rachel nodded. "Sometimes, I'm so angry with myself," she whispered, "for having squandered so much time. After Franz came back from Dachau... and the month in Heijplaat, the years in Haarlem... I was so unhappy. We both were. And if I'd known then how little time we'd have together..." She found she couldn't go on.

"But we can never know what the future holds," Sophie said quietly, her hand still on top of Rachel's. "Maybe that is a mercy."

Rachel let out a shuddery laugh. "Yes, maybe it is," she replied. She thought of herself at twenty-two, naïve and hopeful and so in love. "If I'd known when I'd married Franz what the future would hold for us... I don't think I would have been able to bear it!"

"And yet you have," Sophie returned with a small, sad smile.

"Yes..." Again, Rachel thought of Corrie and missed her and Betsie and their father with a fierce ache of longing. "And you're right, it has been a mercy. God knows what we can bear... and He gives us the strength to bear it in the right time."

Sophie laid a hand on Rachel's bump. "Including this."

Rachel took a deep breath. It was easy to mouth such platitudes about generalities, but this? Her own child? Her child's life?

"Yes," she said, putting her hand over Sophie's. "Including this."

On the last day of November, when the air was frigid and the ground as hard as iron, Rachel went into labor. At first, she ignored the persistent backache and twinging pains; she'd been experiencing such things for weeks, and she was too busy fetching and carrying for Klara and Pfani to pay much attention.

It was only when she felt a contracted band around her middle like a hot iron, leaving her gasping for breath as tears of pain started in her eyes, that she realized what was happening, and she cursed herself and her own stupidity. She might not have time to contact Sophie or Stanisława. How would her baby be saved then?

Rachel staggered back into the barracks with a pail of water, half of which she'd spilled as she'd struggled with the pain of her contractions. Fortunately, Klara was too drunk to notice, and Pfani, a former prostitute, had disappeared from the barracks, as she was often wont to do. All the other women, lying on their bunks, were too ill or exhausted to be of any help, or even to notice.

Rachel stumbled to her bunk, wrapping her arms around her middle as another contraction came upon her like a tidal wave, sweeping her under for a few breathless moments as she struggled to manage the pain.

The contraction receded, the tight bands of pain lessening, but only for a moment. Already, the next one was upon her, and Rachel knew enough from her short time in the maternity ward that she was far closer to delivering this baby than she might have wished. There was no time to call Stanisława or Sophie, or even Klara or Pfani, to help her. How could she have been so stupid, so *reckless*? She'd known her time was near. She should have been more careful, so much more careful…

But now it was too late. She would have to birth this baby alone. She glanced up at the trough in the middle of the room that had served as a birthing bed for so many women. If she labored there, Klara or Pfani would no doubt stumble in, half-drunk or worse, and find her. They would take her baby as they had so many others, and she wouldn't have Sophie or Stanisława to help her hide her child.

Maybe, Rachel told herself, laboring like this was a blessing, if only she had the strength.

Please give me the strength.

As carefully as she could, Rachel eased herself back onto the bunk. Like the other barracks in Birkenau, the bunks were built into the stone walls, so they resembled something close to coffins on three sides. At times, it could be claustrophobic, the air stifling and fetid, but now Rachel was grateful for the privacy it provided. Maybe, just maybe, she could stay hidden…

Another contraction gripped her, and she moaned out loud, clenching her eyes against the pain. She could do this. She *had* to do this. Her breath came out in a shaky rush as the contraction receded and then she felt a warm gush of fluid from between her thighs. As she'd seen with other laboring women, her waters had just broken. Her baby was coming.

Her breath came in pants as she started to push. *God, help me.* Sweat beaded her brows and she kept her eyes clenched shut as she rode through another contraction, bearing down as best as she could.

"Rachel."

Her eyes flew open to see Sophie crouched in front of her, her face pale with anxiety.

"It's your time," she said in awe. She glanced behind her, frowning. "Klara's in her room."

"Stanisława…" Rachel managed to get out through gritted teeth.

"I'll get her, I promise. But first let me help you…"

"No." Rachel shook her head, her sweat-dampened hair sticking to her cheeks. "Get Stanisława. I need her… to hide…" She couldn't manage anymore as another contraction hit her and she began to push again.

"Oh, Rachel." Sophie's eyes were wide as she crouched down to watch her baby come into the world. Rachel was too focused to care about the modesty or lack of it in the situation—she wanted her baby born. She wanted her baby to live.

A thin, mewling cry split the air and then Sophie was wrapping Rachel's baby in a scrap of blanket, her face suffused with tenderness.

"There, little one, there." She glanced up at Rachel. "Rachel, you have a daughter."

Rachel fell back onto the bunk, gasping. A *daughter*. She had a little girl just as Franz had hoped.

"Rachel, look." Gently, Sophie put the baby into Rachel's arms. "She's beautiful. Let me get Stanisława. She can cut the cord…"

Just then, Klara emerged from her room, red-eyed from drink, an ugly look on her face. She could be a mean drunk sometimes, Rachel knew, taunting the women with how she would take their babies away. Quickly, she rolled away, drawing her daughter into her chest. Sophie did her best to put the blanket over them both to hide both the baby and the mess of birth.

"I'll get Stanisława," she whispered. "Rachel, it will be all right, I promise."

"You can't know that," Rachel whispered brokenly.

Tears started in her eyes, and she blinked them back because there was no point. She had to be strong for her baby. If

Klara discovered she'd given birth, she'd wrest her daughter away from her and take pleasure in drowning her like all the others. It was evil and utterly inhumane, but she knew the midwife would do it. And she wasn't strong enough to fight back, not that that would do her or her daughter any good.

This place, she thought in wretched misery, closing her eyes. *This evil, evil place...*

Sophie slipped away and Rachel tucked her daughter into her chest, brushing her lips against her downy, damp head, aching with a desperate love. Already, her baby was rooting around, desperate for both food and comfort. Rachel guided her to her breast, reveling in this moment of motherhood as her daughter began to suckle, praying that Klara would not notice she had retired to her bunk.

The minutes crawled past. Rachel could hear Klara moving around, muttering to herself. Another poor woman had started labor, and she'd had to stumble to the stove in the middle of the room where the women were meant to give birth by herself.

"Where's Pfani?" Klara asked irritably. "Or Rachel? I have to do all the work myself around here."

The work of *murdering* babies, Rachel thought savagely, and burrowed further into her bunk. Klara continued to stomp around, muttering and complaining, as the woman on the stove continued her labor alone. Rachel wished she could help her; she knew all too well how hard it was to give birth by yourself. Thank heaven Sophie had come, but she needed her here now, with Stanisława...

And then she was there. Stanisława swept in, calm and unflappable as ever, checking on the laboring woman while Klara continued to complain, and Sophie hurried to Rachel.

"Listen," she hissed. "Stanisława gave me the scissors. I can cut the cord."

"Do it," Rachel whispered. "Do it if you can." She closed

her eyes as Sophie cut the umbilical cord and tucked the blanket more firmly about her.

"I also have the needle," she whispered. "Rachel, I have to put your number in this little one's arm."

"She'll cry..." Rachel whispered, frantic. "Klara will hear."

"I know. I'll do it away from here, but... Rachel, I'll have to take your baby away." Sophie gripped her hand. "I have someone to take her until this madness ends. But... do you trust me?" Her eyes were dark and earnest as she gazed at Rachel in the dimness of the bunk.

Rachel gulped. Did she trust Sophie? Did she have any choice? "Yes," she whispered. "I trust you."

"What is your daughter's name?" Sophie asked gently.

Rachel had not considered any names; she had not dared. Now she realized she knew it with a bone-deep certainty. "Cornelia," she said. "But I will call her Corrie."

"Corrie," Sophie repeated, and then, with Rachel's heart feeling as if it were breaking right in half, she carefully took Corrie from her arms. The baby let out a tiny cry of protest and Sophie quickly pulled the scrap of blanket over her head. Rachel watched, everything in her aching, as Sophie walked quickly out of the barracks, her baby bundled under her arm like she was no more than a newspaper.

Then, like a spectre looming out of the night, Klara suddenly appeared above her, scowling.

"Well, weren't you quick," she sneered. "Where's your brat, then?"

"The baby was born dead." Stanisława's voice was as steady as ever as she joined Klara by Rachel's bunk. "Too early and too weak, poor thing. I laid him out with the others, God rest his innocent soul, before I went to help this poor woman." She nodded toward the stove. "Now, we have a birth to see to."

Klara swung her head round to glare at Stanisława, who gazed back at her calmly.

"Saves me some trouble," Klara finally spat, and stomped back to the stove.

Rachel let out a shaky sigh of relief. Her daughter was safe… for now. But how many more threats and dangers would she face before they could be reunited again… if they ever were?

CHAPTER 25

JANUARY 18, 1945—AUSCHWITZ-BIRKENAU

It felt like the eerie, unnatural calm before the storm.

Rachel stood in the doorway of her old barracks, shivering in the cold under an iron-gray sky, a few other women gathered besides her, everyone uncertain. There had been no roll call that morning or evening; there had been no work all day. For the last few weeks, their guards had been distracted and tense, rushing to and fro, barely aware of the prisoners they had once been determined to torment and kill, whether it was through the gas chambers or simply working them to death.

The gas chambers had been empty and unused for weeks. The crematoria had been destroyed. Thousands of prisoners had already been taken from the camps, to who knew where. No one knew what was going on, but Rachel had heard through Sophie and her sources that the Red Army had pushed west through Poland. The prisoners had seen bomber planes streak across the sky on more than one occasion. Could this really be the end?

It had been nearly two months since Rachel had said goodbye to her daughter and, with her heart near to breaking, placed Corrie into Sophie's arms. Sophie had tattooed Rachel's baby with her own number, the digits hidden in the soft folds of her tiny elbow, and then had her spirited away, out of the camp, tucked inside in a laundry basket and given to a local woman. Would Rachel ever find her again? All she knew was that she was in a farmhouse somewhere between here and Oświęcim... but at least she was alive. One day, Rachel promised herself, she would find her. God willing, even one day soon.

Since then, she had returned to her old barracks and her work in the bakehouse, almost as if her baby had never been. And yet she thought of Cornelia every day, prayed for her safety and for the woman who had agreed to take care of her. She thought of Franz too, and wished he had been able to meet his daughter. The daughter she was determined to keep safe...

A gunshot sounded in the distance, the single crack splitting the still air. It was a common enough sound there, heaven knew, but it still raised the hairs on the back of Rachel's neck now, when the camp was so quiet and felt so empty.

What was going on?

She glanced at Eva, who stood behind her, her arms wrapped around her waist, a deep line carved between her eyebrows. "I don't like it," she muttered. "What have they been doing all day? What do they *want*?"

"What's there to like about anything here?" another woman returned wearily. "At least it's almost over..." She paused before finishing grimly, "One way or another."

"But to die when we're so close to the end!" someone else exclaimed with a shudder. "I'd rather they'd have killed me at the start than to go through all this and for what? A bullet in the head?"

"Don't say that," someone from the back protested softly. "We've got through this much. We can get through the rest."

But could they? Rachel wondered. Would their captors really allow them to walk out of this wretched place? Considering how empty and still it was now, maybe they would...

Then, suddenly, the camp sprang to life. Floodlights snapped on, sweeping through the darkened yard as several SS officers, dressed in thick winter coats and boots, strode forward, firing their pistols into the air. "*Raus, raus!*" they shouted. "Anyone who can, assemble in the yard. *Now!*"

The women exchanged uneasy glances, uncertain whether or not to obey.

More guards came into the yard, holdings guns and whips, Alsatians straining at their leashes. They were going to be forced to leave, Rachel realized. Either that or they would murder them right in the yard—but no, there were no crematoria anymore to dispose of the bodies, the evidence. They would, she realized, have to make them leave the camp.

"Out, out!" The furious litany continued. "*Schnell, schnell!*"

Quickly, the women in the barracks began to rush around, gathering their few paltry possessions. Hardly anyone had coats; many had holes in their shoes. It was well below freezing, snow blowing across the courtyard under a bitter sky. If they weren't shot, Rachel thought grimly, they would almost certainly freeze to death.

She turned to Eva. "Are you going?"

Eva shrugged. "What else can we do?"

"We could hide," Rachel suggested tentatively. She had no idea where they would be taken, only that it would be even farther from her daughter, and she couldn't let that happen. If she stayed at Birkenau...

"I'm not waiting here for the Red Army," Eva declared. "I've heard they're even worse."

"Don't believe all the stories—" Rachel began, but she was cut off by another woman.

"Look!" She pointed to the sky, where smoke was beginning to billow up, obscuring the horizon. "They're burning the camp down."

"The fire won't get far, in this snow," someone else said. "They can't hide that much."

"*Schnell!*" A guard strode toward the door of their barracks, his pistol pointed right at Rachel as he roughly urged her to hurry. "*Schnell!*" he shouted again, his face contorted with fury, his eyes wild with fear.

Their Nazi guards were *afraid*, Rachel realized with a ripple of terror. Afraid of not just being captured, but of being discovered as the monsters they truly were. And fear was a terrible thing when coupled with power; their guards would become like cornered rats, fighting for their lives, killing whoever they could…

As if to prove her point, the guard pointed his pistol at a woman lying on her bunk, too weak to move, and fired, the sound echoing through the confined space and making Rachel's eardrums throb. The woman's body twitched once and was still.

"Everyone *out*," he snarled before nodding toward the dead woman in her bunk. "You know what will happen if you don't move."

As one, the women began to hurry out of the barracks. Rachel ran back to her bunk and reached for the emerald still hidden in a hollow in the board. Her fingers closed around it and she slipped it into her shoe. Would she be able to find Sophie amidst all the chaos? she wondered. Her friend had been struggling with a cough these last few weeks. How would she be able to march through the cold and the snow all night?

"Are you coming?" Eva asked, and reluctantly Rachel nodded. What choice did any of them have?

All the women of Birkenau, save for those who were too ill or weak to move, had assembled in the yard under the bright glare of the floodlights. Guards were urging the women forward, out of the camp, in lines of five, with dogs and whips at the ready. Every so often, Rachel heard a gunshot and cringed as someone fell. The air tasted metallic with both snow and fear. As much as she longed to slip away and hide, she knew she couldn't risk it.

She'd come back, she promised herself. She'd come back and find her daughter, no matter what it took.

With their shoulders hunched against the bitter cold, the women walked in columns of five out of the camp, urged on by the guards and dogs. After just a few minutes, Rachel's face was numb, along with her fingers and toes. How long would they be forced to walk? To the ramp, to get on a train, or farther still?

She looked around, searching for Sophie, but it was too hard to see anything or anyone. All she could do was put one foot in front of the other... and pray.

The guards drove them from the camp, down the road heading west to Wodzisław Śląski. Already, women were stumbling, falling. One woman in Rachel's column fell to her knees, and without missing a beat, the guard turned around and shot her in the head. Filled with horror, Rachel watched the snow become speckled with red as they were forced to march on. She could not stay here, she realized with a lurch, marching onto her death... and far away from her daughter. Somehow, she had to find a way to escape, to find Cornelia... but first she needed to find Sophie. Sophie could tell her where her daughter was. And so, when the guard had moved forward, Rachel slipped to the end of the row.

"What are you doing?" Eva hissed as she saw her move. "You'll get shot, Rachel, and for what?"

"I have to find my daughter," Rachel whispered back fiercely. "You know I do."

Eva shook her head, sorrowful but also certain. "They'll kill you," she stated flatly, and Rachel gave a defiant shrug.

"Then I must take that chance."

Under the cover of darkness, when the guards weren't looking, she slipped from row to row, her heart beating hard, always looking for Sophie. In the darkness, all the women looked miserably the same—haggard and exhausted, dressed in shapeless gray and shivering from the icy wind. How on earth would she find her friend?

Still Rachel kept looking, slipping from row to row, searching for Sophie. The minutes slipped past and as the moon rose in the sky, she suspected it had been at least an hour since they'd started marching, an hour that took her farther away from Corrie. Should she give up? Turn back and hope she could find Corrie somehow on her own, simply by stumbling through the night and knocking on doors?

It was a terribly dangerous proposition.

Then Rachel heard a hacking cough—a common enough sound, heaven knew—and she glimpsed, under the moonlight, the still-soft curve of Sophie's cheek as she plodded along, her head lowered against the bitter cold, her arms wrapped around her middle.

"*Sophie!*"

Sophie turned, her eyes widening. "*Rachel...*"

"I'm going back for Corrie," Rachel whispered urgently as she grasped her friend's hand. "Tell me, please, do you know where she is? How can I find her?"

Her eyes wide, Sophie shook her head. "Rachel, I'm sorry. All I know is that she's in a farmhouse on the main road to Oświęcim. A wooden house with a thatched roof. The farmer's wife took in laundry for the camps." She grasped Rachel's hand. "Rachel, it will be dangerous. The guards are shooting whomever they like—"

"They will kill us one way or another," Rachel replied. "A bullet in the head or freezing to death in the snow, what does it matter to them? This is my only chance."

Sophie nodded soberly. "Well I know it." Another cough wracked her thin frame. "God help us all."

Rachel squeezed her hand. "Take care of yourself. We will meet again," she promised. "In Henri's, with Hannah and

Rosa." Her voice wavered and then she firmed it. She needed to believe in Henri's now, when it felt both so tantalizingly close and so fearfully far away.

"Yes." Sophie managed a wan smile. "Yes, in Henri's, in June, when this is all over. It *will* be over in June. I know it will."

"Yes, in June," Rachel agreed, trying to inject a certainty in her voice that she could not truly feel. "It's not so far away."

Once more, the crack of a gunshot split the air and a woman near them fell, forgotten in the snow. Rachel slipped her hand from Sophie's and, with a last wave of farewell, she fell back another row, and then another, carefully working her way back through the column of women.

Another hour passed as they marched on. The guards were getting tired, and the cold was so bitter that they hunched their shoulders, keeping their heads down against the icy wind, indifferent to the prisoners around them.

It would not be so hard to melt into the night, Rachel thought, but then what? She might die in the snow, alone and forgotten, miles from her daughter.

Yet what other choice did she have?

Rachel waited until the guards were striding ahead, spurring on stragglers, before she quickly stepped out of the road, crouching in a frozen ditch. There were others, she soon saw, in the ditch—some dead, some barely clinging to their lives, turning to her with fear-fogged eyes. Where would any of them go? Who would help them?

She, to her shame, could not.

Rachel waited until the column had moved on, down the road and into the night, before she turned and started walking alone back to Auschwitz.

. . .

The sky was lightening to a pale pinkish gray by the time Rachel reached the road that led to the camp. She couldn't feel her face, fingers, or toes, and she feared the frostbite might incur permanent damage, but she didn't care. She was close, so close, to finding Corrie. Just a few more kilometers...

It had taken so long to get this far, walking in the trees or ditch alongside the road at first, to avoid notice from any guards at the rear of the march. When they'd finally all marched ahead, she'd dared the road; a few others were stumbling back, perhaps hoping they might find more safety at camp, now that the officers and guards had all abandoned it. Who could possibly know what was safe, how to survive?

The world had never seemed like such a dangerous and unknown place.

She passed the gates of Birkenau, now flung open, the whole place looking unsettlingly empty, and then headed east toward the Auschwitz camp and the road to Oświęcim. Just then, a column of raggedy male prisoners came into view, heading out from the main camp, and being spurred on just as the women from Birkenau had the night before, flanked by guards with whips and dogs. It was another march, and Rachel was standing right in front of them.

She dove into the ditch along the side, crawling on her hands and knees to the cover of a few sparse evergreens. Her lungs burned and her heart thundered as she moved as quickly and quietly as she could and the men marched past. How stupid could she be, she berated herself. Of course, the camps weren't completely empty. There were tens of thousands of prisoners still languishing in them; there would be many more marches, and many more guards on the lookout for those trying to escape. She had to be so very careful.

Rachel lay flat on her belly, the snow soaking straight into her skin, as the men marched past. She watched dozens of them, at various points, attempt escape, diving into ditches or sprinting into the forest. Several were shot and lay where they fell. Rachel flattened herself to the ground as much as she could, praying she would not be strafed by a stray bullet. Finally, they marched past, and it was still again, the smell of smoke from the fires earlier lingering in the wintry air.

Carefully, Rachel rose to her knees and looked around. Several bodies littered the road, blood-spattered and unmoving under a snow-whitened sky. In the distance, she saw a man moving carefully into the cover of the trees. He wasn't wearing the usual male prisoner garb of a striped shirt and trousers. He had a winter jacket on, and a hat pulled down low over his ears. With a ripple of surprise, Rachel realized she recognized the tall, lanky form, the slightly uneven gait. It looked like Jakob, the man who had told her about Franz.

She held her breath as she watched him melt into the forest. He'd escaped. Glancing around and seeing no guards, she started creeping along the edge of the forest, following Jakob's route toward Oświęcim.

Time passed, the sun rising in the sky, as Rachel slowly made her way along the road, staying close to the trees, searching for farmhouses. The area around the camps had been cleared of houses, no doubt in an unsuccessful attempt to hide what the Germans had been doing at Auschwitz. According to Sophie, all the local Poles had still known. How could they not have, with the great smokestacks pointing to the sky, the raggedy ranks of prisoners marching along the road, digging ditches or hauling stones? And then of course there was the fine, slightly greasy ash of incinerated bone and flesh that coated the air for miles...

Finally, after what had to be nearly an hour of walking, a farmhouse came into view, but it was made of brick, with a slate roof, not wooden as Sophie had said. Rachel was too scared to risk knocking on the door; she had also heard from Sophie that many of the locals were deliberately unconcerned with the Jews who filled the camps so near their homes. What if Sophie had had the house wrong? Could Rachel risk it? Did she dare?

Rachel stood under the cover of a spruce tree as she watched the house, smoke curling from its one chimney. Otherwise, there was no movement; it was only a little past dawn.

A crack of a twig behind her had her whirling, her heart slamming in her chest.

A man stood just a few feet away from her, his hands held up in the air. It was Jakob.

"Rachel?" he breathed. "I thought... I thought it might be you."

She nodded shakily as he lowered his hands. "You escaped."

"It was either that or be killed. They murdered almost all the *Sonderkommando*. There was only a handful of us left. I didn't want to take my chances with that march." His expression was somber. "They'll march those poor sods to death, I fear."

Rachel thought of Sophie, the cough rattling through her thin chest. "They can't kill them all that way, surely?" she whispered.

Jakob shook his head. "God alone knows. But what are you doing here?"

"My daughter..." Rachel swallowed. "My daughter is somewhere near here, being take care of by a local laundress." Her voice hitched. "I have to find her. She's all I have now."

Jakob nodded slowly. "Let me help you."

Surprise rendered Rachel speechless for a moment. "You should get away," she finally said. He had to know how dangerous it would be to stay so near the camps.

"It was what Franz would have wanted," Jakob insisted. "What *I* would have wanted, if my wife..." He stopped, started again. "Let me help you."

Knowing she did not have the luxury of refusing—and grateful for the company as well as the help—Rachel nodded.

. . .

They walked in silence for the better part of an hour, keeping to the trees. The day was still and strangely peaceful, but bitterly cold. Jakob took off his jacket and draped it over Rachel's shoulders, although she protested.

"I've worn it long enough," he told her. "God knows I don't need a reminder of what I did to earn it."

"It wasn't your fault," she protested softly. "We all did what we could to stay alive."

Jakob simply shook his head.

"What will you do, after?" Rachel asked eventually.

She felt the need to remind them both that there could *be* an after; that the hell of the last few years was almost over, and the world would once more become a place where they could live as normal people—working, laughing, loving, *being*. She could find her mother, a job as a teacher, maybe in Germany, or perhaps somewhere further abroad. It felt as hazy as the most distant daydream, and yet she wanted to reach for it.

"I was a teacher before all this," Jakob replied. "I taught literature. I cannot imagine doing so now."

"I taught history," Rachel told him, and he smiled faintly, as if to acknowledge the absurdity of them both having once been teachers, and thinking they could be so again, when they were wandering through a forest as escapees from the worst kind of prison anyone had ever known.

What would the world be like, when all this was over? And how, Rachel wondered, could they make it better? The ten Booms, if they were still alive, would be asking that question… and she knew they would be determined to find an answer.

"Rachel." Jakob put a hand on her arm to stay still. "Look!"

There, in the distance, was a wooden farmhouse with a thatched roof. A line of washing had been strung out between the house and the barn, the clothes now frozen and as stiff as boards.

"It must be the place," Rachel whispered. She felt as if her heart had just leapt into her throat. "Let's knock on the door."

Jakob looked hesitant, but then he nodded. "All right."

Their knock echoed through the house and the cold air as they waited for someone to answer. Was this where Corrie had been kept? Dare she even hope...? What if the occupants were hostile to the prisoners, as so many were?

Then, finally, the door opened, and a woman stood there, her face drawn into lines of suspicion and hostility. Rachel's heart sank.

"*Bitte...*" she began, and the woman's frown deepened. She started to close the door.

Jakob stopped her with one hand and then began speaking in Polish, gesturing to Rachel. Rachel held her breath, waiting, hoping, *praying...*

Please let her be here. Let her be safe.

An age seemed to pass as Jakob fell silent and still the woman didn't speak. Then, finally, she nodded and opened the door wide for them to step inside. The smoky warmth of the little cottage was like a blanket being dropped around her shoulders. Rachel closed her eyes and nearly swayed as exhaustion crashed over her. She was so tired, so cold, so hungry, and so hopeful.

Please, please let Corrie be here...

The woman turned and walked down the hallway, leaving Rachel and Jakob alone.

"What did she say?" she whispered.

Jakob gave a little shrug, his forehead creased. "Just that she'd be right back."

Fear clutched at Rachel's heart. What if the woman had lured them in, was calling the police? She'd heard of prisoners who had tried to escape, only to be turned in by locals who feared for their own lives. Could that be happening now?

Then the woman returned... and there was a baby in her arms. A baby wrapped in a hand-knit white blanket, her cheeks plump and pink with good health. Rachel's breath came out in a rush, and she took a step forward as she let out a little cry.

"Corrie..."

Silently, the woman unwrapped the blanket and withdrew the baby's little arm. There, in the folds of her elbow, Rachel saw the tiny numbers, tattooed in black ink. 653126. Her own number. Her own daughter.

With another cry that was close to a sob, Rachel held out her arms and, smiling, the woman handed her her baby.

Rachel gazed down at her daughter with a thrill of wonder. She had not dared hope for this moment, and yet at the same time she'd yearned for it with everything she had, and here it finally, wonderfully was. She had no idea what the future might hold—when the war would end, how she would find her mother or her friends, or even care for her daughter—but none of that mattered now. Nothing mattered but the fact that Corrie was finally in her arms.

Jakob rested a hand on her shoulder. "She has Franz's eyes," he said quietly, and another sob escaped her.

"Yes... yes, she does." She glanced up at Jakob and he smiled down at her, his eyes full of sadness. "Thank you," Rachel whispered. She turned to the woman. *"Thank you."*

"*Komm*," the woman said in clumsy German. "Eat. Drink. You must rest before you journey on."

"Thank you," Rachel said again, overcome with both gratitude and wondrous joy. Smiling at Jakob and holding her daughter, she followed the woman into the kitchen—and the beginning of the rest of her life.

CHAPTER 26

JUNE 2, 1946—PARIS

The café was silent as Rachel finished her story, the women motionless as they absorbed all she'd said, all she'd endured.

Then Hannah wiped the tears from her eyes as Rosa slowly shook her head. "Oh, Rachel. I can't even imagine how it must have..." She broke off as she dabbed at her eyes. "Sophie must have fallen on the march," she added sorrowfully. "She would have been here if she could. I know she would have."

"We made a promise," Rachel agreed, her tone somber. "She told me she would be here, when... when we said goodbye." Her voice hitched. "Sophie was so courageous, so determined... she did so much for me." She shook her head. "I would not be alive save for her. Neither would Corrie."

"And neither would I," Hanna agreed. "Or Lotte."

"Oh, Hannah, I'm so pleased Lotte is alive!" Rachel exclaimed as she reached for her friend's hands. "Sophie told me what happened at the children's home. She didn't know whether Lotte had survived—"

"Being half-Jewish saved her," Hannah explained with a wry twist of her lips. "She was arrested, but they let her go."

"Thank God," Rachel said fervently. "Thank God." She

turned to Rosa. "And you, Rosa? What happened to you during the war?"

"Well..." Rosa gave a twisted smile. "I'm afraid I'm not allowed to talk about it. But suffice it to say I did very *dull* work."

Hannah's eyebrows rose. "That you're not allowed to talk about?"

Rosa shrugged, and they both laughed softly in understanding before subsiding once more into sorrow as they considered what had happened to Sophie and how she should have been there. How she would have, if she'd survived.

"And you, Rachel?" Hannah finally asked. "After you found your daughter... how did you last the war?"

"In a displaced persons camp," Rachel explained. "The conditions were almost as appalling as Birkenau, but at least we were safe and fed. Mostly, anyway." She sighed. "It wasn't easy, and we were released just a few months ago. I went back to Berlin, to look for my mother and grandmother." Her mouth turned down in memory. "I learned they'd been transported to the ghetto in Lodz all the way back in 1941. My grandmother died there, and my mother was sent on to Treblinka. According to the Red Cross, she would have been killed as soon as she'd arrived."

"I'm so sorry," Rosa whispered. "I can't even imagine..."

Rachel shrugged, her expression resigned. "Can anyone? *Should* anyone?"

Again, the women fell silent, weighed down by the sorrow and grief of the years.

"We should have a toast," Rosa said finally, her voice filled with determined cheer, even as it wavered. "We should toast Sophie."

"Yes," Hannah agreed. "Let's toast Sophie."

Rosa went to the bar to order champagne, no doubt at an

exorbitant price. Hannah and Rachel exchanged small, sad smiles.

"What about you, Hannah?" Rachel asked. "You've survived the war, thank God. What will you do now?"

"I'm living in Paris with Lotte and my husband, Michel," Hannah told her with a shy, quiet pride. "He'd been captured near the start of the war, but then escaped. We've all been so fortunate, really, to be here at all. I am thankful."

"Yes, to have survived such madness..." Rachel shook her head slowly. "It truly is a blessing. A miracle."

"What about you? What will you do now?" Hannah asked.

"Well..." A shy smile curved Rachel's lips. "I am going to work with my friend, Cornelia ten Boom. I met her back in Haarlem, and she saved Franz and my lives more than once. Corrie is named after her." She took a deep breath as she squared her shoulders and continued to explain, "She is starting a—an organization, I suppose, to help prisoners and Nazis alike—"

"*Nazis!*" Hannah exclaimed, recoiling at the thought.

Rachel nodded soberly. "They need healing too, in their own way," she told her quietly. "Corrie helped me understand that. To live with such horror and guilt—it is almost as bad. Maybe it is even worse." She fell silent for a moment before continuing, "Her sister Betsie—one of the kindest and most joyful people I've ever met—died at Ravensbruck. And her father Casper—he was so wise, he was known as the Old Man of Haarlem—died in prison, as well. But Corrie is alive, and she wants to start this work. It was Betsie's idea originally, but she is determined to carry it on."

"And you will help her?" Hannah asked, still sounding incredulous. "Working with... with *Nazis*?"

Rachel nodded. "I know it will be hard, but it is right. Everyone needs grace." She smiled faintly. "And God will give me the strength."

Rosa returned with a waiter who carried a dusty bottle of champagne and three coupes. "Here we are," she announced, her voice cheerful and just a little bit brittle. "The three of us." Carefully, she reached into her pocket and withdrew her shard of emerald; the sunlight streaking through the window caught it and briefly seemed to set it on fire. "Have you kept yours?" she asked the others quietly.

Silently, both women withdrew their own slivers of emerald.

Rosa let out a choked laugh of disbelief. "How have we all managed this?" she demanded, shaking her head. "Truly a miracle."

Slowly, as one, the three women held their hands out and silently fit the emerald back together. The missing piece was like a wound, a scar. The jewel now would never be whole.

The waiter popped the cork on the champagne and began to pour it out. It was a time for jollity, for celebration, but the three women were silent and somber as they watched the glasses fill with frothy bubbles, each of them remembering their last toast, on the *St Louis* seven years ago, when their futures had shimmered so brightly and seemed so hopeful.

So much had happened since then. So much suffering and grief and loss... yet here they were, just three of them.

Rosa raised her glass first, her lips trembling before she firmed them into a line. "To Sophie," she said, and Hannah and Rachel followed suit.

"To Sophie," they echoed. They clinked glasses and then they drank, meeting each other's sorrow-filled gazes over the rims of their coupes.

"Rosa," Rachel asked as she lowered her glass, "what are your plans after the war?"

Rosa held up her left hand on which sparkled a sliver of diamond. "Well, I'm getting married," she said with an impish smile. "To Peter. He's a German refugee, as well. In fact, he came with me to Paris. He's waiting outside."

"Is he?" Hannah exclaimed. "But so are Lotte and Michel!"

Rachel laughed. "And so are Corrie and Jakob," she told them. Then, at their surprised looks, she admitted, "I married Jakob a few months ago. He was in Auschwitz with Franz, and he helped me to find Corrie right after the camps were emptied. We were in the DP camp together, as well. He's... he's a good man."

"Well, what are they all doing out there?" Rosa exclaimed with a laugh. "Let's invite them all inside."

A few minutes later, the little café was full of people—Michel with his arm around Hannah's waist, Lotte hugging Rachel and cooing over Corrie, Peter and Jakob shaking hands.

What a motley group they made, Rachel thought as she looked around, her heart filled with happiness—and yet so much sorrow. She thought of Franz, and then she thought of Sophie. Both of them should have been here...

Then the door of Henri's opened again. A woman stood there, thin and terribly gaunt, her blond hair pulled back from her angular face, her blue eyes sweeping the room and then settling on the little group as a weary smile lifted the corners of her mouth.

"I see I'm late for the party," she remarked dryly.

For a second no one moved or spoke. Rosa gaped, while Hannah simply stared, and then Rachel rushed forward.

"*Sophie!*" she exclaimed, and embraced her friend. Then Rosa and Hannah were rushing forward too, and for a moment the only sound was joyful weeping as all four women embraced, incredulous and thankful.

"What... what happened..."

"How did you manage..."

"Why," Rosa cut across them all, her voice filled with her

old, dry humor, "are you so *late*? You almost missed the champagne!"

Sophie laughed as she stepped back, wiping her eyes. "My train was late," she told them. "I came from Berlin. I've been living in the west of the city, working with the Red Cross, to help displaced persons, since the end of the war. I'm amazed I made it here at all, considering the state of everything."

"Sophie, your family?" Rachel asked. "Are they...?" Something in her friend's face gave her the answer, and she fell silent.

Slowly, Sophie shook her head, confirming Rachel's fears. "All gone, even Heinrich, on one of the first transports from Belgium. I only learned it at the end of the war." She swallowed her tears and thrust out a hand. "But now I think I'd like some champagne."

Rosa reached for the bottle and poured her out a coupe.

"We need to toast again," she announced. "To our families and to the future. May the first never be forgotten and may the second always be bright."

"Hear, hear," the others murmured, and all four women raised their glasses before drinking solemnly, their gazes fixed on each other.

This moment that they'd waited and pined for, for seven long years, incredible and miraculous as it was, had finally come —and it was bittersweet, seamed with as much loss as it was with hope. The past could never be forgotten... but the future remained, ready to be forged with faith and determination.

"Sophie," Rosa asked. "Your emerald?"

"Of course." Smiling, Sophie withdrew her sliver, and once more the friends held up their shards and silently fitted them together, finally forming a beautiful, wondrous whole, just as it had been back on the *St Louis*.

The four women stood there for a moment, holding back tears as they smiled at one another and the years turned back to the moment they'd forged their friendship and made this vow, kept against all odds and under unimaginable circumstances. They'd made it. They'd all actually, wondrously *made* it, and now the future stretched in front of them like a golden thread they could follow, to wherever it led.

As they held up their pieces of the jewel, their breath hushed with the glorious magnitude of the moment, sunlight streamed through the window and caught the emerald's facets, its depths gleaming with an inner fire, reflecting its light to a broken yet healing world.

A LETTER FROM KATE

Dear reader,

I want to say a huge thank you for choosing to read *The Girl Who Never Gave Up*. If you enjoyed it, and would like to keep up to date with all my latest releases, just sign up at the following link. Your email address will never be shared and you can unsubscribe at any time.

www.bookouture.com/kate-hewitt

This story was so meaningful to me, as I have always admired Corrie ten Boom and have wanted to write about her for ages. Her story is truly inspiring, and I was so glad to be able to share a little of it with readers.

I wrote this book while undergoing many life changes myself—moving countries, saying goodbye to longtime friends, and my daughter getting married and living in a different country than me! While it was sometimes hard to focus on the writing with so much going on in life, I really felt like I could empathize with a little bit of Rachel's sense of lostness, and the hope she ended up finding. I hope you can too, for we all experience upheavals of various sorts throughout life.

I hope you loved *The Girl Who Never Gave Up* and if you did, I would be very grateful if you could write a review. I'd love to hear what you think, and it makes such a difference helping new readers to discover one of my books for the first time.

I love hearing from my readers—you can get in touch on my Facebook group for readers (facebook.com/groups/Kates Reads), through X, Goodreads (goodreads.com/author/show/1269244.Kate_Hewitt) or my website.

Thanks again for reading!

Kate

www.kate-hewitt.com

𝕏 x.com/author_kate

AUTHOR'S NOTE

Much of Rachel's story, like those of the other Emerald Sisters, is based in fact. The events of those leaving the *St Louis* for the Netherlands are as described, and the conditions were far worse than those for the refugees to other countries.

The part of Rachel's story that I enjoyed most is her interaction with the ten Booms. While Rachel and Franz are fictional characters, the ten Booms were wonderfully real people, and their story can be found in Corrie ten Boom's memoir, *The Hiding Place*, along with several other of her works. Events around the raid of the Beje happened much as I described, and those hiding in the wall space remained there for forty-six hours before they were rescued. All survived the war, save for Mary Itallie, who died of pneumonia.

Conditions for pregnant women at Birkenau were, horribly, much as described. The Polish Catholic midwife Stanisława Leszczyńska, as well as the other midwives, Klara and Pfani, were real people, and, according to records, acted much as I wrote them. Of the three thousand babies Stanisława delivered, only thirty survived, with some being smuggled out of the camp as Rachel's baby Cornelia was.

Other events described in this novel, including the uprising of the *Sonderkommando* and the death march from Auschwitz-Birkenau, happened much as described and have been taken from oral histories.

Corrie ten Boom did start an organization after the war in the Netherlands, to rehabilitate both Jews and Nazis alike. She was convinced to do this work after a guard at Ravensbruck who had been particularly cruel to her sister Betsie asked for her forgiveness after the war. She related that shaking his hand was the hardest thing she'd ever done, and that God gave her the strength to do it.

ACKNOWLEDGMENTS

As ever, there are so many people who are part of bringing a book to see the light of day! Thank you to the whole amazing team at Bookouture who have helped with this process, from editing, copyediting, and proofreading, to designing and marketing. In particular, I'd like to thank my editor, Jess Whitlum-Cooper, as well as Imogen Allport, and Laura Deacon; Sarah Hardy and Kim Nash in publicity; Melanie Price in marketing; Richard King and Saidah Graham in foreign rights; and Sinead O'Connor in audio. I have really appreciated everyone's positivity and proactiveness!

I'd also like to thank my friends, who are not writers themselves but who have always cheered me on, even after I moved away. Thanks to Mand, Cat, and Jo! You guys are absolute stars, and I don't know what I'd do, or who I would be, without you. Thank you for being wonderful friends!! Also thanks to my dear friend Katy Kelly, who has been a stalwart supporter of my writing. I will miss our lunches together and moaning about the state of the world with you! And Emma Robinson and Jenna Ness, my writing buddies both in the UK and the US who have always had my back. Writing can be a lonely profession and I am so grateful to these two who have made it a little less so.

Lastly, thanks to my husband Cliff and my five children, Caroline, Ellen, Ted, Anna, and Charlotte, and also my new and wonderful son-in-law, Jacob! So, so grateful for all of you.

PUBLISHING TEAM

Turning a manuscript into a book requires the efforts of many people. The publishing team at Bookouture would like to acknowledge everyone who contributed to this publication.

Audio
Alba Proko
Melissa Tran
Sinead O'Connor

Commercial
Lauren Morrissette
Hannah Richmond
Imogen Allport

Cover design
Debbie Clement

Data and analysis
Mark Alder
Mohamed Bussuri

Editorial
Jess Whitlum-Cooper
Imogen Allport

Copyeditor
Jade Craddock

Proofreader
Tom Feltham

Marketing
Alex Crow
Melanie Price
Occy Carr
Cíara Rosney
Martyna Młynarska

Operations and distribution
Marina Valles
Stephanie Straub
Joe Morris

Production
Hannah Snetsinger
Mandy Kullar
Jen Shannon
Ria Clare

Publicity
Kim Nash
Noelle Holten
Jess Readett
Sarah Hardy

Rights and contracts
Peta Nightingale
Richard King
Saidah Graham

Printed in Dunstable, United Kingdom